Praise for Jeffe Kennedy's Twelve Kingdoms

The Mark of the Tala

"The fairy-tale setup only hints at the depth of world-building at work in this debut series. What could be clichéd is instead moving as Andi is torn between duty to her father and the pull of Rayfe and his kingdom . . . This well-written and swooningly romantic fantasy will appeal to fans of Juliet Marillier's Sevenwaters series or Robin McKinley's *The Hero and the Crown*."
—*Library Journal*, starred

"A tale that is both satisfying and tantalizing. This promises to be a trilogy that will leave readers enthralled."
—*Heroes and Heartbreakers*

"I thoroughly enjoyed the world that Jeffe Kennedy created here. It was the type of sweeping story that was easy to get lost in, thanks to the interesting characters, the bit of mystery surrounding Andi's mother, Salena, and their otherworldly heritage."
—*Harlequin Junkie*

"This magnificent fairy tale will captivate you from beginning to end with a richly detailed fantasy world full of shapeshifters, magic, and an exciting romance!"
—*RT Book Reviews*, 4½ stars, Top Pick

"I loved every page and the conclusion simply left me stunned."
—*Tynga's Reviews*

The Tears of the Rose

"Kennedy creates a well-constructed world, and Amelia has a solid character arc, moving from unlikable to heroic in her own way."
—*Library Journal*

"New readers will have no trouble following along. . . . Amelia's journey from pampered princess to empowered woman begins with sorrow and pain, until she begins to see her purpose and embraces her newfound strength and power. She is a surprising female character, as is the scarred and mysterious Ash. One of the highlights of the Twelve Kingdoms series so far is that the women are charged with saving themselves and creating their own happily-ever-after, with the men surrounding them just one part of the process."
—*RT Book Reviews*, 4½ stars, Top Pick Gold

"*The Tears of the Rose* strikes gold . . ."
—*Fresh Fiction*

"Certainly, Jeffe Kennedy's characters are not perfect. No, they are flawed, even Andi in the first book, but their flaws are believable and make them relatable. So, even if you don't like them (like I didn't like Amelia at first), you can definitely understand where they're coming from."
—*The Romance Reviews*

The Talon of the Hawk

"The saga of The Twelve Kingdoms returns in grand style! This is a complex world full of danger, subterfuge and secrets with empowering female characters who are not afraid to fight for their future."
—*RT Book Reviews*, 4½ Stars, Top Pick

"Excellent character development and strong action continue to characterize the Twelve Kingdoms, and I'm thrilled beyond belief to know that we will see more of this world in future Kennedy books."
—*Fresh Fiction*

THE PAGES OF THE MIND

JEFFE KENNEDY

KENSINGTON BOOKS
www.kensingtonbooks.com

KENSINGTON BOOKS are published by

Kensington Publishing Corp.
119 West 40th Street
New York, NY 10018

All Kensington titles, imprints, and distributed lines are available at special quantity discounts for bulk purchases for sales promotion, premiums, fund-raising, and educational or institutional use.

Special book excerpts or customized printings can also be created to fit specific needs. For details, write or phone the office of the Kensington Sales Manager: Kensington Publishing Corp., 119 West 40th Street, New York, NY 10018. Attn. Sales Department. Phone: 1-800-221-2647.

Kensington and the K logo Reg. U.S. Pat. & TM Off.

ISBN-13: 978-1-4967-0424-5
ISBN-10: 1-4967-0424-X
First Kensington Trade Paperback Printing: June 2016

eISBN-13: 978-1-4967-0425-2
eISBN-10: 1-4967-0425-8
First Kensington Electronic Edition: June 2016

10 9 8 7 6 5 4 3 2 1

Printed in the United States of America

To all the librarians,
past, present, and future.
Those who put books in my childhood hands, those who
put the books I write on their library shelves,
and those who will continue the work, fighting the
good fight to open minds and hearts.

Acknowledgments

Many thanks to Lynne Facer, who told me she wanted Dafne's story because she herself has no magic, isn't beautiful, and can't swing a sword—but she's hell on documents. I loved that remark so much, I had to give it to Dafne.

Special thanks go to Megan Hart, for being the "fresh to the series" beta reader.

Heartfelt love and gratitude to the rest of my critique partner/cheerleading squad—Anna Philpot, Carolyn Crane, and Marcella Burnard—particularly for reading this unfinished because I was freaking out about it being ALL WRONG. You gals saved my sanity.

Thanks to Anne Calhoun, for always being there.

Love to that Grace person, even if you did steal my award.

An extra-special thank you to my agent, Connor Goldsmith, who is always awesome. And also to Fuse Literary partner Laurie McLean, who goes above and beyond for all the agency clients.

Huge thanks to the Kensington team for all they do, especially my editor Peter Senftleben, amazing production editor Rebecca Cremonese and her myriad minions, publicist Jane Nutter, and communications diva Vida Engstrand. You make my books better, more beautiful, and put them into readers' hands. Extra grog rations for all!

I don't know how to express my deep gratitude to all the readers and reviewers who have loved on these books and shouted that love to the world. All year I've been hearing how much you couldn't wait for Dafne's book. Both tremendously gratifying and terrifying. I hope I did her justice for you.

Thank yous to the staff at RT Book Reviews, and to all the reviewers, bloggers, and readers who have talked up these books. Chocolate, fairy dust, and Jason Momoa pics to you all.

Many thanks to Ruth and Kendrick Frazier, for love and support over these many years, and for the loan of their cabin, where I watched the snow fall and made the final pass on these pages.

Always, I send love to my family, the myriad extended lot of you, who bring joy to my life every day.

I always thank David last, because he's the one who's there for the better and the worse. I love you, my dear.

1

When histories tell of the glorious dawning of a new era, they typically focus on the grand events—wars won, tyrants deposed, glittering coronations. Much waving of pennants and joyous shouting.

The duller truth is that—even though those histories are usually written by people like myself, the humble, nearly invisible keepers of the books—they never mention what consumes the most monumental effort.

Paperwork.

Really, can you blame us?

Since I'd returned to Castle Ordnung, to serve the new High Queen Ursula as her councilor in the wake of her father Uorsin's death, it seemed I'd done nothing *but* record keeping. From the smallest details of ticking off the lists of supplies for restoring the much-depleted resources at the seat of the High Throne, to looking up laws new and old—from niggling to sweeping—to keeping notes during the many interminable meetings, I sometimes felt I might be buried under the avalanche of books, scrolls, and parchments.

Not that I minded, exactly. It was my calling and practically only useful skill. I possessed neither magic, nor beauty, nor warrior skills, but I was a demon on documents.

More, seeing Ursula on the throne at last fulfilled a lifelong ambition of mine. Death to the tyrant. Long live the High Queen. She would be a fair and honorable ruler, if I had to make sure of it myself.

The thing I'd learned about realizing lifelong ambitions? Once you're there, life doesn't end. Neither, apparently, did the long hours and paperwork. Fortunately the avalanche of work kept me mostly too busy to think about it.

Or about the dire prophecy the sorceress Queen Andromeda—Ursula's sister—had told me just over a month before of the threat that loomed following the coronation. She'd sworn me to secrecy, then gave me practically nothing to go on.

There are four men, exotically armored. Tall, broad, and fairhaired. Ursula crowned, on her throne. I don't know them, but they are Dasnarians, not Vervaldr. In the great hall at Ordnung.

Not dire in and of itself, but the prospect had troubled her deeply. The only other hint she gave me was to tell me to have things in order. I was doing my utmost, though the chaos of a new reign made it no simple task.

Which is why I found myself searching for the High Queen in the early morning hours, so she could sign off on a set of sensitive declarations. The messengers were poised to depart to the far reaches of the Twelve Kingdoms—now Thirteen, in the wake of Ursula's inadvertent magical acquisition of Annfwn and subsequent treaty with King Rayfe and Queen Andromeda. We'd met until late, arguing the finer points; then I'd spent the night composing the actual text. The messengers should have gone hours ago, but I didn't like for the missives to go out without Her Majesty's final approval.

For form, I checked her rooms first, not at all surprised to find them empty. She would of course be out on the practice grounds, running her sword forms with her Hawks before court. Some things didn't change, no matter what else had.

I had the one correct—she was working out—but not on the practice grounds.

I'd taken the shortcut from Her Majesty's rooms, through the arcade open only in warm weather. Not for many more weeks. The chill of winter stung the air, promising heavy snows to come, if not that day, then soon. The ring of blades clashing echoed through the dimness, Glorianna's sun lightening the sky but not yet high enough to bring warmth. I found the High Queen with Harlan in her favored private courtyard off the family wing. She'd long been one of the few to use the walled garden. By tacit agreement, most in the castle left her to it. Probably we should make it her private space, as she had little enough of that. I made a mental note to pass the word on it.

I disliked intruding when she'd clearly chosen to be away from everyone. Thus I hesitated in the shadows of the arcade, torn between discretion and the urgency of my errand, then fascinated by the scene.

They'd been at it a while, as they both glistened with sweat. She moved fast, with the grace of a dancer, like a fluid blade herself. Harlan, a Dasnarian mercenary, her lover and probably twice her weight, took perhaps one step for every three or four of hers, fending her off with his massive broadsword as she sought to penetrate his guard, spinning in and out again, moving under his strikes with such narrow escapes that my heart felt like it thumped in my throat and I had to relax my tightening fingers to keep from bunching the scroll I held.

Completely and utterly focused on each other, they moved in sync, a study in synchronicity and opposition. For all that they attempted to best each other, they seemed to be two halves of one whole. Harlan laughed, a deep, sensual sound. "Come closer and try that again, little hawk."

And Ursula laughed with him, sounding carefree as I rarely heard her, her smile fiercely exultant. "You wish, rabbit."

"I do wish."

Abruptly, I became excruciatingly aware of seeing something I should not. As if I'd walked in on them in sex play. Which, it became more apparent, this was, in its own way. They circled, tested, and teased each other, their bodies speaking in a profound harmony of visceral intention.

Definitely intruding, urgent timing or no. I took a step, intending to flee.

Harlan, however, spotted my movement and called a hold before I could escape. He lifted the flat of his sword to his forehead in the *Elskastholrr*, gaze on Ursula as if she shone brighter than the sun. Now that I fully understood the meaning of the vow, the gesture blew through me, leaving ragged emotion behind. He'd pledged himself to her unconditionally, for life, whether she kept solely to him, married another, or took a hundred lovers.

For all that I reminded myself I'd never trade places with her—I was a librarian, not a warrior or queen—unexpected bitter jealousy burned my throat where my heart had been, acrid as I swallowed it down.

I gathered my composure quickly when Harlan tipped his head in my direction and Ursula turned in inquiry. She did shine. Flushed with exertion, yes, but also radiant with love. Perhaps with being loved. Something I'd never know.

Her keen gaze surveyed me. "Problem?"

For a second I thought she meant my state of eternal spinsterhood, of only reading about the adventures of others, never being in the center, but forever on the edges, witnessing and recording the lives and loves of someone else, never knowing any of it for myself. *No, idiot. She wants to know why you're here.* "I apologize for intruding, Your Majesty. The new proclamation." I handed her the scroll. "Would you review it? If you approve, I'll make copies and send it straightaway."

"If you wrote it, I'm sure it's perfect," she replied, but she unrolled it and read. "Interesting. You manage to convey a great deal concisely and in a way that should minimize quibbling. Well done, librarian."

She handed it back to me. Studied my face.

"I'll go copy it, then."

"Stay a moment. Harlan, would you excuse us? It's time to prepare for court anyway."

"Of course." He lifted her hand and kissed it, a courtly gesture that nevertheless carried over the fierce sexuality of their duel. I prayed that my face had not turned red.

After he left, Ursula pinned me with a steely look as sharp as the sword she hadn't yet sheathed. "What troubles you?"

"Nothing in particular." I tried for a cheerful grimace. I wouldn't tell her about Andi's prediction of a Dasnarian incursion, even if I could. Until it happened, there was nothing she could do. "I'll be glad to get this task off my list so I can move on to some of the others. King Rayfe sent back the allied kingdoms agreement with a list of additional stipulations and requests for concessions."

"Anything outrageous?"

"A few you won't like. I'll flag those and we can review after court."

She nodded, with an expression of affectionate exasperation for her brother-in-law. None of us blamed Rayfe and Andromeda for zealously guarding the bounty of Annfwn now that the protective magical barrier that had sealed their kingdom away from the world no longer did. But parts of the Thirteen desperately needed to establish trade for food—one of Ursula's highest priorities—and the back-and-forth had gone on for weeks.

"What else?" she asked.

"I'm sure you've heard from Jepp's scouts, but rumors that the volcano at Windroven is rumbling still continue to come in, along with similar rumors from elsewhere on the Crane Isthmus and from the Remus Isles. Several barges on the Danu River have gone missing, unfortunately with much-needed food supplies, with possibly coincidental and certainly unconfirmed sightings of a giant violet squid or octopus." Once I would have temporized on such a description. No longer.

She listened as I updated her, polishing her sword, the newly embedded ruby in the hilt glinting in the light of Glorianna's rising sun. Until just over a month ago, it had been a cabochon topaz— or so all, including me, had believed. Instead the jewel turned out to be a flawless orb, a gift from her mother, Salena, powerful sorceress and former queen of Annfwn. Now the topaz, the Star of Annfwn, remained in our High Queen's belly, apparently for good, as it had shown no sign of passing through her system. It troubled me, but short of cutting the jewel out of her, there wasn't much we could do. And it seemed to be doing her no harm. We'd replaced the wound in her hilt with one of Salena's rubies. That looked better than the jagged metal, though it would never hold the same power for her.

Most of what I related the queen already knew, but she nodded, checking things off against the list she carried in her head.

"Were you awake all night?" she asked when I finished, taking me by surprise. It never paid to forget her warrior's instincts— and how much she loved the unexpected attack.

"Finishing this missive and a few other things, yes. I'll grab a nap after you adjourn court this afternoon."

"I thought you just offered to go over Rayfe's new demands then."

"After that," I amended.

She gave me a long look.

"I'm fine."

"That's usually my line," she said with wry amusement. "And it's a lie when I say it, too. I'll ask again. What troubles you?"

I fumbled for a reply. As well as I knew Ursula—distantly all her life and more recently, in closer quarters, through serious trials—I never kidded myself that I was anything near her equal. She was High Queen and she had far more important concerns than my personal issues. I'd sworn not to tell her about Andi's vision. More than that, I trusted Andi's judgment that it wouldn't help Ursula to know. But how to give her a satisfying answer that wouldn't sound like another prevarication?

"Nothing troubles me on the scale of the problems we're facing, Your Majesty. You were the one to emphasize that we're too busy to worry about less important things."

"And you corrected me that priorities sometimes should be revisited." She sheathed her sword. "You know, you're valuable to me. Have been to all of us through all that's happened. In the past few days, I've come to appreciate that even more. There are not many people who will look me in the eye and tell me I'm wrong."

"Not wrong, Your Majesty. I only mean to—"

"I don't mind being wrong. And stop trying to make this a formal conversation. I consider you a friend, and it's been pointed out to me, by more than one person, that I don't have many and so should make an effort to be good to the ones I do have." She grimaced ruefully. "However, I'm the first to admit that I have little practice and probably zero skill at it. So help me out. Tell me what I can do for you. How can I make things better for you?"

"Better . . . for me?" I couldn't imagine. It would be easier to go back to the endless task list.

"Dafne. These past weeks haven't been easy and they're not likely to get better anytime soon. I need you, but I can find a way to get by without you. You don't have to stay here. Uorsin's gone. You have no reason to be loyal to Ordnung or the High Throne—and good reason not to be."

Everything clarified then. "Harlan said something to you."

To her credit, she didn't wince, simply met my gaze with calm and clear understanding. "You didn't tell him not to and he felt I should be aware."

I struggled with that. It was true that I hadn't thought to tell Harlan not to mention the long conversation we'd had when he escorted me from Annfwn to Ordnung. The Dasnarian former mercenary, for all his threatening bulk, had a way of worming confessions out of a person. The tradition he followed, the *skablykrr*—both philosophical and martial—included the tenet that internal wounds harmed a warrior as much as or more than external ones. He possessed an uncanny knack for sniffing them out, including my own, which I normally never discussed, asking in such a way that I'd actually answered, telling him my sad and sorry tale.

"I regret that I never thought to ask you about it," Ursula continued when I couldn't muster a reply. "All my life, you were always around. Though I knew on one level that you'd survived the fall of Castle Columba at Uorsin's hands, I didn't give it more thought than that. I'm ashamed of that blindness and I apologize to you."

"You had plenty of your own concerns," I managed, quite overcome. So odd how the pain you easily ignored became overwhelming when another offered sympathy. Ursula had always borne the brunt of Uorsin's rages—and possibly far worse. I'd sometimes wondered but had so little power that I stopped there. It hadn't been my place. My own kind of willful blindness.

"What do you want out of life, Dafne?" she asked then, looking into me nearly the same way Queen Andromeda did. Andi had followed in her sorceress mother's footsteps, but at these moments, I wondered how much of Ursula's uncanny insight into people and politics came from a touch of Salena's magic.

"This." I gestured with the scroll. "I wanted Uorsin gone, Salena avenged, and a good monarch on the High Throne—you."

"And now that you have that?"

Not an easy answer. I'd formed this ambition the moment Ursula had been born, when Salena had handed the indignant baby to me and told me I held the future High Queen. When Salena said things like that, you knew they would come true. It had given me a kind of hope, to channel all that rage and grief over the loss of my family, the outrage of seeing Ordnung built on the bones of my family's home, to imagine their destroyer dead and good coming out of all that death. But then, perhaps hope is simply the absence of despair.

"You told me once that you still see Castle Columba when you look at Ordnung. That you returned with me from Windroven because you felt you owed me."

"Well, that and my deep agenda to see you on the throne,

which didn't seem appropriate to mention at the time." I tried to make it a joke, but that didn't divert her either. She possessed an excellent memory and, now that Harlan had directed her attention, wouldn't let this go. "I couldn't stay at Windroven, couldn't stomach yet another siege and occupation. I didn't care to contemplate how I might have fared at Old King Erich's hands. My place is at Ordnung and I'm fi—I don't need you to do anything for me. I should go copy this. The messengers are waiting. We'll both be late for court."

She didn't move. "They won't start without us and the messengers can wait a bit more. That has been pointed out to me, also, that a benefit of rank is letting go of some concerns."

"You have rank, Your Majesty. I am only as good as the work I do." I tried to pull back my too-sharp words, but Ursula grinned.

"Aha. There you are—the Dafne who doesn't fear speaking her mind. I've been giving it thought. Another thing I never questioned before. Why did Uorsin keep you, out of all your family?"

The weariness of the night shadowed me and I could hardly bear the rise of old grief at her question, on top of my sudden, strange burst of jealousy and longing for something I'd thought I'd long since resigned myself to not having. Ursula would not release me until she'd satisfied herself, however.

"Because I was the only one left." It felt terrible to say. A final truth.

Ursula, however, waved that off. "That might be true, but it's not why he kept you. We both know my late, unlamented father was not a man or a ruler to give succor to anyone not useful to him. It would have been more in character for him to have you killed."

She was right about that. "I think . . . Salena intervened? I stayed with her, in her tent at first. She . . . helped me." A cool hand on my forehead, disbursing the crowding nightmares. Other things. So long ago I barely remembered. Had she called me dragon's daughter?

Ursula nodded thoughtfully. "I could see her doing that. She had a fondness for children, even beyond the high value all Tala place on the young. It's possible she saw you as an adoptive daughter. Uorsin owed her greatly for her role in helping him win the war."

She didn't have to mention Salena's role in bringing down Columba, or that she might have been expiating her guilt by saving me. The words hung unspoken in the air.

"It's more likely, however, that she convinced him of your usefulness in some way. I wonder that he never married you off. As a ward of the Crown, you could have been used to cement alliances. You count as part of the High King's family by law."

"But not in fact. A marriage to me would have cemented nothing, as Uorsin cared nothing for me and all knew it. In point of fact, he did attempt to arrange several marriages for me. All unsuccessful."

She tapped her hilt, both satisfied and irritated by that. "An odd comfort that I can still predict him that well, though I don't recall those conversations."

"It was in my later teens, around the time you were named heir, but before you were heavily involved in discussions like that. Back then I at least had a measure of nubility and potential fertility to commend me to my future in-laws, though clearly not enough for them to commit to an offer."

"That was—a bad time for me," she admitted, the ghost of old pain darkening her eyes. She shook it off. Hesitated. "This is somewhat more delicate, but I need to know. Did you wish to marry?"

"To the men Uorsin proposed? No." Being young, I'd idealized the fantasy. Marrying nobility and going off to some castle, escaping my tenuous, half-alive existence at Ordnung. Until I met some of my prospective grooms—and their arrogance—and had realized that I would be still little better than a servant in those places, too. Only with a fancier title and likely more rules to follow. "And once it became clear that I would not be useful, Uorsin forgot about me and I gained the freedom to study as much as I liked."

"And also to find someone of your own. In his forgetting, you could have married," Ursula prodded.

"I never met anyone I liked enough to marry." Or even spend time with. It had always been easy to decline the rare offers. To stay safe and quiet instead. "Like you, I've been busy with other things." My morning for saying the wrong thing, no doubt due to missing sleep. "That is, until you—"

"Met Harlan? An extraordinary development, true. And, as you witnessed, not something that was easy for me to adjust to. It still isn't, to be honest." She hesitated over something. "It wasn't all being busy for me. I hope there isn't . . ." She trailed off, uncomfortable, and I shared her embarrassment. Both of us so private and protected, in our different ways. She, as always, possessed more courage than I and forged on. "This is more Harlan's area of expertise than mine, but he seems to think I should be the one to talk to you. I have an idea of what it's like to take refuge in being busy, focusing on the goal and telling myself that I didn't need, well, human connection." She huffed out a breath and shook her head. "Harlan would laugh at me for avoiding using the word 'love.' But that's part of it. It takes courage to let another person in, to let them love you. More to open up enough to allow for the possibility of loving in return."

I couldn't quite believe that Ursula—prickly, contained Ursula—was saying these things to me.

She shrugged, a wry smile for my consternation. "The look on your face. I'm trying to tell you that it's worth it, opening yourself to that experience. Even with the fear that you will lose it again. People die. They leave. Sometimes fail to love you enough."

Sorrow and—yes—fear lodged in my throat. "No one could love a person more than Harlan loves you."

She nodded slowly, then tapped her temple. "I know that here." She put her fist over her heart, an echo of the Hawks' salute. "But I don't always feel it here. I think that it's as if the emotional wounds leave scar tissue that keeps us from being able to feel like normal people do."

"But you love Harlan. You feel that. I can see it in you."

"No, I don't always feel it. Not like the poets describe. I know that I love him mainly because I know I wouldn't want to live if he didn't. I'd far rather die than attempt to survive him." She smiled wryly and rolled up her eyes at some memory. "Unfortunately, he feels the same way, so we'll either be racing each other for the privilege of dying first or we'll have to find a way to go together."

It helped to laugh at that, to break some of the discomfort of her confessions.

"The point is, Dafne—I don't want to hold you back from seeking your own happiness."

"You're not. I have the ear of the High Queen of the Twelve—I mean, Thirteen—Kingdoms. What could make me happier than that?"

"And her friendship," Ursula said in a serious tone. "I want you to remember that, especially as I'm not always good at showing it. You've been assiduous in pointing out the precedents we've established in declaring Annfwn an independent ally, justified by Andi's marriage, and that prospective suitors will likely look to widowed Ami to gain the same status. Has it occurred to you that you are also eligible to cement a similar alliance?"

It hadn't. I gaped at her, fumbling for words.

"That's right. And this time it would be different because the person who will be wearing the crown cares for you deeply. It won't take the rest of the world very long to figure that out."

"Are you offering me an arranged marriage?"

"There have been leading questions. No outright offers, but I need to know if that's something you even want to consider."

I stared at her, completely dumbfounded.

She shrugged and grinned. "Take some time to absorb the possibility. I'm telling you that you have options. More than most.

You can pick the life you want. If I can provide something for you, I will."

"A Dasnarian prince of my very own?" I teased her, wanting her off the topic of being concerned for me, for both our sakes, regretting the words as soon as they escaped my mouth.

The fact that Harlan, who'd always presented himself as a humble merc and captain of his own fighting force, the Vervaldr, turned out to be the youngest of seven brothers in the Dasnarian ruling family had caused more than a little trouble. We'd counted ourselves lucky that Dasnaria was far away and had never bothered with our part of the world. With the exception of the Vervaldr and the late Illyria, a priestess of Deyrr who'd seduced Uorsin, our last contact with the Dasnarian Empire went back centuries. Hopefully it would stay that way, as we did not need any other challenges at the moment. Though Andi's foresight warned otherwise.

"Harlan does have six brothers." Ursula smiled and relented, turning at last in the direction of her rooms, finally ready to release me from the uncomfortable inquisition. "Surely one or two remain available. Perhaps the Dasnarians will contact me with leading questions."

As if summoned by her words, Jepp, leader of the Hawks' scouts, came skidding up, out of breath. She looked much better than she had for a while there, the waxy-pale quality gone from her brown skin and her usual vitality restored. Uorsin had nearly gutted her in that final battle, and though she'd benefited from magical healing, it had taken her a while to completely recover from coming so near death. Not much taller than I, she probably outweighed me substantially, all in muscle. With large, dark eyes in a high-cheekboned face and her deep-brown hair in a short pixie cut, she looked like a fairy-tale creature. One that could slice you open before you saw her move.

Normally she had an easy smile and faster jest. Instead her expression communicated urgency, even alarm. A chill of prophecy crawled over my scalp. Ursula went on instant alert, hand going to her sword. "What?"

"Your Majesty—some of my scouts have returned with news."

"Tell me."

"You should hear for yourself. They're waiting in your rooms. I think Captain Harlan should hear this as well, but that's your call. Maybe you won't want him to know."

Harlan. Dasnarians. It was happening.

Ursula was already striding in that direction. "Don't play coy, Jepp. Spill, and then I can hear it again in detail."

I had to break into a jog to keep up with their long-legged pace.

Jepp huffed her unhappiness at the news she bore. "Suffice to say that, unless there are Vervaldr in Elcinea, there's a Dasnarian army headed this way."

2

Though I'd nagged and cozened Ursula into taking over some of the late king's meeting rooms and council chambers, she still preferred to use her private rooms to confer with her Hawks. For once I was glad of it. My thoughts piled on top of each other in distressing disorder. So much to deal with, at least in my aegis. Those who'd opposed Ursula taking the High Throne would be the first to attempt to use this against her. This kind of news, so early in her new and tenuous reign, had to be kept quiet as long as possible.

Which would likely not be long at all.

The two Hawks scouts, whose names I didn't know, which meant they were long-range scouts who hadn't ridden with us on my travels with Ursula, came to their feet as she entered. Dusty and road worn, they clasped their fists over their hearts. Harlan stood nearby, hair damp from bathing, wearing clothes he'd changed into for court. Not his Vervaldr regalia, nor the uniform of Ordnung's guard. None of us had been able to decide how he should be presented, except that he shouldn't be either of those things, yet he couldn't be her official consort either. Ursula continued to be irascible and her most stubborn on the topic, and the whispers had yet to rise to the level of a real problem, so I'd let the issue rest.

In the absence of clear direction, he'd taken to wearing a variation on what he'd worn in Annfwn, leather vest over a sleeveless white shirt, black pants, and boots. With his broadsword strapped to his side, he looked both barbaric and obscurely comforting, someone you could count on for protection. He returned Ursula's inquiring glance with a bare shake of his head. No, the Hawks wouldn't have spoken to him without Ursula's express permission.

"High Queen." The male Hawk bowed deeply and cocked an eyebrow on the side of his face away from Harlan. "We have news."

"If it involves Dasnarians, then Captain Harlan in particular should hear this," she asserted without equivocation.

Puzzlement creased Harlan's brow, a rare expression of surprise. "Dasnarians?"

The female Hawk gave Harlan a cagey glance, then spoke to Ursula. "Captain"—she fell into the familiar title they'd used with Ursula for so long—"we witnessed a caravan of very large, fair-haired men making their way north on the main road out of the Port of Ehas. They are not wearing Vervaldr colors, but perhaps . . ."

She let the question dangle. Harlan's surprise had gone to shock. Another man would have sat at that moment, but not one of his training and temperament. Still he shook his head slowly from side to side, as if dazed. "No. All of the Vervaldr are accounted for. They're either in the Ordnung environs or cleanly witnessed as deceased." He didn't need to specify that he meant either form of death—real or Illyria's monstrous living death. His pale eyes sought Ursula's and held them. "They are not mine."

"Then whose?" she shot back.

He pressed his mouth in a grim line. "Approximate number?"

"One hundred, even, Captain Harlan."

"Colors? Could you make out insignia?"

"A deep burgundy, like the wines of Nemeth. They have a banner that seemed to have some sort of fanged fish on it."

Now Harlan did sit—or at least, folded his arms and leaned back against Ursula's desk—bafflement clear on his face. Then he laughed, completely without humor. "*Hlyti* is playing a fine game with me."

"Who is it?" Ursula asked with more gentleness than I would have credited her with.

He raised his eyebrows, jaw tight. "It appears that my brother Kral is impossibly here, and with his elite battalion."

She cursed. "It's a thriced coincidence that I'd barely heard of Dasnaria before and now we've been three times accosted by them."

"Am I the first of those?" he asked with strained patience.

"I didn't mean that how it sounded. I apologize."

"Accepted." He gave her a wry, affectionate smile, touching his fingers to his forehead, almost absently, as he thought. "Your point is well-taken that this can be no coincidence. That's not a fanged fish on the banner, but a *hakraling*. Large sea creatures that can kill a grown man in seconds, for which Kral is named."

"A 'shark' in Common Tongue, I think," I said. Since Harlan had been willing to converse with me in his language, I'd gotten somewhat better at hearing the similar roots between that and the trade language of the Thirteen.

He nodded. "Sounds like the same derivation. Last I knew, Kral was general of the Dasnarian military, under my eldest brother, Hestar, the emperor. He typically uses them as an advance force. It's entirely possible the entire Dasnarian navy stands off the shores of Elcinea, waiting for the signal to send troops ashore."

"You think he's here for conquest, then?" Ursula asked.

"I can think of no other explanation. My brothers do not mount expeditions to distant lands for other reasons."

Between the two of them, Harlan and Ursula pumped the scouts for what little more detail they could dig out of them, while I carefully recorded it all for future reference. The two Hawks had returned to Ordnung at top speed to give the maximum amount of warning and had not lingered to observe much more than they'd already reported. If not for Ursula's edict that they all travel at least in pairs in this era of uncertainty, one would have stayed behind to spy. As it was, they couldn't be sure how quickly the company had progressed.

Before long, Ursula dismissed them all, asking Jepp to debrief the scouts again with Marskal, lieutenant of the Hawks, after they'd rested. Jepp wanted to stay for the strategy session, but Ursula asked her to assemble all her in-house scouts and make a strategy to disburse them to watch for General Kral. She would send for Jepp and Marskal later.

Creatures of action, they all hummed with the desire to race out and fight off their enemy—and crackled with frustration at not being able to act just yet. Particularly Ursula. Possibly Harlan, too, though he didn't show it as she did with her restless pacing as she listened. A change for them both, to have the responsibility of planning and sending others to fight, instead of leading their forces personally.

At least, I hoped Ursula realized that. For now she focused on strategy, but if she thought she'd go into the field herself, she'd have a fight on her hands. My style.

Meanwhile, I took steps to see that announcements were made canceling court. I sent a page to hand off the job of copying the missives that seemed so imperative an hour ago, so the messengers could go with all haste. Several more pages went to Uorsin's study, which I'd taken over, since Ursula had refused to and most of the important legal documents were shelved there, to gather my texts on Dasnaria. At some point I'd start thinking of it as my study, but not yet.

We all have our responses to crisis, our own weapons to gather.

"If unopposed, they will be here in five days, possibly four. Presuming they continue to head directly for Ordnung." Harlan traced a thick finger over the map we'd spread over the table.

"A company that big?" Ursula argued. "I don't see that. They won't cut through Aerron, unless they're fools, in which case the desert will take care of them for us."

"They are not fools."

"Then they'll go through the hills at the border between Elcinea and Nemeth, which is not a fast crossing. After that they still have all of Duranor, where I can promise they won't go unopposed. At least they're unlikely to encounter Ami and the babies on their journey to Castle Avonlidgh. Whoever guessed I'd be grateful for Aerron's drought?"

"Six days, then, at the outside," Harlan conceded, though he didn't sound fully convinced. "And Kral is no fool. He has other flaws, but lack of strategy isn't one of them. Nor is underestimating his enemy."

"Duranor still has substantial armies between here and there, and also in Avonlidgh." Ursula grimaced for that reality. Though Prince Stefan had decamped with his forces before the coronation, having lost his bid to convince enough of the kingdoms that a young woman who murdered her father in cold blood should not ascend to the High Throne, they had not been gone long and an army that size moved slowly, even without Stefan's foot-dragging. "But they have some back home, too. It's entirely possible they'll take out Kral and his guard of one hundred before they reach the border of Mohraya."

Harlan sat heavily, staring hard at the map.

"I apologize," Ursula said. "I did not mean to wish an ill fate on your brother." A difficult position for them both. This, I realized, was the primary reason she'd wanted to have this conversation first, without any others present.

Harlan gave her an unamused smile. "It's not that, though I appreciate the sentiment. No matter the state of affairs between us, I do not relish facing my own brother in battle. Though there's no question I would, should it come to that. No—every one of those one hundred soldiers could fight off ten men. In a strategic position, they could defeat a force one hundred times their size."

I wrote the numbers out, careful to be exact with the zeros. The state of our military wasn't one of my strengths, but the recent conflicts had severely depleted Ordnung's guard. If we were to assemble an army of more than ten thousand, we'd need to draw on the forces of the subject kingdoms. Not a popular move, given recent events. Particularly as we'd regret stirring the pot with Duranor until those ruffled feathers had settled.

"But they're not in a strategic position. They're traveling in the open, in a land completely foreign to them, where they are unlikely to know the language. They could be cut off and surrounded on all sides. I can't get sufficient forces in place in time to stop them, but they can't know that. I would hope, anyway. As it is, they have no fortifications, no supply wagons. They'll have to buy or kill for food. It seems risky, even foolhardy." Ursula paced to the map, bending over to stare at it, as if by looking long enough, she could see General Kral for herself. "If he's bent on conquest and you believe he has more forces on ships offshore, why not bring everyone on land? He could have taken over Ehas, had the benefit of the city's food and shelter, probably secured all of Elcinea before we even knew they were there."

"I don't know." Harlan sounded grimly perplexed, seething with something darker than the need to fight. "I wouldn't have predicted any of this from him. Unless things have changed dramatically since I left Dasnaria, he wouldn't be here without permission from Emperor Hestar, who's never had any interest in these lands before. It's possible Kral came only with his battalion, though that would be a first for him. And why land all the way around at Ehas? Any one of a number of ports in Avonlidgh and Aerron would have been closer. Did they leave a ship at harbor in Ehas?"

"That would be good to know. It would also be useful to know their speed, but we can't get eyes on any of this or messages back and forth any faster than you think they're moving." Ursula gave the map a black, frustrated glare.

"I have an idea," I put in.

"What?" she asked without looking up.

"Zynda can take a winged form, right? Send her to look. You trust her."

"I should have thought of that." She nodded at me. "Send for her."

I handed a hastily written note to a page outside the doors to take to Zynda. Ursula's Tala cousin, Zynda had returned with us from Annfwn, expressing a desire to see the world beyond the fallen barrier. A shape-shifter who also possessed some undefined magical skills, Zynda reminded me a great deal of Andi—and also of Salena, their common ancestor.

"Where did you bring the Vervaldr ashore?" Ursula was asking Harlan as I returned.

Harlan reached over and tapped a point on the Avonlidgh coast, a port town so small it wasn't noted on the map. "Here. At Ryalin."

"Of course. That's where Uorsin told you to land," she mused. Uorsin's secret importation of the mercenary Vervaldr still rankled her. "You came up the back roads and stayed away from the main trade routes near Windroven, Lianore, and the Danu River, so few would see you pass."

"And we traveled at night, also by instruction," Harlan said.

"Your brother wouldn't have known the best place to land, without someone here telling him."

"No, very little was known of the Twelve and Annfwn in Dasnaria. The Vervaldr had completed a campaign elsewhere when Uorsin sent his offer. We sailed here directly."

"So why Ehas?"

I tapped one of the Dasnarian tomes. "They didn't know, so they had their scholars research what they could find. Remember when I told you the tale of fair-haired giants landing in here long ago and the sorcerers of Deyrr who likely accompanied them?"

"They landed at Ehas." Ursula nodded. "They went with what they knew. That's old information, however, long predating the unification of the Twelve Kingdoms under Uorsin, and yet by the scouts' reports they're heading directly for Mohraya, at least, and the only reasonable explanation for that is they're coming to Ordnung. But how did they know this is the capital, if their other intelligence is that stale? If that's indeed why they're coming this way. If so, perhaps they got wind of Uorsin's demise and think the High Throne empty for the taking. That could be done with a small, highly trained force. Do you think it could be a coup attempt?"

"I have not been in communication with my brothers, so I can't know the answer to that." Harlan's voice had a rare edge to it.

"I never thought it," Ursula returned in a mild tone, turning to lean against the map table next to him. She nudged him with her knee. "Give me some credit. I try not to be stupid about the same thing twice."

Harlan softened and picked up her hand, his thumb rubbing over her palm. They exchanged a long moment of wordless communication and I focused on my notes, giving them that much privacy. "My guess is that Kral is indeed headed straight for Ordnung and knows it is the capital. He'll rely on speed and surprise to move his men here with minimum conflict. He'll know that even the healthiest military cannot be mobilized immediately and likely counts on that to keep his way clear, knowing also that they can clear it themselves of smaller, more mobile forces."

"And would also know that Ordnung itself *would* be fortified and heavily defended by a standing guard. He can't be planning to lay siege. Does he plan to ride up and ask admittance?" Ursula laid her hand over Ordnung on the map, as if she could hold it there. "Unless he knows of our recent conflicts and thinks we're weakened. But that brings us back to how he knows any of this and why he's come."

"This stinks of Illyria and I don't like it," Harlan said.

"It makes the most sense," she replied. "We still don't know how Illyria came to be here. If she was working with someone back in Dasnaria, possibly communicating with her superiors at the Temple of Deyrr, it's possible they know of *her* demise and are coming in response to that."

"If they know that, however, then they'd likely know of my presence and role in your ascension to the High Throne. But how could they have heard any of that news?"

"Maybe she had a way of communicating magically," I suggested, still looking at my notes; I listed that as a possibility.

"Did you see that somewhere?" Ursula asked, so I met her gaze.

"No. There's simply not that much written about the Temple of Deyrr, but it seems possible that magic that includes reanimating the dead could devise a system of long-distance communication."

Harlan was already shaking his head. "The temple is powerful, yes, and tolerated because of that. But no one in the royal family or government would openly traffic with them."

"And yet you say this stinks of Illyria," Ursula returned.

"Yes. Because I can think of no other connection."

"There's still you, Captain Harlan," I pointed out, as neither of them seemed inclined to.

Ursula shot me an irritated glare. "I know I behaved badly in the past, but I trust that Harlan would not betray us that way." She turned her gaze on him, lethal, not soft. "I mean that."

He ran a hand down her back. "I know that. And even if my brothers knew I was here, they would not concern themselves with me." That brooding edge again.

"Why not?" Ursula asked softly. "You've never said."

"You are blessed with your sisters. Not all families are as such."

"My father was hardly a blessing."

Harlan laughed ruefully, still stroking her back. "Nor mine, my hawk. Nor mine."

"Dafne, would you give us a minute?"

My relief at being able to flee was short-lived, as Harlan stopped me. "No need. There is nothing I could tell you that a diligent librarian would not find in the texts. Suffice to say that I am the youngest of seven boys and the only disappointment. They washed their hands of me. There may be lingering acrimony on their part, but more likely utter lack of interest. Kral is the shark and I am the rabbit. He would not be here for me."

I didn't quite believe him and neither did Ursula, by the narrow look she gave him, the one that presaged one of her infamous interrogations. Then Zynda knocked, and I didn't miss the flicker of relief in Harlan's eyes.

She wore her hair long and loose in the Tala style, and a blue dress the exact color of the sea at Annfwn, shades lighter than her deep-blue eyes. Ursula explained the problem and the need for discretion. Zynda eagerly agreed to take wing.

"I'd love to see more of this land," she said. "I will go to this Ehas and ask about a ship, then look for this army with the shark banner and come back here. Just explain where these places are."

"Danu take it." Ursula looked annoyed. "I didn't think of that. How can we describe it so you'll know?"

Zynda's eyes sparkled with easy good humor and she waved a graceful hand at the map. "This is how it looks from the air. Show me on your drawing. But color in the details."

"Can you remember details like in that in bird form?" I asked, unable to restrain my curiosity.

She shrugged and pursed her lips. "Yes and no. It's difficult to explain. I don't *think* the same way in animal form, but it's as if part of me has a . . . filtered access to what my human mind knows. As if it's still there, just not physically present."

"That makes no sense." Ursula shook her head. "How can your human brain still exist somewhere if you've converted it into a bird one?"

She couldn't quite mask the shiver of revulsion, and Zynda grinned at her discomfort. The only one of the three sisters to bear the mark of the Tala, Andi was able to shape-shift. Ami's daughter, Stella, also bore the mark, which had affected Ami pro-foundly during her pregnancy, though she attributed any unusual abilities to the gifts of Glorianna. Still, both Stella and her brother, Astar, had already shape-shifted, so the blood still ran strong. Andi had pointed out that Ursula's unusual fighting speed, strength, and resilience came from latent shape-shifting talents, but the High Queen preferred her skin as it was.

Quite understandable, really.

"Magic, Cousin," Zynda said with a lingering smile. "It allows many things to exist at once. Some say that shape-shifting isn't truly changing forms at all, but rather exchanging a form we exist in, in this world, for one in another. So perhaps in this parallel realm, I am always the bird. Then, when I shift here, I trade places and my human body goes there."

Ursula pointed a long finger at her. "That does *not* sound better."

"Can you imagine the chaos if you lived in the other world, where people changed form because a consciousness elsewhere decided upon it?" I asked, thinking aloud, and Ursula threw me a disgusted look.

"Thank you for making my head ache more," she griped, and Harlan laughed. His dark mood had eased and I realized she'd been encouraging the diversion, for just that reason.

Remarkable.

"I'll lead the Hawks and anyone else I can get on horseback this afternoon." Ursula showed her on the map. "We'll be on this road, which you'll see leading out of Ordnung. Find us along that route and—"

I cleared my throat loudly and she jammed her fists on her hips. "I'm not idling inside Ordnung while a foreign army marches through *my* lands, marauding and Danu knows what else."

I folded my hands and kept my mouth shut.

"Fine." She threw up her hands. "Say it already."

"You can't go."

"Politics can wait, librarian. There's a battalion that—"

"I'm perfectly aware. But your place is on the throne, not on the battle lines. Send all the troops, your Hawks or Vervaldr, even Captain Harlan, but *you* cannot go."

She visibly seethed. "I won't hide like my father did."

"No, you won't. You'll be far too busy. You know full well there's a monumental amount of work to be done to ready Ordnung— including solidifying your relationships with the monarchs and ambassadors whose continuing support you'll need. Regardless of General Kral's intention, you must be in a position of secure power when he arrives."

"Dafne is right," Harlan inserted before Ursula could vent the angry words she had ready. "He'll be looking for weakness. And I'm sorry to say it, but he'll assume that of a woman."

"Then he'll be in for a surprise," she snapped.

"Yes. He will. I'm actually looking forward to witnessing that." The admiration in his eyes did a great deal to soothe her ire. "But Dafne is correct that Kral will capitalize on any divisiveness he detects. Your soundest strategy is in consolidating your seat here. You will need to be High Queen, without question. I will, of course, remain at your back."

"You want me to sit here and wait for his arrival. Knowing your brother, that's what you advise."

Harlan thought a moment, came to a decision with a nod. "Yes. He won't maraud if it's not necessary, if only because it will slow him. I advise passing the word as much as possible that he's not to be opposed and that they should be given any supplies they request. Leave the way clear for Kral to come here and go nowhere else. Move your forces as you can to hem him in on the sides and after he's passed. Clear the path and, yes, wait for him to arrive, knock at the gates, and tell us what he wants. If you don't like what he says, you'll have him trapped."

"And if he does have an invasion force anchored offshore? They could come up behind our troops and have *us* trapped."

"That could happen regardless. The positive there is now we are on alert and you can notify Ehas and Elcinea to prepare for that possibility. Send them reinforcements. It's not quick or easy to invade from ships onto land."

"I've never had to think that way," Ursula admitted. She sighed. "All right. I'll have Jepp's scouts spread the word. I want everyone inside Ordnung with the gates closed four days from today, in case Harlan has their arrival pegged better than I do. At least Andi, Ami, and the babies are out of Ordnung, should it come to the worst." She meant siege, of course. In all the flurry of the past hours, that hadn't occurred to me as a real possibility. For someone with a haunting fear of siege situations, I ended up in them far too often.

"All right." Zynda stood and spoke into the foreboding silence that had fallen. "I'll go this moment. Unless there's more?"

We couldn't think of anything, and we watched, rapt, as the long-bodied woman shimmered, then condensed to the center, and a hummingbird as bright as jewels hovered in midair. Perhaps I'd expected a large raptor, like one of Rayfe's forms, and an astonished, delighted laugh escaped me. The hummingbird, with an iridescent blue throat the color of Zynda's eyes, zoomed a spiral around my head and buzzed musically out the window with enviable freedom.

3

In an unexpected development, the King of Carienne arrived the afternoon Zynda departed, along with an entourage large enough to be another small army. He'd left court in anger years before, long before Rayfe called in the contract on his betrothal to Andi, and Carienne had never sent an ambassador. They unfailingly paid their tithes, but never offered more than required—and forcibly resisted any of Uorsin's attempts to bully them into it. As Carienne had been one of the kingdoms that had not been conquered, but rather had voluntarily agreed to join the original Twelve, for the promise of peace and prosperity, they had succeeded in remaining aloof from squabbles, tending to fall out of mind.

Therefore, no one had been surprised that he had not attended the coronation, and as Carienne had never posed an explicit threat, we'd tabled the question of his fealty for the future.

The presence of King Groningen with his resplendent black beard and hearty laugh recalled better days—those early years of rebuilding after the Great War, when everyone had hope for a better future—which mitigated the tension that had settled over Ordnung amid rumors of more trouble to come. Particularly when he declared immediate loyalty to Ursula, along with his delight and congratulations at Uorsin's demise. The entourage, rather than bristling with weapons and hostility, instead brought the unlooked-for gift of the fruits of an excellent harvest to be shared as needed, in celebration of a new era.

Working quietly with Lise, Ordnung's chatelaine, I arranged to have those provisions stockpiled, just in case celebration turned to siege.

In private, Groningen brought apologies for his tardiness, along with tales of a sea monster recently glimpsed swimming in Lake Sullivan. A freshwater lake in the low mountains to the north, Lake Sullivan was so deep that none had ever determined where the bottom might be. At the center, the deep-blue water looked nearly black, and the lake stayed chill even in the hottest summers.

Ursula offered assistance with the sea monster, suggesting that the Tala might have wizards or shape-shifters who would know how to cope with it, but Groningen laughed, shaking his head.

"You mistake me, Your Majesty. Our sea monster goes back in legend for centuries and is said to be a bringer of good luck and prosperity. And look! Our harvests seemed to double overnight. My people are saying that magic has returned to the land and awakened our totem spirit."

He leaned in, dropping his voice conspiratorially, though the three of us dined alone in the family council chambers, as Harlan had taken the opportunity provided by trusting Ursula to a friendly ally to review Ordnung's fortifications with Marskal. The chambers had been considerably restored, with the many portraits of Uorsin removed, replaced by three of Ursula and her sisters, painted when they each turned fifteen.

"In truth, Your Majesty, you would do better to take note of rumors from the misty recesses of the Phoenix River."

"In Branli?" Ursula toyed with her wine goblet, appearing unstudied. But Branli also shared a border with Annfwn, and that's where the former High Priest of Glorianna, Kir, had disappeared to, thinking himself on a holy mission inspired by Glorianna, not concocted by Amelia in revenge for his corrupt influence on the church.

"Both our side of the river and theirs," Groningen conceded. "My scouts have not, however, uncovered much to be certain of. Still, there are tales of dark creatures and the dead come to life."

I choked a little on my tea and he nodded at me gravely. "As I heard similar stories from Ordnung, I thought you should know."

Yes, though what anyone could do about it was another question.

The morning after Groningen's arrival, Ursula convened formal court and shared what we knew. By then rumors had been floating among the courtiers, carried through the countryside faster than any scout—or even hummingbird—could go. Zynda had not yet returned, though we didn't expect her so soon, so whether Stefan's army would meet General Kral's remained an open question, with no one quite sure which outcome they hoped for. Harlan opined that his brother would easily dodge the slow-moving bulk of Duranor's forces.

Some members of court took the High Queen up on the suggestion that they flee Ordnung, in any direction but Kral's. Others, notably King Groningen, elected to stay and support the High Throne, even should it come to siege.

Zynda returned the following morning, markedly thinner and with an exhausted pallor that belied her story of her human body parking elsewhere while she took on an animal form. In Ursula's private rooms, she reported that Kral would likely arrive closer to Harlan's original estimate of four days and had indeed left a ship at anchor in Ehas, paying handsomely in gold to do so. More richly than he need have, as the harbormaster had been unable to explain the price and the Dasnarians had simply handed over several solid gold coins and departed, leaving a small group of intimidating-looking sailors to guard the ship.

"Not something one would expect of an invading force," Ursula commented.

"I'd love to see what coins he used," Harlan said from a chair by the fire. The weather had grown chilly, though the sun shone brightly enough to satisfy those who worried over omens.

"I couldn't carry them, not in that form," Zynda apologized.

He waved a hand at her. "I'm mostly curious."

"Why?" Ursula frowned at him.

"We have different coins," Harlan replied, "that indicate different treasuries. Gold coins are generally used only by the royal family, the other branches of our government, or agencies sponsored by them. Sometimes for a campaign, special coins will be minted as a kind of luck bringing. It would give a hint as to his intentions." He shrugged. "We'll find out soon enough."

"Yes," Zynda inserted. "I'm glad I made it back in time for formal dinner. I must go bathe and change."

"You don't need to be present," Ursula told her. "Aren't you exhausted?"

Zynda's grin lightened her face. "A bit tired, but I can't miss supporting my cousin and High Queen in public. Salena would come back and haunt me for it!"

Two days later, with all prepared on every front we could think of, the township protected, the road cleared of travelers, we waited those few tense hours for Kral to close the final distance. Ursula offered to take petitions, if only to kill the time, but no one stepped up. To maintain ceremony, along with the appearance of being unintimidated by Kral, Ursula had taken her place on the new throne for the first time since the coronation. It was a truly beautiful thing, a gift from Andi and Rayfe that reminded me of

Annfwn, a different sort of splendor that spoke of the magic of nature. Sitting alone where there had once been so many—one for each of the sisters, for Uorsin, and for Salena, empty ever since her death—the throne did the job of heralding a new era. Ursula wore the crown and new clothes that recalled her fighting leathers and their warrior's menace, but in rich fabrics.

As Harlan refused to leave her side, standing in his place just below the throne, the outer gates were manned with Vervaldr to conduct the initial conversations with Kral. They knew how to handle it—goddesses knew, Ursula had spent enough time going over every possibility imaginable—but she radiated impatience, clearly wishing to be on the walls herself.

I spent the time at my table, noting in my journal as much as I could of what had brought us to this point. I intended to keep a journal of these days and perhaps later write a history, my own contribution to archiving this era. Such important information should not be completely lost. It seemed unlikely that I wouldn't be able to continue the record, but after our disastrous collision with Illyria, everyone anticipated the worst.

At last, Jepp, looking unusually formal and reserved in the uniform of Ordnung's guard, entered the hall. Ursula shifted, coming alert, simmering with impatience as Jepp walked down the long aisle. With Marskal outside the walls leading the Hawks and other forces to close behind the Dasnarians, Jepp had the duty of being liaison. She hadn't liked it either, but Ursula had finally told her that misery loved company and Jepp could damn well be trapped inside the walls, too. She looked better for the days of forced inaction. At least someone had benefited from it.

"High Queen." Jepp bowed, her mobile face alight with interest now that something was finally happening. "General Kral of Dasnaria and Imperial Prince of the Royal House of Konyngrr asks admittance to Castle Ordnung and craves an audience with you."

Another prediction of Harlan's correct. So far he hadn't missed one.

"And his men?" she asked.

"He's willing to leave his battalion outside the walls, if he can bring a personal guard of five."

Ursula's gaze flicked to Harlan, who shook his head and held up three fingers.

"A personal guard of three and I'll receive him immediately."

A grin of anticipation split Jepp's face and she bowed again, a bit more saucily than the occasion merited. She wore a big knife and a set of daggers at her hips. Knowing her, she likely had any number more secreted on her person. She strode out and, again, we waited. At least I had my notes to occupy my nervous energy.

The clatter of heavy boots shattered the tense silence as the Dasnarians entered the hall. From my seated position, I couldn't see them over the heads of the courtiers immediately, but a rustle ran through the assembly, sounding like surprise and . . . awe?

Then they came into view. I expected them to be big. Harlan and the Vervaldr were all taller than our average, most of them with substantial bulk. But even surrounded by Vervaldr in Ordnung uniform, General Kral and his three guards outsized them all. No doubt, limited to only three, he'd picked his biggest and baddest. Even given that, Kral himself seemed enormous, an effect enhanced by the gleaming black armor they wore. They all wore broadswords on their backs, but unlike Harlan or any of the Vervaldr, they also wore heavy helms and gauntlets.

Four armored men. Exactly as Andi had seen. I only wished she'd told me how this would turn out.

Kral moved like a man accustomed to owning the room. Though I couldn't see much of his expression behind the helm, he seemed to study Ursula. He also looked to Harlan and away again, showing no sign of recognition. Stopping before her, the men pulled off their helms, which seemed to be a gesture of courtesy, but did not bow.

"Queen Ursula." His tone made it a question, his accent thick on the words.

" 'High Queen' or 'Your Majesty' is appropriate, General Kral of Dasnaria and Imperial Prince of the Royal House of Konyngrr.

Why do you bring an armed battalion to the High Throne of the Thirteen Kingdoms?"

Kral looked to Harlan's man, Brandur, who'd been the one to lead the conversation at the gates, but Harlan stepped forward and translated Ursula's words. A relief to me that he'd agreed, though he clearly had reservations in greeting his brother's arrival, but I feared my Dasnarian would not hold up to the delicate nature of this confrontation. Hearing the words Harlan chose only confirmed that. Also, it left me free to make a record of the conversation.

Kral paused. Harlan had warned us that Dasnarians rarely came straight to the point, instead preferring elaborate verbal dodging. It surprised none of us that Ursula went straight for a clean thrust, but it did take the general aback.

"I did not expect to find you at the feet of a woman, rabbit," Kral said in Dasnarian. The slight difference in the way he spoke Harlan's name made me think he deliberately meant the animal.

"Answer the High Queen's question, shark," Harlan replied, confirming my suspicion. Though he appeared as implacable as ever, his voice held a tone of suppressed anger.

"Are you a woman's lapdog, then?" Kral sneered.

Harlan did not reply, awaiting the answer, as did Ursula, staring down at Kral with convincing cool menace. Always people called Ami the avatar of Glorianna, an easy comparison to make. At moments such as this, I saw the warrior goddess Danu expressed in Ursula's clear gaze and shining strength. Kral assessed her, possibly rethinking, as if he saw it, too.

No, she was not what he had expected.

He spoke to her now, as he ought to have to begin with. "We were uncertain of the state of affairs here or what our reception would be. It seemed best to come in strength, should strength be necessary."

Harlan translated and Ursula received the words without reaction.

"And your mission?"

Kral did not like being questioned. A muscle flexed in his jaw. "Reconnaissance."

Ursula's gaze went to steel. "General Kral of Dasnaria and Imperial Prince of the Royal House of Konyngrr," she emphasized his titles, pointing out that he'd failed to use hers, "you are on my lands, in my realm, without invitation or diplomatic overtures. You arrogantly walk up to my gates with an armed force and without explanation. Dodging answers to my questions is not in the best interests of your continued good health."

Kral and his men flushed with anger as Harlan translated her words, bearing out Harlan's advice that they would never expect a woman, no matter her rank, to speak to a man so, let alone one of the royal house.

"You dare threaten me? I could crush your tiny realm without losing an eyelash. Your lands are riddled with weakness, ruled by a woman. My armed force traveled here without any opposition. Ridiculous! Your own people gave us supplies."

"Yes, as I commanded them to do. We've been watching you all along. Your ship and guard at Ehas have been impounded pending my findings here. You're trapped and surrounded. I can have you all killed and send your head back to Emperor Hestar with a note suggesting that next time Dasnaria should wait for an invitation."

Kral actually snarled, advancing a step, to be stopped by a fence of blades from the Vervaldr. He glared at them. "Where is your loyalty to your motherland?" None replied, frustrating him further.

"If you are here to start a war, General Kral of Dasnaria and Imperial Prince of the Royal House of Konyngrr, then you and your men will assuredly be the first casualties. We have weapons you cannot imagine." Ursula said, as softly as the whisk of a blade edge on a sharpening stone. "Zynda, would you mind demonstrating?"

The Tala woman stepped forward, flashing the Dasnarians a brilliant, sensual smile that all but Kral automatically returned, appreciation for her beauty in the filmy gown she wore evident in their eyes. Admiration that changed to shock and horror when she transformed in a blink into an enormous tiger. I'd seen only drawings of them in books, and the reality eclipsed even those stunning images. She sauntered toward the men, sat, and lifted a paw bigger than my head, licking it and lavishly displaying wicked claws.

"The claws are real," Ursula informed them. "I have a trained army of such people surrounding your small battalion. Your decision. Either start talking or be the first to die."

Kral lifted his gaze to Ursula's steely one, new respect in his face, and visibly wrestled himself under control. "Forgive me, High Queen. We have traveled long and at great speed. I come here at the direction of Emperor Hestar to answer a number of questions that have come to his attention of late. They would be perhaps better addressed in a private audience."

"Ask your questions and I shall decide whether and in what venue I'll provide answers."

A rush of soft laughter whispered out from the assembly. Ursula would not be bullied and neither would our realm.

Kral looked to be grinding his teeth. "Very well, High Queen. I was tasked to discover the fate of my brother, Harlan Konyngrr, which has been answered by his presence here. Also to determine the veracity of a rumor that he seduced a king's daughter and usurped a throne in a coup, which has been partially answered. Finding him alive, I am to bring him back to Dasnaria to answer charges for the murder of a high-placed priestess of the Temple of Deyrr. Finally, we seek retribution for a magical attack on our empire, which we consider a hostile move and blatant attempt to steal a valuable treasure horde."

To his credit, Harlan translated the damning words without inflection. Ursula considered with apparent disinterest, pursed her lips, and waved a negligent hand at Kral. "Describe the nature of this alleged magical attack."

He looked pointedly at the tiger. "Alleged? You have, perhaps unwisely, demonstrated that you have magic indeed."

"So you can't describe it."

"I can, but I want answers to my questions."

Ursula dropped the façade of boredom and leaned forward slightly, as intent as if she had drawn her sword. "You are in no position to bargain with me, General Kral of Dasnaria and Imperial Prince of the Royal House of Konyngrr. You bring an accusation that my 'tiny realm' has attacked yours. I expect you to back up that claim with immediate detail or withdraw it."

She gave even me a chill. I'd never been at the point of Ursula's sword, but this must be how it felt.

Kral gestured peremptorily to one of his guards, who produced a scroll and handed it to him. "The details are documented here. I assume my brother, at least, can still read his mother tongue."

Instead, Ursula looked to me. *Oh, wonderful.* Feeling my legs shake, I stood and approached the men, feeling smaller and more timid than possibly ever in my life. They watched me with perplexed expressions.

"Lady Mailloux, the High Queen's councilor and scribe, will examine the document," Harlan explained.

I put out my hand for the scroll and Kral narrowed his eyes, almost as if he recognized me, which wasn't possible. His hair was a darker gold than Harlan's, his eyes blue instead of pale gray. He gave it to me with a smirk. "Good luck reading it, *nyrri.*"

Not sure what he'd called me, I made myself return the hard stare and answered in his language. "I don't require luck, General Kral of Dasnaria and Imperial Prince of the Royal House of Konyngrr. I have knowledge."

Proud of myself for surprising the man, I turned my back on him and caught Ursula's slight smile as Harlan translated our exchange for her.

"You may be excused from my presence, General Kral of Dasnaria and Imperial Prince of the Royal House of Konyngrr," she said, smile vanishing. "You and your men will be escorted to a place you may make camp and rest from your taxing journey here. As a sign of continued good faith, we will provide you with food and water as well. I shall summon you if and when I'm ready to discuss your questions."

"If you truly wish to show good faith, release my brother from whatever spell you have him under and allow him to come with us."

Harlan cracked a smile as he translated, and Ursula laughed. "Prince Harlan Konyngrr is his own man, who comes and goes as he pleases. If he wishes to visit you, he will."

"Come with me now, then, rabbit."

"Perhaps later," Harlan said, making it clear he would not discuss it further.

Without further politeness, Kral turned on his heel and stalked out of the hall, nearly outpacing his escort with his furious strides. The hall doors slammed behind them, the sound ringing through the assembly hall. Silence reigned for a moment; then King Groningen stood, bowed to Ursula, and said, "Well done, my Queen. Well done." He raised his voice, "All hail the High Queen!"

With a resounding roar of approval, they did.

4

"Danu, I'd rather take my sword to that man than trade words with him again." Ursula strode into the council chambers, having adjourned court after sending me ahead to study the scroll in more detail.

"Groningen is right," Harlan replied. "You did well. Kral did not expect your talons. As I expected, it was a treat to watch you gut him."

"Hardly. I'm not sure I even scratched him."

"Oh, you did. Believe me. But don't call me 'prince' again." Usually so even tempered, Harlan sounded brusque enough that Ursula gave him a long look.

"I only meant to point out your rank in comparison to mine and his. I might not understand Dasnarian, but I heard the insult in his tone to you quite clearly."

"I know why and I appreciate it." He brushed her cheek in apology. "I, however, put that person behind me. I am no prince of Dasnaria."

"Given what we witnessed today, I can understand that." Ursula dropped herself into the chair beside me, peering over my shoulder at the text as if she could read it. "What does the cursed thing say?"

"I might need Captain Harlan's assistance on a few words. What does this mean?"

"Volcano."

Great. More volcanoes erupting. "So the gist of it is that one of their protectorate kingdoms, I think—not Dasnaria, but an island called Nahanau?" He nodded at my pronunciation. "The island experienced a number of unusual events."

"Nahanau is actually a chain of islands," Harlan explained, sitting on my other side to study the scroll also. "Somewhere between the Thirteen and Dasnaria. It might not be far from Annfwn, in truth, in the waters west of it."

"Danu's tits," Ursula cursed softly.

I nodded in agreement. "The timing seems to match when the barrier fell. Apparently there's a dormant volcano—or the islands *are* dormant volcanoes?"

"Much like at Windroven," Ursula commented.

"Makes sense. Nahanau experienced a tremendous storm with strange elements. Driving rain in different colors, wingless creatures falling from the sky. And, if I'm reading this correctly, something inside the volcano, which is no longer dormant."

"You're reading it correctly," Harlan said in a grim tone.

"The something is . . . a *mo'o*?"

He shook his head. "That's not a Dasnarian word, but the one next to it, *gyll*, means gold."

"People died," I told Ursula, who returned my gaze, eyes dark with sorrow.

"It's my fault." She sighed and scrubbed her hands through her hair, hitting the crown she'd forgotten she wore and tossing it on the table.

"Amelia would say you simply acted on the will of the goddesses," I pointed out. "Regardless, you did what you had to do. None could have known the barrier would collapse and magic blow out everywhere like that."

"Andi knew," she said thoughtfully. "And she thought that maybe the barrier didn't collapse, but stretched, because she could still feel it. Whatever secret magic she does back in Annfwn, she was going to do it and report back. If the barrier moved instead of falling, it could be that Nahanau is now inside it."

"Other parts of the Thirteen experienced similar storms—perhaps from the barrier passing through as it expanded?"

"Could be. I wish we could ask Andi. We don't have all the time in the world."

"We could send Zynda."

"I don't think we need to yet. I'll have to answer Kral's charges first. I don't much like that he's right. At least I can tell him that I killed Illyria, not you," she said to Harlan. "Dasnaria can charge me with her murder if they want to."

"That part makes little sense. The Temple of Deyrr might be angry about it, but the Crown doesn't do the temple's bidding. Hestar would not send Kral all this way over the death of a priestess. Especially as she wasn't acting for the empire, but rather on a private quest of hers or the temple's."

"To obtain the Star of Annfwn," she agreed.

"And we still don't know why." I turned to Ursula. "Can you explain to me what it does—or did?"

"Does, I think." She stretched back in her chair, eyeing the crown. "It was passed down among the queens of Annfwn. Salena gave it to me when I was a girl and told me that it would guide me." She flicked me a look full of irritation. "So vague as to be worthless. I know it responds to my sisters, heating when they're near."

"Even still?" Harlan asked with concern.

She put a hand over her stomach. "Even still."

"I don't like that it remains inside you. That can't be good for your health."

Ursula gave him a slanted smile and raised her brows. "Will you cut it out of me, then? I seem to be fine, and at least we don't have to worry about hiding it from Deyrr. That reminds me, though, Dafne—you should add that to your records, that when I die, it *should* be cut out of me and given to Stella."

Not something I wanted to think about, but I made a note. "You swallowed it before whatever you three did that changed the barrier."

"Whatever we did, yes."

"Could the 'guiding' aspect be that the Star allowed you to determine where the barrier would be?"

She studied me thoughtfully. "An interesting thought. Andi communicates with the barrier, keeps it strong and governs its permeability from what she calls the Heart of Annfwn—and no, I don't know what it is. It's apparently some deep, dark secret and she refused to say. Don't write that down. I'm probably not supposed to have told you."

"Not unlike the secrecy around the Star."

"True. But I don't think I decided to move the barrier."

"What if you did, without realizing it? Protecting your realm is always at the forefront of your thoughts," Harlan said. "The Star might have responded to that and extended the barrier to encompass them all, guided by your will."

"If so, then how did Nahanau, which I've never heard of before this day, get caught up?"

"Andi talked about the barrier like a dome," I said, thinking it through. "What if it's shaped like the soap bubbles children play with when the maids do laundry? The word 'heart' implies a center—what if it has to be a sphere radiating out from there? So when you guided it outward to cover all the Twelve plus Annfwn, it went in every direction, sweeping up Nahanau also."

She closed her eyes briefly, perhaps offering a prayer to Danu. "You want me to tell Kral that I not only attacked Nahanau, but I annexed it?"

"It would be interesting to watch his face," Harlan remarked in some satisfaction.

"Oh, yes, laugh. Keep laughing when he brings down the might of Dasnaria on our heads for it."

"Wait." A thought occurred to me. "If our theory is correct and the barrier didn't collapse, but expanded, how did Kral sail through it to get here?"

They stared back at me with expressions of dawning comprehension. "They didn't," Harlan said. "The ship was already inside, probably in the Nahanau islands. Kral has long been fascinated by the place."

Ursula nodded slowly. "That has to be it. So Kral is bluffing about being sent by Hestar. He's here on his own, with all the men he has."

"It is very much in character for him to bluff like this, yes."

"Then we have an advantage over him and I intend to use it. Perhaps we can knock down his bravado enough for him to let me make amends without him seeing me as weak."

"So, what is this gold that's mentioned?" I frowned at the document and checked my notes. "He said that in his initial accusation, too—'a valuable treasure horde.'"

"One way to find out. Let's have him summoned. Bring him here to talk privately. See if you can convince him to leave the muscle behind."

Harlan stood and kissed her on the top of the head. "Yes, Your Majesty. Remember to put your crown back on."

She glared at it balefully. "I already hate the thing."

Letting her stew, I went to arrange for food. Perhaps food and wine would soothe some of Kral's savagery.

Kral glared as balefully at the food as Ursula had at her crown, then shoved it away. "How do I know you don't seek to poison me?"

Ursula stiffened in offense—she might slit his throat, but a warrior of Danu would never stoop to poison—so, with a sigh, I took a slice of meat from his plate and ate it. "It's not poisoned."

"It could be poisoned with a substance you've developed a tolerance for," he said, his gaze going to Harlan and Ursula. Kral looked different without the armor. Taller than Harlan, yes, but not as heavily built. A leaner, somewhat darker, sharper version. The shark.

He'd brought his guards but agreed to leave them outside the room. He wore his sword, however, so Harlan did also. Ursula had convinced Harlan that he couldn't stand behind her as he preferred, because it would look like protective hovering and Kral would interpret that as weakness on her part. Harlan conceded the point, sitting at the table to translate. Instead of translating that last for Ursula, he spoke directly to his brother.

"Kral. I know we have anger between us and this incident has started badly. However, the High Queen is interested only in protecting her realm. She has no need to kill you if your problems can be resolved diplomatically. Besides," he said with a malicious grin, "she is a highly trained fighter such as you've never seen. She moves faster than a snake heated by the sun. If she decided to kill you, it would be with a blade, not poison."

Kral listened, not looking at Ursula. "She has seduced you. Are you certain there's no black magic at hand? Tell me now and I'll free you." He glanced at me. "The *nyrri* understands, I know, but *she* is no warrior. I can silence her easily if she attempts to speak."

"I have given Ursula the *Elskastholrr*," Harlan told him, then nodded at Kral's astonishment.

Ursula looked between them, gaze sharp. She'd recognize that word if nothing else, along with her name, and she returned Kral's long, assessing stare with unflinching steel.

"You . . . You what? But . . . that cannot be compelled. Which means you have gone crazier than I thought." Unexpectedly, Kral broke out into an enormous laugh, booming like Harlan's, and grabbed the plate back, stabbing a slice of meat with a small dagger. He stuffed the meat in his mouth and pointed the dagger at Harlan. "At least you shall make a colorful contribution to the grand Dasnarian tradition of pledging doomed eternal love to the worst choice possible. Will she make you king?"

"I have no wish to be king."

"Nonsense, every man wishes to be king. Any man with balls."

"Is that why you are here, Kral—do you think to be king here since you will never reach that status in Dasnaria?"

"Perhaps." He nodded thoughtfully, scanning the room. "You know I could bring an army so vast that your queen would fall, no matter the speed of her sword or how many pet magicians she calls to her."

"Ah, but there we know you are lying, Kral." Harlan translated for Ursula, handing her the conversational ball. Like the hawk he called her, she went in for the kill.

It took hours—well into the evening—before Kral cracked and admitted that all had happened just as we'd surmised. He'd been on a mission to Nahanau when the magic storm hit. The devastation had been enough to stymie whatever they'd been there to do, which he would not elaborate on. Not wanting to strain the resources of the devastated islands, they'd left for home, with the intent of returning at another time.

And hit the barrier.

They had sailed south along its edge, seeking a way through, until they found themselves rounding the Crane Isthmus, following land north again in search of human habitation. One of his men was a historian and recognized Windroven's distinctive profile from drawings and recalled the peaceful Port of Ehas as a place that had welcomed Dasnarians in the past.

" 'Welcomed' as in 'were easily conquered,' " Ursula inserted.

Kral grinned at her, still the shark with his flashing teeth, but no longer so hungry. "Would you have picked a different strategy?"

She conceded with a twitch of her shoulder.

"My historian knows enough of your Common Tongue to eavesdrop, especially as your realm is churning with discussion of recent events. A High King dead. A High Queen stepping over his body to the throne. And, against all probability, my baby brother and the Temple of Deyrr, in the thick of it."

"Do not lump me in with Illyria," Harlan told him, and Kral surveyed him, wary again.

"So she was here."

"She was, and, no—I don't know how or why."

"It's bad business to mess with the practitioners of Deyrr."

"Believe me, I did not do so willingly."

"It relieves me to know that. I had bad moments, wondering."

"Then why make a production of accusing us of her murder and threatening to drag me back to face charges?"

"If you were unwillingly chained to your queen, it would have been a good gambit to take you away from her. I knew you could not have killed Illyria, so I offered the people here a scapegoat to pin the murder on, to escape the might of Dasnaria. I thought they might let our ship through the barrier wall to get rid of us."

"I'm surprised you cared so much for my fate."

Kral heaved out a sigh and folded his hands together on the table, a habit Harlan shared. "Many years have passed since you left, and I am not the same man I was. I . . . have regretted the nature of our parting. I would not have sought you out—would not have known how to—but now *hlyti* has brought us together. I knew it as soon as we landed at Ehas and heard your name in the rumors. I wish to make amends with you."

"These are easy, and convenient, words to say." Harlan considered. "Show me you mean to work together with us."

Kral thought a moment. "Illyria's presence here could have had something to do with a man who calls himself a High Priest of the Twelve Kingdoms, who has been consorting with the temple."

I gasped and Harlan sat upright at that. "What do you say?"

"I know primarily from gossip. It's unusual for a man to both wear pink—I saw those pink-garbed priests in your court—and be foreign. But it is a connection. I'm willing to trade information and assistance in return for being allowed to take my men home.

Along with an explanation for the attack on Nahanau and restitution for the damage King Nakoa KauPo and his people suffered."

Ursula had been patient with Harlan falling into conversation with his brother and translating only intermittently. She trusted both of us to fill her in completely later—or trusted her ability to badger us into doing so. But she had caught our alarm and surprise and spoke up sharply. "Translate."

"Kral says that, if I'm not mistaken, Queen Amelia's missing High Priest may have found his way to Dasnaria and is in the company of the Temple of Deyrr."

Anger flared in her gaze and she just stopped herself from putting a hand to her sword. "Then he's a traitor. Don't translate that."

"Kral is offering the information as a token of goodwill. He knows we have him trapped and he . . . wishes to make amends with me for past offenses." Harlan explained the terms and Ursula thought about it while I took out a blank parchment, anticipating the agreement to be drawn up.

"Do you trust him?"

"I don't distrust him." Harlan looked long at her, as if seeking some kind of anchor. "I think you have nothing to lose. The restitution he asks is something your honor and sense of responsibility would compel you to do regardless, especially as these people fall within your realm. You will have to address the issue of any other ships trapped within the barrier, so you'll have to set policy on that. I advise downplaying the accidental nature of the incident and simply offer assistance in helping them return home."

"If Andi can even do it."

"Something we'll need to know," I pointed out. "We're facing the same situation Salena and the Tala did if we're trapped within our own magical barrier, except over a bigger area and hopefully with more time." Zynda and I had debated this during my time in Annfwn. An argument she'd made had stuck with me, an uneasy thought. *What if magic is more like fire and the more fuel it has, the hotter it burns?*

"What about this treasure he thinks we tried to take, the gold?"

Kral smiled easily when Harlan asked. "The Nahanau islands are rich in many ways. Why else attack? Be warned, however, King Nakoa KauPo is most obstinate. He will not see his islands assimilated into another realm easily. Dasnaria has been trying for years."

Harlan studied his brother. "Why not simply take a force and conquer?"

"Far more easily said than done. Your queen will want to send an ambassador to negotiate. Someone nonthreatening." His gaze lingered on me a moment before he pulled it away. "Do we have a deal or not?" He was evading, but Harlan let it go and I agreed with his choice. It likely didn't matter.

Harlan summarized the last for Ursula, who nodded crisply and held out a hand to Kral. "Let's hammer out the agreement, then."

She surprised him only for a moment; then Kral clasped hers in return, flashing a glance at Harlan. "She has sword calluses."

Harlan grinned, looking pleased for the first time since Kral's arrival. "I know. A large factor in her seducing me and bending me to her will."

"Hmm." Kral released Ursula's hand and bowed slightly from the waist, his respect solidified. "I begin to understand the attraction. Are there more like her?"

"Women warriors? As a matter of fact, there are. Once we make this agreement, I shall introduce you."

"Then, let us have at it. Scribe away, *nyrri*." Kral gestured at me. "I find myself hungry for more than meat."

That part didn't take long at all. I had my notes, so we simply reviewed the terms and I wrote it out twice—once in Common Tongue and once in Dasnarian. Kral and Ursula set their seals to both. The logistics would take more discussion, but with relief we left the council chambers with the possibility of conflict resolved. Ursula walked ahead, escorting Kral, while Harlan and I followed behind.

"Will you really introduce him to one of the women warriors?"

Harlan lifted one shoulder and let it fall. "I will pass the word to Jepp of Kral's interest, and she can tell the Hawks. Best to keep it within their ranks. More than one will likely be interested in Kral's offer. They know how to handle Dasnarian men."

I shouldn't have asked the question, because I blushed then. Any number of women at Ordnung had sampled what the Vervaldr offered and talked about the results as very satisfactory. I couldn't see the appeal, myself, much as I liked Harlan.

He must have sensed my unease because he patted my shoulder. "Have no concerns, librarian. Kral may be a shark, but he'd never take a woman unwilling."

"What is that word he calls me?" I asked him. "Is it an insult?"

Harlan grimaced slightly. "Not exactly. I don't think he means it as such, but you might take offense."

Not like him to be less than straightforward. "Just tell me."

"It means a small, female nature spirit, one that lives in the cinnamon trees. Your eyes are very much that color and you are . . ."

"Short," I filled in.

"Which is not an insult," he hastened to add. "But compared to Dasnarians, you do seem unusually . . . I can't think of the right word in your tongue."

Ursula made a snorting sound and said over her shoulder, "Yes, you can. You just don't want to say it."

"It's fine," I said. "I understand now."

We entered the dining hall. Despite the late hour, an astonishing number of people had gathered to enjoy a celebration of coming to accord with the Dasnarians. Ursula asked Harlan to show his brother a seat—now as guest of honor—and to provide him with whatever he wanted. "*I* will pass word to Jepp," she informed him wryly.

"So you can give instructions?"

She smiled thinly. "And so you can talk to your brother. Extract some of those amends he owes you, so I don't have to." Though she tried to pass it off as a joke, her quiet concern for him showed through.

He laughed, a soft one, and shook his head. "Will you fight all the world for me?"

"Yes. Which I don't have time for."

Kral looked back and forth between them, apparently bemused. Harlan lifted Ursula's hand and bowed over it, kissing the back. His fingers caressed her palm as he did and I wondered if she knew how he felt about her calluses.

"Come, shark," Harlan said to his brother. "Let us take a cup of wine together and talk of old times."

"Have you anything stronger than wine, rabbit?"

"I might. I just might."

5

After staying through some obligatory toasts, I passed on the remainder of the party, exhaustion crashing over me. Even so, by the time I left, Harlan and Kral had already put away a fair amount of some liquor Brandur brought from the Vervaldr barracks, and several female Hawks, including Jepp, were matching them shot for shot. Ursula stuck to wine but seemed amused to sit by and watch, nodding absently when I excused myself.

When I awoke, easily an hour or two past my usual rising time, I wasn't surprised to find a page waiting, asking me to attend Ursula in her chambers as soon as I'd had my tea. Feeling more than a little abashed and lazy at sleeping so long, I pulled myself together with a quick wash in the handbasin while my tea brewed, then took the pot with me. Ursula liked the same blend, one from Nebeltfens.

I found her at her desk, surrounded by scrolls and various missives, and filled her empty cup. She looked remarkably bright-eyed considering she must have stayed up far later than I. Since Harlan's advent she seemed to sleep far more and better. All those years of short nights and restless pacing had probably made her more tolerant of lost sleep, and getting more rest these days improved her resilience enviably.

"Where is Captain Harlan?" I asked.

She made a face. "Passed out sometime before dawn. Can't you hear him? Listen a moment."

A rattle, something between an angry bear and thunder, echoed through the closed door to her sleeping chambers just then. "Goddesses," I whispered.

She grinned in fond amusement. "I don't know how I sleep through it, but I do. And you don't need to whisper—he's like the dead. It's rare for him not to notice I've gotten up, and it's been hours. If not for the snoring, I'd be concerned."

"I'm sorry I overslept."

"Don't be. You needed it, too. I've been for my workout, tended to some business, had one pot of tea, and am happy to share another. I'm glad Harlan is still sleeping so you and I can discuss next steps in private."

I got out my notes. "So, you'll want to determine what supplies we can—"

"Not about that," she interrupted. "Yes, we'll have to determine that, but I've already talked to Lise and set a few people to work on deciding what we can spare most easily. Thank Danu for Groningen's largesse. Later today, I'll get Harlan to interview Kral—sober, preferably—on exactly what the Nahanauns will need most and how best to negotiate with this King Nakoa KauPo. Zynda has already left for Annfwn. She'll explain the situation to Andi and come straight back, hopefully by this evening."

"You have been busy this morning. We both know the fastest way to Nahanau would be through Annfwn."

She was already shaking her head. "No way in the Twelve—Thirteen—am I letting Kral get a look at Annfwn's bounty, even if I wasn't sure Rayfe would have my head for it. No, Kral's ship is in Ehas, so you'll travel there and sail around the Crane Isthmus, taking the most important emergency supplies, with our ships following behind later with the less critical. Depending on Andi's reply, she can either meet you there from Annfwn, as she can probably shift into a fish or some such and swim there, or she might be able to control the barrier from the Heart and assist with sending you through from a distance."

I'd been taking notes as she talked. Paused. " 'You'? As in . . . me?"

"I want you to go with them, Dafne."

I felt myself gaping at her, my brain clearly not awake enough. Picking up my teacup, I drank deeply, willing the kick to penetrate to my mind along with the warmth. "You want me to go to Nahanau?"

"Yes," she said, laying her palms flat on the desk. "And from there to Dasnaria."

"But . . . I—I *can't*."

She held up a hand. "Hear me out. If you find a flaw in my logic, I'll reconsider." She stood and started pacing. "This is what I'm thinking. I need someone to smooth the way with this King Nakoa KauPo. Kral told me more last night, when he was well into his cups. The man is a warrior king, very difficult to deal with. The Nahanauns treat him like a god. You can present the supplies as a gift and sweeten him up for later discussions of how to merge our kingdoms. Kral offered to help you with translation from Dasnarian to Nahanaun. You won't need to say much—don't tell him anything about the magic barrier yet; we'll wait until Andi knows more about manipulating this new version. You're good at that kind of diplomacy."

"All right, but . . . *Dasnaria*?"

"If Kir is in Dasnaria and conspiring with the Temple of Deyrr, it's possible that he's the one behind Illyria coming here to seek the Star of Annfwn. He knew something about the dolls Salena left us—at least enough to have interfered with the magical tool Salena left Ami in hers. It's not clear what Deyrr knew before, but it seems they've put their pieces together to come up with a purpose for it. Thus the answers to why Deyrr wants the Star—along with how badly, what they plan to do with it, if they will make an-

other attempt, what we need to do to counter it—all lie in Dasnaria, with the temple.

"You speak Dasnarian; you read it as well, including older books
and documents with their more archaic texts. You know how to do
the research and you're already familiar with Deyrr, to the extent
any of us is. I'd send Harlan to find out, but we both know he's too
stubborn to go, especially with all the unrest here, and besides, he
doesn't have your talent for ferreting out information. Nor does
he have your particular subtlety and guile."

"My . . . my guile?" I couldn't seem to stop stammering.

She gave me a look both stern and amused. "Please, librarian.
You vanished yourself from Uorsin's attention, something that
only Andi also accomplished, and now we know she had magic to
help her. You didn't. And you not only survived the court here,
but lived to see your long-term plans unfold. You manage me better than Derodotur ever did my father—don't think I don't notice
and appreciate it. You manage Andi and Ami equally well, which
means you're very good at reading people and adapting to their
personalities. More, you look like a *nyrri* to the Dasnarians, on
top of being female, so they won't suspect you *and* they'll underestimate you." She stopped in front of her desk, leaning against it.
"You're the perfect spy."

I'd mustered some coherent thoughts while she spoke. "Spies
know how to defend themselves. I do not."

"I'll teach you some tricks. If Ash could get the basics through
Ami's stubborn skull, then by Danu I can teach you. And I'm not
sending you alone. I'm asking Jepp and Zynda to go with you.
Zynda can continue to be our messenger and Jepp can be your
guide and bodyguard. Nobody gets past her knives. Also, she
knows enough of the Dasnarian customs and language by now to
be an asset—even if most of it is related to sex play." She smiled
sourly.

"But you need me here."

Ursula sobered, going intense in that Danu-channeling way she
had. "I need you more there. I wouldn't ask it of you if I didn't.

We need eyes—and ears—in Dasnaria. You're the only one who can do this." It seemed far too huge to contemplate. Harlan's voice echoed in my head: *Hlyti is playing a fine game with me.*

For a time I'd thought *hlyti* meant fate, until I asked him one day.

"*Hlyti*," he'd said, "is more as Queen Amelia believed Glorianna guided her steps in bringing magic back to the Twelve. But not an actual deity."

" 'Fate,' we would say, which does sound like a similar derivation," I'd answered.

He'd rumbled a thoughtful sound, then shook his head. "Perhaps so, but in that case the meanings have migrated. Other words I've found close to *hlyti* are 'serendipity' and 'coincidence.' Still, they are not quite right. It's following one path over another for no good reason other than some sense that it will take you to the place you need to be." He slanted me a sly look. "Perhaps like your desire to learn a language you don't need."

"That is something else entirely. I want to learn because the best fence against the world is a thorough knowledge of it."

"And you feel you must have this fence?"

"Don't we all? Each of us is under siege in some way. You have your muscles, your weapons and warrior's skills. I do not. But knowledge is more than equivalent to force, some say."

"Hmm. A great Dasnarian poet said, 'It takes more courage to examine the dark corners of your own soul than it does for a soldier to fight on a battlefield.' "

His words felt like a prophecy now, of this mission Ursula laid before me. How would I get access to the texts? How would I know where to find the people of the temple and get them to talk to me? I'd have to figure it out, make a plan. But how do you plan for something you know nothing about? All I could do was get through one moment and to the next. *Deep breaths.* Ursula was watching me closely, so I summoned a smile for her.

I could no more refuse her than I could the goddess herself.

"All right, I'll go." I nearly lost my breath saying it. Was I really going to do this? "But I am *not* getting myself married to some Dasnarian prince, if that's what you're plotting."

She didn't laugh. Instead she straightened and put her hand over her heart, giving me the Hawks' salute. "Thank you, Dafne."

A first for me, of course. A salutation for warriors, for the brave adventurers. It gutted me and it seemed in that moment that maybe I could be something more than I'd been. I stood and, instead of curtsying, I returned the salute.

"Thank you, my Queen."

I'd just become one of her Hawks.

The next morning found me doing something I'd never envisioned—learning basic self-defense. And from not just Ursula. I'd reported to the private courtyard at dawn as ordered by my queen to find Harlan and Jepp waiting also.

Ursula scowled at the sight of my fighting leathers. "How old are those?"

"Old. It's not as if I need them often," I answered, feeling more than a little cranky about it all. And it wasn't like I had access to an unlimited wardrobe budget. "Besides, you're sending me as an ambassador, which means I'll be wearing court gowns most of the time. If I have to defend myself, it will likely be in a dress."

She sighed for the truth of it and turned her razor gaze on Jepp. "Dafne has a point. As you travel, you'll have to work with her in her everyday clothes, too."

"Yes, Captain." Jepp winked at me from behind Ursula.

Ursula pointed at me. "But you make time to get a better set made. These offend Danu's eyes."

"I've already spent hours with the seamstresses, and I have so many things to—"

"Consider it payback for all the times you dressed *me* to your standards," she snapped. Also cranky. Now that we'd set the wheels in motion, Ursula had started to worry. It hadn't been a full day since our conversation and already she'd given me more advice, cautions, and caveats than I'd be able to stuff into my memory given twice as many days.

"I'll make time," I told her.

"Speaking of time," Harlan gently intervened. "Shall we proceed with the lesson?"

Ursula rolled her head on her shoulders. "Yes. We should. All right, librarian. We've no time to teach you Danu's forms, which would be the foundation of what you need to know as a fighter. Instead we're going to show you the tricks—all with the intent of you gaining time to escape should you be attacked. For the most part, your aim will not be to kill or permanently disable an attacker. You don't want to be that close for that long. Instead you will focus on hurting a person enough that they can't chase you. We'll lay the groundwork this morning and then Jepp will take over after you leave tomorrow, helping you refine the skills and build on them. Does that make sense?"

"You've no time to teach me the entire alphabet so you're giving me the equivalent of conversational phrases that I can practice and add to as I learn this language."

Her frown cracked and she laughed. "Exactly. You'll do just fine. I know you will."

I knew she meant more than just with knife work and I nodded, hoping to reassure her.

"The first thing you'll learn is what to do when someone grabs you. Jepp, demonstrate. Let Harlan catch you, and break free."

Jepp sauntered up to Harlan and gave him a saucy grin of challenge. "Captain Harlan can catch me anytime." She turned her back, and he launched himself at her, dwarfing her slim form, muscles bulging in his sleeveless shirt as they flexed to restrain her. She seemed to fold in, then burst out, spinning in place and halting with a sharp blade at his throat.

He grinned at her. "Lucky indeed would be the man who could both catch *and* hold you."

"Stop flirting, you two," Ursula said. "Now you try it, Dafne."

"I can't do that!"

"You can and you will." She pressed a short knife into my hand, much like the daggers she and Jepp habitually carried, but made of wood with blunted edges. "Harlan?"

He advanced and I took an automatic step back. "I can't get away from a man that size!"

"You're going to a place where they are *all* that size," she emphasized. "Better to learn with someone you know and trust."

"Maybe I should start with Jepp?" I offered weakly, but Ursula shook her head, a determined set to her jaw.

"Jepp is here to see what we teach you. Today you're working entirely against Harlan and me. You have to experience what it's like to be up against someone bigger and more skilled."

I wished for some of the thrill I'd felt yesterday when I accepted this mission. Being called to adventure turned out to involve a great deal of unpleasant challenges.

I nodded in resignation and turned my back. Harlan's big arms closed around me, trapping my arms against my sides, sending a flutter of panic through me. *Trapped in the dark. Unable to move. My throat on fire. Can't breathe.* I whimpered and his arms loosened.

"Tighter than that, Harlan. Don't go easy on her," Ursula's voice whipped out.

"She's afraid." His voice rumbled against my back, an oddly comforting sensation that worked some to lessen my rising fear, but only a little. "She doesn't like being trapped."

Of course he'd remember, from that story I'd told him, of the fall of my family's castle. Ursula bent over so her eyes were level with mine, bright steel. "Use it," she commanded. "Everyone feels fear at some point. That's healthy self-preservation. It's also the fuel that will drive you to survive. You've called on it all these years. People underestimate you—use that, too. Now, let him think he has you, collapse a little, like you're fainting. He senses your fear so he'll believe it. Let your weight sag, so he's forced to support you, then call on that will to survive. Picture it like a sun burning in your heart. Push up from the ground and rise. Burst up and out. Do it."

It helped not to fight the panic. *Use it.* I let myself collapse as she said, feeling Harlan's arms tighten to keep me upright. That dark space. *Trapped.* The fear burned like a sun indeed, and I wondered how Ursula knew. It wanted to break free, so I let it. Harlan grunted, his hold breaking.

I'd done it!

"Good," Ursula said, "but don't just stand there. Break, stab him with the knife, and run. Hold her again."

Ursula was a relentless taskmaster. I'd seen her badgering Andi all those years to learn to defend herself and also witnessed Andi's wary attempts to avoid the lessons. Ami had stubbornly refused and appealed to Uorsin, who had, of course, indulged her. Which was no doubt why she found herself needing lessons from Ash so many years later.

Over and over, Ursula made me break free, showing me which vulnerable spots on Harlan were in easy reach of my short blade. Due to my much smaller stature, that usually meant somewhere in his groin area. Ursula made me put my hand up between Harlan's massive thighs, to feel for myself the hollows where the arteries ran shallow and where his man jewels hung heavy and vulnerable. Harlan stoically endured it all, but I blushed furiously.

"Get over it," Ursula ordered. "This isn't about niceties. This is about saving your life. Now, break away, and if your position is good, shove your blade as hard as you can up into his balls."

"I don't want to hurt him."

Harlan gave me a reassuring smile. "It won't be the first time—and I've been hit there by people much bigger than a *nyrri.*"

He called me that deliberately, to make me mad, but it worked anyway. Experimentally, I called on that, too. When I broke away, I did as Ursula bade me and brought the wooden knife up hard between his thighs, slicing edge up.

To my shock, Harlan dropped to his knees gasping out a Dasnarian curse. Ursula surveyed me with a delighted grin. "Excellent! Imagine if that had been a sharp blade. He'd be bleeding out. But you still forgot to run. Do it again."

Harlan gave her a sidelong look. "This time, I'm wearing protection."

"I'm sorry," I told him.

"Don't be." He held out a hand for me to help him to his feet. A gesture of courtesy, as he surely didn't need it. He inclined his head. "Be proud of besting me."

"Only because you let me."

"Someone who doesn't know you won't expect this from you," Ursula said. "The element of surprise will make up for it. Once you have this down, we'll work on you not being grappled in the first place, which will be your first and best strategy."

For the next several hours, we worked it, until running as soon as I struck began to feel like second nature. I learned more spots to knife Harlan and then they switched up, having me defend myself against Ursula, with Harlan and Jepp offering pointers. That felt completely different from Harlan's overwhelming strength. With her I learned to stay out of range—not at all easy with her uncanny speed. *Faster than a snake heated by the sun*, Harlan had said, and I fully understood the analogy.

When I missed staying out of her reach, her grip was more like being tangled in a living vine, her body wiry, the vulnerable points never quite where I expected them to be. That shape-shifter magic. No wonder the Tala were so difficult for our troops to meet in battle.

By the time Ursula relented—mainly because she could not postpone the other pressing tasks required for launching our expedition—the sun stood high, and though the air was crisp, I dripped with more sweat than I'd thought my body possessed.

"It's a start," Ursula conceded. "Jepp will teach you how to hide your knives where you can draw them quickly. Practice that. You can't practice that kind of thing too much. Get in the habit of sleeping with your knives."

"I don't have any knives."

"We'll take care of it," she replied in an absent tone, thoughts already going to her next task. "Go clean up. I'll see you in a bit for the meeting with Kral."

We assembled to leave the following morning. I wore one of my new traveling dresses, along with a lovely fur-lined hooded cape. The weather had turned quite chill, so I appreciated the warmth. We'd all ride, so as to go faster, with the most critical emergency supplies also on horses. I wasn't an excellent horsewoman like Andi, but I'd kept up with the Hawks when we rode from Windroven. Another test of newly acquired skills.

Ursula and Harlan saw us off in the quiet outer courtyard. When I hurried out, fearing I'd be the last to arrive, Kral and Harlan were in quiet conversation, Ursula standing well back, giving them privacy. The two men parted, then stepped together for an awkward hug. Kral turned on his heel and left to assemble his men into a ready formation and await us outside the walls. Harlan strode toward us, raw emotion in his face. A kind of grief, perhaps. But he smiled for Ursula's assessing look and turned pointedly to me.

"Kral will watch over you, librarian. There's none better." He dipped his chin to Ursula. "I asked it, as part of his amends."

"Thank you," I told him, moved that he'd asked. Ursula gazed at him for an extended moment and I realized he'd done it for her, as much as for me.

"I have something for you," Ursula said, and handed me a soft leather package. "A gift."

I took it in surprise. "A gift?" I echoed stupidly. "You've already outfitted me and hidden gold and silver everywhere you can think of in my possessions."

"What? I'm sending you off to face Danu knows what dangers, knowing full well you don't truly wish to go. Those are supplies. This is something else. Open it."

I undid the ties and unrolled the leather. Inside lay a set of exquisite, deadly sharp daggers. Slim like the ones she and Jepp used, chased with a script down the blades. I turned one so I could read it. *This is why it's perilous to ignore a librarian.*

"Andi said you said that to her, when you found the designs of the tunnels beneath Windroven, so she could escape." Ursula gave me a narrow look for that and I tried to appear chagrined for what had likely been a traitorous act. But truly the thoughtfulness of the gift left me so astonished I couldn't muster much. "A good reminder for you to have," Ursula continued, "that you're as dangerous as anyone, in your own way. Whether by knife's edge or your mind's."

"I don't know what to say."

"There's one piece more."

She had a funny sound in her voice as she prompted me. I rolled the delicate blades up and unfolded the other half, which was heavier. Another dagger, bigger, worked with the same designs as Ursula's sword, with a shining bloodred ruby in the hilt. One of Salena's.

"You can't give me this," I breathed. "The rubies were your mother's."

She was watching me with turbulent gray eyes. "Yes, and we decided they should be divided between her daughters. It's clear to me now, as it always should have been, that Salena considered you an adopted or fostered daughter. This one is for you to take. The rest of your shares will await your return."

My heart had clenched and I found myself weeping a few silent tears. How had she known I needed this when I hadn't known it myself? "This is a gift beyond measure, my Queen. I can never express how much—or repay it."

"Yes, you can. By coming home safely." She embraced me in a sudden gesture of rare physical affection, hard and fierce. "If you don't," she said against my ear, "I'll hunt you down and you'll be responsible for me abandoning my duties to the High Throne."

I laughed, watery, and hugged her back. "A severe threat indeed."

She let me go. "I mean it, too. Don't make me start a war with Dasnaria over you. Go. Get the information. Come back safely."

"Yes, Your Majesty." I said it with much the same love Harlan put into the title, with all the same exasperation for her impossible orders. Jepp and Zynda had arrived while we spoke, standing a few polite paces back, so I wiped my tears and started to roll up the knives.

"No." Ursula plucked out the dagger and handed it to me hilt first. "*Wear* it. All the time. Jepp has my permission to smack you over the head if she catches you without it."

Jepp gave me her easy grin. "I love my job." Unlike me, she wore no cloak, just the leather layers of her Hawks uniform, her head uncovered, so she looked sleekly lethal. By contrast, Zynda had her own hood pulled up, the white fur framing her black hair and golden skin, making her deep-blue eyes startlingly bright. Exotic traveling companions for my dowdy self.

"I'll be glad to travel south," Zynda remarked. "A few hours back in Annfwn reminded me how much colder it is here."

"Has the climate there seen much impact from the barrier shift?" I thought to ask her. Our meetings the night before had focused entirely on Andi's extensive dissertation on her theories of how the Heart worked to control the barrier and what she could and could not do to adapt it so people could pass through, particularly those with no Tala blood. Thank Moranu for the Tala gift for memory. Zynda had been sworn to secrecy and memorized it all, repeating it word for word, uncannily sounding exactly like Andi at times.

"At the pass, yes, as you saw when we traveled through. Deeper in it feels just as warm, but there have been odd storms. Almost a mix of tropical rain and magic."

"As Kral said the Nahanauns encountered," Ursula said thoughtfully.

Zynda nodded. "I thought so, too. I shared his tales with Andi and Rayfe, so far as I could recall." Which meant perfectly. "They have been working to stabilize the weather patterns and I'm to tell you, High Queen, only if you asked, but I believe this counts, that yes, yes, yes—she remembers about sending rain to Aerron, to stop fretting about it because she can feel you thinking at her."

"Does she mean that literally?" I wondered.

"Probably," Ursula replied in a dry tone, then bared her teeth in a malicious grin. "I shall have to think at her harder and see what kind of results I get."

She made us laugh, no doubt as she intended. Then she embraced Zynda and Jepp in turn, saying something to each, likely another iteration of her exhortation to me to return safely. After that, there was nothing to do but mount up and ride out. I looked back over my shoulder to see Ursula watching us go, leaning against Harlan's bulk for comfort as he held her under one arm, his head bent over her.

I tucked the image away firmly in my memory, so I'd remember I had family back home, at Ordnung.

6

I'd journeyed out of Ordnung twice before in my life—once to Windroven and again to Annfwn. This time, I followed a third road, broader and busier than the goat track to Annfwn or the trade route to Windroven. Teeming with carts laden with the precious fruits of late harvests and watched over by soldiers wearing the uniforms of Mohraya and Ordnung, with former Vervaldr mixed in with each, notable for their height and fairness, this thoroughfare led in a straight, fast line to the Danu River.

Uorsin had improved the road from the backcountry lane it had been in the days of my youth at Castle Columba, first to bring the armies and supplies of Duranor to lay siege. Then, as one of his first acts to demonstrate the prosperity brought by the peace of the kingdoms unified under his power, he expanded it into the primary trade route it had become, running across the continent to the coast of Biah, distributing the goods ferried up and down the Danu River from Avonlidgh to Erie.

I'd read about all of it but never seen it with my own eyes. As we rode, I made notes in my journal. If nothing else, this journey would add to the history I would someday write. I'd even exercised some of my new authority in a completely self-indulgent way and had one of the scribes copy over a miniature map of the original Twelve for me. I kept it folded in the pages of my journal, so I could note where I'd been. Our maps ended to the west with the mountains of the Wild Lands and didn't show Annfwn or the Onyx Ocean north of the Crane Isthmus. Though I lacked good cartography skills, I hoped to add to it as we sailed.

Once relations with the Tala stabilized, perhaps we could ask them to fill in the details of Annfwn.

"I've never seen a woman with her nose so much in a book."

I jumped a little at Kral's comment, unaware he'd pulled his horse up next to mine. To increase our speed, Ursula had provided mounts for the Dasnarian battalion also. We'd leave the horses that the Vervaldr returning to Ordnung wouldn't need in Ehas, to be distributed to other parts of the Thirteen. Better to distribute Ordnung's hoarded wealth, she'd commented, with the added benefit of allowing Ordnung to feed people instead of horses.

"You are not the first person to say so," I told him.

He grunted, whether in agreement or dissent I wasn't sure. "You seem an unlikely ambassador."

"Because I'm small and female?"

"That, too." He scrutinized me, like a shark circling. "More because you do not behave as a proper lady ought. You speak your mind baldly. Even a man sent to the Dasnarian court would be more careful of his words."

Stung, I bit back a retort. I would have to improve my cover. "I'll keep that in mind, General Kral of Dasnaria and Imperial Prince of the Royal House of Konyngrr."

He let out a booming laugh, so like Harlan's but without his spontaneous joy. "See? You have adopted your High Queen's way of wielding a title to slice like a blade. But you are no queen, *nyrri*."

I set my teeth. "I am well aware of that."

"So, my brother has asked me to tutor you in speaking to King Nakoa KauPo and the ways of the Dasnarian court. I understand the latter far better than the former. I am not the most glib of courtiers, but I shall do my best to teach you the correct words and phrases you will need to cloak your true nature."

Surely Harlan hadn't told him I was meant to spy? "My true nature."

"Yes. The Dasnarians would see you—and your companions—as unnatural females. The women of your kingdoms, such as I've met, speak and act boldly." His gaze lingered on Jepp, riding a few horses ahead of us, flirting outrageously with one of Kral's men in decidedly lowbrow Dasnarian. She'd picked up a fair amount from keeping company with the Vervaldr. Brandur rode on her other side, glowering in what I hoped wasn't black jealousy. The heat in Kral's gaze made me wonder if she'd had sex with him, too. "I will teach you," he continued, "and you will instruct your companions. For the safety of you all."

Deciding to exercise some of that diplomacy, I thanked him and refrained from saying more.

"Does she love him, do you think?" Kral asked, abruptly enough that I thought he meant the man Jepp flirted with. For all his talk of elaborate courtesy in the Dasnarian court, he spoke quite bluntly. Probably, I realized, a sign of disrespect. "Your High Queen Ursula," he clarified. "Does she love my brother?"

It occurred to me that he might be thinking strategically, of how he might use that connection, but the truth was there to see, whether we said anything publicly about the *Elskastholrr* or not. Harlan had told his brother about the vow for a reason. And ultimately it didn't matter, as, if Ursula did accept a marriage of alliance someday, she would not be the first ruler to wed one while loving another.

Goddesses willing, it wouldn't come to that.

"She seems to be a very hard woman—not loving," Kral clarified, unnecessarily.

"She loves him," I said, certain he wasn't asking from concern for Harlan, but to ferret out information. I decided to try some ferreting of my own. "The High Queen was concerned about the bad blood that lies between you two."

Kral's expression darkened. "Did he discuss it?"

I went for a nonchalant shrug. "Certainly not with me. I am not privy to their conversations."

"You hear more than most, I think." He watched Jepp, who was attempting to tell some story about a fight or battle, pantomiming slicing a throat. "I withdraw my observation. Perhaps you will make a decent ambassador, after all."

"That is my intention."

"Perhaps so, since I have warned you. But that is not why your queen is sending you."

"It isn't? She said as much to me. Did she imply otherwise to you?"

Kral pulled his gaze off the animated Jepp and gave me a humorless smile. "Better, *nyrri*. Perhaps you can be taught. I do not know your true mission and shall keep my speculations to myself. I shall also do my best to honor my pledge to my brother. But know this—I can only do so much."

"I'm sure Harlan knows this as well."

"Perhaps he does. Perhaps not. He gave up much when he abandoned his birthright. Though he seems to have landed in honey. He ever was the luckiest of us. If your queen truly loves him, that is."

"Do you doubt it?"

"I cannot say." He watched Jepp again, as if fascinated, though his expression seemed to be one of dislike. "Your ways are most strange to me, the way you go from man to man without thought or loyalty."

I restrained the urge to explain that we weren't all like Jepp. Kral didn't need to be assuming that every woman of the Thirteen Kingdoms was like every other, and it would serve him right to learn otherwise. "I've had time to observe the Vervaldr during their tenure at Ordnung. Many of them have gone from woman to woman."

"Yes, but they are men. That is the way of things."

"Perhaps then it is not so much that our ways are strange, but yours are." I said it a bit too tartly, Kral's sharp smile confirming that he'd pushed my temper past diplomatic discretion.

But he considered. "Perhaps so. I shall think on it." And he rode off to speak to another of his men, leaving me to ponder all the subtext in our conversation.

We moved fast enough that we camped on the banks of the Danu River that night. The barge masters kept large areas cleared up and down the river for groups like ours to camp and wait for our assigned vessels. The scouts Ursula sent ahead had arranged for a barge large enough to hold our whole party, including horses, but they were rowing it upriver and it wouldn't arrive till morning.

Jepp, Zynda, and I had our own campfire, a bit away from the Dasnarians. Our Vervaldr guard had thrown in with them for the evening and they'd all fallen into some sort of Dasnarian drinking and gambling game. Jepp glanced over at a particularly raucous group shout they sent up, with cheers and groans. "Men," she muttered.

"You could join them, if you prefer," I offered. "I wouldn't mind and I doubt Zynda does."

"Not a bit," Zynda agreed. "Though I don't think Jepp wishes to."

"No, Jepp does *not* wish to." She made a face. "I've had enough of male egos for the day, thank you. Besides, the High Queen told me to guard you two with my life and I'm not about to let her down."

"Understandable. I would be equally loath to face Ursula with a failure like that."

"Does it bother you," Jepp asked, "that she's with Harlan?"

I blinked at her. "Why would it bother me? I think he's really good for her."

"I just figured that you're in love with her and it's hard when that happens and the other woman picks a man instead. I mean, it hurts when they pick *anyone* else, but for some reason it's worse when it's a *guy* and—"

I cut in then, not wanting to hear more. "I'm not in love with Ursula. That is . . ." I searched for the right way to explain my feelings.

"No more so than we all are?" Zynda offered. "She's an admirable woman who inspires great feelings of devotion."

"I admire her greatly, yes." I sounded stiff, even to myself, badly wanting out of this conversation.

"I would do Ursula," Jepp said thoughtfully. "All that intensity and passion, focused on you in bed? Mmm."

Zynda snorted. "From your tales, it sounds as if you would do anyone."

Jepp grinned, unrepentant. "Well, I do have standards. But they're woefully low. I'm weak—I rarely turn down an opportunity for an honest, vigorous fucking. I prefer cock, in general, but women can work for me, too. I wouldn't blame you if you did have a crush on our High Queen, Dafne."

"I do *not* have a crush on Ursula!"

"I just figured because I never see you with men. And you spend so much time with Ursula. And Harlan." Her eyes brightened with salacious interest. "Unless you're in a threeway with both of them? *That* would be amazing."

I choked on my tea, face hotter than the campfire. "No! Don't put images like that in my head."

"I wouldn't judge," she insisted. "I'd be insanely jealous, but you can tell me. In great detail, please."

"There is nothing to tell. I promise."

"Have you ever been with a woman?" Jepp looked me over far too appraisingly. "They can be a lovely change. Softer, delicate, more precise. And another woman knows her way around your body, so she can—"

"Jepp!" I strangled on her name.

"Why are you flustered?" She sounded genuinely surprised, a perfectly innocent tone, but her dark eyes glittered with mischief. "Are you uncomfortable, Zynda?"

"No." The Tala woman smiled easily. "And no, I've never been with another woman. I have, however, been with a number of men. I've been satisfied with the results and plan to stick with that path for the time being."

"Well, you won't be having any soon, because General Killjoy has forbidden all of his men, including *our* Vervaldr, from having sex with any of us for the duration of the journey. So if either of you want to experiment?" She finished hopefully, then made an annoyed sound when we both shook our heads. "No fun at all, the both of you. How am I supposed to go that long without sex? It's inhuman, I tell you." She kicked at a rock in the ring around the campfire. Interesting that Kral had issued that edict—and that Jepp alone knew about it. Which likely meant he'd given the order because of her.

"Seeing how long Dafne has gone, I suspect you have no room to complain with her."

"Oh?" Jepp brightened with renewed interest in the conversation. "Do tell. It's not fair you talked about your sex life with Zynda and not with me. Throw me a bone here. Or an oyster." She snickered.

"Oyster?" I didn't get the joke, though Zynda clearly did.

"A man's cock is like a bone—hard and straight—and a woman's sex looks and tastes like an oyster," Jepp explained with a wicked smile. "And there's a little pearl that—"

I held up a hand. "Enough. I get it."

"Then stop dodging and tell me what you told Zynda."

"I did not talk to Zynda," I said in the crispest tone I could manage. "She's guessing."

"But I'm right, aren't I?" Zynda's eyes took on the hue of the firelight, like the amber shine of a forest animal, her own version of Jepp's sensual wickedness gleaming. Both of them so comfortable in their bodies, with their many lovers. How had I ended up with such companions?

"What is she right about?" Jepp examined me. Then her face went blank and horrified, looking as if she'd discovered I had some terrible disease and only weeks to live. "You're not . . . You're a fucking virgin?"

"I believe that's an oxymoron," I snapped. "I am a virgin because there has been no fucking." I didn't think I'd ever used that word before. Such was the toll of Jepp's company.

She gaped at me in real shock. "I don't think I've ever met a virgin. I mean." She shook her head. "Not one who was . . ."

"A middle-aged spinster?" I finished for her. "Look your fill, because here's your big chance."

"There's no shame in it," Zynda put in gently. "Just as some prefer the company of their same gender, there are those who prefer to keep their bodies to themselves."

"What—*never* have sex, ever in their lives?" Jepp was flat astounded, assimilating that. "I can't even imagine."

Zynda shrugged. "People are people. I don't judge." She said that last to me, but with a flicker of emphasis for Jepp.

"I'm not judging," Jepp said in haste. Then she reached out to touch my hand, a fleeting gesture, as quicksilver as her moods. "I didn't mean to offend you. If you are happier without sex, then good for you. I don't *understand* it," she added, unnecessarily, but seeming unable to stop herself, "but I do think everyone should do what makes them happy."

"Thank you. Both of you." Then a laugh broke free from me, which helped vent some of the tight embarrassment. "It is not, however, that I am asexual. I simply . . . I don't know. Never quite had the right opportunity."

"This conversation calls for something stronger than tea," Jepp decided, springing to her feet in a lithe movement.

"Oh, no! We're not having a conversation about this," I protested.

"Too late," Zynda murmured. "You'll never get her off your tail until she's heard it all."

"And you were such a great help," I retorted.

"What's the harm? We're all friends. If you can't confide in us, who would you, then?"

"Yes." Jepp plopped herself down and handed me a flask. "Drink and pass. We can help you. What would be the right opportunity? If we know what you're looking for, we can keep our eyes open. Be your scouts!"

Groaning mentally at that prospect, and in order to avoid answering her question for a few more precious seconds, I sipped. Whiskey. Very smooth. Good Goddesses—and unholy strong.

"Goes right to your head, doesn't it?" Jepp took it from my hand, swigged, and handed the flask to Zynda. "Okay, maybe we should back up. What *have* you done? Kissing, at least."

The warmth of the whiskey did help, so I nodded. One of my prospective fiancés had kissed me. And then one of the Tala while I was in Annfwn, Zyr, in his flirtatiousness. "Twice. I didn't care for the first."

"Why not?" Zynda frowned in suspicion at the flask, then sipped.

"It was . . . not interesting. I mostly waited for it to be over. I didn't want him touching me—it made my skin crawl. The second one was better, but still not . . . moving. Not 'wonderful, take me to bed and have your way with me' exciting. Even though he offered that and there was no reason I shouldn't have taken him up on it. I just didn't want to. Goddesses." I took the flask and swallowed. "Maybe I am asexual!"

"Let's not leap to conclusions." Jepp wagged a finger at me in clear imitation. "Did you like the guys who did the kissing?"

"Not the first one." In fact, I'd rather hated him on sight, in all his condescending arrogance.

"Then of course you didn't want him touching you." Zynda held out a hand for the flask. "This is seriously good liquor."

"They distill it in Branli," Jepp replied, her gaze still on me. "I laid in a supply when I was up there. Worth the pain of carting it around. And the second one?"

"I liked him. Um, actually it was Zyr," I confessed to Zynda. "The night we left."

Zynda widened her eyes. "Zyr tried to seduce you and you resisted? Wow." She took a drink and held it in her mouth, pondering. Swallowed. "Wow," she repeated.

"Is that such a rare occurrence?"

"It might be. I don't know of anyone else who's turned him down. Moranu, I wish I'd known! I could have teased him mercilessly."

"He was very gracious about it." He'd been sweet, in fact, saying "Some people share themselves easily, like the bushes that produce clusters of berries, plenty for all to have and enjoy. A few are like the *kalpa* tree, which bears a single fruit, after many years, which is all the more precious for that." Words that had stuck with me. "I don't think you should mention anything to him. I wouldn't want to wound his pride."

Zynda hooted a laugh, an animal sound in it. "Wound his pride? That man has plenty to spare. All the women going on in raptures about him and trying to catch his eye, but you gave him the cold shoulder."

"I told him I'm waiting for someone special and he understood."

"I doubt it. Everyone is special to Zyr. And if all the swooning and sighing can be believed, he's very special to them." She snickered. Jepp rubbing off on all of us.

"Have I met this guy?" Jepp demanded, sitting up straighter. "What makes him so good?"

"I wouldn't know, as he's my brother," Zynda said in that dry tone. "But no, you haven't met him—he hasn't left Annfwn and isn't likely to."

"I just knew I should have gone with you into Annfwn instead of staying back with Brandur! Danu curse me for lost opportunities." Jepp stared sourly at the flask. "I have the worst luck lately."

"Don't you like Brandur anymore?" I asked more to keep the subject off my sex life than from any real interest to know more about Jepp's. Zyr's kiss *had* been excellently executed. I should have taken him up on the offer and at least experienced skilled lovemaking. Shared some berries instead of sitting on my precious fruit. So to speak. I snorted out a giggle at the thought.

Jepp gave me a dubious look and took away the flask. "Lightweight. I like Brandur fine. I've had Brandur—in every way physically possible, as he's had me. We're friends, but there's an extra zing, you know, with some people more than others. Emotional. Special. Or whatever. Danu." She swigged from the flask. "I'm starting to sound like the librarian."

"Hey!"

"No offense," Jepp grumbled, though I knew she meant it more sincerely than she sounded.

"I know what you mean." Zynda leaned back on her elbows, long and sinuous. "There's sex for sex's sake, which is—don't get me wrong—really great. You know. Sorry, Dafne—I guess you *don't* know, but unless your partner is totally self-involved, which can happen, then it's a real gift. But, with someone special, who really *gets* you, then . . . I've lost the thread. What were we saying?"

"The advantage of having lightweights as traveling companions," Jepp announced, "is more whiskey for me. I had sex with General Killjoy," she added. A confessional afterthought that nearly slipped past me.

Then it made its way fully into my fogged brain. "You *did*? I know he wanted to try a woman with sword calluses, but Brandur was right there, too."

Jepp waved a hand at that. "We've never been exclusive. Tell me about the sword calluses thing."

No harm in that, I supposed. "He and Harlan discussed it, after Kral shook Ursula's hand. Apparently the concept of a woman's hands with sword calluses lights up the Dasnarian men."

"Probably exotic to them," Zynda said. "As it seems their women are all soft."

"Probably," I agreed, rubbing my fingertips together. Soft. Though with sore spots from the knife lessons.

"This explains a great deal," Jepp mused. I could almost hear her thoughts clicking over how to use this to her advantage.

"How was the general?" Zynda prodded. "Was it just the once, or will he violate his own edict?"

"Just the one night, but several times. Pretty much all night and then some. The man has serious staying power. As for his edict, I'm pretty sure he did it entirely because he's pissed at me. Mistakes were made."

"You pissed off a prince of the Dasnarian throne, general of their armies, with whom we just created a very new and even more tenuous peace?" I pressed my hands to my eyes, wishing I could banish the knowledge. "Ursula would kill you."

"Well, no. But she would banish me from Ordnung." Jepp gave me a thin smile when I looked up. Waved at me as if she'd just arrived. "Hi."

"That was really a foolish thing to do, Jepp."

She scowled. "I know it. Danu! Do you think Her Majesty didn't nearly take my head off for it?"

I took the flask from her, definitely needing more. "You might as well tell me everything. Especially as it's likely to have bearing on the rest of our journey."

Jepp ran her hands over her short hair and Zynda watched our exchange with interest. I handed her the flask.

"It shouldn't have been a big deal!" Jepp insisted. Always a bad sign, when someone started with the defensive. "He made it clear he was attracted. I sure was. He offered. I accepted. We spent a sizzling-hot night together—"

"Where?"

She frowned at me. "Does it matter?"

"It might. Indulge me."

"His bed."

I groaned. Worse and worse.

"Captain Harlan asked that, too. What's the deal?"

"I don't know that there is one. Except that there's this edict. He hasn't renewed his invitation?"

"Well, after he caught me with Brandur, he made it pretty clear that—"

She stopped when I held up a hand. "You had sex with Brandur, too? After a night and then some in Kral's bed?"

"It wasn't immediately after. Hours and hours. At least eight. Give me that cursed flask."

Zynda passed it with an admiring gleam in her eye. "You have some stamina, sister, I'll give you that."

"What? I was restless. Too much sitting on my ass *recuperating*." She sneered the word. "It's not like I'd made either of them any promises. Brandur didn't mind. Much. Though he did want me to make it up to him." She sounded entirely too pleased with herself for someone who was supposed to be sorry.

"Neither is Brandur a Dasnarian prince who invited you to his bed." No wonder Ursula had been so much crankier than usual right before we left. Not just worried about me, then. But I thought Jepp was wrong about the queen sending Jepp with me as a form of exile. She would have predicted Jepp's presence would annoy Kral. Unless she'd done it on purpose. Ursula rarely did anything by accident.

"What is the significance of Kral inviting Jepp into his bed?" Zynda asked. "For us it means no more than a convenient place to be together."

"For most of us, too," I told her. "But Dasnaria has much more arcane cultural rules—particularly as regards the role of women."

Jepp made a disparaging sound. "They can be real jerks about it, too."

"I don't doubt that. I've been trying to study what I can." This might explain some of Kral's circuitous warnings earlier, especially about me instructing my companions. As if I'd be able to instruct Jepp in anything at all. "You have to remember that the Vervaldr we know have been away from Dasnaria for many years. They've experienced many cultures and have adapted to and more or less understand that our ways are different. In no small part due to the leadership of Captain Harlan, who is an unusually flexible thinker."

"Am I back in school?"

"Shut up, Jepp—I want to hear this. Keep going, Dafne."

"I'm not perfectly certain, because so much of it is embedded in their society and so not always explained clearly in the texts, but it seems that women have essentially two roles to choose from. I use the word 'choose' lightly because I'm not sure the decision is up to them. Women are always either a wife, which is a respected role, as she then has access to everything that belongs to her husband—reputation, rank, wealth."

Jepp had started to catch on, looking queasy, though that could have been all the whiskey. "And the not-wives?"

"Women don't appear to have much of any rights on their own, can't own property or work to make a living. So they're entirely dependent on the men in their lives to provide for them. A woman who has a father or brothers is provided for until she marries—which seems to be a complicated arrangement involving many contracts and ceremonies. If she doesn't marry, she can accept the protection of a man, who will commit to caring for her in exchange. That agreement is much simpler. The word they use is 'rekjabrel,' which translates more or less as 'bed slave.' He offers her his bed, symbolic of giving her a place to live and be safe."

"Danu's tits," Jepp whispered in horror.

"Exactly. It's possible he thought you were exclusively his."

"People don't own other people," she snapped.

"They do in Dasnaria, in a manner of speaking." I shrugged, took the flask, and saluted Jepp. "Always pays to do your research!"

Jepp gave me a sour look. "Aren't you going to tell me this is why it's perilous to ignore a librarian?"

She'd snorted at the inscription earlier, when she showed me how to hide the little daggers on my person without slicing myself. A more patient teacher than Ursula, Jepp had been most helpful. I did like her and she didn't deserve me making light of her situation.

"I'll do what I can to smooth things over with the general," I told her. "I doubt you're in any serious or permanent trouble. You offended his pride and now he's repaying you by keeping you from being with any of his men."

"The old 'if I can't have you, no one will' thing," Zynda agreed.

"But he could have me!" Jepp protested. "If he'd just bend his cursed rules a little . . ."

"Do you want my advice?"

"Even Ursula listens to your advice," Jepp complained. "How can I say no?"

"Then I think you should let it go. You had your night and the aftermath went badly. Call it a bad deal and move on. It's not like you want to go be his bed slave in Dasnaria for the rest of your life, right?"

Jepp pretended to look thoughtful. "It was a really good night."

I groaned and Zynda burst out laughing. Jepp grinned at us. "All right. You have a point. At least I'll please Danu with my celibacy until this journey is done. Maybe the sacrifice will appease Her to turn my luck around."

We could all use some of that.

7

The barge took us down the river at what felt like a stately pace, the brown water flowing with few ripples and the banks crowded with overhanging trees, brilliant in their fiery autumn colors. When we reached a break in the foliage, however, we passed the dock or town far more swiftly than a horse would go.

When Jepp let me take a break from knife practice, I mostly sat on the deck, wrapped in my warm cloak, with my map and journal, enjoying the cloudless blue sky and noting the various villages we passed. Mohraya and then Avonlidgh on the right bank, the broad expanses of Duranor on the left. It made for peaceful travel, especially in the afternoon, with the great river flowing silently and all the Dasnarians napping.

A peace abruptly broken in the most alarming way.

The scream—a man's scream, which is somehow more unsettling—startled me out of my thoughts, and I jumped to my feet. Jepp, who'd been napping nearby, had moved so fast she already stood between me and the increasing shouts, her blades drawn and body coiled.

"What is it?" I asked, unable to see anything, though the noises came from the downstream end of the barge.

"I don't know and we're not going to go look," Jepp replied. "Where is Zynda?"

"She was bored and said she wanted to stretch her wings. I assume that means flying."

Jepp didn't reply to that, just watched, then cursed under her breath. "Put your things away. Have your big dagger in your hand. Be ready to run. Or jump overboard. Which means lose the cloak."

I heard it then, as I hastened to do as she instructed, a beast roaring over the screams of men, along with shouting in a jumble of Dasnarian. A large bird, white, with a long, swooping neck, spiraled over me and landed on the deck, flashing into Zynda, who ranged herself next to Jepp, also in a fighting stance. "Trouble," she said.

"What is that thing?" Jepp asked.

"I've never seen anything like it, but it just swallowed a man whole."

Normally I'd be perfectly happy to cower behind them—and had been thus far—but curiosity got the better of me and I edged around Zynda to peek down the barge at what they watched. A violet haze rippled through the sky and water, as if emanating from some glowing thing. Then a man flew through the air, landing in the water with a splash. He began to swim for the barge, but a violet tentacle rose from the water, wrapped around his waist, and dragged him under.

"On second thought," Jepp said, "don't jump overboard."

"So noted." I sounded amazingly calm, even though the barge started tipping down, our end rising. The panicked whinnies of the horses added to the cacophony.

Jepp looked at Zynda. "Can you fly Dafne off this boat?"

"No. I don't have an avian form big enough."

"Besides, we're not leaving you behind," I said.

"If it's a choice between getting eaten by this monster or facing Her Majesty with the news that I let *you* get eaten, I'll take the monster," Jepp replied in a grim tone. "Danu—look at them. The cursed Dasnarians are fighting it all wrong."

"They've never fought a magical creature before," Zynda said. They exchanged glances. "They need help. Advice."

"We have to stay here. It's our duty to protect the librarian."

"If they all die, we go down with them and we've failed to protect her anyway."

Instead of pointing out that I was standing right there, I said, "Zynda can get Kral, bring him here. You give the advice and I'll translate."

They only looked surprised for a moment before Zynda took off running. She came back after a long stretch of minutes during which violet tentacles pulled more men off the barge and the surface tilted enough that we had to grab handholds not to slide.

"We'll roll straight down its maw soon enough," Jepp predicted. "I should tie you to something."

"The barge will break in half first," I told her. "Then likely sink. Tying me would just ensure I'd drown."

She grunted but didn't disagree. The barge made groaning, creaking noises, bearing me out. "Here he comes."

Kral jogged up, Zynda pulling him along. He gave Jepp a vicious glare. "What? We're a little busy saving your pretty asses."

"And fucking it up, too!" Jepp retorted in her coarsely broken Dasnarian. I stepped between them.

"General," I said. "Jepp and Zynda have both fought magical creatures before. I suggest you listen to their advice."

He nodded curtly.

"He needs to pull his men back," Jepp switched to Common Tongue. "No solid ranks. Think wolves worrying a deer. Fast, sharp attacks. In and out."

"Stop cutting off the tentacles," Zynda added. "For each cut, two or three more grow. Pour salt on them instead to get it to release the boat."

"Give it a decoy." Jepp again. "It's eating wood and men alike. Give it something big and metal that it can't swallow. It'll choke."

"And use this." Zynda handed him a blue glass ball. Then she took a knife and cut her finger, squeezing blood onto a cloth. "When you're ready, wipe the blood on the globe and throw it down the monster's throat. Don't delay. Then take cover. Get the tentacles off the barge first."

I translated as fast as I could, stumbling here and there over the terms that had never quite come up in polite conversation. When I got to the point of putting the blood on the glass ball, Kral gave me an incredulous look.

"Tala blood carries magic," I told him. "I'd trust her."

Without a word, he took the blood-soaked cloth, turned heel, and ran back down the barge.

"You're welcome," Jepp muttered, shifting restlessly, clearly wanting to join the fight.

"He listened," Zynda told her. "See?"

Jepp hadn't bothered to put me behind her again, so the action down at the other end became easier to follow, especially with the ranks of big men retreating back to the center. A team of five worked to break the chain to the big anchor at midship.

"Smart," Jepp commented. "The man is a jerk, but he's no slouch."

Another team of Dasnarians brought out sacks of salt, knifing them open as a small crew distracted the monster, worrying at it and darting away again.

"How do you know the salt will work?" I asked.

"I don't," Zynda admitted. "I'm guessing. But it's a freshwater creature and it doesn't have scales, so the salt should burn, if nothing else."

The results were spectacular. As soon as the soldiers poured the salt on the tentacles, deep-purple steam billowed up and an unearthly shriek filled the air. Quick as snakes disappearing into grass, the tentacles unwound from the barge and slithered into the water.

Jepp gave Zynda an impressed nod. "Good guess."

"Tala children learn early to be careful of taking a freshwater animal form and jumping into the ocean," she said in a wry tone. "No one makes *that* mistake twice."

Muscles flexing, the men with the freed anchor carried it to the monster's screaming maw. I couldn't make it out very well, as it wasn't very much above the water level. The men chanted, swinging the anchor. A bright blue flash of light sailed through the air and the men let the anchor fly. They all dropped flat in an instant, curling into balls that presented only their hard armor to the outside. Jepp reached to grab me, but Zynda stopped her.

"We're fine here."

For a long moment, nothing happened, except the monster thrashing, wailing like a pitiful thing, violet tentacles reaching up from the water and slapping down again. Then the air seemed to ripple, hot and then cold. A boom of unheard thunder vibrated in my bones.

And the creature was gone.

Nothing to be seen but the glasslike sheen of the river and the thick forest lining the banks.

"Good trick," Jepp commented.

Zynda nodded, looking unhappy. I felt much the same. The monster had been beautiful in its way, and now we'd destroyed it. At least, I thought so.

"What happened to it?" I asked her. "Is it dead or . . . gone elsewhere?"

"You know how I explained that the shape-shifting can feel like parking one body in another place? That spell sent it there."

"Oh." It seemed a dire fate.

Jepp gave us both a disgusted look. "It was the enemy. Never feel bad for defeating an enemy that tried to kill you."

"It didn't actually try to kill me," I pointed out.

"Not something you want to wait and see about," she insisted. "Sentiment is for books and poetry. There's no place for it in a battle with a hungry monster. Sentiment makes you hesitate, and a blink of hesitation is sometimes all the space you have between living and dying."

"I have you," I said, "to not hesitate for me. So thank you."

"I will echo the thank-you," Kral said, walking up to us and using the Common Tongue phrase as he nodded with respect to Jepp and Zynda. "It was good advice and has saved us when we might otherwise have perished. Have you more of those blue globes?"

Zynda looked amused when I translated the last. "I can make more," she replied to me in Tala, "but tell him that it takes me much time and effort."

I did and Kral studied her, wheels clearly turning in his head. He looked at Jepp then, grudging respect, simmering anger, and something else in his expression. Longing, perhaps. The same mix I'd seen the day before as he watched her while riding. It seemed he wanted her as much as she did him. But the rigid set of his body showed he would not unbend.

"Ask them if they would train my men in these tactics," he said without looking at me. "It seems we have things to learn if we are to survive this journey."

Though we debated whether to get off the river, ultimately Kral cut off the discussion by asking if there was any reason to believe, given the randomness of the reports of strange and magical creatures, we'd be less likely to meet one on land. Given that we'd go faster on the river, we stayed that course.

Zynda, however, took a nocturnal animal form, to keep an eye out while we slept. I hadn't known she could make spells like that. Shape-shifters and wizards, the tales always said of the Tala, and stories of the Great War implied that Salena, or others in the armies she brought from Annfwn to fight for Uorsin, had performed feats of magic. I'd seen some during my time in Annfwn, but most of the tricks I'd seen had been for entertainment—mak-

ing colorful patterns in the sky and conjuring pretty toys for children—or involved the staymachs, which were shape-shifting animals guided by trainers.

So far as I knew, while Andi could control the barrier using the
Heart, she couldn't make spells like Zynda's. But when I mentioned it again, after Kral stalked off to assess the damages to his
battalion, Zynda put me off in such a way that I felt as if I'd invaded her privacy. Given that she'd been open and forthcoming
about sex, I found it interesting that this topic would be off-limits.
I respected it, however, much as it piqued my curiosity.

The Tala had their secrets, to be sure.

By early morning we'd reached the confluence of the Danu
River and the Del, which flowed out of the mountains of Avonlidgh. It marked the nexus of three borders—the point where
Duranor, Avonlidgh, and Aerron meet—presided over by the imposing bulk of Castle Avonlidgh. Though Ami preferred Windroven, where she and Prince Hugh had made their home after
their marriage, Castle Avonlidgh traditionally had been the seat of
the kings of Avonlidgh. It also marked the point of our debarka-
tion, as the mighty river would begin to fracture into swamps as it
crossed through the intensely dry heat of the southern coast and
spread into a vast delta that led to the Sea of Elcinea.

We passed by Castle Avonlidgh, a stern edifice with little to
recommend it. No wonder Ami had no affection for the place, beyond that her despised father-in-law had lived there. Was she still
in residence or would they have moved on to Windroven already?
Ursula had told her not to, but Ami was nothing if not stubborn.
And she'd become a committed ruler. She'd want to see if the volcano posed a danger to her people.

Riding hard for several more days, we traversed the hills in the
north of Aerron. From their still-green swells, the view of the vast
desert below struck me hard. Ringed around with fertile farm-
lands, the yellow sand seemed a barren blight, another kind of
monster, eating its way ever deeper. The days remained clear and
dry, the sun burningly intense this far south and east. We'd packed

the fur cloaks away and Zynda had happily returned to her usual light garb, when she wasn't assuming some animal form to run or fly alongside. She said it kept her in practice to shift into a variety of forms, especially the farther we traveled from Annfwn and the Heart. Privately I thought she enjoyed unsettling the Dasnarians as much as anything.

Coming through the pass that marked another nexus, this time the four-way point between Duranor, Nemeth, Aerron, and Elcinea, we stopped for the night at the great Watchtower there. Standing on the tallest peak, the tower stood as high as fifty men, built of stone laboriously gathered by generations of Elcineans, to keep a lookout for incursions from their aggressive northern neighbors. Not that it had helped. Elcinea had been the first to fall to Duranor's acquisitive ways—leading to the conscription of a young Elcinean fisherman named Uorsin.

As we traveled through Elcinea to the Port of Ehas, with the landscape softening, becoming lusher with every passing hour, it seemed ever more paradoxical that such a hard man had come from such a gently beautiful place. The one must not inform the other. After all, Ash had come from the harshest of backgrounds and had become the most gentle of healers. Harlan and Kral could not be more different in aggressiveness and their regard for others, yet they'd grown up in the same family. It was interesting to ponder.

When we topped the last rise above Ehas, I gasped as I took in my first view of the Sea of Elcinea as the poets wrote about it. Dazzlingly clear, showing the famous white sands beneath the calm waters, intensely blue in others. Not the aquamarine of Annfwn's sea, but a deeper set of colors. The city—the largest I'd ever seen—rolled over the hillsides, all the low, rambling houses facing the sweet breezes off the sea. The buildings became denser toward the city center, coming to a point at the great harbor. Possibly a hundred or more ships sat tied to the docks or at anchor in the harbor.

"There," Kral said, pulling up next to me and pointing. "That galleon with the crimson sails? That is mine. The *Hákyrling*."

I followed the line of his finger and smiled at the pride in his voice. "The *Lady Shark*?"

He grinned, a happy expression for a change, without his usual angry malice. "You are learning, *nyrri*."

"And you are relieved to find your ship where you left it."

His smile dimmed and he lifted one shoulder, let it fall, just as Harlan would. "It occurred to me that your High Queen could have been bluffing and sent us to chase our tails."

"With me the sacrificial dove?"

"In truth, the fact that she sent you along is what convinced me to accept this plan. You may be a woman, but your queen clearly values you. I did not think she would use you as a *bynde*."

"A *bynde*?"

"A piece in a Dasnarian game of strategy. The *bynde* can be easily sacrificed to gain ground for pieces with more power."

Ah. Closer to my role in life than he thought. "It seems to me that someone who is 'only' a man can be a *bynde*, also."

"I meant no offense. Simply an observation."

"You pointed out to me, General, that our cultural differences are vast. You may give me offense whether you intend to or not."

He eyed me thoughtfully. "In Dasnaria, a man does not apologize to a woman. But I believe that applies to Dasnarian women. I shall consider you a third gender. A woman of the Twelve Kingdoms; therefore, I apologize for my offense."

"Accepted," I replied, as that was likely a major concession from the general. So interesting, the arcane reasoning of the Dasnarian male mind. In some ways I understood Harlan better, having a deeper perspective of the culture that bred him, but it also pointed out how much he had changed from that. When I returned, I'd have questions for him, if he'd answer.

Would Jepp fall into Kral's third-gender category? Very tempting to ask, but unless it became diplomatically relevant, I wouldn't touch it. Jepp could fight her own battles there. I might not like the role of women in the Dasnarian culture, but my job was to understand Dasnaria in order to preserve peace, not to change them to my liking, much as I might want to.

We spent little time in Ehas, proceeding directly to the harbor in order to board the *Hákyrling*. Adventures do not lend themselves to sightseeing, unfortunately. The urgency of the mission overrides more frivolous concerns such as exploring a fascinating new city. The sight of not one, but several booksellers gave me a pang, however. And then a library—a large one. The general, who'd continued to ride by my side, asking for translations of the various signs or explanations for different sights, asked me what I stared at so wistfully. I explained and he grunted his disinterest.

"When you return home, perhaps you can spend time in this 'library,'" he offered, not unkindly. I nodded, not mentioning that coming all the way to Ehas to go to Ordnung would not happen. Ursula didn't want Kral to know of the closer ports and none of us would tell him.

Thus we sailed out of the Port of Ehas within hours of arriving, Kral delighted to catch the tide—and possibly to see the last of Brandur, who planned to stay—and me standing at the rail, watching the Thirteen Kingdoms fade into the distance behind me.

8

Soon I discovered that my thoughts had been overly dramatic. We sailed parallel to the coast of Elcinea, then Aerron and Avonlidgh, for some time. Some days I saw only open sea; then we'd draw nearer, enough to see the white sands turn to the parched yellow of Aerron's desert. It wasn't until we sighted the rocky cliffs of Avonlidgh that we struck out for open sea. Kral's shipmaster, Jens, had spent the waiting time in Ehas speaking the universal language of all sailors—navigational maps—and was following a new route for the return voyage.

He patiently answered my questions, showing me his charts from the sunny, windswept upper deck while Jepp practiced her dagger forms nearby. Several of the Dasnarians eyed her with longing, but—so far as I knew, and Jepp was anything but reticent on the topic—they'd all obeyed Kral's edict. They left me alone as much as they did Zynda. The Tala woman they regarded with superstitious fascination, particularly after she leapt overboard to shouts of alarm and transformed into a dolphin midair, cleaving into the waves and popping up to cackle a laugh at the men preparing to rescue her.

For my part, I confused them with my interest in their tasks and the questions I asked. They'd begun to treat me as Kral's third gender. Not the way they spoke to other men, but no longer using the verb forms I'd begun to recognize as being specific to addressing a woman. Harlan had always used the male forms with me. Probably a deliberate gesture of respect, as the female forms seemed to be more directive, more command language, and also left less room for back-and-forth dialogue. Not as helpful for me in learning the correct—and polite—language forms. No wonder Kral had declared me not suited to diplomacy. I'd talked to him as a man would. However, the fact remained that I would not be able to sustain my cover as ambassador if limited to language appropriate for females. So I pointedly used male language with the Dasnarians as a form of practice, paying close attention to what they became accustomed to and what made them so uncomfortable that they ended the conversation.

Jens seemed impossible to offend. Happy to have someone to talk maps with, he showed me the path he believed they'd taken on the way in, where they'd circled far to the south to avoid the treacherously shallow, and to him unknown, waters of the jagged islands around the isthmus. Now, equipped with more knowledge and better maps, he planned to save time by cutting a diagonal across open water to the point of the Crane Isthmus, where we'd follow a meticulously charted route of deeper water through what the sailors at Ehas called the Sentinels. Jens pronounced the name not in Common Tongue, but in old Elcinean, which I found interesting. Clearly an old place name, then, and not one I'd heard before.

The shortcut had its perils, apparently, but nothing like risking an encounter with one of the treacherous winter storms farther south.

We'd reversed our seasons again, but over the course of two days, sailing from the warm summer of Elcinea into the deepening autumn of Avonlidgh. The Feast of Moranu would come before much longer and the days grew markedly shorter, the wind's bite sharper. Zynda complained she felt warm only in the water, which made no sense to me, as the icy spray confirmed how cold that water could be.

"It's because my animal form is adapted to cope with that environment in a way my human one isn't with this one," she told me in our shared cabin, hands cupped around a hot mug of tea, a blanket wrapping her. "If I could stay in that form until we reach warmer weather again, I would."

"Why don't you?" Jepp asked, listening as she worked through one of her forms as the narrow space allowed. We'd all taken shelter indoors until the morning crossing, as the stinging rain and bitter wind made it miserable on deck. "I would if I could. This being stuck in a little room makes me crazy."

"Are you sure it's not the celibacy?" Zynda teased her.

Jepp stopped midspin and pointed her twin daggers at Zynda. "Don't taunt an armed woman. Unless either of you has changed your mind about tasting the fairer sex, I don't want to hear about it."

"Sorry." Zynda sounded truly contrite. "The general hasn't relented? He watches you constantly."

"Does he now?" Jepp brightened considerably. "Good. He should suffer for being an ass. I don't know if he'd relent, as I haven't offered. And I won't. I have my pride . . . of a sort. I'm holding out for a willing island boy. I'm imagining tanned, lean muscles from swimming. Mmm. Speaking of swimming, you didn't answer my question."

"Maybe she didn't want to, Jepp," I said mildly. For the most part we got along fine, the three of us, but being confined by the weather in close quarters would test anyone's friendship.

"I don't mind," Zynda said in a thoughtful tone. "The Tala don't generally share such information with mossbacks, but it's likely good for you to know my limitations. The more we understand each other's strengths and weaknesses, the better we can support and protect each other." She gave me a narrow look, some of that Salena steel in it. "But don't write this down, Dafne."

I set down my quill and attempted to look as if the thought had never crossed my mind.

I didn't fool her, but she nodded in satisfaction. "We can't stay in our animal forms for an extended time because we begin to lose contact with human thinking. Dafne—you asked me how much I knew in bird form what my human mind knows, and I told you it's not so much having it, but keeping contact with it. The longer we remain in animal form, the more tenuous that connection becomes, until it breaks entirely."

Jepp looked horrified. As it did Ursula, the thought of changing her body into something else made her deeply uncomfortable. "Then you're trapped as an animal forever?"

"Yes. It's one of our greatest punishments for lawbreakers—to trap someone in their animal form so long that they lose themselves."

"How do you trap someone in their animal form?" I asked, fingers itching for my quill.

But Zynda laughed, shaking her hair back. "That, I think, I shall not tell you."

"What if we need to know," Jepp asked, clearly as curious as I, "in case it happens to you and we need to intervene?"

"It won't. Nobody without Tala magic and knowledge of our ways could do that."

Hopefully that wasn't overconfidence, as we would be dealing with foreign magic and sorcerers in Dasnaria, but I didn't say so. Another thought occurred to me, however. "What about relaying messages to Andi—what if Nahanau is so far that you can't change back to human shape along the way?"

Seeing Jens's maps had given me an idea. The landmass of the Thirteen was more or less the same distance east to west as north to south—depending on how much of the Northern Wastes I counted. Or rather, how much Ursula considered her responsibility, if our theory proved correct. If I drew a straight line between the farthest points that she legally held claim to, and made that be the diameter of a circle a dome would make, the barrier wouldn't be *that* far out. However, Andi controlled the barrier from what she called the Heart, which implied the center. Assuming the

I Ieart lay somewhere near the cliff city where she and Rayfe dwelled, that could make for a very large circle indeed. If Nahanau lay on the far western edge of the barrier, it could be as far from there to Annfwn as from the west coast to the east.

Zynda sobered. "That occurred to us. Andi *thinks* the barrier is not so expanded that they can be so far, but we don't know. It is one of the uncertainties. And some forms allow for more brain space than others."

I didn't much care for uncertainties, but as the Dasnarians had on the way in, we would be sailing into uncharted waters. Jens had kept charts of their journey in, but he lacked knowledge of Annfwn's coast, which was, naturally, not on the maps he'd obtained in Ehas.

"We'll fight that battle when we reach it," Jepp declared in her pragmatic way. "All we can do is be ready. Speaking of which, librarian, get your knives. Time for some practice."

I mentally groaned, but—knowing she was right—went to do so.

By morning, we'd come within sight of land again. I braved the chill, my furred cloak and hood firmly tied closed, and stood on the upper deck with Jens to watch him delicately maneuver the ship through the Sentinels. They'd taken down the sails so a wayward wind wouldn't dash us against one of the jagged rocks that speared up all around. Instead the Dasnarian soldiers took on the job of rowing the ship through the narrow passages. They'd removed sealed coverings from ports I hadn't known were there, pushing through long oars, and chanting as they worked.

Jepp checked it out, of course, just as she'd scouted every inch of the ship, and pronounced it a fine sight, the men working up such a sweat that they stripped to shirtless or less despite the chill outside. I, however, declined to see for myself. Apparently, though, the men were bored and restless enough with the enforced inactivity to embrace the exercise. Jepp seemed more than a little disappointed that they wouldn't let her join in, saying that her smaller size and pull would throw off the rhythm.

I was happy enough to stay on deck, withstanding the numbing cold on my fingers so I could sketch the sights in my journal. The scenery was far from pretty—rather, imposing in a dreadful way. The reason for calling these islands the Sentinels became obvious. These were not the rounded humps visible from the cliffs at Windroven. They reminded me more of the rock formations in caves that I'd seen in books, if someone had lifted away the cave ceiling. Nearly black, with a glasslike sheen, the rocks pointed at the sky, rearing up around us taller than the mast—sometimes two or three times as much. Fog curled around them, the waves hitting, then splintering against them. Farther away, larger islands loomed, looking more like a normal assembly of rocks. I imagined that with these, the ocean had worn away all but what remained. A kind of core of obsidian. We seemed far from Windroven, but perhaps that volcano had spewed her lava this far. Or her sister volcanoes. I needed to read up more on the properties of volcanoes, particularly given where we headed on the way to Dasnaria.

It took the better part of the day—short as the light was and with such painstaking maneuvers—to make it through the passage, and we all breathed a sigh of relief at the sight of open water again. Not just to have escaped without becoming wreckage like so many ships we spotted remnants of, but because those rocks cast a kind of pall over us all. The way the wind howled through them sometimes sounded like the screams of the doomed, and more than once I startled at a curl of fog that seemed to move of its own accord, reaching out to me. I refused to be superstitious, but my skin crawled. It might have been my imagination that the ghosts of drowned sailors lingered there, trapped among the unforgiving, unchanging obelisks that guarded the isthmus, but if they did linger, they deserved to go to Glorianna's arms at last.

Once we were clear of the dolorous place, the clinging miasma and sense of gloom fell away. The furling sails caught the wind with a vivacious snap and the *Hákyrling* leapt forward, as if the ship was as happy as we to escape that place. We slept well that night, the calmer waters palpably soothing after the rough seas off Avonlidgh. The rising sun showed us deep-blue ocean, with hints of aquamarine in the distance. How close would we go to Annfwn?

Zynda stepped up to the rail next to me, eyes focused along the same lines.

"Tempted?" I asked her.

She flicked a glance at me and restlessly pulled her hair behind her neck, holding it there as if contemplating knotting it, then letting it fall free. "After the Sentinels? Yes. I didn't care to even touch the water there. And now I imagine I can smell the flowers of Annfwn on the wind."

"You could go. Swim there from here. I doubt we'll be closer than this."

"Fail in my first adventure?" She huffed out a sigh. "No. I'm thinking that journeys of this sort are meant to be painful at times. Moranu guides me where I need to go, to grow and learn. To become more than what I've been. Change is rarely easy, and with growth comes pain."

I mulled her words long after she jumped overboard to swim a while, with a jaunty promise that she'd be nearby. Watching her leap and dive through the swells caused by the ship, I nursed a little envy of her ability to take on a form like that. What did it feel like, to swim so freely?

The *Hákyrling* sailed fast, with a good following wind that made Jens grin. All the Dasnarians became lighter hearted, cheerful at the prospect of being able to return home, and they sang as they worked, chants with multiple harmonies made for male voices.

Within another two days, the lookout sighted Nahanau. According to Jens's charts, that made my supposition that the Heart remained at the center of the barrier the most likely eventuality. At a nod from Jepp, Zynda disappeared to swim ahead and scout what she could. Jepp, always keen to gather information, had a way of subtly conscripting scouts to her cause, and I wondered if Zynda realized she'd been recruited.

Kral joined me at the forward rail as I scanned the horizon for my first glimpse of the islands. Jepp, nearby as always, scowled at him, but he ignored her as if she didn't exist. He watched her only when he thought she wasn't looking. "You won't see them yet, *nyrri*," he said. "You'd need a long-distance glass. But see there?" He pointed at a cloud that billowed up, then caught some high wind and streamed away like a river in the air. "That's the plume from the volcano."

"Does that mean it's erupting?" I asked. Surely we wouldn't go ashore if so. Or I wouldn't, which would be disappointing. Not seeing much of Ehas was one thing. I'd likely never have another chance to the see Nahanau.

"They make the smoke without the lava at times. We shall see when we get there."

"How far is the barrier from the islands?"

"Not far, though we didn't take the shortest route before, so we're not certain. We'll stop here long enough to drop off the supplies and meet with King Nakoa KauPo. Hopefully we'll be able to convey to him who you are and to expect more of your people."

"What do you mean—does he not speak Dasnarian?"

"No." Kral seemed surprised. "Why would he? The Nahanauns are only a protectorate. They are very unlike us. Very different language and culture. You have no idea how different." He glanced away, suddenly ill at ease.

"But you know their language?"

He shook his head. "I have no gift for tongues as you do. I limp along—I know the words for food, water, shelter."

"But you promised to translate."

"Don't be concerned. I'll speak for you, as I do for all under my protection. If he agrees to meet with you, I shall inform you." He nodded at me and I wanted to stomp on his foot for his arrogance. He strode off again. Fine. I would piece it together on my own. Perhaps it would be similar to the Tala tongue, with them being more or less neighbors.

"Did he say you didn't need to talk and he'd speak for you?" Jepp sidled closer.

"Yes. You're getting quite good."

"Nothing like boredom to make even language lessons interesting." She shrugged off the praise, but she seemed proud. Jepp hadn't thought she could learn another language, beyond a few useful curse words and sexual requests, but she'd demonstrated a surprising facility for it, once she actually focused. Both she and Zynda were getting reasonably fluent, a good thing, as I might not be always with them to translate in Dasnaria. That had been the key to getting Jepp to learn—she recognized the strategic value, if nothing else. "Anyway," she continued, scowling at his back, "he's an ass, but we won't be here long enough for it to be an issue. I don't know volcanoes, but by the look of that plume, you might have to stay on the boat."

I fumed at that, feeling much like the mountain in question, much as I'd felt at the base of the pass into Annfwn when Ursula commanded me to stay safely behind. I had no wish to be foolhardy with my choices, and Goddesses knew, I lacked many survival skills, but I'd already spent much of my life taking the circumspect way, playing it safe by keeping my head down and my mouth closed. I knew exactly what that got me, which hadn't been a bad life.

But I wasn't at all sure it was the best life, either.

We sailed into the harbor of the biggest island a few hours later. By then the volcano towered overhead, dominating the sky much like another Sentinel. Only instead of fog-wrapped, glassy silence, this one rumbled as a disturbed god might, not yet angry, but leaning in that direction. Like Uorsin had been most days toward the end—quiescent for the most part, then erupting at the least thing. Never predictable. I really wished I'd thought, in my pack-

ing frenzy, to include a few books on volcanoes, and what set
them off.

As I looked, I recalled some scrolls I'd found in the Tala's col-
lection in Annfwn. The drawings, vividly inked, had caught my
eye and stayed in my memory. They showed islands dominated by
perfect conical peaks, draped in jungle foliage—and dragons flying through the sky. No dragons in sight here, but the islands
were uncannily like those.

Ash filtered through the air like snowfall, settling on my arms
and leaving dusty smears behind, like the wings of moths. A heavy
stink filled my nose, burning acrid at the back of my throat unlike
any smoke I'd encountered—though I recognized a faint cousin
of it from the depths of Windroven. The narrow entrance to the
harbor stole all my attention. Formed of two points that came
close together but did not meet, sporting two great beasts facing
each other.

Dragons.

They'd been carved from the rock of the landscape and then
built up with matching stone. As fearsome as the Sentinels and
probably twice as high as the tallest, they reared up toward the
sky, toothed jaws gaping wide. As we passed between them, the
detail became clearer—their great tails looping down the rock
ridges, the scales exquisitely executed. The wings, like those of
bats, lay folded against their backs, but so lifelike that the membrane seemed as ready to take wind as the sails of our ship. A
shiver ran through me as we passed between the towering sentinels. Warning received.

As Zynda had reported, the harbor appeared to be far more
elaborate than I'd expected of such a remote realm. No city or
many buildings were in evidence, though the heavy jungle foliage
could easily obscure anything but a castle. Piers and docks of the
same elaborately carved rock, however, vividly displayed the high
level of civilization. Everywhere sculptures twined through the ar-
chitecture. Cranes and pulleys stood waiting, with a cart-and-rail
system beyond to convey goods. No space wasted that could be

decorated. Cranes and herons stalked in stony splendor along the pylons of the piers, the floor of which formed the back of a sleepy tortoise. Snakes twined to form the pillars of the arcade.

The place was eerily empty, however, with no ships at harbor. The ghost twin of the Port of Ehas, as abandoned as that place bustled.

"Are they all dead?" Jepp wondered in a hushed voice. Between the abandoned harbor, the fuming mountain, and the lingering hangover of doom from passing through first the Sentinels and then the dragons, she sounded as I felt. Not afraid, precisely. But ready to be.

"No," Kral replied, striding up. He'd donned his full armor again—they all had—and I felt exposed in comparison. It seemed another ill omen that they dressed as if preparing for war instead of a diplomatic mission, though Kral told me not to be concerned, as it was protocol. Maybe I'd been around the Hawks, Vervaldr, and Tala too much, with their more relaxed ways and preference for fighting leathers over mail, but the armor made me as nervous as it had that day the general first strode into Ordnung's hall. "They moved the ships to protect them from burning. Look there. King Nakoa KauPo and his entourage."

I followed the line of his finger to see the group emerging through a vine-draped archway and striding onto the stone dock. Surely that was the infamous King Nakoa KauPo, leading the way, just as Ursula would want to do. Our ship drew up to a berth at the deserted pier, the men throwing out ropes to secure the *Hákyrling* in place, and I tucked myself into a corner of the rail out of the way, where I could observe and take notes in my journal. As the king and his party came near, it became clear that the Nahanauns were as naked as the Dasnarians were armored. Darker skinned than Jepp, King Nakoa KauPo's chest was bare, decorated with tattoos a few shades deeper. They reminded me of the dragons and other creatures carved into the rock, the muscles of his chest and abdomen similarly hard and ridged as the volcanic formations. As if he'd been created of the same substance and then animated. A fanciful thought indeed. Something about this place brought out my imagination—in a dark and twisted way.

He wore his black hair loose like the Tala, but not as long. Instead it coiled around his shoulders like a living thing, and what I took at first for ash dusting the dark locks turned out to be silver and white streaks threading throughout, like lightning spearing through thunderheads. More than his coloring evoked that image, as his expression was also stormy, brooding and stern. Some of what I'd taken for tattoos turned out to be what looked like flexible scaled armor at the vulnerable points of his shoulders, elbows, and ankles and over his groin. His only other garment was a sort of skirt—though that seemed the wrong word for it, as it wasn't feminine in the least. More like the *kyltes* the Vervaldr sometimes wore when off duty, short and mainly to cover the groin. He went barefoot as they all did, with some sort of similar shields over his ankles, and wore a copper torque at his throat.

Utterly fascinating.

Male and female warriors attended him, the women with the same scaly plates over their breasts, but their slender, toned waists also bare. They carried bows and spears instead of swords, and all looked as fierce as Jepp. None had the white streaks King Nakoa KauPo did. Was it a sign of age or something else? Not age, I thought, as his face seemed not lined enough. Ridged, yes, set in those brooding lines, but not wrinkled. I found myself sketching that face, rapt.

At that moment, though I hadn't moved, he looked up, fixing me with a stare so penetrating I startled. His eyes were black as the obsidian Sentinels, and equally as sharp and forbidding. He studied me, as if equally fascinated by me, though I couldn't imagine why.

"Danu take me." Jepp whistled. "We *have* to go ashore, if only for one night. Look at those people. I'll never forgive myself if I don't taste one—male or female. I wonder if they'd be willing to do a threesome with me. I'll ask. What can it hurt? After all, we're only here a night, if that."

"You'll have a difficult time asking," I told her quietly, as if King Nakoa KauPo could hear me. It seemed as if he did, as hard as he stared at me, a ridiculous thought, as he couldn't understand Common Tongue. "Remember—they don't speak Dasnarian."

Jepp gave me an arch look. "You might be the smart one with all your knowledge, but the language of the body is one I know and communicate in very well. Some things don't require words."

Between Jepp's salacious remark and the discomfort of King Nakoa KauPo's intense regard, I flushed. His expression didn't change from the stark lines, but his full lips curved into a slight smile, though he couldn't possibly guess at our conversation. He dipped his chin and turned to greet Kral, now that the gangplank was down and the general, along with his own set of guards, strode ashore. They raised hands, palm out, and King Nakoa KauPo gestured to the ship. Kral pulled something palm-sized from his pocket and handed it to Nakoa, who glanced at it, at me again. Nodded.

Then he turned and beckoned to me.

9

Jepp stepped protectively in front of me, even before Kral made the turn to face us.

Kral frowned at Jepp, a black scowl that seemed to indicate he thought she'd done something to incite him. He spoke to the king, using dismissive gestures. Even Jepp could read that body language, and she growled under her breath. "Why did the king gesture to you like that?"

"Perhaps that is him agreeing to meet?" I peered around her, seeing the men argue, growing more annoyed with each other, getting nowhere at all. "He was staring at me before that."

"I noticed that, but I thought it was because you look so different. Now I wonder," Zynda said as she came up on the conversation. "There's something about him and this place . . ."

"What?" Jepp's body took on battle readiness and she watched the king and his guards with wary aggressiveness. "Be specific."

"I can't necessarily," Zynda answered, tersely for her. "Magic isn't a black-and-white thing. But there's the sense in the air of some pending spell, for want of a better way to put it."

"I don't like it," Jepp told her. "Can you do something? Get one of those blue globes ready."

"No." Zynda said it firmly enough that Jepp risked a glance at her. "I won't. I won't use my magic against another human being. Not under these circumstances."

"If Dafne's life is—"

"If it comes to that, I will consider options."

"Better start considering fast," Jepp muttered in worsening temper.

Below, King Nakoa KauPo gave up his explanation and moved to the gangplank. Bemused and still scowling, Kral stepped aside and walked with him up and onto the ship, throwing Jepp glances all the while that managed to be both annoyed and cautionary.

"Wrong woman, boyo," Jepp said under her breath. "This time it's not my fault."

"It's not mine either," I said. "I didn't do anything."

King Nakoa KauPo walked toward us with graceful strides, his lightning-streaked locks shifting as he walked, black eyes fixed on me with the intensity of a snake about to strike. Jepp squared herself between us and Zynda flanked her. The king stopped before them, assessing the knives in Jepp's hands and her fighting stance. With his height, he looked over them easily, to me, where I pressed up in my corner, holding my journal over a heart that pounded unreasonably.

He spoke, smoothly, in a mellow singsong tongue. I sighed for it mentally. Another pitched language, by the sound of it. Ever so much harder to learn and nothing like Tala, from what I could tell. So much for the hope that I'd be able to piece together some of it quickly. He held out a hand toward me, saying the same thing again, only more gently, like one might speak to a skittish animal. His forbidding expression, however, did not reflect his tone. He transferred his gaze to Jepp and her knives, stepped closer. She struck out.

A warning swipe, but fast enough to demonstrate her considerable skill and determination. The king's guards shouted in anger, leveling their spears and arrows. The Dasnarians drew their swords. Nakoa KauPo only raised his brows—also black-

and-white threaded together—holding up a hand that told his guard to stand down, even as Kral snapped out Jepp's name.

"You can't attack King Nakoa KauPo," he said. "Don't be an idiot. You'll get us slaughtered."

"I will if he tries to hurt Dafne. That comes first."

"He won't hurt her. He's interested in her."

"How do you know?" I retorted, standing straighter at the mild insult. "Can you understand what he's saying?"

King Nakoa KauPo listened to me intently, lips moving slightly as if he tried to parse my words. He said something to Kral, then held out his hand to me. Preemptory. Demanding.

"Maybe he wants your little book," Kral said. "Give it to him."

I clutched my journal tighter. Not that. All my notes and drawings. The sketch. That must be what it was. He saw me sketching him and thought that I'd stolen a piece of his spirit, just as the Remus Islanders believed. Goddesses protect me that all he wanted was the journal, much as I hated to give it up. *You'll get us slaughtered.*

The volcano rumbled, the sound traveling through the ship, sending waves through the harbor, water clapping against the wooden sides of the hull. King Nakoa KauPo glanced at the mountain and back to me, extending the hand he still held out to me a bit farther, repeating the same words in that coaxing tone that belied his stern expression.

"Just give it to him, Dafne," Jepp said.

With a sigh, I complied, passing the journal between my friends and reaching to place it in his outstretched hand. King Nakoa KauPo took it with an expression of interest and a nod of acknowledgment that surprised me. He didn't seem angry in truth. As I became accustomed to his brooding visage, I read him better. He seemed . . . curious. Intensely interested. As he flipped through the pages, even showing care to keep the loose notes and maps in place, his eyes skimmed over the words and lingered on the sketches. He then turned to the page I'd been on, studying the drawing of himself.

Making a sound of maybe satisfaction, he looked at me again, eyes so black I couldn't make out a pupil in them, though surely he had to have them. Unless he wasn't fully human. His full lips curved as they had before. Not a smile exactly, but a lessening of his sternness.

Then he handed the journal back to me.

Surprised, relieved, and grateful, I reached to take it and clutched it again to my breast. I inclined my chin to show my gratitude and added a curtsy. He watched, then held out his hand, saying the same thing, more slowly, with insistence.

"Not the journal, then," Jepp noted ruefully.

"He wants Dafne to go with him somewhere," Zynda said.

The king waved his hand at the volcano and held it out to me again.

"The magic is getting thicker," Zynda said in Tala, so only I understood. "It's like a wave cresting, ready to break. I could shift to defend you, but I can't fight this level of magic easily, and not at all in animal form. You have to go, Dafne. Convince Jepp before this gets ugly."

Wonderful.

"Let's just see what he wants," I told Jepp. "I'm supposed to meet with him anyway. You can stick with me and so can Kral's men. You'll be ready to protect me and there's not so many of them. Harlan said that the Dasnarians could take on a force ten times their size."

"I don't like it," Jepp replied. "Kral is an idiot about many things, but he wouldn't think we'd be slaughtered were that not true in this circumstance." But she moved aside enough to show her cooperation. She spoke directly to King Nakoa KauPo. "I know you don't understand me, but listen to my tone. This woman is under my protection. I will not allow you to harm her."

"Is she threatening King Nakoa KauPo?" Kral asked me with curt anger. "If she gets my men killed . . ."

"You guaranteed her safety," Jepp told him in Dasnarian, giving him a thin smile for his surprise. "If your men die defending her, then you're only living up to your word."

"Don't presume to lecture me on questions of honor," Kral growled at her.

King Nakoa KauPo looked between them, then turned to Jepp, putting his back to Kral. He pressed his palms together in front of his heart, saying something to her in a respectful tone. Then held out his hand to me.

"As good as we're going to get," Jepp decided. "Go slowly, though, Dafne."

She didn't have to tell me that. My heart thudded as I stowed my journal safely in a pocket of my full skirts and made myself take the first step, then another. This close, the tattoos that wrapped over his biceps and chest resolved into finer detail. Despite whatever overall symbol they made, each was composed of smaller pieces, scales like a lizard's.

Or a dragon's.

Probably a dragon, because the copper torque around his neck appeared to be one. Again, much like those illustrations I'd seen in Annfwn. Remarkably lifelike, the sinuous creature seemed to coil around his thick throat, inset ruby eyes glinting.

He said those words again, encouraging, soothing.

I placed my hand in his.

He covered it with his other hand, fingers closing over mine, hot as the sun behind the cloud of ash. The volcano rumbled and the ship rocked. His mouth moved in that not-smile. "Nakoa," he said.

"Dafne," I managed, stilling the urge to pull my hand away. He held it, not tightly, but so firmly that I wouldn't be able to withdraw my hand without causing offense.

"Dafne," he echoed. Then smiled in truth. He said something longer that sounded pleasant and ended with my name. Then he bent over my hand, still holding it in both of his, and pressed his lips to the back of it. He said something, kissed my hand, and repeated it a third time.

"Uh-oh," Zynda whispered, using the Tala idiom for trouble.

"What?" I asked, almost afraid to. Except even I could sense something of it. The thickness in the air, like the static before lightning strikes. Zynda didn't reply.

Nakoa raised his head, studying me with that intent stare. He tugged my hand and turned slightly, inviting me to come with him. I followed, Jepp falling in behind me, muttering various curses and warnings under her breath. For which of us I didn't know. Nakoa guided my hand through his bent elbow, laying my palm on his forearm and covering it with his other hand. Intended as comforting, judging by his touch, but also effectively trapping me.

I breathed into the panic, trying to let it go before it swamped me, and concentrated on the present.

I almost expected his skin to feel scaly, so realistic were the tattoos, but it was silky smooth, without hair like most men have on their arms. And hot, as if he burned with a fire within, not unlike the volcano. He escorted me off the ship, his people forming a double line that we walked through. They bowed as we passed, murmuring something that sounded reverent, pressing their palms together before their hearts as their king had done. Nakoa paused at the end of the dock, looking down at me. He patted my hand reassuringly, then let go and crouched to my feet, assessing my boots with both curiosity and disdain. As he unlaced them and drew them off my feet, I searched Zynda's face for clues. Her tight expression did nothing to reassure me.

Nakoa's people watched us also with tense alertness, faces showing hope, trepidation, and the bright anticipation of witnessing something of great moment. Setting my boots aside, Nakoa slid his hands up my calves, under my skirt and over my knees. I stopped him, in a flare of embarrassed alarm, and Jepp took a half step toward me. Nakoa frowned up at me, glancing at Jepp, and saying something while tugging at my sock.

"Fine," I told him. "But *I* will take them off." The knit stockings that tied over my knees were too hot for the muggy island heat anyway. I pushed his hands away and reached under my skirt, trying not to raise it too high, and untied the ribbons. Pulling off the stockings, I rolled them carefully so my hidden daggers would not fall out and stowed them in another pocket. One reason skirts were so much more convenient than fighting leathers, though it might have been better had I been dressed as a fighter. I felt oddly naked and vulnerable to be barefoot. At least I had my other knives, hidden away.

Satisfied, Nakoa stood and offered his arm again. All of this was so strange. He raised his brows at my hesitation, so I took it. He patted my hand in approval and I began to feel like one of Andi's horses, trained to accept the bit and saddle. Holding my hand in place again, Nakoa led me down three steps off the stone pier, my bare feet sinking into the soft, damp earth.

A flash rang through my head and the ground seemed to move under my feet.

No, it *did* move. The island shook and a plume of smoking ash roared up from the volcano. I cried out and clung to Nakoa's arm for balance.

He planted himself, steadying me, holding me upright even as his people sent up an excited chant, singing in the direction of the volcano. Nakoa did not sing, but kept his gaze on the volcano, stroking my hand. My head cleared, though a dull ache remained in the wake of whatever that had been. Jepp had hold of my other arm but was turned away, in furious conversation with Zynda, who met my eyes over Jepp's shoulder. She gave me a small shake of her head, more communicating that she couldn't do anything than that she didn't know what had happened.

The chant finished and Nakoa gestured to a path that seemed to lead in the direction of the volcano, walking us both forward. Jepp and Zynda fell in behind, and it was an obscure comfort to hear Jepp's mutters. I didn't blame her, feeling the urge to send up a prayer of my own. We stood on foreign land, but the extension of the barrier might put these isles under the protection of the Three. Following instinct, I drew Glorianna's circle in the air with my free hand, inscribed Moranu's crescent, and bisected it with Danu's sword, adding a fervent, wordless wish for this to turn out well.

Nakoa took note of my gesture, interest softening some of the sterner lines around his mouth, but did not slow or break stride. We went up the path, soft packed dirt, that wound and switch-backed along the mountainside. As we climbed, the vista fell away below us, the sea shimmering blue-green, the *Hákyrling* clearly visible in the harbor. I'd fortunately gained some conditioning, going up and down Annfwn's cliffside roads. A year ago I could not have sustained the pace. As it was, I grew out of breath keeping up with Nakoa's much longer strides. He glanced down at me in puzzled concern—apparently none of the island women spent more time reading than climbing volcanoes—just as I yelped, stepping on a hot ash I missed seeing.

Frowning in such a forbidding way that I flinched, Nakoa stopped, turned me around, and picked up my foot, inspecting it just as I'd seen Andi check horses' hooves countless times. Which did not do anything to defuse my earlier sense of being trained like one. His thumb passed over the burn and the tender skin of my foot, already sore from the unaccustomed friction of going barefoot on the increasingly rock-strewn path. In one smooth movement, he put my foot down and scooped me up in his arms—a dizzying sensation that stole both my breath and my equanimity—turning and showing me to Jepp, saying something as he did.

She didn't like it any more than I did, but she nodded curtly and spoke to me in a deliberately even tone. "You're no more vulnerable than you were and in some ways less so. You can more easily get a knife into his throat from there, if you need to. Better to save your feet anyway."

In case we needed to run. I nodded back faintly and Nakoa, clearly considering the matter settled, set out again at an increased pace. At first I kept my arms folded, hugging them to myself, but I only felt more like helpless baggage that way. And I tended to slide down instead of looking forward. Tentatively at first, in case I earned one of those black frowns, I put a hand on Nakoa's bare chest, snatching my fingers away again at the astonishing sensation. He glanced down at me, amusement clearly etched in his face, and said something, adjusting his arms so I sat up higher. Testing my understanding, I slid a hand behind his neck, anchoring myself, and he responded by lifting me into a much better position. Now all I had to do was assimilate the unprecedented feeling of hot male skin under my hand, slick with exertion, his thick, curly hair brushing my hand, shoulder and neck muscles undulating as we climbed.

Unbidden, an image came to mind of experiencing this exact thing, only with us both naked in bed, and him rising over me to plow my body with his. I kept my face averted, gazing steadfastly forward so he wouldn't guess the direction of my thoughts. Not at all my normal sort of thinking. Whatever the king's agenda, it had nothing to do with that. Not with me. Not for a man of his power, surrounded by the tall, lethally beautiful women who guarded him.

Goddesses only knew what was happening to me.

We reached a clear area under the summit before much longer, the air ironically clearer than lower down. The heat, however, radiated up through the rock around us, making me profoundly grateful not to have my bare feet on it, no matter how discomfiting the alternative. Nakoa stopped at a ledge that looked over a dazzling horizon, ocean as far as the eye could see, the humps and dots of other islands visible in the distance.

And below us, a bubbling lake filled with lava.

Stricken, I clutched at my captor, though if he planned to toss me in, my feeble strength would be no match for his. Mastering myself, I dropped the hand I'd braced on his chest and found the small dagger I'd secreted in a hidden pocket of my skirt, ready to draw it.

I looked over his shoulder at Zynda and asked in Tala, "Do they mean to sacrifice me to the volcano?"

"I don't *think* so, but I don't know what they do mean to do."

"Stop talking around me," Jepp snapped. "What's going on here?"

"A ritual," Zynda answered. "A powerful magical one."

Nakoa's people began a slow, humming, hypnotic chant, the sense of portentous magic looming large over us. I couldn't help staring at the lake of lava, mesmerized by the possibility of my imminent death. From where we stood, Nakoa could simply drop me and I would fall with nothing to break it. Would it hurt or would I die instantly?

My chest hurt from holding my breath and a tear slid down my cheek. That or sweat from the menacing heat. Nakoa frowned at me and shook his head.

"He's too close to the edge," Jepp whispered furiously to Zynda. "I can't get to him without risking losing her. But we have to stop this immediately."

"I don't think we can. It's like an avalanche of magic, already crashing down too fast to halt."

"Nonsense. A good blade stops anything. Pull your dagger, Dafne, and put it to his throat. Do it *now!*"

10

For once grateful for Jepp's relentless drilling and my unthinking obedience to her snapped orders, I moved before I thought about it. Faster than I'd ever thought I could, I had my blade out and pressed to the soft spot at the pulse point of Nakoa's throat. It looked ridiculously slim and delicate against his corded neck, but the glint of the words Ursula had inscribed there heartened me. I might be small and strengthless compared to this barbarian king, but I had fangs of my own that should never be ignored.

The chanting, however, did not slow, and Nakoa only dropped his black gaze to mine. He did have pupils, though so nearly matching the irises that I barely made out the delineation of them. Oddly, he smiled, ever so slightly, the tone of which I couldn't quite interpret, but with something of that same interest he showed in my journal. Holding my gaze, he slowly and deliberately leaned into the sharp edge. I lacked the fortitude of my warrior sisters, else I would have kept it in place instead of playing the coward and not resisting. If my hand had not been shaking so badly, the blade would not have bit at all.

As it was, I sliced him. Not deeply, but enough to draw bright blood that ran in a rivulet both along my little dagger and down his throat. Nakoa spoke a few words, a hiss behind them. His arms tightened and he gathered me closer, completely ignoring the blade.

And fastened his mouth on mine.

Stunned, I did nothing at first, unaware of anything except his startlingly hot and hard lips. This was not Zyr's artful, sensual kiss, nor my suitor's sloppy, indifferent promise. If Zyr's kiss had felt like a song not written for me, this one drilled to the very core of my being, filling my body and blood with a sense of homecoming, of feeding me some necessary food I'd lacked all my life. I drowned in it, overcome, forgetting the blade in my hand, my friends watching and worrying, the dire, strange circumstances in which we found ourselves.

I lost everything except my connection to Nakoa and the rumbling of the volcano around us. It thundered through me, stirring my heartbeat into a matching rhythm, as if my quiet, closeted heart had opened up and become part of a much greater, wilder one. Nakoa's mouth seemed to feed on mine, coaxing something from me, pulling me closer and deeper. I clung to him, no longer questioning any of it, viscerally desperate to meld my skin with his. His heartbeat pounded in time with mine, synchronized. Mine. His. And something else, even larger.

The realization struck me and I started to pull away, but Nakoa slid a hand to clasp the back of my head, holding me there, even as he let me slide down his body, gradually lowering my feet to the ground, the heart of the mountain taking me under deeper, thoroughly, the avalanche of magic searing my blood with unaccustomed heat.

My feet touched the burning rock and the volcano boomed, making Nakoa stagger and wrenching apart that endless kiss, though he caught his balance and kept me upright, pressed close.

Expecting lava to rain down on us, I threw back my head to see. If I was to die here, at least I'd witness one of the greatest events of nature for myself. For once I'd be in the middle of it all.

The cloud of ash and steam billowed and swirled. Breathless, my body charged with a combination of dread, excitement, lust, anticipation, and terror, I focused on the smooth peak rising just above us. Soon lava, bright and molten like the lake below, like the blood boiling through my body, would spill over the mountain and carry us with it.

So unfair, that I would meet death moments after the most interesting thing that ever happened to me. That I would die a virgin. The perfect sacrifice.

Instead of regret, however, I felt mainly the exhilaration of imminent release.

Nakoa's heart still pounded with mine, a profound connection that linked us, that made me feel as if our bodies both circulated the liquid rock that surged up inside the volcano. It burgeoned, grew, swelling to explosive levels. The volcano itself seemed to draw in. Impossible that a mountain could move in such a way, but if rock could melt, then it could also—

Crumble.

Not an explosion, but a peeling back.

And out shot a dragon.

Glittering gold, it cut through the steam and ash, cleaving it like a knife separating flesh and leaving shreds behind. Moans of reverence and shouts of dismay followed in the dragon's wake as it speared straight up into the sky, a glittering, vertical comet trailing ash, magic, and awe. It nearly vanished, so high above us it became like a star. The shuddering of my heart, feeding blood to the ascent, went with it. Paused there at the apex.

Then the dragon returned. It grew to the size of a full moon, diving ever closer. I shrank against Nakoa, absurdly seeking shelter from the captor who brought me to this literal and figurative precipice.

With a snap that echoed in my bones, the great wings unfurled. Zynda cried out in protest, shouting something in Tala about shattering wings. But they held, the dreadful dive converting into a glide, a great sweeping circle of soundless grace.

I became aware of the still silence then. The rumbling of the volcano had ceased. Nothing more erupted from the peak, and the fall of ash thinned, diminishing with each moment, like the last gentle edge of a snowstorm, after the blizzard winds move on.

"What the fuck was that all about?" came Jepp's harsh whisper.

I struggled, suddenly acutely aware of being held against Nakoa's naked chest. With the magic releasing its hold, along with the keen peak of awareness imminent death had brought, all that remained was a grim sense of exposure. I wanted, needed, to hide away somewhere. Some of that black, remembered panic rose, and I fought the restraining arms as I hadn't before. Nakoa frowned at me as I struck him. I'd lost my dagger and had no wit to pull another, but he set me away from him, taking my wrists in each hand and speaking soft words that made no sense and didn't soothe. My feet burned.

"Let her go," Jepp said, her words sharp as the edge of the blade she put between Nakoa and me. "Whatever this was, it's over and she needs you to release her. Now."

Nakoa ignored her, studying me with that intent expression as I tugged away from his implacable grip. He asked me a question, the tone concerned, and I nearly screamed at him that I didn't understand his words or any of this, but my heart had fluttered up into my throat, my skin icy with sweat as cold as the rain that had dripped down the black rocks that had entombed me.

Lithe arms wrapped around me from behind, the scent of the vines of Annfwn with them, catching me when Nakoa released my wrists. Zynda leaned her cheek against mine from behind, cradling me against her as we both sank to the hard, heated rock.

"You're okay," she murmured in her singsong tongue. "Relax, librarian. All is well."

I flinched at the brush of her magic, like hot water hitting a sunburn, but then it took the rawness and sting away from my soul. My blood cooled, and rational thought—something I'd never expected to fail me—returned.

"I'm all right," I told her.

"Yes, I can feel that, but give it a moment until we see how things lean."

Jepp and Kral were arguing furiously, her Dasnarian full of sexual insults. Behind them, King Nakoa stood, arms folded, still as a carved statue, only his dark eyes glitteringly alive as he watched not them, but me. Above, the dragon circled, enormous wings extended as it rode the air currents like a golden-scaled eagle above the heights at Ordnung.

"Let me up—I need to translate." Zynda hesitated and I pulled away. "Seriously, Jepp is making things worse with her malapropisms."

She stood, with that supple strength she shared with Ursula, helping me up. My feet still burned on the hot rock, but I could ignore them for a while. The last thing I wanted was for Nakoa to pick me up again. Or touch me at all, given how completely he'd rattled me. Feeling more centered, more in my realm of expertise, I put my hands on Kral's and Jepp's shoulders, drawing their attention and stopping the barrage of epithets.

"Jepp," I said to her in Common Tongue, "this battle falls to me. My weapons are better. Let me translate. What do you argue for?"

She speared me with a hot, angry look. "We need to get off this island immediately, but lunkhead here says the danger is over and we should give the king the lead."

At least she possessed enough discretion still not to use Nakoa's name aloud. I translated for Kral, cleaning up Jepp's opinion considerably. He eyed Jepp as I spoke, jaw clenched.

"We can't flee for the boat," he ground out. "It will be seen as a sign of weakness. King Nakoa already invited us to a welcome feast when we first arrived and I accepted. Given the scarcity of their supplies, it's an enormous offer and we'll give fatal insult if we renege now."

"Even after he . . . all he did?" I amended, careful not to look at the man, though he'd caught his name, by the way he shifted in my peripheral vision.

Kral shifted his gaze to me, a tinge of regret there but still righteous in his conviction. "A kiss, no more, *nyrri*, and you are none the worse for the wear. From what I gather, this"—he waved a hand that encompassed me, Nakoa, and the circling dragon— "was an exceptional ceremony. An honor to you."

"He accosted her," Jepp inserted in terse Dasnarian, using the word that fell one shading shy of rape. It spoke volumes about the Dasnarian culture that they had so many words for varying levels of sexual consent. And about Jepp that she'd learned them well enough to choose the correct one.

"What he did," Kral said directly to her through gritted teeth, "is take nothing that shouldn't be accorded to any foreign dignitary under normal circumstances, and even you must admit these are far from normal events."

Jepp leaned in. "We of the Twelve Kingdoms do not offer up *any* of our citizens, male or female, as party favors to anyone at all."

"But we're not in the Twelve Kingdoms!" Kral shouted.

"General Kral of Dasnaria and Imperial Prince of the Royal House of Konyngrr," I snapped, his title cutting through his frustration as I'd hoped. "If we're to draw new borders, as the document you recently signed designates, then these islands *are* within the *Thirteen* Kingdoms, which makes me, as adopted sister to the High Queen, and as her envoy, the ranking decision maker here."

I surprised even myself with that. Where had that come from? Both Kral and Jepp gazed at me in identical astonishment. King Nakoa moved then, snagging my eye. He gave me a nod, then spoke and gestured down the mountain.

"Fine," Jepp said. "You rank. What's your call, Lady Mailloux?"

I ignored her sarcasm, figuring it justified and deserved. "Let's do the feast. Do what we came here for. Especially as it seems at least one danger has passed. No one seems concerned about the dragon. Let's get through tonight and put this place behind us in the morning."

She accepted with ill grace, giving Nakoa a baleful glare, which seemed to amuse the man, if I read his expression correctly. I shifted, one burning foot to another, and he noted it, stepping forward with clear intent. I held up a hand to stop him. I couldn't bear to be so near him, even as part of me felt that our hearts still shared the same blood, along with the impossible monster winging above. I needed time to assimilate this. Surely there would be tales to inform me?

"You can't walk down the mountain barefoot," Jepp said, considering my reddened feet. "Perhaps one of Kral's men?"

"I will carry you," Zynda decided. "A demonstration that we are not helpless, should escape become necessary."

"Thank you," I told her with heartfelt gratitude. She shimmered beside me, that sense of nighttime magic, of the shadows, glints of moonlight and animal eyeshine washing over me. Like and yet not like the magic of whatever had happened with the releasing of the dragon. I watched Nakoa carefully, so I caught the flicker of surprise when Zynda became a gray mare beside me. No more than that from this controlled, savage man, however.

A murmur ran through his people, not shock so much as that sound of reverence. Of course, we'd just seen a dragon emerge from a volcano, so a woman shape-shifting into a horse might seem commonplace. Zynda knelt down to make it easier for me to climb on, which I did quickly to forestall any contradiction from Nakoa. He simply gestured down the mountain again, then took position beside me, walking close enough that his bare arm occasionally brushed my calf. I tried to pretend that the brief points of contact didn't send sparks through my blood.

As we descended, I lost sight of the dragon, though that newly opened sense in me still tracked its presence. Perhaps it had landed somewhere. The Nahanauns sang as we walked, an eerie, multilayered harmonic that seemed to speak of joy and triumph. Glimpses through the thickening foliage showed the vista clearing, the water gaining sparkle. Freed of the sulfurous stink, the air carried other scents—of flowers, the loamy soil, and cooking food. My stomach rumbled, reminding me how long it had been since I'd eaten—not since dawn, and now the sun declined to the horizon—and Nakoa, nearly at head height with me, glanced over at the sound and very nearly smiled. The language of the body, indeed. In that we managed to communicate. He patted my calf, a caress that slid down my leg, where his fingers lingered briefly, easily encircling my ankle.

I tore my gaze away, wishing fiercely that I dared put on my stockings again.

We could get through this feast. I could get us through this. If I'd managed to survive Uorsin all those years, I could find my way around this unpredictable king with his dagger-sharp eyes and lingering touches. Why he'd picked me of all people for his ritual that freed the dragon, I didn't know. I might never know, which— much as the possibility rankled—I'd trade for putting distance between me and this island. I'd done my part, so he should have no reason to prevent my departure.

Goddesses make it so.

We passed the way to the harbor, heading down another branching pathway that led around the curve of the island. A fresh breeze off the water greeted us, cool on my sweat-damp brow, where my hair clung in soaked curls against my temples. The Dasnarians in their armor must be sweltering, but they showed no sign of it, striding along in stoic silence. Jepp, walking on the other side of Zynda from the king, gleamed with sweat also, though she looked good with it, brown skin shining with golden light. She'd calmed on the walk, though I knew from keeping company with Ursula that this was the peace of preparing herself for battle, not of conflict resolved.

We traveled through a tunnel of trees, clearly tended so their branches wove together in an arch overhead. They dripped with panicles of flowers in soft hues of lavender, pink, and buttercup, like a rainbow at a rainy sunrise. As we emerged, a golden palace came into view. Not at all what I expected from a king who went barefoot.

Where the cliff city at Annfwn rises vertically, built into both human-made and natural caves, this place sprawled out over ledges and terraces. Columns held up balconies that contained only gardens, and large expanses of the polished gold stone, big enough to be ballroom floors, led to steps that descended directly into the crystal blue water of the sea. In the gloaming, torches and candles gleamed from the interior, reminding me of Annfwn with a kind of nostalgic homesickness.

Under me, Zynda shifted and huffed out a long breath, making me wonder if she felt it, too. Though Annfwn *was* her home and never mine. Thus it shouldn't feel like homesickness. Odd that I connected that feeling—that lingering ache of loss for my family home at Columba—with Annfwn and now here. Maybe because I'd been happy in Annfwn and had come to associate that feeling with this sort of sight.

Nakoa touched my ankle and gestured at the palace, asking me a question, eyebrows raised. Did he ask what I thought?

"It's very beautiful," I told him and he tilted his head, listening.

We started forward again, winding down the hillside. When we reached the land-side entrance of the palace, another broad expanse of polished stone, Nakoa spoke to Kral, making it clear that he and his men should wait. Kral halted, giving us a warning look that we hardly deserved. Nakoa walked the three of us forward. At least he allowed Jepp to remain.

His warriors peeled off to the sides, taking up stations around the perimeter, holding their spears butt-end down before them. Then the doors opened, spilling light into the fading evening, and children came dancing out. Unlike Nakoa's warriors in their scaled armor, the children were dressed in pastel scarves, like the panicles of blossoms in the arbor. They sang as they moved, creating a complicated pattern of color, and dropped handfuls of white flower petals, perfuming the air.

A group of young women followed, all luminously beautiful and dressed the same way. The foremost carried a wreath of white flowers with exotically trailing petals. She smiled at me, a reserved, closed-mouth curve of her lips very like Nakoa's. Family resemblance or cultural? Nakoa gestured to the young woman, who stopped before him.

"Inoa," he said, then put a much-too-proprietary hand on my knee. "Dafne."

She inclined her head, saying something much longer with my name, then handed the flower wreath to Nakoa. He lifted it, making it clear he wished to place it over my head. The children halted their dance, holding whatever pose they'd been in—a fantastic demonstration of athletic skill—their song falling similarly silent.

"I don't like this," Jepp grumbled. I was beginning to wish I had a jewel for every time she said it.

"And I don't see a way to refuse this without insult," I replied. I leaned down, and Nakoa, catching and holding my gaze, placed it over my head. "Thank you," I told him, hoping that's what this was about.

Inoa clapped her hands together over her heart and bowed, the children bursting back into song and movement at the signal. The other women added their voices to the song, augmenting the sweet sopranos with darker harmonies and languid hand motions that seemed to go with the song. It all seemed directed at me, a kind of joyful welcome.

When they finished, Nakoa spoke and the other young women approached, concern on their faces. He touched my ankle again and Inoa moved to look at the bottom of my foot. They exchanged words and seemed to come to a conclusion that involved Inoa sending the other women on an errand. Nakoa held up his hands to lift me down and Inoa stepped back.

"Do you think you can stand?" Jepp came around Zynda to be ready to guard my back. "The sole of your foot looks pretty torn up from here."

"I don't know. They ache but are mostly stiff, I think." But I couldn't ride Zynda into the lovely palace. The floors seemed to be inlaid with intricate wood patterns that her hooves would likely scar. Bracing myself, both for touching Nakoa and in anticipation of pain, I swung a leg over Zynda's neck, making sure to keep my skirts tucked between my thighs as I did, then set my hands on Nakoa's shoulders. He put his hands on my waist and nearly encircled it, they were so big. With great care, he lifted me, then lowered me to the ground, Inoa giving him advice the whole while, by the sound of it.

My toes touched the ground. Thankfully Nakoa still held most of my weight, because I nearly blacked out from the sudden shock of pain. It rolled over me in a nauseating wave—far worse than I'd been prepared for. Vaguely I recalled reading somewhere that foot injuries hurt the worst of any. And here I was, living the reality I'd only read about.

Had I longed to be in the center of events instead of at the periphery? A wish I'd take back at that moment.

Nakoa instantly swung me up in his arms again and carried me into the palace, while Inoa trotted alongside, speaking nonstop in a chastising tone. He looked blackly angry and I longed for the words to point out that if he hadn't taken off my shoes and stockings, this wouldn't have happened. Jepp and Zynda—back in human form—brought up the rear. By the set of Jepp's jaw, she blamed herself for this.

After a maze of hallways, we entered an enormous bedchamber, ringed by nearly a full circle of balconies that looked out over the tranquil sea. I didn't see much, what with the pain and concentrating on not being physically ill on the king of a foreign nation. With more gentleness than I'd have credited him for, Nakoa set me on the bed, laying me against a mound of pillows and keeping one arm braced under my calves, so my tender feet wouldn't touch the covers.

Inoa slid a cylindrical pillow under my legs, replacing Nakoa's arm, and, edging him out of the way, adjusted the pillows under my head. Worried about crushing the gorgeous flower garland, I moved to pull it off over my head, but she stayed my hands and gave me a small shake of her head and an unmistakable warning look. She smiled when I subsided.

Then, speaking sharply, she indicated that King Nakoa should leave. He lingered a moment, paying no attention to her, but studying my face. He said something to me and touched his index finger to his full lower lip. Inoa answered in a tart tone. With one last scowl for her, he left.

11

The other young women streamed in, bringing various supplies, Inoa directing them in a much less sharp tone now that King Nakoa had departed. Jepp took up a guard position at the head of the bed while Zynda prowled the room, investigating.

"Okay," I said to them in Common Tongue, both because we needed to talk and because I needed the distraction from my throbbing feet, "what do we make of all this? Think Inoa is related to King Nakoa KauPo?"

At my words, Inoa looked up, gave me a far warmer smile than before, placed her hand over her heart, and said, "Inoa KauPo."

"I am honored to meet you," I told her, returning the smile. "That answers that. Wife or sister?"

Zynda returned from her explorations, climbed onto the bed on my other side, being careful not to jostle me, and settled into a cross-legged sitting position. "Sister or other relative, unless the king has multiple wives. You're currently in his bed."

"Danu's tits," Jepp swore, a sentiment I shared.

"How do you know?" I asked Zynda, though I didn't disagree. The few things I could see from my vantage echoed Nakoa's tattoos and jewelry, including the sinuous dragons that formed the posts of the bed, holding the frame from which very light fabric hung, gathered at the four corners.

"Besides that everything here smells of him?" Zynda smiled wryly. "He set his weapons down over there. This is his space."

"Can you smell that well?" I asked her. I hadn't really noticed a strong scent to the man, but then I'd been distracted.

Zynda slid a look at Jepp, weighing how much to tell, apparently. Then she shrugged. "If we spend enough time in an animal form, we can retain some of those aspects. Human senses aren't all that different from those of animals; we just emphasize the information differently in our minds. Being an animal that uses its sense of smell extensively teaches us to pay more attention to what our human noses scent."

Oh, yes, Jepp would want to take advantage of that. I started to say something, but Inoa put a hand on my ankle, interrupting us. She spoke to Zynda, miming holding my ankles down. Wonderful.

"Hold on." Zynda patted my hand. "They have some ointments, so hopefully those will numb the pain. Just get through the application."

She took over for Inoa, holding my ankles in a relentless grip. Thoughtful of Inoa, to have my friend do this instead of one of her people. After that attack of panic on the mountain, I might not be able to withstand being trapped again so soon by someone unknown. Bad enough to endure it at all. To my surprise, Jepp took my hand. "Squeeze hard if you have to," she advised. "Seems strange, but it truly helps."

Inoa asked a short question. Assuming she asked if I was ready, I squeezed Jepp's hand and nodded. The cool slap of ointment on both feet at once made me cry out, tears stinging my eyes, the nausea rising again, the edges of my vision going black with crimson bursts. Adventure was definitely overrated. Inoa's ladies crooned an encouraging sound, adding more of the stuff. Gradually the pain lessened and my feet did go blissfully numb. I realized I held Jepp's hand in a death grip, crushing her knuckles, and apologized.

"You did good, librarian," she said, keeping my hand when I would have let go. "Worthy of any of the Hawks. Foot wounds sting like Danu's tits. But you're not through this yet."

She called it. Inoa's ladies brought over a wash basin and pulled up a table covered with gleaming tiles of all colors to set it on. They set to bathing my feet, which I felt even through the numbing ointment. Worst was when they picked up tools with sharp edges and pointed ends, digging into my flesh, making me grateful Zynda held me so securely, as I could not have done it myself.

"They're picking stuff out," Jepp told me. "Little rocks, dirt, stuff like that. That's good because it means they know about preventing infection, but it's probably better not to look."

So I lay back and stared up at the ceiling. Like the floors, they were also formed of long strips of wood, shading from dark brown to pale sunlight, coming together at a peak. Recalling the way I'd lectured Jepp on ignorance of Dasnarian customs and accepting Kral's invitation to his bed, I sighed to myself.

"It's probably a really bad sign that I'm in his bed, isn't it?"

Zynda tossed her hair over her shoulder to look at me without breaking her grip on my ankles. "He's clearly taken a personal interest in you."

"If that kiss was any gauge, yes." Jepp gave me a crooked smile, a shadow of her usual cheeky grin. "Seriously hot from the outside."

From the inside, too. I didn't want to think about that. "It was part of that ritual."

"Definitely." Zynda nodded. "But, speaking from an animal perspective, all of his body language toward you shouts possessiveness."

"To this mossback, too," Jepp said drily.

"Wonderful."

"We'll figure something out," Zynda reassured me.

Jepp squeezed my hand. "We won't leave you alone. Zynda and I will take turns standing guard. He's had all he'll get of you, I promise you that."

I didn't tell her not to make promises she couldn't keep. Jepp blamed herself enough for this. The ladies finished, adding more ointment and wrapping my feet in a light cloth like the bed curtains. Inoa approached with something steaming in a cup covered with the same bright tiles as the table. She showed it to Jepp, bowing slightly, and took a sip from it. Jepp took it from her and tasted it tentatively.

"It tastes familiar," she said, "like one of our sedative teas. But I don't know for sure."

Inoa gestured from the cup to me, giving me a hopeful smile and nodding as she spoke.

"If they wanted to kill me, they could have already instead of spending all this time healing me. I'll drink it." Though much abated, the pain in my feet would likely keep me awake otherwise.

"I'll take first watch," Zynda said. "In an appropriately daunting form." She shifted, becoming the large cat, stretching out beside me and casually flexing her claws.

The ladies gasped, one making a small shrieking sound, but Inoa, with the same equanimity as Nakoa, only widened her eyes slightly, then bowed to Zynda in a gesture of exaggerated respect.

I took the cup and drank from it, while Jepp made herself comfortable in a chair by the open windows. Fatigue and drowsiness overwhelmed me, the cup nearly falling from my fingers before Inoa neatly took it. I might have dreamed it, but I thought she bent over and kissed my forehead. I let myself fall into oblivion, unutterably grateful for Zynda's warm purr and Jepp's steadfast presence by the windows.

I might be trapped—a siege of another sort—but I wasn't
alone. Not this time.

I woke to bright sunlight and the startlingly fierce and brooding face of Nakoa, watching me intently from a chair by the bed.

"He's been there since not long after you dropped off," Jepp
said, coming into view. "He came in and sat down. They've brought
him food, but he's refused to leave. He hasn't tried to touch you, so
don't worry about that." She looked weary. So much for taking
shifts. I doubted she'd slept at all.

I struggled to sit up and Nakoa reached to help me, adjusting
the pillow under my knees and plumping the ones under my
back. Stiff from lying like the dead all night—that tea was powerful stuff—I groaned a little. Nakoa frowned at me, asking a sharp
question.

"I'm fine," I answered. Then huffed out a laugh, thinking of
Ursula saying it was always a lie when she said it, too. I shrugged
my shoulders, rolling them in demonstration. Then pantomimed
yawning. "Just stiff from sleeping so long."

He seemed mollified. Then he glanced up at Jepp and back to
me. He gestured to my feet and asked a question.

They felt okay. Sore, but not anything like the night before.
"Better," I told him. Then tried their gesture of laying my hands
over my heart. "Thank you, King Nakoa KauPo."

He shook his head, frowning. "Nakoa."

Okay, then. "Thank you, Nakoa."

"Thank you," he echoed, trying the words, and I smiled to reward the effort. He gestured to Jepp, waving her away.

"I'm not leaving you," she replied, fingering her daggers for
his benefit.

"Could you maybe go to the windows and watch from there? I
don't know what he wants, but . . ."

She sighed heavily. "Point taken. We need him happy, if we're to convince him to let you go." She crossed the room and turned her back. "Just yell if you need me, for the least little thing."

He watched her go, then gestured to my feet again, placing his index finger on his lower lip, tugging it and casting down his face with a sorrowful expression. An apology then.

"It's all right. You didn't know." I pointed to his feet, then tapped the palm of my hand with my nails. "Yours are tough. Mine"—I changed the gesture to stroke my palm lightly—"are soft."

Moving slowly, he took my hand and mimicked the motion, brushing his fingers lightly over my upraised palm. The sensation shivered through me and I caught my breath as my heart thudded and blood surged to the surface of my skin.

"You okay?" Jepp asked without turning around.

"Yes." Except I wasn't. I needed to think, something that became impossible when this man touched me.

Nakoa flicked Jepp an irritated glance. He gestured to her and said something longer, using both my name and his. Still holding my one hand, he made encompassing circles with the other at the ceiling, sea, and me. It sounded very solemn. He finished by touching the garland still hanging around my neck, sadly crushed and wilted now.

I wanted to say I didn't understand, but I suspected I did, all too well.

"What was all that?"

I glanced at Jepp, who shifted impatiently from foot to foot. Nakoa tapped my cheek lightly, turning my gaze back to him. "*Ayh*," he said sharply, shaking his head. He gestured to Jepp and said the sound again. "*Ayh*." Then pointed back and forth between him and me. "Nakoa. Dafne."

"Please stay quiet unless I call you," I told her, not taking my eyes off Nakoa. This felt much like negotiating with a predator intent on eating me if I made the wrong move. More wolves surrounding me. Or a dragon, stalking.

I held up my hand, asking for his patience, and eased the other from his grip. Plucking a wilted petal from the garland, I pointed to the sea out the windows and moved the petal as if floating it on the waves. I set my finger on it, saying my name, showing the petal sailing to the palace. "Dafne came here on a ship to help you." I showed him the petal sailing away again. "Dafne cannot stay." I added a firm shake of my head. "Dafne must leave again."

Nakoa's expression grew thunderous. He touched the garland, then laid a palm over my heart, pressing me against the bed. Speaking long and in a commanding tone accompanied by much head shaking, he made it clear that I would be going nowhere. I flinched back a little at his touch, but he held firm, gentling his tone. Then he picked up my hand again, uncurled my fingers, and placed a kiss on the inside of my wrist.

If the previous caress had been a shiver, this was a bolt that shot into my already pounding heart. I imagined I felt the echo of Nakoa's, beating in the same rhythm, along with that other, wilder heart. In the distance, a musical roar sounded. Nakoa cocked his head at it meaningfully, then kissed the tender skin of my wrist at the pulse point again, watching me as he did. I tried to keep calm, hide my reaction, but it made no difference. His lips curved in an unmistakably sensual smile. "Dafne *mlai*," he said, and kissed my wrist again.

I stared back at him, my thoughts scattered. Somehow I'd gotten myself engaged or, Goddesses forbid, married to this foreign king, and I had no idea how to get myself out of it.

Ursula was going to kill me.

Apparently satisfied that he'd won the argument, Nakoa stood and went to the doors, opening them to admit a smiling Inoa and her entourage of ladies, bearing food and likely more healing supplies. One of them carried a garland like the one I wore, only fresh. Nakoa took it from her and came back to me, placing it over my head and around my neck with that same sense of ceremony. Only then did he remove the wilted one, handing it back to the same woman, who received it on upturned palms with a reverent nod. Nakoa turned back to me and held out an expectant hand. Guessing, I laid mine palm up in his and his lips curved in approval. Well-trained Dafne.

He pressed a final kiss to my inner wrist. *"Mlai."*

The ladies all beamed and sighed, their dark eyes shining, as if they found it romantic. Nakoa said something more, then left. At last. Inoa set a tray over my lap with a few murmured words. It held fruit and some kind of tea. I gestured to the tea and mimicked yawning. She shook her head. *"Ayh."* Then used her fingers to make her eyes look wide and alert. Good enough. And at least I knew their word for "no."

Much good may it do me with the dragon king.

A large raptor dropped a bag on the balcony and landed on the rail. Zynda shimmered into human form and picked up the bag again. She and Jepp had a brief, quiet conversation, then came over to the bed, where the ladies were delicately unwinding my bandages.

"How are you feeling?" Zynda asked, her eyes deep blue with concern.

"Much better. I don't know if I can walk yet, but my feet don't hurt nearly as much."

Jepp and Zynda moved to where they could see as the ladies unveiled my wounds. "Oh, yeah." Jepp nodded. "Not nearly so raw. Scabbed up in places. The blisters all popped and are nicely pink, healing up. You can probably put your weight on them in another couple of days."

It sounded like forever. "Days?"

Jepp gave me a rueful shrug. "Feet are hard—all you can do is stay off of them."

I couldn't stay here for days. With every passing hour, it felt as if my chances of getting back to the ship and escaping the island slipped away like sand eaten by the tide. If I knew why Nakoa had fixed on me, I could find a way to talk him out of his certainty that I had to stay. All I knew was it had to do with that ritual on the volcano. "Any sign of the dragon?"

"No," Zynda drew out the word thoughtfully. "And I flew around quite a bit looking for it. Could it have gone back to sleep? The volcano seems to be quieter, too."

"Hmm." We all fell briefly silent, contemplating the import of that. No one wanting to broach the obvious issues we needed to discuss.

"I guess we didn't sail out on the morning tide, huh?" I finally said.

Zynda grimaced. "The supplies have been unloaded, but your King of the Volcano and his people won't answer Kral's attempts to inquire about or see you. We're going to have to carry you out and I'm afraid we'll need the Dasnarians to do it."

"At least Kral is trying." It reassured me on one level, as I hadn't been at all sure of Kral's loyalties. Or agenda.

"Not nearly hard enough," Jepp replied. "Not yet. But I'm working on him. He knows at least some of their language. It will be up to him to insist on getting you out of here."

"It might not be possible."

"Why not?" she demanded. "What happened between you and Na—him?"

Inoa looked between us, brow gently wrinkled for the tone of our words. She patted the top of my foot and gave me a bright smile with it. Clearly she thought they were healing well, too.

"Thank you," I told her, putting my hands over my heart. She nodded back, pleased, then set her ladies to cleaning the chamber and various other tasks. "Keep your tone of voice as light as you can and smile, as if we're talking about how happy we are," I told

Jepp and Zynda. "Here's what I think is going on. Taking an educated guess, I'm now engaged or possibly married to the volcano
king. Keep smiling, please."

Jepp plastered on a fake grin and cursed through her teeth.
"Danu take the bastard!" She singsonged, and Zynda burst out
laughing, which at least helped with the whole pretending-to-be-
happy façade.

"You are terrible at this," she told Jepp, then set the bag on the
bed and climbed on. "I brought your hairbrush, your writing
things, and a change of your lightest clothes. Tell me more."

Gratefully, I took the brush and at least set order to my hair. It
didn't take much and I felt better. "As I said, I'm guessing from
what we observed and what the volcano king tried to convey to
me. But he seemed to be saying that he and I are connected and
that I'm not going anywhere."

"Then he doesn't know what he's up against!" Jepp did a better job of sounding reassuring instead of darkly pissed.

"We can't fight them, even if Kral threw in with us, which I
don't think he'd do."

"Then we break you out by stealth," Zynda promised, making
it sound like she offered to take me on a picnic.

"Yes," Jepp agreed. "I'll talk to Kral and go from there. Whether
he agrees or not, we'll get you out of here and onto the ship. This
place is hardly a fortress. You lie still and build up your strength.
We'll take turns staying with you, and tonight—tomorrow night at
the latest, as Kral is anxious to go—we'll act. Don't worry."

"All right," I said. I expected to feel a sense of relief. If anyone
could spirit me out of this mess, Jepp and Zynda could. Oddly,
though, I mostly felt a sense of loss. I couldn't possibly stay here.
I'd be failing in the mission Ursula had entrusted to me and desperately needed me to succeed in. Also, I'd be facing an even
worse exile than I'd already lived, with people even farther from
being family to me.

More than any of that, I could not be Nakoa's wife or concubine or whatever he had in mind. Those sensual smiles and kisses

left little doubt of his plans for me. I had not come this far to become the bed slave I'd so thoughtlessly teased Jepp about bungling herself into.

"Don't worry," Jepp repeated, more reassuring now. "We'll take care of you."

"I know. Thank you." I had to stop myself from laying my hands over my heart.

12

I spent what remained of the day doing as Jepp ordered—lying in bed. Inoa, my constant companion, made sure I always had food and drink at hand. I tried not to think of her as my jailer. She was kind and helpful, even gathering the ladies to help me hang over a chamber pot. They giggled and I blushed, but the relief was so great I nearly didn't care.

The few occasions I painfully barked my feet confirmed I'd be going nowhere under my own power. I didn't think Nakoa had planned this to ensure my captivity—he'd seemed to be trying to convey genuine regret—but the injury had me effectively trapped, which I tried not to dwell on overmuch, as I could do nothing about it.

Inoa and her ladies helped me undress so I could sit on the edge of the bed and give myself a sponge bath, then assisted me into new clothes. Not the ones Zynda brought, but a filmy gown like theirs—which felt good in the afternoon heat but had no place to hide my little daggers. Inoa found them, of course. She didn't take them away as I expected. Instead she laid them in a neat line on the tiled table beside me, even the ones she dug out of the stockings rolled in the pocket of yesterday's gown. Shaking out the socks, she considered them with bemusement until I pantomimed pulling them over my feet. Her eyes widened in astonishment and she nodded in understanding, giving me the distinct impression she'd decided I needed them to shore up my poor, weak feet.

Sitting, she poised a foot over the opening, looking to me for permission. Why not? I waved at her to go ahead, and, with more giggles, she pulled them on. I showed her how to tie the ribbons at the top to hold them up and she pranced around, holding her sheer skirts above her knees, the heavy knit of the stockings a marked contrast. Then the other ladies all had to try them, laughing and talking. I taught them my word for the stockings and they eagerly joined in the game, giving me the names for various objects.

I memorized as much as I could, writing the words in my journal, spelling them phonetically, though I quickly ran out of ink in my pen's tiny reserve. Zynda offered to go to the ship to restore my supply, but Inoa caught the tenor of our conversation, sent one of her ladies running, and presented me with a lovely blue-glass bottle full of a gorgeous thick ink that retained a black gleam on the page even when dry. The lady also brought extra sheets of paper, of some of the finest quality I'd ever seen—both thin and surprisingly sturdy.

At least they understood about books, ink, and writing. If Kral's diplomacy and Jepp's strategy failed to free me, I'd have that much.

The ladies took my clothes and stockings away, demonstrating that they'd be washed. As the sun declined to evening, they changed me again, this time into a much grander dress, in shimmering shades of copper. For the first time all day, Inoa abandoned me and left me to her ladies, who set to fixing me up, using my hairbrush after thoughtful inspection and adding colored ointment to my lips, cheeks and eyelids. Jepp arrived as they fussed over me, wearing her dress uniform, confirming that we'd be attending the feast that had been canceled the night before due to my injuries.

"They're setting up for a major event," Jepp told us. "Kral says he's never seen them do anything on this scale."

"Does he know why?" I asked.

"No, but we can all guess. Be prepared for anything, is my best advice."

"I'd best go change, then," Zynda said. "I'll meet you there."

"If you can shape-shift back to a fully dressed person, why can't you change clothes the same way?" Jepp asked.

Zynda looked a bit surprised. "I never thought about it. I always just shift back to whatever I was wearing originally."

"If *I* could shape-shift, that's the first thing I'd want to learn. Practical." Jepp was keeping things lighthearted, but she clearly worried about the evening's events. Distracting all of us with her poking at Zynda. "Besides supersenses, of course. Hey! Maybe you could create extra weapons, too."

Zynda laughed, as Jepp wanted, and shook her head. "I'll work on it."

"Speaking of weapons"—Jepp eyed the array of little daggers on the table—"I brought your knife. *Which* you should have been wearing yesterday." Inoa watched but did not interfere as Jepp fitted a lovely belt over my gown, adjusting it so the sheath draped at my hip, the ruby glinting.

"This isn't mine." I traced the lovely gold-worked leather, set with small jewels.

"No." Jepp sounded gruff, even for her. "It's mine. Rather, it was my mother's, but it's yours now."

"Jepp, I can't take this. What if—"

"Especially what if," she replied. "You'll keep it and, more important, you'll wear it. Besides, it was always too fancy for me."

And yet she'd carried it with her, one of the precious few belongings she could bring on her journeys, along with the weight of

Branlian whiskey. Jepp always seemed so brashly confident and unsentimental. Keeping something like this was not what I would have expected of her.

"Thank you." I felt unexpectedly weepy at the gift—and afraid of its import. "Any news?"

She shook her head. "Lunkhead wants to see what happens tonight, as he's not at all convinced the volcano king means to keep you here. However, he also plans to set sail in the morning, barring anything to interfere with that, so . . ."

So, be ready for anything. All right, then.

Not long after Inoa and her ladies finished primping me, Nakoa arrived. No surprise there. He stepped into the room, carrying a fresh garland of flowers, and bowed to me with his hands folded in front of his heart. Still bare chested and barefoot, he'd traded his scaled armor for festive-looking metal armbands made of copper that matched his torque and my gown, also figured to look like twining dragons. Naturally. He wore a pleated skirt of the same hue. It should have seemed odd for a man to wear such a garment, but it somehow made him look that much more masculine. Enough to spike that desire he seemed to stir in me, though I thought I managed to disguise it behind bland disinterest.

He approached me where I sat on the edge of the bed. I wondered where he planned to sleep that night. It would be difficult for Jepp to extract me, if he wanted to sleep in his own bed. Or sit and watch me again. No doubt she had a plan and would let me know what to do.

Nakoa said my name and replaced the flower garland around my neck as he'd done that morning, then indicated that he'd pick me up. I frowned and shook my head. I'd had enough of that. I indicated a chair. "*Ayh*, Nakoa. Why can't I sit in a chair and be carried that way?" I tried to demonstrate with gestures.

He frowned back. "*Ayh*, Dafne." Despite his obvious negation, I got the distinct impression that I'd amused him and he echoed me on purpose. He said something longer, gesturing back and forth between us as he'd done before.

"My take is no one carries you but him," Jepp offered, not at all helpfully.

"So I gather also." I folded my arms and scowled at Nakoa, who returned the look implacably, with the air of a man who'd wait forever and still get his way.

"Just get through tonight," Jepp soothed me. Later I would take time to reflect on the irony of our role reversal.

"Fine." I gave Nakoa the go-ahead and he rewarded me with a small smile, taking my hand, clearly intending to kiss my wrist. I made a fist so he couldn't. "*Ayb*," I told him.

His smile deepened, as if I'd amused him further. Keeping his hold on my wrist, he picked up one of my slim daggers from the bedside table and offered it to me with another word I recognized from the afternoon naming game with Inoa and her ladies. "Open."

Uncertain, I opened my hand and he nodded in satisfaction that I'd understood. He laid the dagger on my palm instead, holding my gaze for a long beat, waiting for something from me. An acknowledgment, maybe, that I was not without the ability to refuse him at least that. I took a deep breath and let it out, then closed my fingers around the now-familiar heft of the hilt, inclining my head to him. Nakoa touched the scab on his throat where I'd cut him, his lips twitching in a wry grimace. I gave him my best insouciant shrug in return.

To my surprise, he laughed. A deep, musical sound, as pitched as his language. Without further ado, he carefully slid his arm under my knees and waited for me to loop mine around his neck.

"It's fascinating to watch you two communicate," Jepp said.

"I'm glad to entertain you."

"I'm just saying you're getting really good at it. Maybe you can talk him into letting you go after all."

Optimism from Jepp worried me. It made me think she wasn't sure how to get me out of here, even if it wasn't a fortress. "I'll try."

Nakoa carried me through the spacious hallways and I took advantage of the opportunity to look around, being far more clear-headed than the night before. As in Annfwn, much of the palace stood open to the tropical environment, with outdoor spaces furnished in the same way as the interior. The lovely wood floors and ceilings gave way to polished stone in the same colors outside, but otherwise the rooms were alike, with sitting and eating spaces. They spoke of people who spent time enjoying themselves and their island kingdom. Artwork—almost always animals, of all varieties—stood in niches or sometimes in the center of sitting areas.

Our small procession turned in the direction opposite of where we'd come in, toward the sea, and we emerged onto that great expanse I'd glimpsed from the hillside. Now it thronged with people seated at long tables scattered around the periphery, while others danced in a clear center area.

At the sight of Nakoa, the music and dancing stopped, the seated people standing up, and everyone turned to face us, sending up a soaring song of welcome and joy, by the sound of it. Nakoa held me up and out, as if displaying a prize, gazing down at me with a glow of pride and the least forbidding expression I'd seen on him yet.

"I don't like this," Jepp muttered.

Neither did I.

Nakoa settled me in a high chair, padded with pastel cushions, and seated himself next to me. Inoa sat on my other side, radiantly happy and wearing dragon armbands that matched Nakoa's. Almost certainly his sister, then. Jepp joined Zynda, Kral, and the other Dasnarians at a table one level below us and to the side, sitting where she could keep an eye on me.

It was an elaborate celebration, indeed, and one focused on me. I ate off of a series of small plates that people brought to me, offerings of exotic, artfully created delicacies that exploded with flavor. I worried that they strained their resources to put on this feast but could hardly cause insult by refusing.

One after another, Nakoa's people performed dances and acrobatics for us. I'd seen the Dasnarian acrobats perform at Ordnung, but Nahanauns outdid them in flexibility, contorting their bodies into astonishing shapes and folding into each other to create living sculptures. A group of two dozen or so nearly naked men and women slowly assembled into one that, when complete, looked like the dragon itself, with extended bodies moving like great wings.

In the awe of the accomplishment, the extraordinary beauty and athleticism of it, I laughed and clapped my hands, forgetting myself. Nakoa looked over at me, pleased, and patted my knee, then called out something to the performers, who disassembled and bowed deeply to me, ecstatic grins on their faces. Inoa waved a hand and baskets were brought to the acrobats, a treasured reward, it seemed by their exclamations and bows of gratitude.

After that I made certain to show my enjoyment. These people had worked so hard to please me and should not suffer because of my fears or need to show Nakoa my displeasure.

Nakoa, however, paid close attention and displayed an uncanny knack for knowing which performances I loved best, rewarding those most generously.

Finally, the dances and acrobatics finished, Nakoa called Kral up to speak with him. They exchanged a version of pleasantries, Kral mostly in Dasnarian and using a few of the Nahanaun words, most of which I already knew. Nakoa clearly thanked him for the supplies and Kral told him more would be coming, which I wasn't sure Nakoa completely understood. I considered attempting to make it clear the supplies came from us, but it felt like the wrong moment, given my tenuous status. If I won my freedom, I'd attempt to convey that to Nakoa. If not . . . Well, I'd have plenty of time for that.

Jepp came up to join the conversation, earning a glare from Kral that she cheerfully ignored. "General Kral of Dasnaria and Imperial Prince of the Royal House of Konyngrr," she saluted him, then bowed to Nakoa. "King Nakoa KauPo. I ask you to agree that Lady Dafne Mailloux will leave with us when we set sail in the morning." She spoke in Dasnarian and used gestures to communicate her meaning, much as I had.

Nakoa stilled, sending a prickle across my skin and making me feel as if I sat next to a quiescent volcano. My volcano king, indeed. He asked Kral a sharp question, and the general, with a baleful glance at Jepp that promised retribution for cornering him like that, attempted an explanation. Halfway through it, I wanted to bury my face in my hands. How could these Dasnarians claim a protectorship of these islands and understand the language so badly? I'd been on the island less than two days and could parse enough to get that Kral had no sense that tonality altered meaning.

Stubborn arrogance on their part that spelled ill fortune for my fate.

I carefully didn't look at Nakoa so as not to draw attention to myself—though as the subject of the conversation, I didn't have much hope of that—but I sensed him growing angrier, like the heat of lava radiating from that lake of fire. Like the dragon awaking. Jepp kept her gaze trained on me, waiting for clues, and I gave her the smallest shake of my head.

This was not going well.

Kral was talking about gold and something else. Nakoa answered him with some sort of taunt that angered Kral enough to gesture to me and say—what? Something about bringing me to him. But I caught a word Nakoa had used several times with me, one Kral also knew and I connected to his original charges to Ursula. *Mo'o.* The dragon?

Finally, Nakoa cut Kral off with a sharp chop of his hand and rose. Everyone had gone silent and Inoa reached over to touch my arm, her eyes wide in anxious alarm. Nakoa called out for a servant to attend him—a phrase I'd heard a number of times already, though I hadn't parsed the exact words yet—and a young man ran up with a curved, dauntingly large sword. Confronting Kral, Nakoa issued an obvious challenge. Inoa's nails dug into my arm and she said something pleading.

Kral looked to me for the first time. "I cannot duel for you, scribe. Do you understand that? I have responsibilities to my men, to get them home again."

Jepp cursed, rounding on him. "Then pretend to stand down and we'll smuggle her out."

For once, Kral didn't respond to her with anger. Instead he seemed regretful. "The king has people watching the *Hákyrling.* Even if we managed to get her past them, he'd make sure of her presence here before he let us sail. I should have listened when you told me he means to keep her. I didn't think it would play out this way. I, ah, apologize for my role in this." Definitely guilt there. What had he handed Nakoa when we arrived?

"Save your half-assed apology!" Jepp spat.

He spread his hands, oddly not rising to Jepp's challenge. "I've never seen him behave like this and I have no power to gainsay him. Emperor Hestar would have my head if I created bad blood with the Nahanauns, especially over a foreign scribe, no matter how connected to royalty." He bowed to Nakoa and stepped back, leaving Jepp alone in confronting the king.

She didn't hesitate, but pulled her daggers and faced Nakoa. "Then I accept the challenge, if this coward will not take it."

Nakoa assessed her and raised his sword. Zynda stood and edged closer, ready to back Jepp.

"No!" I shouted at them both. "*Ayh!* Nakoa."

He backed up a step to be able to see me without turning his back on Jepp. A wise man, not to underestimate her.

"Shut up, Dafne," Jepp hissed.

"I won't. Kral is right." I held out a hand to Nakoa, the small dagger on my open palm. "Nakoa. I will stay." Unable to think of another word to fit, I said, "Dafne open."

Jepp glared at me in helpless fury but relaxed her stance. Nakoa lowered the sword and came to me, grim satisfaction on his face. Plucking the dagger from my palm, he took my hand and placed a firm, lingering kiss to my inner wrist.

Beyond him, Jepp seethed. She would have been happier fighting, even if it meant her death. "You don't know what you're doing," she said in Common Tongue.

"Maybe not, but I won't watch you or anyone else die on my behalf. I've had enough of wars. I can't be the cause of one." And better this way than to lose our mission entirely. Time for me to face that reality.

When Harlan explained *hlyti*, he failed to mention that—goddess or no—she could be cruel.

The party disbanded and Nakoa carried me back to his rooms, looking thunderous. Jepp and Zynda gamely followed behind. He started to set me on the bed. "*Ayh*," I said and pointed to a chair. "There."

Shooting me a bemused glance, he set me in the chair, then gave me an exaggerated bow. Maybe I shouldn't give him orders, but I needed to draw lines. Particularly if I was going to be trapped here with him. Possibly for the rest of my life.

I couldn't think about that.

"Leave us, please," I said, hoping I sounded more polite, though the phrase was one I'd heard used with the ladies who fetched and carried for Inoa and might not be at all appropriate for a king. "I want to talk to Jepp and Zynda."

He looked at them and back at me. For a moment, it seemed he wouldn't agree, but he went to stand on the balcony outside, back to the rail, watching us with folded arms. As good as I'd get, apparently.

"I'm *not* leaving you here," Jepp threw out, voice tight. "If we can't get you out, I'm staying with you."

"I will, too." Zynda sat and took my hand. I squeezed it, grateful for the contact.

"You can't stay," I told them. "Either of you. You have to leave me here—there's no other option."

Jepp exploded. "Don't you tell *me* there are no other options. I'm charged with protecting you, and by Danu, I'll do it."

I didn't ask her to modulate her tone or still her pacing. Nakoa, like a carved statue silhouetted against the night, a black stone sentinel of a man, would know exactly what we discussed.

"Listen to me, both of you." I waited for Jepp's attention, snarling as it might be. "You have to go. Zynda will make contact with Andi regardless, to get the Dasnarians through the barrier. She can pass a message back to Ursula. The additional ships might not have left yet. They can bring more effective rescue and, in the meanwhile, I'll learn the language and customs and will be ready to start diplomatic relations between King Nakoa KauPo and the Thirteen."

Nakoa, hearing his name, dipped his chin slightly, eyes catching the torchlight and glittering with amber sparks.

"You're suggesting I go to Dasnaria without you?" Jepp sounded incredulous. "I can't fulfill the mission. I don't know how to unearth secrets from books! I can scarcely read Common Tongue, let alone Dasnarian."

"You're Ursula's best scout. You know how to find out anything you want to know. Just establishing if Kir is really there would be significant in itself."

She subsided, fuming, so I turned to Zynda. "Promise me that you'll make sure Ursula doesn't come after me herself."

Zynda blinked at that, then pulled her hair over her shoulder, braiding it as she thought. "I don't know how I'm going to do that. I don't have your gift with her."

"Recruit Harlan. Speak to him privately and convince him. Then make sure that, whatever you tell her, it doesn't sound like I'm in any danger. Which I'm really not, because I don't think the king will harm me or allow me to be harmed. Ursula can't leave the High Throne unattended, whatever happens. That's more important than what happens to me."

Zynda nodded slowly. "I'll do my best."

"He might not harm you, Dafne." Jepp sat, knees spread, hands folded between them, her large dark eyes somber. "But you will not emerge with your virginity from this. I've seen the way he looks at you and touches you. Even if we manage to eventually extract you, that will be the price you'll pay."

She looked so serious, so worried for me. We'd come a ways from her blithe teasing and plots to divest me of that virginity. "I don't think he'd force me." My gaze went to Nakoa, watching us in silence.

"Perhaps not." Jepp tapped her fingers together. "But if he thinks you are his wife or betrothed, he'll expect it. Putting you in his bed gives a clear message that way."

"Now you see that?" I had to tease her a little about it, but she didn't smile.

"I learned my lesson, yes. I wouldn't wish the same on you."

"Are you worried about going to Dasnaria—what your status will be there?"

"I can handle myself." She waved that off. "And I can handle Kral. The question is, can you handle the dragon king?"

"Why do you call him that?" I asked, a bit taken aback to hear my secret thoughts spoken aloud.

Jepp gave me a funny look. "The tattoos look like scales to me—don't they to you?"

"And he wears a torque in that shape," Zynda agreed. "Also there is . . . some connection there."

"Do you really believe some magic he worked released the dragon?"

She tilted her head, solemn. "Not just him, but you also. Dafne, watch yourself with him. We don't know their culture, but if sex seals the marriage, diplomacy might not get you out of it."

"If you don't want Her Majesty going to war over you—as she no doubt would," Jepp added, "then you'll have to hold him off. However you manage it. That's the best course of action. If you can," she added in a dubious tone that made me bristle.

"Of course I can. I've held off all my life. If I'm practiced at anything, it's that."

"Not with someone who affects you like he does." Zynda nodded at my confusion and Jepp joined her. "Your body language shows it, too."

"I'll have to find the strength." I said it in a dry tone for her absurd observation—and yet, part of me knew it to be true. Nakao did affect me as no other man had. I would be hard-pressed not to give in to the attraction. But I would. I must.

That was the way of adventures, it seemed. You stepped up, not because you were brave, but because you had no other choice. Courage wasn't required. Only fortitude.

Hopefully I'd find it in myself to withstand the patient assault of King Nakoa.

13

Jepp and Zynda stayed for a bit after Inoa returned with a couple of her ladies. She shooed out her brother with her usual scolding words, which he accepted from her with an affectionate scowl. I'd do well to cement the friendship she seemed to offer, and perhaps recruit her to my cause.

My feet ached from sitting up so long, swollen and hot. Figuring it would help my efforts to keep Nakoa away from me, I didn't fight the tears that sprang up when they put new ointment on my feet. Inoa clucked in sympathy and petted my hand in comfort. Fervently I wished for some of the ice we stored in the cool depths of Ordnung, but that wouldn't be possible.

Still, I felt better with new ointment, a fresh, cool gown, and my feet propped up on several pillows. I refused the drowsy tea, not wanting to miss saying good-bye to my friends. Inoa gave me a stern look but set it next to the bed, then climbed in next to me. Settling herself in firmly as my jailor. Zynda kept her human form, saving her energy for an emergency, I suspected, and curled up in a chair while Jepp took first watch.

It seemed silly, as I'd have no protection after tonight, but they insisted, promising to wake me before they left.

I slept in fits, my mind racing. In my dreams, I awoke, dressed, and left with Jepp and Zynda for the ship. Sometimes we already stood on deck, making me wonder how I'd escaped. Other times I went out to the balcony, leapt off, and flew over the water. Over and over, I left my luxurious prison only to wake to find myself still in Nakoa's bed, feet aching and body stiff from lying on my back.

I thought I lay awake still, but Zynda woke me with a gentle touch, the room black with night, no torches lit. The gauzy curtains drawn around the bed while I slept caught a faint glint of moonlight, moving ghostly with a bit of welcome breeze off the water. Inoa breathed deeply in sleep, far on the other side of the big bed.

"Is it dawn?" I whispered, feeling the bleak hopelessness of that darkness, an abandoned ghost, myself.

"Not quite, but if we're to be aboard to sail with the *Hákyr-ling* . . ."

"Of course."

"It's not too late," Jepp said quietly from behind her, a deeper shadow. "You can still change your mind."

"And do what—gallop out of here on Zynda's back? Have you lower me over the balcony with rope and hope no one sees?" I felt bleak enough that I considered those as options. If only I could shape-shift and fly away in truth. Inoa stirred, rolling over and blinking at us, then sat up and lit a candle. "There are no doubt guards outside the doors. No matter what, they'd simply pull me off the ship again."

"I meant that I can stay." Jepp fingered her knives, even as Inoa got up and moved around the room, lighting torches and retrieving a gown for me. "I think I should."

"You can't. We made a treaty to help the Dasnarians get home. Ursula needs that information. And I debated whether to tell you my suspicions—for that's all they are; I have no proof—but I think Kral deliberately brought me here, as some sort of trade with the king."

Jepp looked simultaneously pissed and astonished. "How—"

"I don't know. See what you can dig out of him."

"Oh, I'll be digging, all right." Her grim smile nearly made me pity the man.

As soon as Inoa had me dressed—and I strapped on the knife belt in response to Jepp's significant glance—she opened the doors and Nakoa walked in, dressed in his exotic armor, as he'd worn the first day, and trailed by a dozen of his people. He eyed Jepp and Zynda warily, then gestured them to the door, his expression more stony than ever, if possible. Jepp glared back, spine stiff and fingers twitching for her knives.

Zynda came over, sat on the side of the bed, and embraced me, her hair silky on my cheek. How she could smell of the flowers of Annfwn when she'd been so long away, I didn't know. "I'll be back, just as soon as I can. I promise," she whispered. "I brought all your things from the ship. They're beside the bed. Though all those heavy clothes won't do you much good."

"Don't come back if it's a risk. I'll be fine. I'm counting on you to persuade Ursula of that."

She nodded, eyes dark with misery. "I'll do my best."

Jepp broke the stare-down with Nakoa and, pointedly turning her back on him, she bent over and hugged me hard, uncomfortably so after Zynda's gentle embrace—nearly cracking my ribs. Despite the set of her chin, however, the look on her face showed how conflicted she felt. "You're going to make me a promise," she informed me, gripping my shoulders. "You are going to hold out, because you are strong and smart. The High Queen believes in you and now I know why. You promise me that I won't have to face her and explain that because I abandoned you—" She broke off on something perilously close to a sob and looked away.

I wrapped my fingers around her wrists. "I promise, Jepp. I'll be fine. When we see each other again, we'll drink your Branlian whiskey, you can tell me about your sexual adventures in Dasnaria, and I'll give you back your mother's knife belt."

She nodded, then cupped the back of my head and kissed me hard on the mouth, shocking me. Giving me something of her cocky grin, she patted my cheek. "If you manage to hold out against your dragon king, I'm definitely taking a shot at seducing you. Never could resist a challenge."

Behind her, Zynda shook her head, some of her misery abated by Jepp's bravado. "Good-bye," I told them. "Safe travels. My thoughts go with you."

They left, escorted out by Nakoa's guards. He, however, remained behind, even as Inoa discreetly slipped out. I braced myself. Would he force himself on me after all, now that we were alone? I felt brittle, hollowed out, as if Jepp and Zynda had taken some of my strength with them. I didn't know if I'd be able to muster the spirit to fight him off, my situation felt so hopeless. Nakoa moved toward me and my hand fell to the dagger Ursula had given me. He paused, stern face going troubled. Laying a hand over mine on the hilt, he touched my cheek, a fleeting, light caress. "No, Dafne."

"I'll use it, if I have to," I said, not caring if he understood me or not. Needing to say it aloud for myself, so I'd believe. "My High Queen and my friend gave this to me. I might not be a warrior, but she taught me how to use this. I won't disappoint her by failing to."

He listened intently, then stroked my hand on the blade and let go. Holding out his arms, he said, "Open," with a twitch of an amused smile. What went on in his head, behind that impenetrable face? Definitely a keen intellect, collaborating with me to find words we both understood, no matter how much we altered the meaning between us. As if we created our own intimate language.

"Open," I agreed, with a sigh, for my tattered emotions, fragile paranoia, and enforced vulnerability.

He took the fresh garland from around his neck and replaced mine, setting the wilted one aside. "*Mlai,*" he whispered.

I raised my arms in resignation, letting him lift me and carry me out of the room. He turned in a different direction than before, climbing a set of stairs that started straight, then began to spiral as they narrowed, ascending to a tower. Ironic if he took me to some prison cell.

Instead we emerged onto an open veranda that provided the most astonishing view I'd yet seen. Glimmers of dawn showed all around the horizon, as if Glorianna's sun might rise from any point at all, brightening the sky from gray to blue. The volcano loomed, a dark silhouette against the sky, the top broken now from the dragon's emergence, like the curl of a broken lip. The harbor over the next ridge also showed clearly, with the *Hákyrling* rocking on the gentle swells, a few of her wine-dark sails going up, one by one. I imagined Jepp and Zynda somewhere under the dense foliage, making their way to it.

A lookout bowed to Nakoa and discreetly left as the king strode up to the polished stone wall that bordered the veranda waist-high to him. I looked down as he lowered me. The drop was precipitous, a long way to the tiled roofs in the morning shadows below. Suddenly terrified he meant to pitch me off the tower, I clutched at him, fingers digging into his hard muscles and surprisingly soft skin. He gave me a long look that I couldn't read and waited for me to let go.

"Sorry," I muttered, relaxing my grip. I'd left half-moon nail indentations, and, chagrined, I brushed them with my fingertips, as if I could smooth them away. He said something in a soft tone and pressed a kiss to my forehead. Forgiven, I supposed. The inherent sweetness of the gesture moved me, smoothing away some of the rawness inside.

Moving more slowly, Nakoa settled me on the broad ledge, with my feet dangling over. Standing behind me, he wrapped an arm securely around my waist, making it clear without words that the last thing he'd do was let me fall.

We stayed there, without speaking, holding a vigil of sorts. It reminded me of observing the Feast of Moranu, waiting for the sun to rise and begin the new year. Only I'd never done so with a man holding me like this, solidly pressed against my back. I didn't lean against him, but neither did I pull away. Not only because I didn't want to fall. The still steadiness of Nakoa provided a kind of comfort that I didn't care to examine too closely. Whether he'd brought me here to witness my ship's departure as a way of demonstrating my final captivity or out of sympathy, it didn't matter.

Much as it grieved me to watch, I wanted to see them go.

Slowly, the *Hákyrling* moved out of the harbor, passing between the enormous guardian dragons like a mouse creeping between two sleeping cats. Just beyond, the ship seemed to pause and her sails rose with the sunlight, blazing bright red with rosy dawn. They billowed, catching a wind I couldn't feel, and she seemed to leap ahead. Then sailed out of sight around the curve of the island.

Leaving me utterly alone.

The bright day blurred and I realized I wept in a steady stream, my face wet with it. Nakoa, the king of patience, made no move to go, so I tried to wait it out without wiping my tears away, unwilling for him to see me so wrecked. Despite his gentle reassurances, I wouldn't deceive myself that he was my friend or ally. We played a game of strategy, and if I'd learned anything from Ursula, it was to keep a brave face and never let your enemies see you flinch. Unfortunately, she hadn't taught me *how* to do that.

Nakoa let out a long breath and turned to seat himself beside me, facing the opposite direction, switching arms to keep one securely around my waist. I turned my face away. Then gave it up, scrubbed at my cheeks, and made myself look at him. In the bright morning, his black eyes showed lighter, like thinner slices of obsidian that might let light through if I held them up to the sun, the pupils distinct windows. He studied my face in turn, seeming to be deep in thought. Lifting his other hand, he brushed a finger under my eye, tracing the still damp skin there, metaphorically wiping away my tears.

"Sorry," he said, mimicking my Common Tongue word. He

touched one of the marks on his chest, where I'd broken the skin enough to draw a bit of blood, then the healing wound on his throat, tapped me softly over my heart, then brushed away the imaginary tear again. "Sorry," he repeated, his tonality giving it the lift of a question.

I nodded. "Yes. Sorry."

Holding my gaze, he bent his head and pressed another kiss to my forehead, letting his lips linger this time, cool against my brow. I might be a bit feverish from my injuries, which would help explain how fragile I felt. Nakoa moved, pressing another kiss to my cheekbone, just under the corner of my eye. With a finger under my chin, he turned my face and did the same to my other cheek. The sensation fluttered through me, warm sun on a winter's day, cool water running over dark stone, salving my thirst. For once the memory didn't feel quite so edged. I let my lids close, savoring the relief from fear, if only for the moment.

Nakoa kissed my eyelids, light as butterfly wings, lifted my chin, and, after a pause, brushed my lips with his. There and gone. Then again.

I likely should have stopped him already, but Jepp's warnings, my resolve, all seemed centuries old instead of hours. I was lonely and the kisses filled me with a golden comfort. While they lasted, I didn't feel hollow and abandoned, but . . . cherished. No one had ever touched me this way, and it felt like the thing I'd longed for, waited for. One part of me stood back and knew it wasn't, that it was all an illusion. Still, I'd made the hard choice, and indulging in Nakoa's physical presence seemed like the one bright spot.

Kisses didn't seal marriages. But they did feed me in a way I desperately needed at that moment.

His lips moved over mine with warm insistence, deepening the kiss, and I parted mine, allowing the flavor of him in. Desire rose in lazy, lapping waves. Not the volcanic, hard and desperate passion of our kiss on the mountain. No echo of a third heartbeat this time. Just Nakoa and me. *The language of the body is one I know and communicate in very well.* Nakoa would be like Jepp that way, knowing how bodies spoke to each other. His tongue touched mine, an intimate caress, and his hand trailed over my throat and down my back, petting me with long brushes, soothing and arousing at once.

I lifted my fingers to his cheek. He made an approving sound against my mouth and leaned into my touch. Encouraged, I threaded my fingers through the curls at his temple, imagining that the white locks felt different than the black, somehow more like coils of banked lightning. He echoed the gesture, touching my temple and then running his fingers through my hair, kissing me all the while, coming back to my temple when he reached the ends, combing through over and over.

Drowning in it, I let go, feeling only the warmth of his kisses and caresses, letting the fear and worry disperse. I leaned against him, his hot skin burning now, and reveled in simply being held.

Then I made myself stop.

I pressed a hand to his chest and levered myself away, expecting him to press me or give me one of those thunderous frowns. But he looked serene. Very nearly happy, his full mouth curving in a sensual smile, gaze slumberous. He took my hand from his chest and turned it over, pressing a formal kiss to my wrist. "Dafne *mlai.*"

"Nakoa."

His smile widened. "*Ae.*"

The word for "yes," most likely. Daunting how much it sounded like no. A slight difference in the vowel tone, a bigger change in pitch. One I'd have to be careful to get right. Pulling my hand from his, I tried it out, pointing my thumb up, "*Ae,*" then down "*Ayh.*"

He tapped my temple and nodded. Absurdly I flushed with pleasure. Or the residual heat of those kisses. Nakoa tipped his head toward the stairs and asked a question.

"Yes," I told him in his tongue, and he lifted me. It would be really good when I could walk again, but for the moment, I enjoyed our temporary truce and relaxed in his arms, even resting my cheek against the bulge of his tattooed chest muscles. I realized I did recognize his scent, something like warm earth and banked coals, distinctly him.

Inoa waited for us in his rooms, anxiety and hope both in her wide eyes. She had the bed turned down for me, a sleeping gown laid out, ointments ready and tea brewing. The sleepy tea, by the smell of it. A wave of exhaustion crashed over me, as if I'd already drunk the potion. I didn't regret refusing it the evening before, but the fitful night, on top of the worry and tension, fatigue from my now throbbingly tender feet, and the hangover of Nakoa's drugging kisses all robbed me of the ability to think.

Obediently, I took the cup from Inoa and drank it down, vaguely aware of her and Nakoa conversing quietly. She wasn't scolding him for once and they were probably discussing me, but I couldn't focus enough to listen for words I knew. I turned my face away from them and stared out the deceptively open windows. A colorfully winged bird flew past, taunting me with its freedom. Tears leaked out of my eyes and I let them.

And fell asleep before Inoa even had the bandages off.

Evening had descended when I rose from the deep dregs of the sleep. And, thank the Three, I was alone. I hadn't been fully alone in weeks. Not since we'd left Ordnung. A strange experience for me, as in the past I'd spent entire days seeing people only glancingly and sometimes speaking to no one at all.

I supposed it spoke to their confidence that I could not escape the island. My prison had expanded, but I wouldn't forget that it was one. Uorsin had done that, early on, giving the conquered kingdoms unasked-for bounties and luxuries the people hadn't known, lulling them into believing they were better off under his rule. Arguably they were. As long as they tithed appropriately and did as they were told.

Not something I'd ever been good at, though I'd faked it well enough.

Inoa had left my feet bare this time—probably a good sign—and the cooler sunset breeze from the balconies brushed against the sensitive soles. Nakoa's rooms, and probably the whole palace, evinced ingenious design with the way the openings facilitated cross breezes. The only time it grew unbearably warm seemed to be midafternoon. Probably no one stayed inside then, but instead moved to one of the cooler open courtyards or outdoor rooms.

Taking advantage of my unexpected privacy, I brought up my foot so I could see. Goddesses—no wonder they hurt so cursed much. Jepp and Zynda had been generous in their descriptions, protecting me, as always. I didn't much like being the person who couldn't be told the truth. Scabbed over, yes, but also looking like one of the animals the Hawks had brought down and skinned for roasting during our travels. Tentative, I poked at it, feeling the pressure but nothing else. Numbed by the ointment, then. Checking the other foot, I found it in the same condition.

If I could have, I'd have told Jepp exactly what I thought of her comforting lies. No wonder she'd been so concerned about getting me to the ship, however.

The ever-thoughtful Inoa had left my journal, ink, and food by the bed, so I ate and worked on recording all that had occurred and my speculations about Nakoa and his agenda. I also added to my growing dictionary of Nahanaun. An advantage of *not* being a warrior—I didn't have to have working feet to do what I did best. I might not be able to challenge Nakoa to a duel for my freedom, but I could think my way out of this situation.

He'd recognized something about me from that first moment. It had been important that my bare feet touch the soil of the island. I hadn't imagined that instant shock at contact, the way the dizzying magic swirled through me, nor that sense of connection to the dragon. Something of that ritual had both released the dragon, then quieted the volcano. Or vice versa.

And Nakoa had known it would from the moment he saw me.

How? Had he truly sent Kral to bring me to the islands, and if so, why me?

I needed answers and I would find them. Answering the riddles of High Priest Kir and the Temple of Deyrr might be beyond my reach, but the information to resolve my immediate problem lay here. Nakoa knew something that I didn't. If they had ink and paper, it logically followed that they had books. Maybe even some in Dasnarian, if I was lucky. I had nothing but the leisure of forced inaction now.

All I could do was use my waiting time wisely to make Nakoa give up his secrets, one way or another.

14

The door to the rooms eased open so softly I didn't hear it, absorbed as I was in my journal. But the movement caught the corner of my eye in time for me to glimpse the wide, dark eyes of one of Inoa's ladies before the door closed again.

Moments later, Inoa herself came in, talking cheerfully and ordering her ladies about. She took the journal and writing implements from me and set them nearby with firm resolve. They set up the sponge bath basin and I let them undress me, pleased to get clean. The day I could do for myself again—and take a full bath!—would be a happy one. They managed to maneuver me to a chair, urging me to lean back so they could wash my hair.

It felt wonderful, but the extra level of primping aroused my suspicions. Ones that were confirmed when Inoa tried to dress me in a gown that would be entirely transparent. Something a bride might wear on her wedding night. Oh, no, no, no.

"No," I told her firmly in her tongue.

Her brows drew together in a frown very like her brother's. All of his stubborn temper in her lovely face. "Yes," she said.

"No, Inoa. I will not wear that. Give me one of the other dresses." I pointed to the cabinet they kept them in.

She folded her arms and stomped her foot, speaking rapidly and holding up the confection. Demanding, with a coaxing edge to it.

"No," I repeated, losing my own patience. Ursula may have taught me to use a blade, but Amelia had shown me the value of a well-timed fit of arrogance. I might be hurt, but I wasn't going to be meekly herded about. Also, if I'd become betrothed or married to the king, I should have some measure of rank and accompanying power. I snatched the towel from the lady comb-drying my hair. It was short enough to dry on its own soon, even in the island humidity. I wrapped the towel around my naked self. "Fine, I'll get one on my own." I made to stand and the ladies all cried out and rushed to stop me, Inoa scolding me much as she did Nakoa.

"Then get me a dress." I used the phrase for fetching and the word I thought meant a general garment.

She threw up her hands in exasperation and went to the cabinet, returning with the copper gown I'd worn the night before. It would do. "Thank you," I told her in her language, but without the accompanying gesture. I wasn't feeling that generous and she wasn't being gracious about it either. I let them finish fixing me up, however, while I contemplated how to handle Nakoa when he inevitably arrived.

I dug in my metaphorical heels again—if only I could in truth—when they tried to reinstall me on the bed. I had enough disadvantages facing Nakoa without that suggestion. They gave way more easily this time, acceding to my wishes and, by dint of joining together to scoot me in a chair out to the balcony, set me up there with a stool to prop my feet on and a table for my journal and other supplies. From that vantage, I could see the evening activities of the palace, far more interesting than staring at the walls, no matter how decorative the art.

As I'd suspected, the place came alive as the afternoon heat receded, torches like the ones on my balcony blazing into light. Servants and other workers bustled about, engaged in what appeared to be repairs to part of the palace. From what I could tell, part of a wing had broken off as the ground gave way beneath it, probably during the magic wave and volcanic instability. Had Kral and his men spent their time lending their considerable strength to rebuilding? There must be villages, too, on other parts of this island and the others. Maybe asking for a map would be a good opening to finding out what kind of library they kept.

"Greetings, Dafne *mlai*," Nakoa said, coming out onto the balcony and taking in my arrangements with interest, but not anger. The salutation he used might mean more 'good evening,' but I wasn't entirely clear on it. It seemed they used pitch to convey the time of day and possibly the pleasantness of the weather. Because a pitched language wasn't difficult enough to learn without adding complexities like that.

"Greetings, King Nakoa KauPo," I replied, approximating his pitch as precisely as I could.

He raised one white-threaded eyebrow at that, registering the formality, then came around to look over my shoulder at my journal. "May I?" he asked, or something close to that, dipping his chin in satisfaction when I handed him the book. He sat in the chair beside me and studied my drawing of the work on the broken wing, making a hmming sound that sounded like interest.

A thought occurred to me and I picked up my pen. "May I?" I tried his question and he handed me the journal, watching as I spread it on my lap and began sketching a dragon in the sky. "Did the dragon do this?" I asked in Common Tongue, tapping the point on it. "Dragon? *Mo'o*?"

Nakoa huffed a sound that might have been a laugh and took the pen and journal, turning to a new page. He frowned a little as he drew, concentrating. Something about that made me itch to touch him, to trace the firm line of his lips as he pursed them. Bare chested as always, he wore none of his usual ornaments, only the simple pleated *kylte* he favored. Short when he stood, it rose even higher on his muscular thighs as he sat, making me wonder what he wore beneath.

If anything.

My face heated at the prurient thought—one completely counter to my resolve to keep our relationship unconsummated—and I made myself look away before he caught me staring. With a grunt of satisfaction, he showed me the page and a surprisingly deft drawing of the volcano as it had been, with a rounded top, and below that, the palace wing unbroken. The drawing next to it showed storm clouds with lightning bolts and people running away from the volcano with smoke billowing. As I looked, Nakoa turned the page back and tapped the dragon I'd drawn.

"*Mo'o*," he said, and I repeated the word, immensely satisfied that I'd called that one. He nodded in approval and said the word for night, using a downward pitch that seemed to mean unpleasant weather. A stormy night, perhaps.

"I know about the magic storm," I told him, pointing to the lightning bolts, then repeated his word, pleased when he agreed. I smiled at him and he touched my cheek, happy also that we'd managed a kind of communication. He leaned in to kiss me and I put a hand on his chest to stop him.

"No, Nakoa."

His initial puzzlement darkened and he asked me a question I couldn't quite parse.

I gestured to the bed inside and to him and me. "No. I will not share my body with you."

"*Mo'o*." He used his word and tapped me over my heart, then touched his own chest, keeping it going in a heartbeat rhythm, evoking that three-way synchronization of our hearts.

"I don't understand," I told him, letting frustration infuse my tone.

With a grimace, he took the journal from me and opened to another new page. He sketched quickly, a bust of a woman with shoulder-length hair and a flower garland around her neck. Me. The likeness was quite good, though odd to see myself through his eyes. He pointed to it and to me. "Dafne. *Mlai*."

I hadn't heard anyone else use that word and didn't enjoy contemplating the import of it. Giving him a narrow stare, I answered, "Dafne, yes," and moved to take off the garland.

He shook his head, stopping me, though not irritated. More amused. He flipped back, finding the drawing I'd done of him from the ship's deck. "Nakoa. *Mlai.*" Adding a flower garland to my sketch of him, he gave me a stern smile that barely cracked his brooding visage, then set the book down. Guiding my hands, he had me grasp the flower garland, remove it, and put it over his head. "*Mlai,*" he repeated, then put the garland back on me and waited expectantly.

So it had happened that first evening, when I accepted the garland from him. A mistake of monumental proportions. Nakoa watched me patiently as I rubbed my temples, trying to think how to explain this. Drawings only went so far. "I didn't know," I finally said, hoping my tone would convey it, tugging at the garland and shaking my head. "My people don't do marriages this way. I can't be your wife. *Ayh mlai.*"

He shrugged, holding his hands palm up, not bothering to argue, clearly indicating that it didn't matter what I knew, that the deed was done.

With a huff of exasperation, I took up the journal and drew Ordnung. "This is where I live. This is my life. Not here."

He examined the drawing with great interest, tracing the stark lines of Uorsin's fortress with his finger, then gave me that same shrug, tugging at my garland with a slight smile. "*Mlai.*"

I was beginning to hate the sound of that word, particularly when he took the journal and drew two figures entwined together, a much shorter woman and a man. Naked. The blush rose in my face as he added his bed behind them. Behind us. He set the journal aside, satisfied that I'd seen it, then tipped up my chin with one finger, studying my face before I, mortified by my own embarrassment, pushed his hand aside and turned away to face the sea, a graying glint in the darkening evening.

If only I had taken Zyr up on his cursed offer, I'd be better equipped to handle this. Able to make my refusal clear without seeming like a flustered girl.

The tense silence spun out between us, Nakoa considering me while I wished desperately that he'd go away and leave me alone. The night might see an end to my virginity after all, and I had no idea how to prevent it.

Well, I had one idea, but didn't know if I could pull it off.

Time to show some strength. Turning to face him, whether my face burned still or not, I leaned closer. He watched me with wary curiosity as I reached out and laid my hand over the bulge of his manhood, the lines and heat of it startling through the thin fabric, totally different from the awkwardness of having to grope Harlan there, but I was grateful now that Ursula had pushed me to do it. I had that much experience at least. Before I lost my nerve—or Nakoa got the wrong idea—I put my other hand on the ruby-hilted dagger. "I'll cut it off," I told him. Common Tongue, but hopefully the tone and gesture would say it all.

His member moved under my hand, shocking me so that I started to snatch my hand away, but he was quicker, encircling my wrist with his fingers and holding it there. He said something to me, slowly, a curve to his mouth, but my thoughts had scattered too much for me to try to find meaning in the words. The sensual warmth in his voice undid me. Instead of warning him off, I'd only encouraged him.

I wrenched my hand free, belatedly realizing he hadn't re-sisted, and held it to my chest as if I'd scalded it. Hating feeling like such a fool, I reflexively put my feet down, wanting nothing more than to put distance between me and my miserable failure to show defiance. The shock of bright pain as my feet smacked the ground cleared my head immediately, and I gasped at it, tears pricking my eyes. Nakoa spoke sharply and put his hands on my shoulders to hold me down. *Stupid.*

"I know." I batted at his hands, furious with him and myself. Not caring if he understood me or not. "I forgot, okay? Just, please, leave me alone." My voice came out ragged with emotion, the agony in my battered feet tearing away what little poise I'd managed.

He let me go. Then bent over and picked up my feet, gently settling them on the cushion Inoa had arranged for me, stroking my calves as he did. I dropped my face into my hand, bracing on one elbow and covering my eyes. I really didn't want to weep again, especially in front of Nakoa.

He stood and went inside. It would be too much to hope that he'd leave, but the reprieve gave me a bit of time to compose myself. Sure enough, he spoke to someone in the other room and, after several minutes, returned with a flagon, two goblets made of colored glass, and my jar of ointment. Setting the things on my table, he filled the glasses and pushed one into my hand. It smelled flowery and fragrant, with a bite to it. So far I'd had fruit juices here, but no wine. He touched his goblet to mine, the glass making a clear chime, and raised it to his lips, ostentatiously waiting for me to drink.

I sipped and the liquid burned smooth and glorious, spreading warmth through my belly. As strong as Jepp's Branlian whiskey and far easier to drink. It would go straight to my already addled head. Getting me drunk could be my dragon king's next plan for seduction. Not that it mattered. We both knew he'd called my bluff and that I wouldn't use my blade against him.

Setting the liquor down, I picked up the glass jar, but he took it from me. He pulled the cork stopper and put it aside, then sniffed. With a sound of approval, he moved his chair next to my footstool, sat, and grasped my ankle, deftly smoothed the cooling lotion on. I sighed for the relief and his gaze flicked up to mine, a slight smile curving his mouth. He had good hands, a touch that continually surprised me with his meticulous care, so at odds with his fearsome visage. Also, he seemed to know even better than Inoa's ladies just how much to put on and to work in. He'd used it on himself, then, for his own injuries, the smile an understanding and sympathetic one.

A group of servants came out, bringing additional torches and lighting them, along with a second table. What new game was this? A game, indeed, it became clear, as they set out a beautifully inlaid piece of stone. Jewel-toned tiles formed spirals that moved out from the center, bisected by concentric lines, making it look much like a spider's web. Small statues of either light blue or deep green and carved in the shape of animals were arranged in a circle at the perimeter.

In the center sat a glittering, faceted dragon. I picked it up and Nakoa watched me, bracing his forearms on his knees, fingers laced together. It was carved from a ruby—a huge one. All the pieces were made from gemstones, it seemed. A flagrant, or casual, display of wealth in just this game. Some of the treasure the Dasnarians sought?

Bemused, I set the dragon back in the center position.

Nakoa gestured to the game, a question in his voice, something of both a challenge and a peace offering. Playing would keep a table between us and at that point I'd seize on anything to forestall the inevitable. It seemed I would learn to play this game.

Nakoa showed me that the deep-green pieces would be mine and made the first move with one of his pale blue ones, demonstrating several countermoves I could make. Some animals were confined to a particular color spiral, others could move from one to the next, but only at certain junctions. The smallest, resembling the seabirds that sometimes flew past, could leap an entire color. Fish could move three spaces at a time, while small dogs went one by one. Moving my piece onto a space occupied by one of Nakoa's let me remove it from the board.

The object seemed to be to reach the dragon, which felt counterintuitive to me. Wouldn't one want to avoid the dragon? I certainly did.

We played in silence for the most part, a relief to my overworked mind to not think about words for a while. Nakoa corrected me when I made both illegal moves and foolish ones, demonstrating how I'd lose an important piece, then backing up the game so I could choose differently. Both the delicious liquor and concentrating on something besides the real-life puzzles that plagued me worked to relax me and I found myself actually having fun.

Nakoa was, too, black eyes sparkling as he watched me contemplate my next move, even laughing when I groaned at my mistakes. It took hours, what with all the backing up and fixing of errors, but we made it through an entire game. Nakoa awarded me the dragon's capture with a bow from his waist.

"Thank you," I said. "Though I only won because you made sure of it." It didn't matter that I didn't even try to say it in his language. I'd play better the next time, some of the convoluted strategy making more sense now. I finished the last of the liquor in my glass, noticing that Moranu's moon was rising over the ocean, waxing toward full. We faced east, then. Somewhere across that water lay Annfwn.

Though the thought made me wistful, the sense of loss had abated, not so keenly felt. I'd actually enjoyed Nakoa's company. Wise of him, to find something we could do together that didn't involve either attempting to communicate or having sex.

Though that was no doubt next.

"I suppose it's time to go in," I said, gesturing to the interior, stilling the flutter of nerves. He'd been waiting for the signal and stood, but he moved around the balcony, putting out the torches, then came over to scoop me up. Instead of heading for the bed, however, he sat again, keeping me on his lap, turning his chair so we both looked out at Moranu's luminous moon.

I'd never sat on a man's lap, especially one so unclothed, and I wasn't sure what to do with myself, perching there on his strong thighs, riddled with tension again. Nakoa said my name, caressed my bare arm, and coaxed me to lean against him, pressing my head to rest on his shoulder. Gradually I inclined against him, his warmth comforting as always.

He stroked my hair, combing through with his fingertips, seeming to enjoy the texture of it. Mine was both finer and lighter than that of any of the women I'd seen here, and I wondered if he found me attractive. A question that raised all kinds of conflicts, as I didn't know if I wanted him to or not. That is, I didn't want him to because I really did not want to go to bed with him.

Didn't I?

That firm resolve from earlier had blurred with playing the game and the morning's kisses. And that liquor, no doubt. Being in such close contact, too, fanned flames inside me. I found myself wanting him to touch me more than the light caresses on my arm and hair.

I really wanted to have a real conversation with him.

"This is when we'd talk," I said to him, my voice coming out dreamy, "and we'd tell each other our histories, hopes, and wishes. That's how we'd know if we are even compatible. Which is a ridiculous thought, since this isn't about romance. I never expected that for myself, but I did think that I'd have the opportunity to know something about the man I married." Of course, I had talked to my other potentials, and that got me nowhere.

"Still, if I could, I'd explain how I'm better at books than relationships and that I've never been with a man before—or a woman, much as Jepp wheedled." I laughed at my own joke and Nakoa shifted, moving so he could see my face. He seemed to be listening intently, though he couldn't understand a word I was saying. It helped, though, to at least speak these things aloud. "I don't know why you picked me out, Nakoa. I'm not even sure what my legal status is. Here I am, waiting for a rescue that may never come, or may not be politically possible. I never thought I'd have to make decisions like this. It's ever so much easier to read about these things, or to help others make the plans that change the world. I'm a librarian, not a queen." *Or king's concubine.* A toss-up there.

For some reason, he caught that word. I'd used it before with him, so I supposed that made sense. "Queen," he repeated, tapping over my heart, then tapping himself. "King."

He used the Dasnarian word. "Yes, King Nakoa KauPo. But I am *not* a queen. I'm just Dafne, last of the Mailloux family of Castle Columba, orphan, and adviser to High Queen Ursula."

"Queen Dafne Nakoa KauPo," he replied, immovable as the volcano itself. Moving slowly, he put a hand on my ruby-hilted dagger, drawing it and wrapping my fingers around it. Then, before I could ask what he intended, he cupped the back of my head and kissed me. I braced my empty hand on his chest but lost the reason for refusing the moment his lips touched mine.

15

The kiss caught me up with a swooping sensation, as if I flew like the dragon, my heart pumping hot blood. Each time he kissed me became more familiar, but also totally different in tenor. This time was about hunger, a fast-rising need that billowed between us. A moan rose out of me and he drank it from my mouth, echoing the sound.

As if I'd said something he understood and returned in kind. *The language of the body.*

I dug my fingers into his chest, kissing him back fervently, and his hands tightened on me, one buried in my hair and the other gripping my waist. I'd felt small against him, but now that didn't matter so much. I wanted into him, to understand who he was, to have him inside me. It made no sense, but sense, logic, words—all had failed me and left me with only this.

Nakoa and I. Not the blade between us. Only fire.

His hands smoothed over my hip, back up my waist, as if he traced the curves, learning my shape. Stroking up my side, back to my waist, each time rising higher, until his fingers brushed the bottom curve of my breast. I caught my breath at the sensation, my nipples tight and my breasts hot. He broke the kiss but not his hold, face a handsbreadth away, eyes catching the silver glint of moonlight, holding my gaze. He brushed my ribs though the silky gown, measuring my response, then moved slowly higher until he cupped my breast, weighing it in his hand.

I held still, wanting to move and afraid to. Nothing had ever felt like this. Extraordinary that he could touch me in ways I daily touched myself and have it feel so totally, mind-shatteringly different. Biting my lip, I waited for what would come next. His one hand moved through my hair, his eyes roaming over my face, as he held my breast with the other. His thumb brushed over my taut nipple and I lost the breath I'd been holding in a sharp cry of startlement and exquisite pleasure.

"Nakoa!"

He smiled, a hint of wicked mischief in it, and stroked my nipple again. Without thinking, I let go of the dagger, leaving it to lie in my lap, and clapped both hands over his on my breast, holding it still. I might not be able to bear much more of that. It did no good, as he simply moved under my hands, now pinching my nipple between thumb and forefinger, rolling it between them. Undone, I let my hands fall and arched my back into it, closing my eyes and actually squirming. The knife clattered as it fell on the polished stone and I didn't care a whit.

I'd never been this person but could no longer remember the reasons for it. Taking the invitation, Nakoa bent his head to my exposed throat, kissing my collarbone and the hollows there, all the while stroking my nipple so my body moved in answering undulations. His hand moved down my back, supporting me while he briefly left my breast alone to tug the loose strap of the gown over my shoulder.

He dragged the soft fabric down my arm, slowly baring my breast to the warm night air. I opened my eyes, uncertain, watching his face. His expression was rapt as he gazed at my naked breast for a long moment; then his eyes flicked up to my face.

"*Mlaipua*," he said.

"I don't know what that means. I don't—Goddesses!"

He'd taken my sensitive nipple into his hot mouth and I clutched at his head, overcome, his hair wiry silk in my hands. I couldn't quite catch my breath again, only able to gasp and groan as his tongue swirled over the hard nub. I'd moved into completely uncharted territory, and I thought of the maps and how at the edges they said, "Here be dragons."

I experienced the truth of it, as my dragon king devoured me, shredding my reserve with hands, lips, tongue, and teeth. Leaving fire behind.

Growling a little, he pulled at my dress, tearing the delicate cloth in his rush to bare both of my breasts. Pushing the garland aside so most of it dangled down my back, he moved from one breast to the other, laving my skin with generous licks and kisses, nibbling my nipples until I cried frantically, then soothing me again with long strokes of his tongue.

I had lost my mind long since.

When he moved a hand to my knee, slipping under the hem of the gown, I stilled. Nakoa kissed me, tenderly, a kind of reassurance that went beyond words. He pulled me close against him, so my naked breasts crushed against his muscled chest, the shock of skin-to-skin contact exhilarating and bewildering. His hand stroked up my thigh, moving from the outside in, and I cringed a little when his fingers skidded over the fluids slicking my skin.

But he groaned, almost a sound of pain, and he murmured my name against my mouth, then a soft question. "Open?"

I sighed my breath back into him, and opened my lips and my thighs.

One part of me stood back in amazement at my complete capitulation and willing participation. The rest, however, soared on the exquisite sensations of being made love to. I felt like Zyr's *kalpa* tree, at long last bearing a fruit I'd had no ability to imagine. All I knew was I'd lost any connection to any thought but having Nakoa's hands on me.

He took my mouth in a drowning kiss and his hand moved to cup me under my skirt, the fragile silk of the pantalets barely any barrier. The intimacy of the shocking contact rattled through me. I clung to him, crazy with it, holding his head with my hands in his hair, rocking my hips wildly. His manhood stood stiff against my hip and he laughed, saying something, nudging me over slightly so I didn't press against him so hard.

"Sorry," I managed, but he kissed me, sweetly.

"No sorry, Dafne *mlai*." Then he moved his hand, pushing the silk into my folds, watching my face. Bereft of his hair, I held onto his shoulders, assimilating the extraordinary invasion of his big fingers against my sensitive and swollen sex, so very different from my own touch. Like a sun compared to a candle.

"Nakoa," I breathed, not at all sure what I meant to convey.

He stroked me, fanning the flames, and the climax built in me, irresistible, inevitable. Something it seemed impossible to share with another person, even in the moonlit-shrouded shadows. How it had come to be this man, so enigmatic and forbidding, remote and exotic as the dragon, I didn't understand.

But, against all reason, it was him.

I came apart in his arms, nails digging in as I convulsed with pleasure unlike anything I'd ever known. My own small orgasms in my private bed were pale, timid moments compared to the blood-pounding release that wracked my body. I ground against his hand, throwing my head back to cry out the ecstasy. No wonder the poets used that word for it. Nakoa feasted on my breasts, murmuring words in his musical language. Moon. *Mo'o*. Me.

When the claws let me go, I collapsed against him, breathless, laid waste. He stood and carried me inside, something I only vaguely tracked until he set me on the bed, carefully laying me on my accustomed side of it. His erect manhood jutted out, delineated by the thin cloth of his garment, snagging my gaze, which I quickly averted. Abruptly self-conscious, I covered my naked breasts with my hands, hiding them from the revealing lamplight.

Nakoa went back out to the balcony, returning with my forgotten journal and the other things. Then he moved about the room, snuffing the candles and torches, leaving only the candle on my bedside table lit, the flame still behind its curved glass protection. He brought over the ointment and, after propping my poor feet on their pillow, treated them once more.

I considered the change of activities with some bemusement. Finished with my feet, Nakoa unbuckled the belt Jepp had given me, returned the blade I'd forgotten to its sheath, and set it by my pillow with a quirk of his mouth and a cocked eyebrow.

Then he regarded my torn gown, hanging in tatters around my waist. Fisting his hands in the cloth, he tore it down the middle, leaving me clad only in the silky pantalets the ladies had given me. I gasped and, ridiculously, tried to cover myself there, too. "Please, Nakoa—no."

His dark gaze found mine, opaque, with something like frustration in it, but also resignation. The Nahanauns were casual with their nudity, more like the Tala. Not at all how I'd come up. I'd been naked in front of other people more here than ever in my life. There hadn't been ladies to wait on me, or any family to be casual with.

I didn't know how to handle this. My nails had left red scratches on Nakoa's shoulders from my passionate frenzy of only moments before, but I blushed furiously now, unable to meet his eyes.

To my surprise, he sighed and drew the sheet over me and placed a kiss in the center of my forehead. Drawing the gauzy curtains closed, to protect me from the biting bugs, he gave me a slow smile full of some satisfaction, though the prominence of his unsated manhood gainsaid that. Without a word, he blew out the candle and left.

It was a long time before my throbbing body cooled enough for me to sleep.

Inoa was not happy with me.

She made that much clear with her disapprovingly pursed lips and the terse orders she gave her ladies as they helped me bathe and dress. I assumed she knew Nakoa and I had not fully consummated the marriage. Which I might as well call it, as that seemed to be the case. Even if I could have explained to her, I would not have wanted her to know more than she clearly already did. It wasn't her business, what Nakoa and I did or did not do together.

Besides, it hadn't been my decision. Nakoa had done a thorough job of seducing me, very little of it attributable to the liquor in the end. I would have let him finish the job, no doubt. A few more of those devastating kisses and I'd have crumbled.

I didn't know why he'd stopped for sure, except possibly out of consideration for me. Maybe because of my feet. More likely due to my obvious trepidation. Certainly not out of a lack of desire. Unless he'd taken that impressive erection elsewhere.

The thought annoyed me unreasonably, making me feel as cranky as Inoa was behaving.

When Nakoa arrived with my fresh garland, she shooed the ladies out, shut the door, and lit into him, waving her hands as she berated him, tossing me a glare every once in a while for good measure. Nakoa waited her out with obvious patience, affection in his expression. She wound down and he said something in a gentle tone, but firm.

Something that set her back, because she shook her head and left.

Though I was fully dressed, the heated interest in Nakoa's eyes raked me as if I still lay there naked before him. "Greetings, *mlai*," he said, shading it toward morning and pleasant weather. Indeed, it looked glorious outside, the ocean breeze sweet and cool.

"Greetings," I echoed him, sitting up from the pillows so he could trade my wilted garland for the fresh one.

He put a finger under my chin, raising it and looking stern, an exceedingly daunting sight on his already brooding visage. "*Mlai*."

I frowned back, steeling my spine. "I'm not saying it when I don't know what it means. I already got myself into this fix by going along and being polite. You won't cow me into doing everything you want." I used mostly Common Tongue, substituting words from his language where I knew them.

Narrowing his eyes, he leaned closer, changing the grip on my chin to a feathering caress down my throat that made me shiver, melting what little steel I'd mustered. "*Mlai*," he insisted, his breath whispering the word over my lips, hovering there.

"Nakoa." I'd gone breathless, my body responding to him with a savage hunger for a replay of the delights of the night before.

"Yes. Nakoa. *Mlai*."

I pressed my lips together, clinging to that much stubbornness. He laughed, a soft sound under his breath, and brushed my lips with his, as sweet and gentle as the morning breeze. I tried to hold firm, but he continued to coax me with teasing kisses, urging me to open, with both the word and caresses that made me forget what I'd been thinking. With a sigh, I opened my mouth, letting my tongue tangle languidly with his, forgetting that I'd been drawing a line and losing myself in the heat of desire.

He kissed me long and thoroughly, then broke off with a look of regret, gesturing to the windows, indicating he had to go. I surprised myself with the sting of disappointment. Of course he had things to do. Goddesses knew, I had extensive experience with how much Ursula packed into any given day. Once I'd been in the thick of it, too. Useful. Not bedridden and essentially only valued for being Nakoa's . . . whatever I was.

I needed to do more than that. Be more.

I picked up my journal and held it out, pretended to read it, then drew a stack of books, along with shelves showing scrolls. Nakoa tilted his head, seeming surprised, then nodded crisply and indicated he'd carry me. I gathered my things and piled them on my lap, and he scooped me up. This time his hand passed familiarly over my breast, where my nipple still peaked from those stirring kisses.

"Hey!" To cover my response, I smacked him on the chest, which might as well have been a wall, for all the impact I made.

He grinned at me, almost boyish, completely unrepentant. "*Mlai*," he reminded me.

"Yes, yes, I heard you." I tried to sound grumpy, but in truth that smile dazzled me. A rare, full smile of warmth and maybe even affection. "But I'm still not saying it."

He adjusted me in his arms, lifting me a bit higher and cuddling me against him, then nuzzling my temple, making nibbling noises. Against all probability, I giggled. Tried to pull it back to being serious, but the giddiness of his attention made me feel slightly drunk. A playful Nakoa was more difficult to resist than a thunderous one.

Pleased with himself, he carried me out of the room, assuming his usual stern expression as soon as we passed through the doors. How much of that was a mask he wore? People bustled through the halls, much busier at this time of day. Several times courtiers or possibly nobles, judging by their dress and bearing, stopped him to ask questions. They acknowledged me politely but paid no more attention than the occasional curious glance as Nakoa answered questions and gave instructions. Something about other islands and birds. Some of his good cheer dimmed with news people brought, concern creasing his formidable brow.

Frustrating not to know everything discussed as I normally would.

In this piecemeal way, we made our way to a part of the palace I'd not yet been in. A servant hastened to open double doors for us—unusual, as not that many rooms I'd seen that weren't bedchambers had doors at all. By that point, guilt riddled me for taking up so much of the king's time on an obviously busy day. Of course if he'd delegate my carting about to someone else, he wouldn't have this problem.

I caught my breath at my first sight of the library. It was enormous—by far the largest I'd ever seen, with standing shelves in rows holding hardbound books, as well as lining the walls, and doors opening into more rooms beyond. Cabinets with shallow drawers probably held maps or documents that couldn't be rolled. Others likely held scrolls. Though there were windows, these were the first I'd seen with glass in them. A controlled environment, to keep the damp from ruining the paper—a concept the Tala had cared little for. The amount of knowledge collected there was incalculable. More, it told me the Nahanauns cared about preserving these materials. Nothing was more important than that.

If I could have stood, I'd have jumped for joy.

"Yes?" Nakoa asked and I gave him a radiant smile, feeling hopeful for the first time in days.

"Yes! Thank you." Impulsively, I kissed his cheek and he turned his head to capture my mouth in a longer, lingering kiss. Several people had gathered at the king's arrival, so I pulled away, self-conscious, and he raised his brows in wry amusement. Striding over to a table, he gave instructions to a man who listened intently, nodding and throwing me interested looks. He had the same graceful beauty as Inoa, with dark hair long enough that he tied it back with a colorful ribbon. Nakoa set me on a chair and a servant ran up with a cushioned stool for my feet. It took a bit of arranging, but they got me situated at the desk, with my feet propped up beneath.

Nakoa opened my journal to a blank page, tapping it and raising his brows in inquiry. I showed him my map of the Twelve and tried sketching one of a series of islands, marking one with a volcano. With his sharp mind, Nakoa grasped what I wanted quickly, giving orders the others scurried to follow. They all seemed thoroughly intimidated, which made me feel better for my lack of spine with him. Seeing Inoa's attitude had skewed my perceptions. Nakoa tapped the page again and I tried to think of a way to explain what I needed.

I pulled out a few loose pages and set them in a stack next to the journal. Laying a hand on one, I said the Dasnarian word for king, then put a hand on the other and used the Nahanaun word.

Nakoa frowned in puzzlement, then called over the long-haired man, who seemed to be in charge, then indicated I should repeat myself. I did. Then added "Dasnarian" on the one and "Nahanaun" on the other. The man's serious face brightened. His assistants brought several maps and laid them on the table, bowing and looking hopeful.

"Yes!" I said, spying the volcano on a detailed map, then another on a smaller scale that showed what might be the Sentinels. "Thank you."

Nakoa spoke approvingly and they beamed in obvious relief. I studied the second map and Nakoa set a hand on the back of my neck, caressing me absentmindedly, looking over my shoulder. The head man returned with two scrolls and set them before me, unrolling them and setting weights to hold them in place. They looked to be the same length. The one in Dasnarian described a tale, a myth involving the creation of the world that sounded quite similar to one common among the Twelve Kingdoms. The other scroll . . . I had to sigh. The undeniably beautiful script used what looked to be pictographs instead of an alphabet.

But it was a start.

"Thank you." I folded my hands over my heart and started to bow, but Nakoa stopped me with a hand on my shoulder.

"Queen," he said, giving me a slight smile, adding the word he'd used when correcting me on illegal moves in the game of strategy. The librarian kept a straight face but seemed amused. I nodded my acquiescence. I would have to get used to this kind of thing. Nakoa tapped my journal again, raising his brows.

"Mo'o?" I asked, using the word he'd taught me. Several of the attendants murmured. In dismay?

"No," Nakoa replied, sounding regretful. Though it wasn't clear to me if he meant that there were no books on the dragon or that I could not see them. If the latter, I would find them myself, once I regained mobility.

"Then this will keep me busy. Thank you." I laid my hands on the documents, palms down. Nakoa sounded satisfied and gave some final orders, which I interpreted to mean they should give me whatever I asked for.

He picked up my hand, turning it over and placing a formal kiss on my inner wrist. "Good day, *mlai*." And waited.

"Thank you, King Nakoa KauPo." I smiled sweetly and he shook his head, huffing out a laugh, to my relief.

He left, meeting several people who waited anxiously by the doors—and who started asking him questions immediately. Salving my guilt with the resolve that I'd be less of a burden if I educated myself, I turned my attention to learning his language.

16

The man who seemed to be the head librarian sat himself down at the table also, clearly prepared to devote his time to getting me whatever I asked for. He put a hand over his heart and introduced himself. "Akamai."

"Greetings, Akamai," I tried, working on my tonality. He didn't seem confused, so I'd at least said something reasonable. "I am Dafne."

He flashed me a bright, easygoing smile and shook his finger at me. "No. Queen Dafne Nakoa KauPo."

I stopped myself from arguing and instead bent my attention to the scrolls before me, while Akamai quietly copied some document. It seemed forever ago that I'd given myself the same task, copying those missives, when my biggest concern was finding the right temple priests and priestesses to bless Ursula's coronation. Not worth contemplating the irony of all I'd made Ursula go through for a formal coronation, not to mention all those discussions of matrimony and who could and could not elevate a spouse to the throne. Nakoa thought he'd made me queen by tossing a flower garland around my neck, and no one seemed inclined to argue.

As I worked, I made notes of likely Nahanaun words that might correspond to Dasnarian ones. I added a third column of the Common Tongue translation, to help keep my thoughts straight. Between those three languages and the Tala I'd acquired, it became easy to forget which one I attempted to translate to. Half the time, instead of the Dasnarian word I sought, the Tala term popped into my head. As if my brain offered anything for "foreign word for this concept" rather than from the appropriate language.

Not at all useful. The fact that the Tala also used a kind of pictography instead of an alphabet also just confused things further—particularly as it seemed to share nothing with the Nahanaun one. Tremendously annoying. How could the realms be so relatively close geographically and share so little culturally? Though the same was true of Annfwn and the Twelve and they at least shared the same landmass. In the past each of the Twelve had their own language unique to that kingdom, but they'd all shared certain commonalities of structure and etymology. Common Tongue had arisen long before Uorsin, driven primarily by trade. Some scholars argued that Common Tongue used to be the language of all the Twelve and the individual languages of the various kingdoms were dialects developed during periods of isolation.

I tended to agree with the latter interpretation, more so over time, as I encountered these wildly different languages from other places.

This effort felt almost more like cryptography than anything else—something I wished fervently I knew more about. I listed the pictographs that occurred most frequently, comparing them to the same in the Dasnarian document and trying to line them up by location in the text. It would be a bad assumption to think that Nahanaun word order was the same as Dasnarian. In fact, I knew it wasn't. The Nahanauns tended to, at least in speech, put an object first, then describe the circumstances around it. Dasnarian had been easier to learn because it used a structure like Common Tongue, typically subject, verb, object. In both Dasnarian and Common tongue, I'd say "I ate an apple." Dasnarians added descriptors after the object where Common Tongue generally put them before—"I ate an apple red" as opposed to "I ate a red apple."

In Nahanaun, though, they seemed to say, "Apple red I satisfied have eaten," with the concepts for past tense, "red," and "satisfied" expressed in the pitch and tonality. All in how it was spoken, and I knew well from studying Tala that what they spoke and what they wrote down could be substantially different. I'd always attributed that to a written language being an afterthought for the Tala, but now, beating my head against this Nahanaun scroll, I reconsidered. How did they designate tonality and pitch in a pictograph? Slight deviations I detected in the same character might indicate that. Or might be only variations in handwriting.

And I was getting nowhere.

If hope is the absence of despair, then that explained how quickly my hopefulness eroded as the frustration grew. It chewed at me, distracting me and increasing my certainty that I could not win out of this situation. Not a good place to be.

By way of taking a break, I set my lists aside and looked at the maps. The Nahanauns drew in a more florid style, an artistic sense that echoed through all the sculptures. Almost more liquid, with few straight or bold lines. That's part of why Nakoa's sketch of me had seemed odd to my eye. He'd drawn me smaller, slighter, more feminine than I thought of myself. My face more piquant and my eyes large and lightly shaded. Like the *nyrri* Kral had taken to calling me. Perhaps my eyes, though brown, seemed as odd to him as his opaque ones did to me.

Likewise the maps showed land edges in light lines and the ocean in varying shades of gray. Perhaps to show depth, as Shipmaster Jens had taught me his navigational charts depicted, though in a different way. Instead of names to indicate places, small sketches appeared at salient points. Not exactly pictographs, but definitely images. Those had to be the Sentinels—their stark, sharp edges unmistakable. They stood amid a depiction of a scattering of islands at the far eastern boundary of the map. Larger islands at the top right corner were likely those at the western border of the

Northern Wastes. Where Annfwn would be, or anything else of
the west coast of the Twelve, Nakoa's map showed only ocean.
His island chain sat in the middle of the map—and took up the
entirety of the larger, more detailed map of Nahanau. I found the
volcano on the detail map and compared the shape of the island
to find it on the big map. Not the first in the chain or the biggest,
but the farthest east of a long archipelago of islands.

There had to be hundreds, streaming easily as far as from Elcinea to Erie. Surely they weren't all under the same rule? At the
far left edge of the map, however, seemed to be a land mass that
had to be Dasnaria, from what Jens had explained.

"Akamai?" I asked and he raised his head, bowing slightly.

"Yes, Queen Dafne Nakoa KauPo?"

I nearly grimaced. No wonder Andi always resisted being
called by her title and full name. "Is this Dasnaria?"

He came over to look. "Dasnaria, yes."

I put my finger on the island I'd identified from the detail
map. "King Nakoa KauPo is king here?"

Akamai drew a circle around the entire archipelago. "King
Nakoa KauPo," he said, pitching the words with pride and the
tonality I associated with the sense of pleasant weather. Maybe it
meant more "flourishing." I made the change to my list of words.
Akamai watched, head cocked. "May I?"

"Yes." I pushed the list over to him and he braced his hands
on the table, studying it.

He tapped a pictograph next to a Dasnarian word. "This is not
correct," he told me, a phrase I'd learned well from Nakoa teach-
ing me the game. Taking a fresh sheet of paper, he drew the pictograph and wrote the Dasnarian word next to it.

I stared at it, almost unable to believe what I saw, realization
overcoming doubt. Could I truly have stumbled on such a stroke
of incredible luck?

Akamai gave me a worried smile and bowed. "Queen Dafne
Nakoa KauPo? I did not mean to offend."

I knew that one, too, from Inoa's ladies—though it seemed

only lower-tier people said it to those of higher rank. "No offense!" I switched to Dasnarian, almost afraid to hope. "Do you speak Dasnarian?"

He hesitated, then shrugged and answered in the same language. "Some. I am not perfectly fluent, Queen Dafne Nakoa KauPo." He used the Dasnarian word for "queen," confirming that much. I'd really hoped for a translation problem there. But the aggravation was minor in light of this enormous development.

"Why doesn't King Nakoa KauPo employ you to translate for him when the Dasnarians visit?"

Akamai seemed torn. Probably not supposed to say—as this had to be deliberate obfuscation on Nakoa's part—but also forced by protocol, and a direct command from his king, to answer my questions. "Perhaps you should ask King Nakoa Kau—"

"No. I'm asking you. Explain this to me, please."

He sighed, resigning himself and pulled over his chair to sit beside me. "It serves King Nakoa KauPo's purposes to allow the Dasnarians to believe we don't understand their language. They can be . . . overbearing."

I laughed, both at his word choice and with the sheer delight and relief that I'd found a teacher. "I agree. Akamai, will you teach me your language? If I'm to be queen here, I need to know."

"I'm not sure if I'm meant to, Queen Dafne Nakoa KauPo." He frowned, deeply troubled.

No way would I let him off this hook. I'd found a teacher, one I desperately needed, and I'd have to be ruthless in securing this opportunity. Coaxing would only weaken my position. Drawing myself up and giving him my best version of Ursula's steely stare, I said, "King Nakoa KauPo commanded you to assist me. This is the assistance I require. I'll take responsibility for any consequences."

"Thank you, Queen Dafne Nakoa KauPo!" The sheer relief on his face, the way he bowed and kissed the backs of my hands, seemed like an overreaction, which meant I'd possibly promised him a great deal more than I'd intended. Still, whatever that might be, it would be worth it to gain this knowledge. Knowledge might be my best fence against the world, but it could also be the active weapon that might gain me my freedom.

Akamai proved to be an excellent teacher, using the scrolls he'd brought me to demonstrate the bridges between the two languages. Profoundly grateful I'd followed my whim—or *hlyti*—in learning Dasnarian, I soaked up the information, putting together a number of fragments fairly quickly.

We worked for hours, me snacking on the ubiquitous platters of fruit, meat, and breads servants kept refreshed. Akamai refused to partake, abashed that I offered, but also wouldn't leave me. It seemed wrong to take advantage, but I'd learned so much already that I hated to stop.

I did only when Nakoa arrived, a relief, as I very much needed to answer the call of nature and had been at the point of trying my feet. He hadn't thought of that, I suspected, in his dictatorial insistence that only he carry me.

"A pleasant afternoon to you, *mlai*." He had shed his entourage but wore his armor, making me wonder what he'd been up to.

Unfortunately Dasnarian had no good corresponding term to match "*mlai*"—or Akamai didn't know it—but he had verified that it meant something like beloved or lover, shaded with possessiveness. No great surprise there, but increased incentive for me not to say it.

"A pleasant afternoon to you, also, King Nakoa KauPo."

An arrested expression on his face, he processed that. "You have learned much this fruitful day."

"It has been an educational day. Akamai is most happily gifted and wise." Nakoa's brows drew together and Akamai quailed.

Nakoa spoke sharply to him, going too fast for me to catch it all, but questioning his decision.

"Am I queen?" I interrupted, earning a glower from Nakoa and an alarmed gulp from Akamai.

I refused to let him intimidate me. *I have stood up to Uorsin, far more of a tyrant than even you, and to Ursula, as well.*

"I have said so, *mlai*. Why do you unpleasantly question me?"

"I do not mean . . . an unpleasant question. I have learned much, yes, but am as a child in understanding." I fumbled my way through, but some of Nakoa's dark frown lightened. "If I am queen, Akamai is to obey me, yes?"

Nakoa nodded. "Though he obeys his king wisely first."

"I told Akamai I would take responsibility for . . ." I looked to Akamai for assistance and said the Dasnarian word for "consequences."

Hesitant, he offered several words to Nakoa, bowing humbly as he did. Nakoa looked astounded but no longer angry, shaking off the further discussion. "I would not undo your gift. Are you ready?" He held out his arms in the gesture of offering to carry me.

"Yes, thank you, King Nakoa KauPo. I shall . . . be here"—I'd forgotten how to shade for the immediate future, curse it—"another day?"

"If the sun shines, Queen Dafne Nakoa KauPo." Akamai bowed deeply and Nakoa lifted me from my chair, carrying me from the room.

"It will be a pleasant day when you . . . are not required to carry me," I offered, hoping I'd gotten all of that right.

Nakoa looked down at me and flexed his fingers on my thigh and just under the curve of my breast. "Not happy. Perhaps I will forbid you to walk, so I may always carry you."

At least, that's what I thought he said. Something that simultaneously pissed me off and made me flush, both of which Nakoa observed.

"A king of so many islands is too . . ." I trailed off, not knowing the word for it. "Responsibility?" I tried.

"You are *mlai*," he replied, with a shrug that edged his hand so his finger brushed the bottom of my breast.

"I don't understand." I'd made Akamai teach me that phrase. I'd no doubt be using it a lot.

"I have not pleasantly shown you?" He stopped, bent his head, and, since I turned my face away, kissed under my ear. Taking my earlobe in his teeth, he nibbled at it, making me gasp while he murmured something against my skin that involved pleasant demonstrations.

"Not here, Nakoa." I pushed at him and he chuckled warmly. But he resumed carrying me to my—his—no, *our* rooms. I couldn't have it both ways, claim right of rank and also deny my new reality.

To my relief, Inoa and her ladies were waiting for me, Inoa simmering with impatience. "You go unhappily slow, young brother," she scolded him, and I was pressed to keep from smiling.

"My burden is precious," he replied, setting me carefully on the bed. "We shall play *kiauo*, Dafne *mlai*?"

"Yes, Nakoa." Though I felt suddenly tired enough to collapse back and sleep. Working the mind so hard could be as exhausting as riding all day at Hawks' speed.

"You have to—" was all I got of Inoa's next words, though I guessed well enough what she was telling him. Especially when he cut her off.

"I am wise in this. You are unhappily not," he told her, teasing, but firm, then sent me a look to see how much I'd understood, smiling at my blush. Nothing like having everyone discuss your sex life.

As soon as the door closed, the ladies blessedly helped me use the chamber pot and then to bathe. To my surprise, my feet felt tremendously better, barely hurting when I bumped them. They chattered as they worked, but now I could decipher much more of their conversation. With Nakoa gone, they dropped some of the formalities, speaking to each other quickly. And about me. I gathered up the fragments, letting them think I still understood no more than I had before.

Unhappy luck that he has not bedded her.
Stormy days loom.

What shall happen to us if?

He is not wise in this. That last from Inoa, accompanied by pursed lips. *She is beautiful but does not understand the importance.*

They gave me much to ponder, especially the word *mlaipua*, which I thought meant "beautiful." Nakoa had used it when he bared my breasts and Akamai had translated the Dasnarian word as such, in relationship to the description of the birth of Glorianna in the scroll. Still, no one ever in my life had described me as beautiful, not even my prospective bridegrooms or Zyr, the rumored master of seduction.

Inoa hopefully offered the transparent nightgown, commenting to one of her ladies that if I'd only put it on then her little brother—she might be saying baby brother—would see a . . . truth? And the sun would shine again. They used so much metaphorical language, mostly tied into good and bad fortune, that deciphering meaning became nearly impossible.

As I had the evening before, I refused. With resignation, she brought out a new garment, this one of a lovely dusky blue, and I agreed to wear it. She checked my feet, telling me in simple words, with exaggerated slowness, that they looked much better.

"May I have my stockings?" I asked, using my word that I'd taught her, as they had no such thing and therefore no word for it. I'd surprised her, but she had a lady fetch them for me. I put them on, though the warmth of the day made them a little much. Experimentally, I put my feet on the floor and added some weight. Not unbearable. Seeing what I was doing, Inoa surprised me again by offering her hands, supporting me as I attempted to stand. She didn't dislike me, but something about the situation with her brother and me had her upset. I couldn't blame her for that. If I had a younger brother, I'd feel the—

It hit me hard, that thought, and I swayed on my feet, Inoa clutching my hands in a fierce grip. I did have a little brother. Or, rather, had long ago. Two of them and an older sister. When had I forgotten them?

I must have looked ill, because Inoa told the ladies to fetch juice and bade me in more polite terms to sit. "My feet are happy good," I told her. "May I go outside to the . . ."

"Balcony," she supplied, giving me a more genuine smile. "So you may play *kiauo* with my baby brother instead of seeing to your responsibilities." She shook her head in annoyance, fortunately missing that I understood and—once again, as always—blushed at it. "No balcony, heart-queen. A storm approaches. See to understand?"

The sky outside the windows had grown dark and thunder rumbled ominously, the air suddenly thick and close, dense with humidity. As if it had been waiting to be noticed, the rain released with a roar, sheeting down in great waves. The air nearly as full of water as the sea.

Extraordinary.

Instead servants set up the game and lanterns, just inside the balcony, along with food and more of the liquor Nakoa had given me the night before. Close enough to smell the rain and feel the cooling breeze that came with it, but out of the downpour.

My feet throbbed by the time I walked to my chair, but I didn't care, it thrilled me so much to get there under my own power. As they finished up, I added a few notes to my journal and planned my strategy. Both for the game and for dealing with Nakoa.

Inoa made sure I had all I needed, then shooed everyone else out, closing the door and studying me, biting her lip as she frowned in thought.

"See to understand," she finally said, and picked up three pieces of fruit, setting them on the table before me. "See?"

What was she about? Inoa kept glancing nervously at the door, as if expecting to be caught. She moved her hand in a hurry-up gesture. "*See?*" she insisted, tapping each fruit in turn.

"One, two, three. Yes." I counted in Common Tongue, but she nodded in relief, then took away two pieces, tapping the remaining one. "Not happy good."

To have only one? I frowned at her, puzzled.

She heaved an exasperated sigh, her eyes welling with tears. "See?" She sounded desperate, knocking the fruit to the floor. "Gone!"

The door opened and Nakoa came in, taking in the fruit on the floor and Inoa's tearful expression. He told her she couldn't do something and she wept in earnest. He took her in a gentle embrace, speaking to her so softly I wouldn't have been able to catch any of it, regardless. She nodded, leaning against him. He said something more that fired her up, so that she tore out of his hold and smacked him hard on the chest with both palms, clearly furious.

With one last significant—pleading?—glare at me, she left.

17

"A pleasant evening to you, *mlai,*" Nakoa said as he closed
and—interestingly—bolted the door behind his sister.

"A beautiful evening, yes, Nakoa." I gestured to the tropical
rain. "Beautiful storm."

He set down the liquor bottle he'd picked up and, frowning,
came over and lifted my chin. "Dafne is beautiful, not the storm."

"Ah. I am not correct."

That must have sounded odd also, because his lips twitched
before he went stern. "You will call me *mlai.*"

"I will not." I held his gaze, not backing down. Let him be
angry.

Instead, however, he smiled knowingly. "You will. What is
this?" He plucked at my stockings, my feet once again propped on
the stool.

"Stockings," I told him, giving my word. "To make my feet
happy. See to understand?" Putting my feet down gently, I took
the hand he offered and stood. They hurt more than before, from
walking, no doubt, but I could do it.

Nakoa's smile broadened, reflecting mine. "Excellent!" He
put his hands on my hips and drew closer, making me acutely

aware of his physical presence and how slight I was in comparison. "I did not wish to hurt you when I take you to bed."

Definitely what Inoa and her ladies had been discussing. My face burned and I had to look away. "Shall we play *kiauo?*"

He laughed softly and helped me sit, lifting my ankles onto the stool again. "I will see these stockings."

"You saw them before," I protested, lapsing back into Common Tongue, flustered enough that I couldn't find the right Nahanaun words as I held the hem of the gown in place while Nakoa tried to lift it.

"I am king—you will obey me," he insisted.

I would have argued except his eyes sparkled with that playful mischief I found difficult to resist. Not good for me that he seemed to have figured that out. "*I* will show you," I told him.

He let go of my gown, so I raised the hem to just over the knees, where I'd tied the ribbons into bows. Nakoa knelt down, fingering the satin. "Beautiful." With a fingertip he nudged the hem slightly higher, so a bit of skin over my stockings showed. He kissed me there, lips hot, tongue flicking out to taste me. "*This* is beautiful—understand?"

"I . . ." I'd gone hot, moisture surging in my woman's core, already so attuned to him. An image of Nakoa pushing my skirt higher and kissing me there had me at a total loss for any words, in any language at all. Except that of the body, which Nakoa heard and understood perfectly.

"Beautiful *mlai,*" he murmured, kissing my other thigh, slightly higher up. Involuntarily, I moaned and his glittering black gaze flicked up to my face. "Will you open?"

I wanted to. Goddesses help me, I did. I craved more, and some animal need had urged me to spread my thighs even before he asked. Still, so far I'd failed in every mission that had been set for me. Jepp had charged me to keep this marriage unconsummated and I would at least do that much. Giving in the night before had only made my ability to resist more imperiled.

"Nakoa . . . I can't."

He studied me, not angry at least. More that interested expression. "You can."

"I don't want to."

Watching me, he stroked the skin above my stocking with a light finger, and I shivered in response. "This is not correct," he said with a hint of a teasing smile.

I huffed out a sigh of frustration. Conversing better with him only elevated our ongoing duel to another level. "I am more than my . . ." Thrice-damn it, I didn't have the word. Instead I gestured to my body, then tapped my temple. "I am this also."

He knelt up and leaned in and tapped my temple. "This is beautiful also."

"Thank you," I replied, disconcerted, not entirely certain I'd gotten my point across.

"I shall play with this"—he kissed my forehead—"before this." A last kiss to my thigh. Then he rose and poured us both liquor, which at least gave me a moment to regain my composure. He meant to seduce me through the game, then. *I am wise in this.* How he'd seen through me so easily, I didn't know, but calling my mind beautiful had unlocked something inside me, more than any of the kisses, orders, or manipulations.

It was probably a deception. Nakoa had made his intent clear, as well as his single-minded determination, which meant he'd likely say and do anything to get what he wanted. I, however, was not without my own fortitude. I'd withstood all sorts of sieges. This would be no different.

If I could keep my head from being turned by pretty compliments.

Nakoa gestured to the board, inviting me to make my opening gambit. An uncomfortable position for me, as I found it easier to react to his moves than make my own. A fine metaphor for our interactions, there. I opened with the same move he'd started with the night before, thinking to keep conservative until I better understood the strategy. With a glittering glance, Nakoa captured my piece, using a move he hadn't yet shown me.

Oh, was that the way of things, then?

It was, indeed. Nakoa played to win, aggressively decimating me with a ruthlessness that spoke volumes. Another kind of language, this demonstration of his superior strategy. He waited patiently as I deliberated each move, answering immediately with decisive and inevitably devastating maneuvers.

I lost badly in no time at all, which rankled my pride no end. It shouldn't, I knew. After all, I'd barely learned the game and I'd spent the day stuffing my head with a totally new, annoyingly complex language. Attempting to be gracious, I picked up the dragon and offered it to him. He didn't take it, smiling at my scowl.

"I wish another *kama*," he said.

Uh-oh. "I don't know that word." I pitched it with irritation, which only made him smile wider.

"Not the dragon. Dafne."

Back to this, then, which I should have seen coming. "This isn't . . ." Fair. Did they even have that concept? "Correct."

He shrugged, a ripple of masculine muscle. "I am king."

Hlyti apparently liked to surround me with megalomaniacs. "What *kama*?"

Reaching across the table, he tugged at the strap of my dress, drawing it down my shoulder so it sagged over my breast. I had to hold the cloth in place and he gave me a pointed look. "I will see."

"You did before."

His smile going wicked, he agreed, tugging at the fabric. "I want to see now. My *kama*."

My nipples had gone hard, taut against the fabric, and his gaze caressed them as he waited me out. Playing with my mind meant more than I'd even guessed. Capitulating, not even sure why I'd given in, except that something about the exchange had me feeling giddily excited, very unlike my normal self, I dropped my hand. Nakoa drew the silk down slowly, letting it drag over my skin and catch on my peaked nipple, an excruciating tease that had me pressing lips and thighs together, as if by doing so, I could keep myself from succumbing to his relentless seduction.

The silk scraped, then fell, revealing my breast, and I closed my eyes against the rawness of the exposure. Nakoa said nothing. Didn't touch me. Finally I opened my eyes to find him watching me with still intensity.

"Thank you, *mlai*," he said softly.

I moved to pull my dress back up but he stopped me with a gentle hand, instead threading my arm through so the dress sagged away from my side. Nervous, I glanced out at the rain, wondering if we had spectators. Unlikely, even if someone braved the downpour.

"No one can happily see," he said, "but we can go to bed. Or play again."

"I can't play like this." My face burned and I shifted in my chair, impossibly aroused by this game of his. Though I couldn't let him know that.

"Then we go to bed," he agreed in great good humor.

"No! I mean—" I took a deep, steadying breath. "I wish to play again."

Equally pleased with that, Nakoa reset the game pieces while I tried to ignore the fact that I sat there with one bare breast, the flower petals of my garland brushing my skin, and—worse—that if I didn't get focused on strategy, any further forfeits would . . . It didn't bear thinking about. Ursula always said the appearance of victory could be as vital as the actual accomplishment. I needed to play to win.

This time Nakoa made the opening move and I contemplated mine carefully. To his credit, he didn't attempt to distract me by teasing me over my state of undress, though he did make it clear he enjoyed looking at me. I ignored him as best I could, setting up my long game. When he fell for a ruse, capturing one of my pieces that then put me in position to take several of his, I savored his surprise. And gave him a cocky grin when he nodded in acknowledledgment.

The game lasted much longer. He played more defensively,

taking longer to decide on his moves, which indicated my foreign strategy put him in a position where he could not predict as well. The last game had been such a swift win I suspected that stratagem was one perhaps often used against an inexperienced player. With each move, I discarded my first response, going for whatever would be most counterintuitive and still serve my overall goal.

The evening deepened to full night, the rain pouring in darkness, and still we fought for each and every piece. With three tokens left on the board—two mine and one his—he blindsided me by taking both in one shocking maneuver. He actually whooped in delight at my consternation.

"This is not correct!" I complained, retracing the move. But it had been legal. I just hadn't seen it coming. Goddesses take the wily man.

Nakoa simply grinned at me and tapped his chest muscle, claiming his forfeit. I nearly snarled, decidedly ungracious in the face of this second defeat. I had nearly won, thrice-damn it. Not nearly as self-conscious this time—the loss annoyed me too much—I took down my strap and let the dress hang around my waist, held in place only by my knife belt, both breasts naked, the garland hanging just short of long enough to cover me. "There. Happy?"

"Oh, yes, *mlai*. Excessively happy." He radiated satisfaction, too. "Another game?"

"Yes. You're not getting out of a rematch."

I made my opening gambit, going in more aggressively this time, using a pattern I knew from an Elcinean game of strategy. Nakoa responded more easily to my moves this time, seeming to predict me better, much as I tried to keep to counterintuitive moves. I set up a careful trap, wary of the one he'd caught me in that last time.

Then he ambushed me.

I had nineteen pieces on the board, all positioned to draw into a net that would capture his most powerful piece—an intricately scaled lizard with nearly unlimited ability to move around the board—when he captured my own lizard with a lowly fish. One I hadn't even noticed creeping up on my perimeter.

It so stunned me that I scrambled to assimilate the loss. I'd been so certain this time, and he'd undercut my strategy so cleverly I hadn't had a glimmer. We could keep playing it through, but I'd lost. I glared at him and Nakoa gave me a gleeful grin of triumph, shaking his white-streaked hair back and raising his arms to flex his muscles, as if he'd accomplished a mighty feat.

Danu take the man. As a warrior he belonged to Her and I had some serious complaints to take up with the goddess.

"Fine," I hissed through my teeth, my blood truly up, racing with a ferocious pulse, and went to pull off the gown.

"No, *mlai*." Nakoa picked up the gaming table and set it aside, then knelt before my chair, expression full of sensual mischief. I was in for it now. Still, I wouldn't give him the satisfaction of seeing how much I hated losing. He put his hands on my stocking-covered ankles and slid them up under the hem of my dress, traveling up my bare thighs. My mouth fell open as I perceived his intention. Oh, no. He kept his hands to the outsides until he reached my hips, then grasped the pantalets and tugged, a challenging gleam in his gaze.

Bracing my hands on the armrests, I lifted my hips, refusing to back down from his stare. With a twitch of a smile, he drew them down my legs and over my stockings, pulling them over my feet with care and tossing them aside without a second glance. My mouth had gone dry and my breath shallow as I tried to anticipate his next move, to prepare my strategy.

Wrapping his fingers around my ankle, he picked up my foot and moved it up and out. I stayed, as if frozen in place by his hypnotic stare. "I will see," he murmured, shading it with a pitch I hadn't heard, but that shimmered through me with erotic impact.

With his other hand, he pushed up my skirt, holding me open for his gaze while I, amazed at myself, allowed it. No—wanted it. Draped in the cushioned chair, my breasts naked and hot, while lanterns shed warm light around me, a storm raged outside, and a barbarian king knelt at my feet, I longed for more. I didn't want to go back to being who I'd been. I was tired of having regrets.

Savage desire surged through me and I embraced it.

Nakoa bent and kissed my inner thigh, murmuring something I had no mind left to translate. He draped my knee over his shoulder and caught my eye. "Yes?"

"Yes."

He paused to lay a hand over my heart, making me stir as he brushed my breast. "Thank you, *mlai.*"

Then he bent his head, like a monk in prayer, and put his mouth on me.

A cry escaped me at the startling sensation, so incredibly intimate, that sent ripples through my body. I arched my back and dug my fingers into his hair. Unable to catch my breath at all, I panted and sobbed, each stroke of his tongue transporting me into some dark, piercing place I hadn't known I carried in me. He licked and nibbled at me, holding my hips still when I writhed, testing my responses in the same way he'd tried my strategy, drawing me out and chasing me back.

Settling into a devastating rhythm, he steadily stripped away my poise, reducing me to a mindless creature clinging to him and begging for more.

I came apart and he chased me there, too, staying with me as my hips bucked and I shattered completely.

He didn't relent, adjusting his technique and coaxing me up again. I'd thought myself spent, but no. The desire flared anew and I groaned but didn't protest when he slid a finger inside me. It felt big in my narrow passage but oh so gratifying. Licking at my pearl, he worked his finger inside me, curling it so a bolt of pleasure radiated out from deep within, connecting to the brighter pleasure his tongue elicited.

"Nakoa, please," I begged him, not at all sure what I asked him for, and he raised his head to look at me.

"All, *mlai,*" he said, and pressed the heel of his hand down as he curled the finger inside.

I screamed, a long, wild sound that I only vaguely recognized as my own, my vision going black, spiked with torch flares of fire. In the distance, thunder rolled through the storm. Or a dragon roared. Or the volcano rumbled.

None of it mattered. Only the soul-shattering release that dragged me under.

Regaining my senses felt like swimming up through the depths of the Onyx Ocean, only to look into the intricately patterned ceiling and torchlight instead of the blue skies of Annfwn, disorienting me momentarily, as if years had passed instead of only minutes. Nakoa still knelt between my open thighs, a look of utter self-satisfaction on his face, transforming it from brooding to something nearly beatific.

"Beautiful, yes?" He tilted his head, a teasing glint in his eye. "An excellent game."

I laughed without sound, still breathless. "I suppose you think you won that part also." Which, in truth, he had. I realized I'd spoken to him in the wrong language, but he didn't seem to mind, giving me a smug smile.

He helped me to my feet, the dress catching on my knife belt. With his eye on my reaction, Nakoa unbuckled it, which set the gown slithering off. I moved to grab at it, but he stopped me so I stood there naked in the pool of fabric, wearing only my stockings. Still kneeling there, he caressed my ankles and calves, tracing up over the ribbons to the bare skin above. Maybe he'd shattered the last of my modesty along with all my reserve, because for once I didn't mind him looking at me.

It felt good to be seen, in truth.

And the way he'd pleasured me left me languid, full of liquid fire, a bit savage myself, naked in the torchlight with my dragon king. He cupped my bottom and pressed a chaste kiss to my belly just over my pubis, lingering there and murmuring a prayer. I stilled, stricken by the possibility that he hoped to get a child on me. An emotional avalanche, triggered by the thought, crushed my thoughts, making it difficult to breathe.

Like in that dark hole, licking at the water, a flicker of hope keeping the despair at bay.

I'd had that dream once upon a time. A lovely—and ridiculous, it had turned out—fantasy that I would have babies and rebuild the family I'd lost. But I'd given it up after the failed arranged marriages and as the lonely years passed, one after another. So thoroughly had I abandoned the idea that it seemed startlingly new—which made the pain fresh, as I gave it up again. Just as with that lapse where I'd suddenly recalled the siblings who had died more than three decades before, whose lives I'd blocked out, along with so much of that blood-drenched nightmare. I'd planned to name my babies after them.

And then I'd given up thinking about any of it.

Grief won out, swamping me with things I hadn't thought of in ages. As if a door opened in my taxed brain, memories of my older sister letting me try on her gowns and putting up my hair, our little brothers doing everything to taunt us and get in the way. Playing games of chase through the meadow under the summer sun, while our mother and father looked on, judging the winners of various races.

All in the days before Uorsin arrived and destroyed our simple pastoral existence in the back of beyond, grinding joy to shreds of flesh scattered across a trampled meadow.

And like that, the grief became rage. All of it gone, never to return. The same as my aging womb, the time long since passed for it to bear a child.

Too damn late.

In a burst of fury, I pushed Nakoa away, punching my fists against his shoulder. Like hitting a wall, but that got his attention. He held on to me, which pushed me over some edge of panic and rage.

I slapped him. Hard.

18

We stared at each other, frozen in equal bemusement. My hand tingled with shock, wrist already aching, echoed by the quiet throb of my overused feet. How out of character for me. How utterly girly—and how ill-advised. Nakoa looked as if no one had ever struck him so in his life, which was likely true.

Good Goddesses—I knew better than this. What was wrong with me?

I braced myself for the thunderous anger, the retaliating blow. I'd seen Ursula on the receiving end of Uorsin's fist, a scene that had filled me with cold terror. Being who she is, she'd handled it with astonishing resilience. My own fortitude came from a different place, and I would never hope to do as well. Perhaps he'd kill me after all.

Nakoa moved and I flinched, bringing up my hands in a weak defense, my heart thundering. No, the volcano. Nakoa flicked a glance in the direction of the volcano, then back to me, considering. Moving more slowly, he picked up the discarded knife belt and drew my dagger. I swayed, my thighs going weak and feet ready to give out, a sob of terror leaking out of my stricken lungs.

206 • Jeffe Kennedy

With an impatient shake of his head, Nakoa pressed the hilt into my hand and put the point at his throat.

Then he grasped my hips, holding me upright. He asked me a soft question. I stared dumbly at him, unable to grasp the words, though the meaning hovered somewhere at the edge of my memory.

He pressed his lips together in a frustrated line, growling under his breath, brow furrowed. "Sorry. Why is Dafne sorry?"

That was it. The shading for a storm, an abrupt event like the volcano erupting. He was asking me what was wrong.

It broke me. Sympathy from an unexpected quarter can do that, as if someone else's caring undermined the carefully constructed walls meant to keep out assault, but vulnerable to concern. I clutched the dagger between my breasts, fisted over my heart, aghast at the second sob that ripped out of me.

"I don't know," I managed, unable to draw breath, my heart pounding furiously at the lack of air, my throat closing over any possibly of getting some. That is, I knew the why of it, but not the reason that the enormity of panicked emotion pressed on me. Or how I'd ever explain it to another soul, even if we shared enough of the same words. "I don't—" I ran out of breath entirely. I struggled to make my lungs move.

Failed.

That decided him. Without further questions, Nakoa swept me up in his arms, knocking the game board and pieces aside so they clattered to the wooden floor, chiming brightly. Instead of laying me on the bed, he sat, then stretched out, turning me so my back was to him and his long body curved all around mine. He put one hand on my belly, pressing me back against him, and the other under my head to wrap around my forehead.

I should have felt trapped, but I didn't. Instead the firm grip calmed the wild panic inside. I felt protected, safe, and secure.

Maybe for the first time since Uorsin destroyed my world.

Gradually, my throat opened and my starving lungs dragged in a fistful of air. Then another. Nakoa murmured something to me. Had been all along, speaking softly in a soothing tone, shading it with pitches of comfort, happiness, and pleasant days. He used different words, some I knew, some I didn't, as if seeking ones that held meaning for me.

I seized on ones I'd heard in reference to my injured feet.

"I will not hurt you," he said.

And I believed him.

We lay like that for a long time, the torches burning low. How late was it? The rain had dropped back to a soft patter and the palace had gone silent of human activity, the only sounds those of the high-pitched tweeting of birds. Only they didn't sound exactly like birds. More reverberation and more chirping than a song. Some other creature? I would have to find out.

The return of my natural curiosity loosened the last of my paralysis. Unwrapping my death grip from the dagger's hilt, I flexed my fingers and took a long breath, letting it out slowly. *It takes more courage to examine the dark corners of your own soul than it does for a soldier to fight on a battlefield.* I would not be a coward.

I turned in Nakoa's arms to face him.

He watched me, the black of his pupils deep pools ringed with the glassier shine of the iris.

"I'm sorry," I said. "For hitting you. For my . . . storm."

He lifted a finger to trace my cheek. "No sorry, Dafne *mlai*," he said, using my word. And returned my wobbly smile at the reminder. In some ways we did better with these small phrases we'd established between us, each understanding the emotion behind it, if not the more complex thoughts we still struggled to convey to each other.

The immensity of it all staggered me. We were like two people lost in that storm, unable to see or hear, drenched and in danger of being washed away by something much larger than ourselves. Finding and losing each other again after a brief point of contact.

And with me at least having no idea where we journeyed.

I wondered if even Nakoa knew. Were these uncharted waters for him, too, or did he follow some hidden map? He studied my face, deep in thought. If nothing else, I presented him with an enigma. Probably I seemed like a crazy woman, as mercurial as I'd been behaving.

He tapped the dagger I still held. "You always have this."

"I know." The ruby gleamed a deep red, a beacon of another life that seemed impossibly far away. Nakoa sought to reassure me still, not understanding the root of my fears, what I truly sought to protect myself from. How could he when I didn't understand myself? I couldn't have explained even if we spoke the same language. I felt I owed him something, though. "My queen gave me this. A . . . special gift."

Tracing a finger over the ruby, much as he had my cheek, he gave me a solemn smile. "You are precious to your queen. For such a happy gift."

"Yes." I blinked back the emotion. Still not steady.

"Precious also to your king, Nakoa *mlai*."

Oh. I wasn't sure how to respond to that. "I don't understand."

He made that rumble of frustration. "No. I know you do not."

He seemed to be torn, waiting for some answer from me, some kind of promise, perhaps. Only I didn't know how to convey that I'd try to be patient. Or that Ursula should be sending people to rescue me, whatever form that might take. Guilt pricked me that I hadn't warned Nakoa of this. Though I didn't owe my captor an explanation that I'd sent for help. How thoroughly he'd seduced me that I even worried about the lapse.

I am wise in this.

And yet, he'd comforted me in my panic. Taught me a strategy game I enjoyed, given me everything I'd asked for—with the salient exception of my freedom. Even now he laid with me quietly, skin to skin, me naked but for the stockings, not pressing his advantage. Waiting for my answer.

"I will . . . see to understand over . . . pleasant days," I tried, using Harlan's trick of cobbling together approximate words and phrases.

Nakoa smiled, though it had a tinge of regret in it. "Sleep, *mlai*. I will go." He moved to lever himself up. Where had he been sleeping? Following the impulse—maybe a bad one, but instinct seemed to be all I had left—I stopped him with a hand on his arm.

"Stay?" I gestured to the bed, the room. "Nakoa's place, yes?"

"Yes." He regarded me gravely, but with a flicker of mischief in his face that also banished the sadness. He patted my hip. "Also Nakoa's."

I made a face at him even as I, ridiculously at this point, blushed. "Stay. It is a . . . large place."

"No sorry?" He searched my face, unconvinced, and it occurred to me that my outburst had wounded him in some way. He wasn't at all sure what had gone wrong. That made two of us.

"No sorry." I said it firmly, for him and for me. A little hesitant, I unwrapped my fingers from the dagger—they would surely carry the imprint of the carving for some hours—touched his cheek and leaned in, giving him a soft kiss. He held still for it, not pressing me, but mirroring the pressure, returning in kind. "Thank you."

"All, *mlai*."

I opened my eyes to a silent room, filtered sunshine, and an emotional hangover. The gauze curtains remained drawn around the bed, but Nakoa was gone. We'd gone to sleep, curled together, my back to his chest, after he'd found me a sleeping gown and helped me out of my stockings. I suspected he normally wore nothing, because he stripped off his armbands, but retained his *kylte* for my benefit. He didn't exactly understand my nervous modesty, but he made allowances for it. Another of his courtesies.

I'd touched him from time to time during the night, or the few hours that had remained until morning, unused to having a furnace of a man in my bed. He'd responded to my confused disorientation with murmurs of reassurance, gathering me against him in that way that oddly made me feel safe.

He must have risen to see to his duties, leaving me to sleep. Ever the dedicated ruler.

Not sure why Inoa and her ladies had not yet invaded, but grateful for it, I parted the curtains and set my feet on the cool floor. Stiff, a little swollen, but tremendously better. I made it over to the chamber pot behind a screen, delighted to have the privacy for such a thing. Not having to rely on others for assistance for the most basic of body functions was something I would never again take for granted.

The same with dressing myself. I gave thanks for the simple autonomy of choosing my own gown—albeit not actually my own, as mine were all far too heavy for the muggy heat, but I wouldn't tarnish the moment with details—and brushing my own hair. And finding places to secret my little daggers. I held one up to the midday light streaming in the windows, turning it so the script glittered. *This is why it's perilous to ignore a librarian.*

I could hide only a few in the filmy garment and my stockings, but I felt more secure for doing it. Interesting that Nakoa seemed to understand that, reminding me of my weapons even as he attempted to disarm me in every other way.

The flower garland lay in a wilted heap on the bedside table, where Nakoa had tossed it after handing me the sleeping gown. I hadn't given it much thought then, beyond exhausted and frankly grateful to sleep without it. The crushed and bruised petals seemed somehow accusing in the morning light, as if I'd broken them in carelessness.

And Nakoa had not given me a fresh one.

Because he'd let me sleep. It had no more import than that. But, feeling a little superstitious about it and maybe a bit of nostalgic affection for how patiently he'd held me the night before, I put it on anyway. I would find the library—I was pretty sure I knew the way—and Akamai. Nakoa would look for me there. Taking the latch on the door, I found it bolted still, refusing to budge under my hand. Panic-filled anger rushed into my head, swift to flash to that emotion.

Then, chagrined, I recalled how Nakoa had manipulated the bolt and I found the catch to undo it. Panicking over nothing at all. He'd simply given me peace and privacy. I'd slept into the afternoon, the palace quiet and almost no one about. The few I saw were in intense conversations in the open shaded courtyards, some casting me strange looks. Mostly the place seemed unusually silent, almost empty.

I took a couple of wrong turns—the palace wound from room to room with few central hallways—but I finally found the distinctive double doors of the library.

As with the rest of the palace, nobody seemed to be inside, though the extensive space, shelves, and cabinets could hide any number of people, not to mention the rooms beyond I hadn't explored yet. Which I longed to do, but my thrice-cursed feet ached from the walk, so I hobbled to my table, no doubt looking like a person mincing as quickly as possible over hot sand, and gratefully plopped myself in the chair. All of the notes, books, and maps remained exactly as I'd left them—a rare luxury for me, who'd always been a person of questionable status, forever acceding to the priorities of others.

Apparently it was good to be queen.

To test my memory—and to immerse myself in trying to think in Nahanaun—I reread the scroll in that language, seeing if I could get through it without cross-checking to Dasnarian. It would be a tremendous relief to get past childlike pidgin talk with Nakoa, even if we'd still have a gulf of understanding to bridge from there. One step at a time.

It posed a challenge, but I made myself wade through it, sounding the tones and pitches in my head, going straight through without obsessing over the words I couldn't parse. Next I'd try writing it out in Common Tongue, which would really pin down the holes in my understanding.

"My queen!"

I jumped like a cat coming across a snake, squeaking out a cry that had Akamai's eyes going wide with alarm, sending him into a deep bow and a torrent of apologetic Nahanaun that coursed far too fast for me to follow.

"Akamai—speak more slowly or in Dasnarian, please."

He fluttered his hands in dismay. Then, with a deep breath and obvious effort, he folded his hands. "Queen Dafne Nakoa KauPo—are you hurt? I am so sorry!"

No sorry, Dafne. Why that silly, stilted phrase made me want to smile, I wasn't sure. "It's happy good," I replied in Nahanaun. The more practice, the better, even if Dasnarian would be easier. "You, ah, were sudden."

"I surprised you," he offered, seeming relieved, and I mentally noted that very useful word. "I did not expect you here on this unhappy day."

A curl of dread wormed in my stomach. "Why unhappy?"

His face crumpled in dismay, his interwoven fingers wringing each other. "You don't know?"

"I only awoke this now."

"Oh." His eyes slid to the side. "Perhaps it is not correct that I—"

"Akamai . . ." Giving up on practice, as the subject was too important, I switched to Dasnarian. "Please tell me what is going on. I need to know and you are probably my only friend here. If you won't tell me, who will?"

He paled and took a step back. "I am not your friend!"

The rejection stung a surprising amount. I'd just assumed, since Akamai seemed so familiar to me, with our shared perspective and love of books and caring for them. "I apologize," I said, somewhat stiffly, not in small part due to the Dasnarian form of apology being a particularly unyielding, unapologetic thing to speak.

"No, no." He washed the air clear of his words. "I'm upset and speaking badly. I cannot be your friend because I am lowly— an orphan, without family or wealth. I am your forever servant,

Queen Dafne Nakoa KauPo." His gaze flicked to my wilted garland and away again. "No matter what may occur."

"Akamai—I greatly appreciate that." I tamped down the pang at hearing his background. Probably a ward of the Crown, much like me. Interesting that he'd found the same sort of usefulness as I had. I wanted to ask more, but his anxiety, along with Nakoa's absence, gave me a bad feeling. "Now will you sit and explain what is going on? Where is everybody?"

He obeyed and eyed me hesitantly. "Has King Nakoa KauPo told you of the troubles he faces?"

"No," I replied, making an effort to keep my voice calm, much as I wanted to throttle him in my frustration. I'd never been a violent person and this unaccustomed quickening to anger was not always easy to manage. "Because Nakoa and I can barely talk to each other. We don't share a common language."

Beyond the language of the body. My blood heated at that, anger going quicksilver to desire, bringing back the memory of our intense game of *kiauo*, the rainstorm, and all he'd done to me with his devastating mouth. Before I'd melted down a different way.

"Ah, yes." Akamai shook his head. "I am a fool with this worry."

"And the worry is?" I coaxed.

"We were not to speak of it, lest our words incite the ancestors to make it true, but I think it is already true and there's no harm in saying it?" He looked to me doubtfully.

"I'm sure that's so. And you're not speaking to tempt the ancestors, but to increase my knowledge so that I may know what to do to help prevent it." I sounded very reasonable, all things considered.

"It may be too late for that. The dragon is gone."

"Is that a bad thing?"

"King Nakoa KauPo proved his worth by bringing you here, to release the dragon and settle the volcano. But the dragon has not been seen. This is a sign of terrible fortune and that another should be king. King Nakoa KauPo has said that he is wise in this and needs only time. Now there is no more time."

I am wise in this. My heart sank a bit more into the growing puddle of dread in my gut.

"What will bring the dragon back?"

"Perhaps King Nakoa KauPo knows, but he cannot be questioned. There was great hope when you arrived as promised and the two of you worked the . . . I don't think there is Dasnarian for it."

"That's fine. Tell me what you can." I could guess, regardless. Great hope. That celebration. I'd thought there'd been more to it than one ship bringing a few supplies in the wake of the storm. Salient, the bit about Nakoa somehow bringing me to the island.

I felt sure Kral had played a close game of his own, manipulating events. He and Nakoa must have conspired. Kral might have had a mission he never revealed, another reason for his concentrated approach to Ordnung. Had he subtly suggested to Ursula that she send me as ambassador to Dasnaria, all the while intending to deliver me to Nakoa? If so, he was a masterful performer.

And none of it explained how or why Nakoa picked me.

"What has happened now?" I prompted Akamai.

"There is another chief who challenges King Nakoa KauPo's right to rule. He calls upon the original portents, that the magic storm came as punishment from the ancestors, proving that King Nakoa KauPo is a bad king. King Nakoa KauPo replied that the ancestors challenge us all from time to time, and the measure of a king is in how he responds to strife, that any person may have character on sunny days, but the true test is how we withstand the storms."

That sounded so like Nakoa—though how I could think so didn't make sense, as little as we'd talked—that I smiled.

Akamai nodded. "See? He is a very good king. Chief Tane would be a terrible king."

I set that aside. Akamai's fervent loyalty to and pride in Nakoa could not be discounted. I'd seen enough to know that few people possessed the self-awareness and critical thinking skills to assess whether or not their ruler—especially a charismatic one like Nakoa—would be better or worse than another. After all, for most of her life Ursula could not be persuaded to see Uorsin as anything less than the hero of her childhood mythology, the shining figure that existed only in tales he'd paid or bullied the minstrels into composing.

Ursula liked to say that history is written by the victors. I knew better. History was written by whoever controlled the writers. You could say it's the same thing, but it isn't. Not always.

"So, when I arrived and King Nakoa KauPo set the dragon free, calming the volcano, Chief Tane had to back down from his claims?"

"Yes. Everyone was overjoyed! You were there. You saw."

"I remember. But . . . the dragon then disappeared?" Good riddance, to my mind.

"A terrible sign. Chief Tane gave King Nakoa KauPo three days to change the winds of fate, to prove his worthiness to the ancestors. He has not done so. A terrible day."

"He's gone to fight this chief then?"

"No. He must prove his fitness to rule another way. By defying the volcano itself."

"Which means?" Though my skin crawled at what I could guess.

"He will swim the Lake of Lava. If he survives, the ancestors have blessed him. If not . . ." Akamai buried his face in his hands.

19

"Goddesses save me from superstitious ignorance," I muttered to myself, grimacing belatedly for the irony. Still, it was one thing to call upon the goddesses for guidance, a way of accessing greater knowledge, and another entirely to devise ridiculous trials that supposedly revealed the will of people long since dead. In my experience, even those like Ami who did their best to channel Glorianna's will still relied on their own intelligence and common sense.

Something I'd love to knock into Nakoa's thick head. Why didn't he simply tell Chief Tane to test the will of the ancestors by trying to take the throne? Nakoa's warriors could keep an enemy army from gaining traction on the island. This chief couldn't have that many supporters, if he had any beyond his chiefdom. Nakoa could have rallied the might of all those hundreds—maybe even more than a thousand; I hadn't counted yet—islands in his domain. That's what I would have advised him to do.

If he'd asked. But he hadn't even alluded to there being a problem.

Inoa had. *Three days to change the winds of fate.* Was that what she'd been trying to tell me, with her three pieces of fruit? *Gone!*

She'd wanted me to bed Nakoa within those three days. And he had been firm that no one tell me. How it could possibly make a difference, how it would demonstrate the will of the ancestors, if I had sex with Nakoa, made absolutely no rational sense. But, then, we were dealing with superstition, not logic at all.

It explained a great deal of Nakoa's determined seduction, but not why he hadn't simply forced the issue. He could have, at any time. Not only because he had the physical advantage, but also because we'd both discovered my vulnerability to his touch. Had he pressed, I likely would have given in. Something I would have expected a man to do, if his life rode on the line.

Something I might have given in to, if he'd only explained the stakes.

But he hadn't even attempted to. More, he'd apparently forbidden anyone else from telling me. Why?

No, instead of confiding in me, he'd left me sleeping while he went to his certain death.

That was the only clear and immediate point in all of this mess, that Nakoa intended to throw himself into the lava, where he would be instantly immolated. I didn't have a stake in whether he remained king. But it was my fault—in a convoluted way—that he faced this fate. He might have conspired to bring me here and then kept me captive, but he'd had good reasons for it, and he'd been kind to me. Even caring.

I understood now, his pretense of finding me "beautiful"—whatever he meant by it—and for tending to me so carefully. Once I'd rebuffed his physical advances, he'd changed his approach and attempted to seduce my mind. Which had absolutely worked. I couldn't let him die because of me, no matter how foolish his decision to do so.

If only because the prospect made me feel ill. He might be dead already and the thought of that gutted me, that I might not match wits across the *kiauo* board with him again, or feel his smooth skin or hear that rich laugh as he teased me. *No sorry, Dafne mlai.*

I didn't know how I'd stop him, if it wasn't too late, but I had to try.

"Akamai—can you get me a horse? Immediately."

The request set off a flurry of dismayed activity. Apparently horses were not within Akamai's purview. He did his best but met with resistance—mainly of the flustered-confusion variety. From what I could gather, Akamai had no authority over the stables and the ones who did were away with Nakoa and pretty much everyone else.

Finally, feeling the press of time, I stood and mustered my best Ursula-defeating certainty and borrowed a line from Nakoa. "I am queen," I said, loud enough to cut through the chattering arguments of the group of servants Akamai had summoned, sending them into a flurry of bowing and apologies. "I need a—" Goddesses take it, I should have listened for the word Akamai used. "Something to carry me up the volcano."

Not as dramatic a command, with the language scramble at the end, but that did it. Galvanized, one of them threw up their hands, just as Inoa would do, and went to see to it. Akamai stayed with me as I slowly walked to the front entrance of the palace. Or the back, as it seemed they thought of the ocean side as the front.

We emerged just as a group of six male warriors strode up, carrying a litter festooned with flowers.

"Seriously?" I said to Akamai in Dasnarian. "Can't I just have a horse?"

"We don't have horses, Queen Dafne Nakoa KauPo. I am so sorry to fail you."

That explained the reaction to Zynda taking that form—not only the shape-shifting, but the animal she'd become. "It's not a failure, but you might have explained."

"You were in a hurry." A pointed reminder that I had no time to quibble about the conveyance. The men lowered it so I could sit and, raising the litter again to their shoulders, set off at a brisk pace, then broke into a jog. Hopefully Nakoa would not give me trouble about having other men carry me. Maybe removing my garland and leaving me behind meant he'd severed our relationship and that rule no longer pertained. Or he might be dead already and the whole thing moot.

Regardless, we could fight about it later if he survived.

The men sang as they ran, a chant that likely helped synchronize their pace, which yielded a surprisingly smooth ride. I felt like an idiot, of course, acutely aware of my disheveled state—wilted garland, knitted stockings that looked absurd with the silk gown—carried along like a goddess from mythology. This is what resulted when one threw about royal commands. Lesson learned.

If Nakoa lived, we'd straighten this out once and for all. I did much better behind the scenes, dispensing advice, than assuming the mantle of authority.

The journey took less time than it had seemed the first time. We moved at a much faster pace than we had before, with the large group and me going at my short-legged pace. That these men could run uphill, carrying me, chanting all the while, impressed me no end.

In my haste to get to Nakoa, I'd left my journal behind. It would be safe with Akamai in the library, but it would have helped me plan my strategy if I could have written it out. Actually, I was grasping at straws—I had no idea what kind of situation I rushed into and therefore could plan for nothing.

As I suspected, they were all gathered in the same spot where Nakoa had kissed me that first day and we released the dragon. Only this time, a huge crowd of people filled the plateau, thronging over the mountainside. My carriers, forced to slow by the mob, ceased their chant so the leader could call out demands to make way for Queen Dafne Nakoa KauPo. Feeling more ridiculous than ever, I tried to look calm, poised, and as if I knew what I was doing. I would have advised anyone else in my position to go for regal or queenly, but I knew my limitations. I might be able to convey knowledgeable confidence, but that was the best I could do.

The people acted with excited consternation, the ripples of their whispers growing louder as the news moved away from us in a wave. I was a rock dropped in the center of a previously still pond. For good or ill.

As they became more aware of our incursion, the crowd parted more willingly, opening an aisle up to the ledge that overlooked the Lake of Lava. A number of tall warriors stood there, making a tight circle and blocking whatever they surrounded, even from my elevated vantage. Many of them wore different armor than I'd seen, with feathers and flowers of other colors—likely marking them as belonging to Chief Tane or other islands. Of all the crowd, this inner circle made no note of our arrival, intently focused on something else.

The dread that had pooled in my stomach threatened to rise into my throat, burning there until I swallowed it down. Would I be faced with the grisly sight of Nakoa's burned body? For the first time since I'd made the choice to try to stop this, it occurred to me how tenuous my own position might be. I owed my false rank entirely to Nakoa—and possibly any guarantee of my safety. He might have locked me in to protect me, a precaution I'd thrown to the winds.

Ah, well. I'd been living with the specter of imminent death so constantly these last days, I'd nearly become accustomed to it. Maybe this was how the warriors did it. *Fear is like pain—it alerts us to a danger.* Ursula had told me that once and I understood her meaning better now. You paid attention to the warning, but had to let it go after that.

"Queen Dafne Nakoa KauPo demands an audience with King Nakoa KauPo!" the leader of my carriers called out—not how I would have phrased it, if I'd comprehended correctly—but it finally snagged the attention of the inner circle. The guards came to attention, throwing curious, even shocked looks my way, then opened up to reveal what they'd blocked.

Almost afraid to look, I steeled myself; then Inoa's glad cry rode on the hot air currents. And Nakoa stepped out from behind another taller, bulkier man. He wore none of his armor or jewelry, not even the dragon torque, and carried no weapons.

The shadowed reverse of Inoa's smiling face, he glowered at me, taking in the men who carried me and nearly snarling at the sight. He strode toward me, ignoring the man who spoke sharply to him, and barked a command at my bearers. They set the litter down with haste, dropping to their knees on the hot ground, pressing their foreheads down and staying there in complete obeisance.

I stood and stepped off the litter. The heat of the rocks warmed the bottoms of my feet through the knit stockings, uncomfortable but not painful. Still, I must have winced a little, because Nakoa moved to pick me up, hands reaching for me, then stopped himself, fingers flexing in frustration. He settled for looming over me. "What do you here?" he hissed through gritted teeth.

I'd cobbled together a few phrases in preparation and kept my voice low also. "I did not understand the consequences. You cannot enter the Lake of Lava—you will be injured beyond healing."

He listened, the black anger lightening ever so slightly with wry amusement. "You have so little faith in the will of the ancestors, in my fitness to be king?"

"I have faith in what is real. Solid." I thumped the hard muscle of his chest, not knowing the word. "Lava burns flesh. You'll die, no matter if your ancestors are happy or not happy." I'd shredded the pitches and tones in my urgency and exasperation, but something got through to him, because he considered me thoughtfully.

"Who spoke this to you?"

"I understood on my own," I replied with calm defiance. We both knew it to be a lie, but I wouldn't implicate Akamai.

He gave me a knowing look, then shook his head. "The time has passed. I must do this. I cannot protect you, understand? You should not have left our rooms. You will go." Then he frowned at

222 • Jeffe Kennedy

the litter, clearly not certain how he could send me away without having someone else carry me.

"You will carry me then, back to the palace?" I asked with as much innocence as I could muster.

A muscle in his jaw flexed and his white-threaded brows drew down. "You understand I cannot."

"Then I stay."

"No. These will carry you. It is . . . the time has passed."

Behind his stern mask, I caught a glimpse of something else. Pain, perhaps. Resignation deepening the lines of his face. He knew very well that this would be suicide. In one sense, that came as a relief, because I'd felt sure he was too intelligent to cater to a superstition like this. On the other, he planned to embrace his own death and abandon his people. Never mind questions of who would make a better ruler. It went against everything I believed in for me to be the cause of him failing his sacred duties.

I couldn't let him walk away from his throne any more than I'd stand by while Ursula did.

Nakoa spoke to the litter bearers, telling them to take me away and not come back, by the sound of it. But I wrapped my arms around his waist, lacing my fingers together, burying my cheek against his skin and clinging like one of the barnacles that festooned the *Hákyrling*. "*Mlai*," I said, kissing the skin over his heart, the rippling black scales of the dragon tattoo.

That caught him off guard and he froze momentarily, not embracing me back. Then he spoke gently. "No. This is incorrect."

"Nakoa *mlai*," I insisted, tipping up my chin so he could read my expression.

He searched my face, looking for something. I showed as much sincerity as I could—a very real desire for him to live. "You do not mean it."

Thrice-damn it. "I want to mean it."

"It is not enough."

"It *is* enough!" Inoa grabbed his ear, tugged him close, then lit into a rush of hushed instructions, her tone growing more urgent.

I didn't know all her words, but I knew the pitches she shaded with, future hope, sun after the storm. Consequences and responsibilities.

"The time has passed," Nakoa cut her off, stubbornly immovable, and Inoa cast me a helpless look of pleading. She didn't think so and she struck me as no fool. There must be a way to forestall the test. If the other chief brought the challenge, perhaps he could be persuaded to withdraw it. Or postpone. Which would bring me back to the same crossroads of whether to bed Nakoa—but I'd confront that choice later.

"I will help." Impulsively, needing to get Nakoa's full attention, I transferred my grip to his neck, standing on tiptoe and leaning against him for balance as I kissed him, hard. He didn't return the kiss, still didn't put his hands on me, a question forming in his opaque expression. "I understand this," I told him gesturing to the man who must be the challenging chief, watching us with mixed curiosity and suspicion. "This is what I do. For my queen. I will do this for you." I really wished I'd been able to bring Akamai along to translate, but all diplomatic posing was essentially the same, right?

Nakoa made that grumble of exasperation, my sleeping dragon awaking. "Dafne *mlai*, you—"

"Is this she?" The other man, surely Chief Tane, came up, interrupting. He gave me a dubious look. "She is small for such big stories."

I let go of Nakoa and faced the other man, ready to assess the situation.

"Queen Dafne Nakoa KauPo, Chief Tane," Nakoa corrected, with very little intonation. Was I the only one who heard the simmering offense in it? "Your queen, to be treated with respect."

Chief Tane grinned, not nicely, a leer in it. "Yes, mine to possess when you inevitably fail the ancestors. I won't hesitate to—" He used a euphemism that I caught only part of, but the words I did get were enough to put heat in my face and fire in my heart. I'd heard plenty of salacious terms for sex, especially traveling with the Hawks and Vervaldr—not to mention with Jepp—but this felt deliberately crude. Behind me, Nakoa rumbled in restrained fury. A volcano about to blow.

Rapidly I revised my opinion to side with Akamai. Chief Tane was of Uorsin's ilk. Full of ambition, cruelty, and raging hunger for power. Such men understood only one thing. He saw me as weak, something to taunt and use up. Never.

"I would kill myself before I let you lay a finger on me," I sneered, liberally mixing Nahanaun and Dasnarian, trusting that he'd get the gist.

He threw back his head, laughing heartily and for show, obviously mocking me. "I would break you in half, little *cala*."

Inoa gasped, ready to spit in her fury. A female insult then. Maybe just as well I didn't know what it meant. Glad I'd thought to hide some on me, I palmed one of my slim daggers, then made it suddenly appear. One of Jepp's tricks, to unsettle the enemy by seeming to do magic. "That is incorrect."

The chief laughed again, but with a shade less confidence. He spoke to Nakoa, something rapid, a pitch that sounded like an insult. Notable that I hadn't heard it used before this moment. It seemed he reminded Nakoa of a promise and, reluctantly, Nakoa stepped back, stroking a hand down my arm finally, then dropping his hand. Constrained by agreement not to touch me, then. Or perhaps intervene at all. *I cannot protect you.* Chief Tane smiled, clearly believing he'd already won, and held out his hands, opening his body to me, making an apparently inviting target.

"Show me, little *cala* queen. I call you false as our former dead king."

It chilled me, the pitch he used to refer to Nakoa, as if he were already dead. My feet burned in earnest, but I ignored them. Everybody else stood barefoot; I could toughen up, too. A thousand instructions from Ursula and Jepp raced through my mind. If only I had something of their speed and skill. I'd love to spin in and slice at him, shocking everyone as Jepp had done with the

Vervaldr early on. I'd missed that demonstration, but the women of the castle had talked about it with great pride and satisfaction for days. She wouldn't be afraid to teach this bully a lesson.

Everyone feels fear at some point. That's healthy self-preservation. It's also the fuel that will drive you to survive. You've called on it all these years. People underestimate you—use that, too.

Chief Tane took me for a fool, so I walked into his trap, slicing at him, making it look a little wild and desperate—not difficult to do, with my heart flapping like a captured bird against the cage of my ribs. With a malicious smile, he dodged my little blade and grabbed me. Trapping me and plastering a sloppy, disgusting kiss on the side of my face. So big.

But not as big as Harlan.

Envisioning myself back in the courtyard at Ordnung, Ursula bickering with Harlan, a grinning Jepp egging me on, I sagged, collapsing, palming a dagger in my other hand also. Tane relaxed his grip, groping my breasts and repeating that foul promise.

I burst up and out. Lashed out with both blades at once. Caught him with a shallow slice to the belly and the hilt hard up against the sweaty balls beneath his *kylte*.

This is why it's perilous to ignore a librarian.

The knives sang the song in my head even as I put substantial distance between me and Tane. I couldn't run away from this entirely, but I could get well away from his reach. Tane roared his outrage and fury, echoed by the shouts of the crowd, Inoa cheering wildly, a fierce glint in her eyes. Nakoa had folded his arms, standing back, ostentatiously not involved, but I thought I saw a glint of amused pride in his face before I resumed my place in front of him, ready to confront Tane.

Blood ran freely down the chief's abdomen, and he clutched his groin, white pain contorting his face. He gained his feet, flexed his hands, and started for me.

I drew my big dagger, letting the bloodred ruby catch the sunlight, and spoke in the iciest, most dismissive intonation I could manage. "Try it, and I will slice off your man jewels this time."

Only I used the crudest word I knew for it—a Dasnarian one, naturally. "Nakoa is *mlai* and you will not injure him."

His face twisted with rage, and I braced myself. I would do it. He'd kill me, but I'd have that much satisfaction. Ursula would know that at least I went down fighting.

Tane halted his forward lunge. Not because of me, though.

The rumble of the volcano did it.

And the trumpeting call of the dragon.

20

The gathered crowd called out, the harmonies of reverent joy rising from thousands of throats, prickling the hairs on my arms, despite the oppressive volcanic heat.

Inoa stepped forward on a triumphant shout, finger pointed to the sky. "*Mo'o!*" she proclaimed, along with some other rapid-fire remarks that seemed related to Nakoa, the right to rule, and various negotiations. Chief Tane glowered, a man thwarted, but he did not argue with Inoa. Instead he focused on Nakoa.

"Do you fail?" he asked, insult replete in the tone. "Are you afraid to test the will of the ancestors as you vowed?"

I didn't wait for Nakoa to answer. Knowing him, he'd agree to the test despite the opportunistic arrival of the dragon. I didn't believe for a moment that it portended anything, any more than Nakoa's death via lava would mean that the ancestors had turned aside from him. Though part of it niggled at me. Ami insisted that all three goddesses had worked through the sisters to remove Uorsin from the throne, so that Ursula would kill him as part of Danu's justice, with Glorianna's loving benevolence and Moranu's healing magic, to soak the land with the king's blood and restore balance. That wasn't explainable by any logic I understood.

Perhaps the dragon's return meant something more than I believed, also.

"The will of the ancestors is clear," I said, hoping I had all the intonations right. "There is time yet for King Nakoa KauPo to prove his right to rule."

"He had three days and the dragon did not—"

I interrupted Tane, both to undermine his power and to prevent any seeds of doubt he might sow in the listening ears. "Does the dragon"—curse it, I had no idea if they even had a concept of a timetable, much less a word for it—"arrive at your command? Do the ancestors call for three days or is that a man's idea?"

The people murmured as Inoa threw me an approving glance. I wished I could risk a glance at Nakoa, to assess his reaction, but I couldn't afford that weakness. Nor, it seemed, could he weigh in on this discussion.

"He is no king if he is no man." Tane grinned at me, that nasty leer in it. "Do you deny he has not . . ." Again with that vile euphemism that had Inoa sizzling with offense next to me. I put a hand on her arm to restrain her.

"King Nakoa KauPo is a great king." I let my voice ring with conviction, pitching it with a tone Inoa had used, that of optimism and hope for the future. "He has care for all. My feet were injured." I made it sound as bad as I could, shading it with all the storm and ill-luck tones I knew. The people near enough to hear studied my stockings, discussing them, bits of concern for the fragile, tiny foreigner drifting on the sulfurous air. "I could not . . ." I floundered, out of words to explain.

Thankfully, Inoa took over, weaving quite the tale from what I could make out, employing languid hand gestures that added to the story, amplifying the cadences she used, making it into almost a dance. She made it sound as if I'd fallen into a fever, too weak to move, sorely afflicted by my injuries, a queen so precious and delicate, her skin had never seen the sun. A sign that I was to be protected, with skin as pale as sand, scattered with flecks of fire like the sunlight burn of my hair. Along with the prettiest description of my freckles I'd ever heard, it sounded good as long as it seemed to be about someone else—and I only caught about a third of it, if that.

Still, I understood more than I might have, the movements of her hands and body lending an almost magical quality. She played to the crowd, convincing *them*—a brilliant move.

She made us sound like star-crossed lovers, separated first by cruel distance, then by one who thought the dragon and the ancestors served his orders. Never saying Tane's name, she nevertheless embroidered on my logic, making that sound absurd. Now I bravely risked relapse—see the pain on my face?—to fulfill my promise to my beloved.

Mlai.

She had even me convinced.

And everyone else, too. By the end of her storysong, people were crooning along, adding melodies and harmonies of celebration and good fortune. Several women rushed up, coaxing me to sit on the litter again, to save my feet. I hesitated, putting them off, risking a glance at Nakoa, who glowered indeed.

"A fine tale," Tane agreed, trying to sound benevolent and not succeeding very well, "and I could be persuaded. But the dragon has gone again. The foreign *anâ* is beautiful, but I cannot go against what the ancestors have advised me . . ." He pitched the words with sorrowful, sincere regret.

Just like High Priest Kir, all over again. Seemed no culture was immune.

"You will see for yourself." Taking the risk, I went to Nakoa instead of seating myself on the litter. Absolutely the more painful choice, as standing that long on the hot, sharp-edged stones had my feet aching enough that I was hard-pressed not to limp. But if Inoa had convinced them that only my injuries had prevented this dragon-taming magical consummation, then my believably promising it would happen forthwith depended on making it look like I had healed enough.

Nakoa wasn't fooled, watching me with a glint of exasperation in his eyes. "King Nakoa KauPo, will you take me home and make me your queen?"

The crowd fell silent, at least those near enough to hear. People farther back called out questions and were hushed, whispers passing back, more ripples in the pond. Nakoa narrowed his eyes at me, just slightly. Just enough to promise retribution for cornering him like that. I didn't care. We needed to get him off this mountain and back to the palace, where we could regroup and strategize. Nothing we did could persuade the dragon to do . . . whatever it was that everyone seemed excited for it to do, but Chief Tane could be dealt with in other ways.

"Nakoa. *Mlai*." I moved closer, laid my hands on his chest, and gave him a stern glare, whispering, "No sorry, yes?"

His lips twitched, though his arms remained folded. With one last thoughtful searching of my face, he looked up and called out to the crowd. "Is this your will?" He kept it neutral, shaded with neither a happy outcome nor an unpleasant one.

The people cheered wildly and, with an ear-splitting trumpet, the dragon flew into sight from beyond the volcano, circled, fixed on us, and headed our way. Gliding on the hot air currents like a jeweled seabird, its wings outstretched an impossible length, the dragon plummeted without a sound, zooming straight for us. "Goddesses!"

Then Nakoa had me in his arms, better than an invocation of any goddess. He stood firm, even turning slightly to meet the dragon head-on. I wound my arms around his neck, missing the feel of the torque but feeling much safer. It made no sense, as the dragon could eat us both in one bite. At least Nakoa could run—that would be a logical reason for feeling reassured.

Nothing to do with the fact that just the scent and feel of his skin worked to calm my instinctive terror.

Nakoa's lips brushed my temple. "See to understand, *mlai*."

I couldn't have torn my eyes from the sight regardless. Like a fiery golden blade cleaving the sky, the dragon grew in size, lethal, fascinating, extraordinary. Ruby flames lit its eyes, taller than Nakoa—and real flames flickered in its gaping maw.

"See?" Nakoa murmured, his voice as full of awe as I felt. "Beautiful."

It was.

A roar sounded in my bones as it approached, my heart pounding into synced rhythm with Nakoa's. No, the roar came from the sound of air rushing over the great membraned wings. Amazingly Nakoa laughed and the dragon passed just over us, as if I could have reached out to touch it, and the turbulence of it tossed Nakoa's lightning-threaded locks so they lashed against my cheeks. All of it welled up in my chest, a kind of terrified elation that burst out in my own laugh. All around us, the people—even Chief Tane—held their hands up to the sky, as if savoring the sensation of the passage of the majestic beast, singing out their song of awe and celebration.

Nakoa carried me down the mountain in a kind of triumph, leading a procession of thousands, all talking and laughing loudly, about the king, the dragon, and the foreign queen. Chief Tane walked beside us, rendering conversation between Nakoa and me unwise. Besides, with the cacophony, we would have been barely able to hear each other.

Still I caught Nakoa flicking me the occasional searching glance, a line between his brows as if he sought to solve a puzzle that perplexed him. Inoa, on his other side, also caught my eye with significant, long-eyed stares, silently communicating something. That, at least, I could make a good guess at.

Yes, I would do what I needed to do to save Nakoa's life and get him through this absurd challenge to his throne. Far more important considerations than this eternal preserving of something that meant nothing if not used, enshrined for a day that would never come. Nakoa had been gentle and patient with me and, better, his touch worked for me more than any other person's had. It would be pleasurable, I'd be done with this spinster-virgin status that made me feel like such a pariah, and . . .

Well, we'd deal with any political or marital repercussions later.

The celebratory chorus ratcheted up another level as we approached the palace. I took advantage of the opportunity to refresh myself on the layout, now that it was more familiar to me, able to identify our rooms from the position of the broken wing, and the grand escarpment overlooking the sea, which I thought of as the formal ballroom, in their version of such things, along with the library in its protected central location and the high tower where I'd watched the *Hákyrling* sail away without me. The thought didn't quite pain me as much or leave me with the same sense of panicked breathlessness at being abandoned.

Very likely because I had far more acute crises to worry about.

Taking note of my absorption, Nakoa paused a moment at the viewpoint, allowing me time to take it in. Not my intention, exactly, as I'd been partially distracting myself from other thoughts. Chief Tane stopped also, a few paces ahead of us, fists on hips—a decided acquisitive light in his eyes as he glanced back at Nakoa.

"A grand place, my new home," he taunted.

"It is not yours," Inoa hissed, curling her fingers into her palms.

"It belongs to no one but the dragon." Nakoa inserted the implacable words between them. "We live here by her indulgence."

"Her?" I asked, pricked by curiosity into speaking before I meant to. It wasn't exactly the female tonality for human women, but I caught it for the first time that way.

Nakoa's night-black gaze moved to mine, slumberous under the white lightning in his brows, a hint of teasing in it, though his face didn't move from its composed lines. "Of course. Females of all species are the most fierce and dangerous." His lips twitched and he adjusted me in his arms. "No matter her size."

"She must be a dragon under the skin, to have held off such a mighty king," Chief Tane said, tone riddled with contempt that twisted the words. He added a euphemism I didn't quite get but that sounded like an insinuation that my woman's passage contained sharp teeth to sever a man's member. Judging by Inoa's silent, furious expression of insult, I had the gist of it.

"If such is true," I said to him, "then best hope King Nakoa KauPo succeeds in his efforts tonight, lest your own *bqllr* be at risk." I used the Dasnarian word for "cock," as it had a satisfyingly lewd sound to it.

Tane's temporary bafflement gave way to icy rage. "Careful, little *cala* queen. I would take your knives and use them to make new holes to fuck."

Nakoa had turned his back, carrying me swiftly away before Tane finished his vile suggestion, but I pieced the words together as the chief followed behind us, calling out more of the same.

"Why do you allow him to come with us?" I asked Nakoa in a low enough tone that we could not be overheard.

He kept his stony gaze focused forward. "The palace belongs to all. No one can be forbidden entrance."

That explained a great deal. Would he have banned the Dasnarians, even Jepp and Zynda, if that weren't the case? I suspected so.

"Not even someone who so blatantly challenges you?"

"He is a chief, with a people to be responsible for. He annoys but is within his rights."

"I'm surprised he seeks to insult me." It seemed the smart course of action would be to cozen and court me, if he sought to make me his queen instead of Nakoa's. Of course, I had none of the dragon-capturing witchcraft they ascribed to me, but they believed so.

"It is not you he wishes to offend." Always taciturn in the best of moods, Nakoa seethed under the skin with volcanic fury, so tightly contained I hadn't sensed the full scope of it until that terse statement.

"Ah. He hopes you will challenge him, as you did General Kral."

He flicked a glance at me. "Yes. Or to distract me with such fear that I will not bed you."

"You cannot believe that I have teeth . . . there. I mean—you already know better." Impossibly, I blushed, recalling how he'd touched me.

Some of the polished implacability of his expression softened and he pressed a kiss to my temple. "Do I? It has puzzled me, what you guard in there so fiercely."

Not really the place to have this conversation, but with his rapid pace down the path giving us privacy, celebratory songs fading behind, the palace now rising above us, along with the looming prospect of what would happen once we gained our rooms, I'd better speak up. "I never have. Bedded anyone."

He gave me a quizzical look. "I know."

"You do?" How? Could he have felt it in my body? Perhaps my lack of experience showed.

"Yes. You waited for me as I waited for you."

Maybe I hadn't heard that right. Or the combination of heat, pain, excitement, and the impending crash of exhaustion from fighting through the last few hours had my brain muddled. I couldn't seem to do more than gape at him like an idiot.

"Understand?" He frowned, searching for words I knew. "I never have bedded anyone. You are for me. I am for you."

My turn to struggle for words. They'd all escaped my grasp, even the ones I thought I'd known well. "How—how can that . . ." I floundered utterly.

He misinterpreted my concern because he gave me another

kiss, this time under my ear, and murmured, "Don't worry. I know what to do."

That did it. I covered my face with my hands in utter consternation. It had been easy to agree to—no, to insist on—this step, up on the mountain, his life and throne hanging in the balance. Now there would be no backing out.

The welcome cool shadows of the palace enveloped us, the sweetly scented breezes from the gardens wafting over my heated skin, along with the oiled-wood aroma of the inlaid floors and ceilings. Familiar.

And entwined with the warmth and scent of this so-foreign man who claimed to have waited for me as I'd always felt I'd waited for someone. Impossible, and yet . . .

"Open, *mlai*," Nakoa said, and I dropped my hands, startled by his use of that intimate instruction in public. His eyes sparkled with humor at my reaction, however, and he dipped his chin at the doors to his rooms. "The latch," he added, pitching it with urgency.

At least my face couldn't get redder at this point. Oh, wait, yes it could.

Chief Tane caught up to us, along with several of his guard and others who seemed to be various nobility and elders. "We will witness!" he proclaimed, a nasty kind of lust in his gaze.

Oh, Danu. Please don't let it come to that. I directed the prayer to Danu, as Her bright blade seemed the most likely to cut through the twisted lies Tane spun. And Nakoa would belong to her, he being my support both figuratively and literally.

My dragon king, of course, came through for me, aided by Danu or not. "No. The outcome will not be in doubt. Go. Enjoy the fruits of our harvest." Nakoa's guard materialized around us, easing out of the crowd in the hallway with silent grace and grim purpose. They'd been with him all along, attending his signal. Not something to forget.

Tane surveyed them, clearly weighing his options, and Inoa appeared at his elbow, amazingly composed, regal and only slightly out of breath from catching up. She'd smoothed over her insulted fury and, very politely and with elaborate descriptions, invited him and everyone to a feast. Nakoa nudged me as she spoke, so I slipped a hand down to free the latch. We were inside, Nakoa's bulk against the door, so fast that Tane barely got out a protest.

"Lock it, *mlai*," Nakoa urged, and I was glad I'd had occasion to learn the mechanism that morning. He sighed with relief as the bolt slid into place, and moved away from the doors. "I shall owe my sister for this."

"Me too," I agreed fervently. Some shouts echoed outside the doors and someone pounded; then all went abruptly silent. Hopefully they wouldn't be listening. My gaze went to the open balcony windows, allowing in the blessed cross-ventilation—and, as Jepp had noted, anyone with the ability to climb.

"No worries," Nakoa said, following the direction of my thoughts. "We will remain alone. You are safe with me." He said something else that might have been about his guard.

"All right." I nodded, attempting a sanguinity I did not feel. "I suppose we'd best get this over with."

Nakoa studied my face and I realized I'd slipped into Common Tongue, likely using a tone that communicated a task to be completed, an unpleasant chore most easily dispensed with if done immediately, not allowing time for dread to build up. Which probably accurately conveyed how I felt. After all, if I'd lost my cursed virginity ages ago, I wouldn't have built up so much expectation and emotion around this act. All those years I simply hadn't been interested, that sense of waiting for the right moment that never arrived—had I been waiting for this?

You waited for me as I waited for you.

I'd learned a great deal more about magic in these last years than I'd ever expected to. I should have known the texts hadn't lied, no matter how extraordinary some of the tales. If people could change shape and Andi, someone I knew well, could forecast the future and wall off an entire realm with a thought, then I could be connected to a man I'd never met. Someone so impossibly far away that I would never have encountered him if events hadn't aligned exactly as they had. Some of which I'd influenced myself. Perhaps my plans had operated to bring me to this place, to Nakoa, when all along I'd thought I'd been working toward something else.

Hlyti, indeed.

21

Instead of taking me to the bed as I expected, Nakoa took me to the chair where I'd sat to play *kiauo*, just inside the balcony He went to get a bowl and filled it with water. As was his wont, he knelt on the floor, bringing us eye to eye. He maybe did it for that reason, aware of how his height and bulk intimidated me. With care he undid the ribbons holding up my stockings and slid them off, then picked up my feet one by one, examining the soles and gently washing them in the basin.

I hissed at the sting, then again when he slathered on the salve. They'd just been getting better, too. The protection of the stockings had helped, but only so much. I reached to pick one up off the floor. They'd burned through, great ragged holes in the knit. Nakoa pinched a few of the straggling yarns together, shaking his head at the destruction, then looked up at me.

"Sorry for your stockings."

It made me smile, his concern for something he knew I valued that did not belong in his world. Moved, I sat up more, tossed the ruined bits away, and leaned to brush a finger over his cheek, as he liked to do to me. "No sorry, Nakoa."

He shared the smile, but it carried a sorrowful edge. "Yes sorry. This." He touched my shredded stockings, then over my heart, and to the bed. "All this. I do not wish you unhappily defeated."

The term he used came from playing *kiauo*, meaning to lose the game. He meant that he had not wanted to force me—though he'd made that abundantly clear—and had concern that I'd been cornered into this. Which, in truth, I had. But the stakes were hardly worth it. My virginity, even if it meant being sealed forever into this marriage, didn't compare to a man's life and the well-being of an entire people. A lot of people, judging by the size and spread of Nakoa's island kingdom.

"It's not important," I told him. "A small thing."

He didn't like that and frowned at me. "It's not small. This is a big, most important thing."

For some reason a joke that Jepp liked to tell ran through my head, one where lovers argued about two different issues, the man believing she insulted the size of his member and he insisting it *was* a big thing. I couldn't help it—I giggled. Then, at the incredulous consternation on Nakoa's face, broke out into a full laugh. His puzzlement only made me laugh harder, until I was pressing my hands to my belly, a few tears of laughter squeezing from the corners of my eyes. A release, I supposed, of the tension and fears of the day.

By the time I composed myself, out of breath and far more relaxed, Nakoa wore a full smile, along with his bafflement. "I do not understand," he said.

"I know." I shook my head at myself. "I'm full of emotions these days." I put my hand over my heart. "I feel so much, so strongly, that I . . . I do not understand."

He sobered, nodding wisely, laying his hand over mine. "You are full of fire and fury, like a dragon trapped in her cave. This is to be expected."

Not how anyone had ever described me. And uncannily close to my childhood entombment. Enough to make me catch my breath at the dank, unsettling memory of blackness and trickling water.

"What troubles you?" he asked, searching my face as if he could read the memory in it. This was what he'd asked me after I struck him in my anger and panic. "Is it me?"

"No." Well, not really "no," exactly, and it wasn't fair to him to lie. "Yes. I mean . . . Ergh! I don't have the words." I'd curled my fingers in frustration and he took my hand in both of his, carefully uncurling them as he'd done when he laid my little dagger in my palm, then sealed it between his. Not trapped, but held.

"Try," he suggested.

"Shouldn't we be—" I gestured at the bed with my free hand.

He shook his head. "We have until morning. Find your words."

And it was only late afternoon. All right, then. *Find your words.* It sounded so simple, but I lacked the knowledge I needed to explain the enormity of how I felt. Perhaps even to myself, to be honest. If only I had my list of Nahanaun words. But I'd left my journal in the library and there would be no risking facing Tane and his cronies to get it now. I acutely felt the lack of it, my best fence against the world.

What lurked in the dark corners of my soul—and why did that place feel like the hole where I'd been trapped? Maybe I'd left a piece of myself behind in it, as if the girl I'd been had actually died there, entombed with the rest of her family, and I was . . . some sort of shape-shifted alternate form. Like in Zynda's metaphor, my real self stayed in some other realm, living on a trickle of rainwater, while I used her shape to move about the world, a part of me forever trapped and under siege.

Ursula had been speaking to this, when she tried to explain that it took courage to let another person in, to open up enough to allow for the possibility of loving in return. Though this challenge wasn't about love. I was much too old and cynical to believe in that fairy tale; my fence of knowledge worked far too well for that. This was about opening. Odd to recall that had been one of the first words of Nakoa's I'd understood.

He watched me as I read a book in a language I only partially understood, as if he could divine my thoughts from my expression, which maybe he could.

"When I was a girl, the palace, my family home, was . . . attacked." It wasn't exactly the right word, but I shaded it with the disaster and storm tonalities and Nakoa nodded thoughtfully. I kept going, using Nahanaun where I could, resorting to Common Tongue where I had to, so I wouldn't lose courage. "I don't remember very much except the awfulness of the siege, how afraid and angry everyone was. Boredom and moments of stark terror. Being hungry." Other, darker things that I didn't care to examine.

Nakoa squeezed my hand, dark eyes full of sympathy.

"I remember weeping and the shouts. People disappearing, never to return. The wounded, screaming in the night and the silence after somehow worse. Everybody died except me. The story is that a healer dug me out of a hidey-hole buried under rubble. Four days after the siege ended. I nearly died, they said, but it rained, so they think I lived on the rainwater that leaked through a crack. I don't remember it."

"You lived in a cave," Nakoa said, "and I sent you rain."

"You—what?" I reran his words in my head, checking my comprehension. How could he have known that? My practical-minded self insisted on the impossibility of such a thing. And yet . . .

"I saw you. Afraid. Death all around. Trapped and thirsty. I gave you rain." He explained it slowly, as if the simple words would make the extraordinary sound more sane.

"How?" I settled on the one word to express all of my incredulity.

"I am king." He shrugged at my scowl. "It is . . . within my power, even when I was only Inoa's little brother."

"You will always be Inoa's little brother," I retorted, making him laugh softly.

"Yes." He sobered. "And always *mlai* for Dafne."

I still didn't know how to assimilate that. "Show me the rain."

With a raised brow for my command, he gave me a slight smile. "Yes, my queen." He stood and went to the window, raising his hands to the sky. Thunder rumbled in the distance, then closer. The sunny afternoon dimmed, clouds gathering with unsettling alacrity. The air grew dense and thick with moisture, pressing against my ears until they popped. Rain began to fall, pattering down gently, growing stronger until the skies seemed to pour water.

The Nahanauns treat him like a god.

For the first time, I wondered if I'd completely misinterpreted and Nakoa could have swum in the lava and escaped unscathed. A sense of intense awe swept over me, my skin prickling with goose pimples. Though that could have been the coolness of the storm. Or the presence of magic, as with Andi or Zynda and their skin-crawling power. Regardless, the intimidated part of me fluttered, light wings of the beginning of panic.

Then Nakoa turned and grinned with boyish mischief. "Rain."

A smile broke out of me, wobbly from my uncertainty, but still elicited by his unabashed pleasure in showing off for me. "So I understand."

His expression shifted, perhaps observing my timidity. "See to understand." In three strides he had swept me up in his arms and carried me out into the rain. I shrieked as I never had in my life, half laughing, half in protest, as the rain immediately drenched me. I pushed at him, but Nakoa held me, laughing also in earnest delight, the rain running in rivulets over his dark skin, soaking his hair so the white streaks stood out in even greater contrast.

I found myself grinning like an idiot in return. "Rain," I agreed.

"For my queen," he replied, sobering, gaze going fiercely intent.

My heart skipped a beat, clenched, desire flaring deep inside at that look. "Did—did you make it rain last night, too, to keep us inside?" All the better to seduce me.

He didn't hesitate. "Yes. I needed to. Needed you. Understand? Open, Dafne *mlai.*" He kissed me, the rain slicking between us, conducting the desire that seemed to grow with every touch, each intimacy.

For a moment longer I quailed behind my walls, the near hysteria of the moments before tearing at me.

It takes courage to let another person in.

I'd learned fortitude, how to hunker down and survive the onslaught. But never how to open the gates again once the war had ended. A small thing, perhaps, for another woman. Huge for me. Feeling as if I laid my heart stripped bare, I dropped my walls, letting in the light. Freeing, perhaps, that other self, long trapped in that dank hole, fenced in as much as I'd fenced the world out. Releasing a dark and passionate flame I'd never known lived there.

Nakoa had given me rain. I would give him fire.

With a cry of longing, I gave into the kiss, into him, taking his hair in fistfuls, kissing him with all my might. For once I felt like the dragon he'd called me, ferocious, my wrath transmuted to passion. He inhaled me, mouth meeting mine with a long-starved hunger that managed to feed my own, groaning in a way that articulated my own need. I'd been wandering the world in search of this. Physically, in my circumscribed way. Mentally . . . I'd scoured all the universe of knowledge seeking this moment, this vital connection to another human being.

Maybe I had been looking for him after all.

I didn't know and, more, I'd lost the ability to think. Impatient to be even closer, I pressed to him, as if we could merge the margins of our bodies and become one being. He felt it, too, tearing

244 • Jeffe Kennedy

at my clothes to bare my breasts. The sound of fabric ripping echoed the fraying of my boundaries and I embraced it, shrugging out of the torn cloth and melding my rain-drenched skin to his. We burned together, tongues tangled, hearts pounding in that now-familiar synchronicity.

Needing to touch him more, I turned in his arms, wrapping my legs around his waist, my core, as wet as the rain but burning hotter than liquid rock through thin silk, pressed against his ridged abdomen. It felt glorious.

It wasn't enough.

I tore my mouth away, gasping for air I hadn't noticed I lacked till that moment. "Nakoa *mlai*."

This time, he didn't question it. "Yes, Dafne *mlai*."

He carried me inside, to the great bed, and dropped us both upon it, uncaring of how we dampened the soft sheets. Or how they tangled between us as we rolled, over and around each other, kissing with the desperation of long-separated lovers. My garland broke, the petals shredding a pale fragrant cascade over the white sheets, gleaming with florid luminescence where they stuck to his dark skin. I picked one off his shoulder, following with my tongue, licking Nakoa's skin as his mouth fastened on my throat. Salt and sweet combined, flagrantly masculine flavors simmering with the fragility of the crushed blossoms.

He groaned as I licked at him, pressing my head to him with his hand. Loving the sound, and that I could evoke it from him, I bit, taking the satin skin and the bulge of muscle between my teeth. Growling louder, he returned the favor, sinking his white teeth into the juncture at my neck and shoulder. I cried out, releasing him and arching against the exquisite sensation. Taking advantage of the opportunity, his hands roved over me, ripping away the last of my tattered gown. The pantalets went with a snap that snagged my attention. Automatically, I moved to cover myself, but Nakoa brushed my hands away with gentle urging.

"Let me see you," he murmured. "I need to see." *See to under-stand.*

Sitting up and turning me on my back, he trailed light fingers over the length of my body, tracing the curves and hollows. Expression intent, he examined every inch of me, lifting my wrists and stretching my arms above my head to drape across the bed. I felt full of languid grace, the fire boiling in my veins but coaxed into channels with every brush of his hand. I lost my shyness in the utter sensuality of it, splayed naked before him in the rain-filtered light.

"I like these." He caressed the constellation of freckles below my collarbones, where the sun found me. "Where they are and where they are not."

True to that, he paid equal attention to my freckled extremities as to the pale inner curve of my elbow, the hollow under my arm, the curve of my breast, the rounded slope of my belly, and the curling hair over my mound. He stroked me without opening my thighs, savoring the texture with a smile of curiosity. Then continued on his journey, learning the round of my thighs, the narrowing of my ankles, taking a moment to study the abused soles of my feet.

"Painful?" he asked, brushing the side of my foot, and I shook my head, mute with wonder over being touched—even worshipped—like this. Maybe I'd feel it later, but for now the only thing that mattered was this sweet, transporting seduction. With a sly smile, he replaced his fingers with his mouth, kissing the top of my foot, then the hollow by my ankle bone.

In this way he worked his way back up my body, caressing first with light fingers, then molding with full hands and following with his mouth. Again, he did not part my thighs, though he kissed the hair on my mound, moving on to trace the line of my hip bone with his tongue. I shifted restlessly, the urge to have him touch me more intimately, to be inside me, rising with fierce-edged intensity. He prevented me, though, sitting over me so his knees pinned my thighs together, sliding slickly now.

"Nakoa." I breathed his name, a plea in it, writhing as much as I could and grasping at his knees. With a slow shake of his head he took my wrists and moved them back over my head, holding them there in one hand as he resumed his slow perusal of my body. Before long, every part he kissed felt as alive and sensitive as every other. The underside of my breast as much as the taut nipple above it. The pulse beat in my throat, the hollow under my arm, the inside of my wrist. He finished kissing each finger, drawing them in one by one to torment with his teeth and tongue, and I held my breath, hoping that this would complete his journey. Indeed, he returned to my mouth, lavishing me with a deep kiss that cleaved me open.

I had no secret shadows anymore, it seemed. All of me, every quiver, breath, moan, and shaking sigh, spoke of things without words. He pulled them in, took me in.

Then turned me over and started anew.

He laughed, a soft chuckle at my cry of frustration, especially when I lost it in a sighing groan at the press of his mouth to the small of my back. Working his way up my spine with the same slow technique that unraveled me past imagining, he finally reached the back of my neck, moving my hair aside to kiss and nip at the tendons there.

It drove me wild. Enough so that he laid his weight on me, pressing my palms flat to the bed as he ravished my neck and my senses. In that position his cock thrust hard against the back of my thigh, hot through his thin garment. Not above payback, I wriggled against it, hoping also to urge him on. With a sharper bite of reproof, he moved his hips away, then took himself back down my body, leaving me to curl my fingers in the sheets and moan helplessly as he found each new secret place that undid me that much more.

The dimple of my buttocks.

The unscathed arch of my foot.

The thrice-damned backs of my knees.

At some point I gave up trying to urge him on. I might as well schedule the rain. He kept at me until I melted utterly, completely pliant to the least caress. When he stretched over my back again, hands over mine, mouth on my sensitive nape, his weight somehow gloriously satisfying, it took me a moment to realize he'd shed his *kylte* and lay naked against me.

I moaned and he hummed, matching my tone and following the undulation of my body. Sliding his hands beneath me, he gathered my breasts in one hand and slid the other into the desperate heat between my thighs.

I'd been on the edge of climax for so long, had become this single throbbing organ of sexuality, that it almost didn't matter— his touch there no more devastating than any other. But he slipped a finger inside my slick channel and pressed his hand tightly against the rest of my sex, rocking there. Then he pinched my nipple and bit the juncture of my neck and shoulder. Hard.

I came apart in glory. Like the dragon exploding from the volcano, soaring to numinous heights, anchored by Nakoa's body, wrapped around me in relentless warmth.

Before I regained myself, another surge pushed me up, his hand giving me no surcease, two fingers inside me now, driving the ache to be filled as he murmured florid words in my ear that meant nothing to me, but still burned with unquenched fire. I buried my face in the sheets, gripping as if to hold myself to the earth, and this time he let me spread my legs, meeting at least that one urge. Shattering again, this time I cried out his name, begging him for more, for anything.

Still in the throes of the climax, I felt him turn me over, but his face so close to mine took me by surprise. As did the brief glimpse of his large cock as he positioned himself between my thighs. Goddesses, would it—

I lost the apprehension in the drowning kiss he lavished on me, desire washing away whatever I'd been thinking. Our hearts pounded together, echoed by that third great heart. Together. This was Nakoa, and I clung to him, digging my nails into his muscled shoulders, opening myself to him, welcoming the hard intrusion against my opening. He stretched me wider and I tensed, but he spread a hand against the small of my back, lifting me so the angle of my hips changed and he thrust inside me.

All at once.

Flashing pain. Astounding ecstasy.

Filling me as I'd never been, skin to skin. As if I'd carried a hollow space that could be completed only in this way. A wracking shudder took me, my breath rattling in panting mews. No, the island rocked, the bed swaying as if we lay in one of the *Hákyrling*'s rope hammocks.

Nakoa levered himself up, seeming not to notice, face set in lines of ferocious determination. He withdrew slightly, then pumped in again, sending ripples of fire through me, forcing a cry of strangled pleasure from my mouth.

A cry echoed by the nearby trumpet of the dragon.

Slowly, picking up pace, Nakoa thrust in and out, bracing himself on one arm and holding my hips with the other. Each stroke inside me sent ripples from my center outward. Circles of brightening light that radiated to my toes, fingertips, even the tips of my hair. I held on to his shoulders, receiving him over and over. If the volcano erupted, if the island broke apart beneath us, none of it mattered.

Only this.

His body tightened, face going blood dark. He threw back his head and roared to the sky as he erupted inside me, the near violent thrusts of his body lifting me from the bed. I cried out with him, not with a climax, though it seemed I'd never quite stopped, but with the excruciatingly intense sense of connection. For a moment I saw myself through his eyes, damp and flushed, my eyes unnaturally bright, like amber jewels. And I saw the sky, the sea, the scatter of emerald islands amid the sapphire waters.

Blood surged through my heart, air pumping into my lungs with each massive stroke of my wings.

I flew. I flew so high the blue sky darkened to black and Danu's stars glittered in unforgiving icy points. Moranu's moon and Glorianna's sun danced a waltz around our world of ocean and island. I flew under. I had no air to breathe.

Then I plummeted back to earth.

22

I gasped for air.

With a murmur of apology, the hot weight crushing me moved. Nakoa turned onto his side, keeping an arm around me, pulling me close as he leaned his forehead against mine and withdrew from my body. Bereft of his intrusion, my woman's passage closed with an aching sting. I hissed at it and Nakoa drew the sound from my mouth with a soft, searching kiss.

"Sorry?" he asked.

"No sorry," I managed. I sounded ragged, so I smiled and kissed him, edging closer, pleased when he draped a heavy thigh over my hip. We lay there, breaths evening out, hearts slowing but still thumping in synced rhythm. The island did not rock or sway, but we were sticky, the bedsheets damp and tangled. Unabated, the rain poured outside the windows, the room fading to gray with no lamps or torches lit.

Now what?

"Did it . . . the dragon?"

Nakoa leaned up on his elbow, propping his head on one fist. "She is pleased." He brushed a finger over my heart, following the curve of my left breast. "Do you not feel her?"

I did. Or I felt something. Nothing that made sense to my mind. The repletion of my body, however, communicated a deep sense of balance and rightness. Whatever the future might bring, I would carry something of the ultimate peace of this moment with me. What lay between me and Nakoa might not be meant to last. He had duties to his throne and people, me to my queen and people. I would never be the woman to throw away my responsibilities for pleasure, no matter how keen, regardless of how this man dressed it up as a fateful star-crossed connection.

His life and throne were secured. Whatever brought me to this moment, naked, sweat soaked, body throbbing from a literally earthshaking sexual encounter, I was glad of it. No wonder Jepp thrived on sex so, if it was all like this.

Though I doubted it was. This had been extraordinary. Even if it couldn't possibly last. I couldn't stay here, trapped on these islands, so far from everyone and everything I'd ever known, turning my back on the promises I'd made and meant with all my being. And, obviously, Nakoa could never leave. The day would come when I'd have to go and we'd part, probably with acrimony. Hopefully without violence. He wouldn't forgive or understand, knowing him, but I'd have this memory to sustain me regardless.

Nakoa touched my bottom lip, tugging it down. "Why do you have sorrow?"

"I'm not. I'm happy." My stomach growled and I clapped a hand to it, grateful for an excuse to turn away from his too discerning gaze. "And hungry. And sticky. Safe to call servants—food, a bath?"

He cocked his head, as if listening for something. "Yes, *mlai*, but I shall do so."

"Fine by me." I waited for him to get up, then straightened the sheets so I could crawl under one. He did not bother to dress again, striding naked to the doors. I'd seen drawings of nude men, artistic sketches that lovingly detailed the masculine lines of a muscled back and flexing buttocks. Seeing it in the flesh . . . well, naturally, it stirred me in a different way. But I'd also not expected a man to be beautiful. Sinuous and simmering with vitality.

I'd noticed before that Nakoa's tattoos extended over his back as well, but had not had occasion to observe that they tapered into a scaled tail that wrapped around his hip and ended in a bladed point over the crest of his right buttock. Dragon king.

He spoke to someone through the opening of the doors, waited a moment, then took something and shut the doors again. When he turned to me, I caught my breath at the sight of him. I'd seen his chest plenty of times, but not the way his abdominal muscles narrowed, like an arrow pointing to his cock, hanging heavy from a nest of lightning-streaked black hair. Difficult to believe that had been inside me, though the growing ache there gave testament to it.

Yet still, I dampened for him, my body apparently lacking all mindfulness.

His eyes glittered black with intent as he crossed to me, a fresh garland in his hands, to replace the one whose tattered remnants scattered over the bed. "*Mlai*," he said, holding it out, the barest hint of a question in it. Holding the sheet over my naked breasts, I sat up and let him drape it over my head, moved by the ritual. He held my gaze, male satisfaction in his eyes, but also a level of affection I hadn't expected. My heart throbbed as raw and tender as the place between my legs, as if he'd had me there also.

Which, I supposed, in a way he had, penetrating to the core of me. Ripping me asunder.

He handed me something, which I took automatically, then studied with some bemusement. The dragon torque. Fashioned of precious metals—gold, copper, and silver—forming exquisitely detailed overlapping scales. The dragon's eyes inset rubies that matched my own, that is, Salena's ruby. Nakoa watched me, waiting, and I looked for the hinge. Finding the catch, I opened it, and Nakoa, with a twitch of a smile, bowed his head. I still had to kneel up and hold the spring open with both hands, so the sheet fell away. Fitting it around his thick neck, I triggered the catch so it would lock into place.

Before I could withdraw, however, Nakoa wrapped his hands around my wrists, holding me there, the question in his eyes.

"*Mlai*," I whispered, as if saying it without force wouldn't bind me to him too strongly. As if I hadn't already lost that particular battle. He read something of that in my face, a line forming between his brows, but he nodded and let me go.

Then ducked his head to drop kisses on the upper curve of each breast. Taking hold of my hips, he lifted me and bent lower, placing a lingering, reverent kiss over my womb. Instead of the panicked rage, this time a deep sense of peace filled me, like an underground river filling in the cracks of my ragged soul.

I threaded my fingers through his hair, taking a moment to assess. I'd become a character in a story: bedded by a king, somehow connected to a dragon, buffeted by magic or fate—the same thing?—whatever had impossibly brought me here.

Or I was an imposter, dragged into a tale meant for a princess or sorceress. *You are no queen.* Even Kral knew that much. Perhaps I'd wake up in my chamber at Ordnung, a book creasing lines into my cheek. I'd write down as much of the dream as I could recall, and the parts I couldn't, I'd embellish. Though my imagination could hardly create a wilder tale than this.

Still holding me, Nakoa glanced up, surveying my expression. No doubt wary of an emotional fit as I'd had the last time he'd done that. But that particular earthquake had come and gone. If he hoped to get a child on me, he'd be disappointed. I would not be, as I knew better. Low expectations made an excellent defense against disappointment.

Someone tapped on the door and Nakoa let me dive under the covers, drawing the gauzy curtains around the bed for added privacy. This time he donned his kylte before letting in a stream of servants who carried a large copper-colored tub, buckets of water, and trays of food. I'd more than half expected Inoa, with or without her ladies, but they were likely off entertaining Chief Tane and his cronies. That's what I'd be doing, were I in her position.

Did they know we'd consummated the marriage? Hopefully there would be no display of the sheets, as some of the Twelve did, retaining that barbaric custom of old. Ours were satisfactorily bloody and would have to be changed. I fingered one of the smears, contemplating cleaning it myself.

Nakoa banished all the servants and they slipped out as silently as they'd arrived, giving me a glimpse of his warriors standing guard in the hall, faces carefully averted. He locked it behind them, then came to get me.

"I think I can walk," I said, wrapping the top sheet around me. I slid off the bed, pausing a moment to test my feet—stiff, but barely at all sore—and Nakoa's gaze went to the bloodied sheets as well. He stopped me with a hand on my arm. "Are you well?"

"Yes." Chagrined by this level of exposure, I ducked my face. Of course he lifted my chin with a finger, studying me with a dubious expression.

"I hurt you."

"Nakoa." I laid a hand on his chest, the glittering scales so satin smooth, despite the trick to the eye. As marmoreal as any of the sculptures decorating the palace and harbor, but living flesh. "You gave me pleasure, too. Though I don't understand how you knew how to do it so well."

One side of his mouth tipped up. "There are ways of knowing without doing, yes?"

"The story of my life," I commented in Common Tongue, needing that phrase to satisfy the wryness of my feelings. He couldn't have understood, but he seemed amused and took my hand, lacing his fingers with mine before walking with me to the bath. At some point I would become accustomed to the difference in our sizes, but for the moment my hand felt dwarfed in his. Surprising, really, that we'd fit as well as we had, sexually. But then, he'd been careful of me.

Had been from the beginning. Something to remember.

I had to climb over the tub rim, it stood so high, Nakoa keeping my hand to balance me. Despite the earlier cleansing, myriad cuts and burns on my feet briefly stung. With determined swiftness, I submerged myself, using the cover of water and Nakoa's convenient inattention to scrub the blood and other fluids from my now quite sore nether parts. He turned back with a carafe of his favored liquor and a pair of beautiful glasses, handing them both to me to hold as he poured.

The bowls of the goblets were wide, fitting into my cupped palms, crystal clear. On them, dragons formed of metallic-gold glass climbed up one side, tails wound around the stems, bat wings wrapped around the bowls and chins propped on the rim, inset ruby eyes glinting. Amazingly clever.

And special. Crafted for this occasion, I suspected.

Nakoa dropped his *kylte* and stepped into the tub, surprising me, though it shouldn't have. Big as he was, there was still room for us both. He took one goblet from me and clinked it against mine. "To our prosperous future," he said.

"Yes," I answered, guilt digging at me that I made it seem as if I planned to stay. My tone came through, or it wasn't enough, because he frowned slightly. Thrice-damn it that diplomacy failed me now, when I needed it most. I knew how to lie convincingly. It should be easy to repeat back his toast and make it sound sincere. But I couldn't bring myself to do it, so I sipped instead, offering him a smile I hoped would be more convincing.

I would have to do better, in the days to come.

In the morning, I awoke from a sleep so deep that I couldn't remember where I was. Annfwn? Not Ordnung. Not with the tropical breezes flowing in from the open sunny windows, the fragrance sweet as honey on the tongue. The sheer white netting around the bed shimmered. Nahanau. Nakoa. I didn't regret the choices of the day before, but . . . how complicated could this situation get? I groaned softly, closing my eyes.

Nakoa's arm came around my waist, pulling my back against his chest as he nuzzled my neck, unerringly finding one of the places that went straight through me. Another sound escaped me, this one darker, full of need that sprang full-fledged to life.

"Better," he murmured against my skin. He palmed my naked breasts and slid his other hand down my belly. "Sore?"

"Some," I answered on a sigh, not really caring as my body hummed from sleep to heated arousal. Somewhere in the back of my mind, thoughts worried together restlessly. I didn't care about them either. Turning in Nakoa's warm embrace, I snuggled up against his chest, delighting in the way our legs tangled together and how easily our mouths found each other. We'd become more practiced at fitting and, at moments like this, moving into touching him felt like coming home.

For once, the idea of home didn't dart around my mind dragging a train of jagged memories, the kind that hissed and slithered along.

"Let me see," Nakoa said against my mouth, softening the deep kiss into a series of smaller, sweet ones. He rolled onto his back and, grasping me by the waist, lifted me.

"Nakoa!" I squealed his name, laughing, grabbing for his forearms to keep from tipping over. Then gasped in far too maidenly shock as he positioned me so I straddled his head. He'd seen me there before, but in the bright light of morning . . .

"Beautiful," he murmured, holding me still with one hand and opening my sex with gentle fingers of the other. I squirmed, gasping, not from pain, but from the delicious sensation of his touch. He lowered me, licking with utmost delicacy, eyes flicking up to my face. "Sore?" he asked again.

"No," I breathed. I would have lied convincingly for that, so he wouldn't stop.

He grunted in approval, then set to exploring me with his

mouth. I went dizzy, leaning my palms against the polished wall of braided golden wood, anchored by that, his arm around my waist, and the decadently wicked work of his lips, tongue, and teeth. Within bare minutes, I was panting, crying his name, bucking wildly.

The orgasm took me harder than I expected, my vision going momentarily dark, the spinning in my head from Nakoa lowering me to the bed again, cozying me in his arms. I started to roll onto my back, expecting the rest, but he stilled me. The tang of disappointment also surprised me.

"What's wrong?" I asked.

"Too sore." He stroked my cheek. "We have all the prosperous future."

Thrice-damn me and my guilt. We'd had full intercourse only the once. I'd been relieved the night before, especially as the sting of my torn tissues made themselves known. We'd played several games of *kiauo*—and I nearly won twice. But then we'd simply gone to sleep, Nakoa seeming as drowsy as I.

Now I wanted that again, him inside me and our bodies joined. If only to stop the plaguing thoughts that I would inevitably wound him when I left. Something he'd just as inevitably take as a betrayal, though I'd never asked for any of this.

Still, his cock thrust against my thigh, large and hot—and the prospect of it abrading me again did seem like a bit much. Curious, as I hadn't had the opportunity to explore him as he had me, I pushed away from him and dragged the sheet down, the sheer white cloth a lovely backdrop for his dark skin. Bemused, Nakoa watched me, willingly rolling onto his back when I nudged him, then closed his eyes with a groan when I wrapped my hand around his shaft.

It probably wasn't appropriate to be taking mental notes, but his organ fascinated me. So long and hard, compared to my oyster and pearl. His skin was even silkier there, moving subtly in my grip over the turgid tissues beneath. My fingers barely encompassed his girth and I marveled anew that he'd fit inside me, knowing what

I did of my own shape and size. But then, I'd watched Ami give birth, the babies' heads far larger. A woman's channel was meant to stretch, it seemed.

Looser, more ruffled skin like my own sex, covered the head, easily pulled back to reveal the darker, slicked skin beneath. I checked Nakoa's expression to be sure I wasn't hurting him, though he hadn't moved to stop me, and the set, even tense expression arrested me. "Painful?" I asked and his eyes flew open, the black as hard and bright as diamonds.

"Not how you mean," he said, voice rough.

Encouraged, I rolled the skin down to expose him, running a fingertip over the pearly seed that swelled from the slit at the top. Curious, I tasted it with a flick of my tongue and Nakoa rumbled, his hand coming up to tangle in my hair. I tried it again, swirling my tongue over him as he'd done to me, judging my success at pleasuring him by the tightening of his fingers. But I wanted to do it right, to give him what I could in bed, so he'd have some pleasant memories of me, to compete with the sour. I shouldn't care, but I did.

"Have you done this before?" I asked, and he nodded carefully. I had to kick aside the ridiculous flare of jealousy at imaging the lovely Nahanaun girls doing this for him. "Show me what to do."

Gently, he wrapped his hand over mine on his shaft, showing me how to move it up and down, much harder than I had been, all the while watching me with his obsidian gaze. "And this?" I asked, using my tongue.

With a light touch, he held my hair and thrust farther into my mouth, so my lips surrounded him. I sucked him in deeper and he made a growling sound, his hips flexing. I couldn't get him far into my mouth, but the more I did the more he liked it, his palm going hot over my hand as I stroked up and down, no longer guiding me, more hanging on. He thrummed under my touch and I tasted the giddy sense of power at having him thus harnessed.

"*Mlai*," he gasped, body going tense, fingers going tight in my hair almost painfully—except that the pull shot straight to my groin, already aroused again from ministering to him. No wonder he hadn't minded so much, those evenings he'd played my body and received no satisfaction in return. In response, knowing how it had felt for me, I intensified my efforts.

He climaxed, calling my name, hips and thighs bucking beneath me, much as I'd done only a bit ago. His seed spilled salt and sweet across my tongue, tasting like another variation of his skin, of new life and the fertile sea.

Letting go of my hair, he seized my arms and dragged me up along his body, bringing me to his mouth like he would a goblet, kissing me with a passionate fervor that left me shaken. He'd taste himself on my lips and tongue—but then so would I my own body. An odd realization, but it seemed right, that we would intertwine in this way. A way I'd never imagined possible for myself.

I returned the kiss, drowning in him, threading my fingers through his hair as he'd done with me, holding him captive and close. All mine. He held me with same fierce zeal.

For once, we understood each other perfectly well.

23

A preemptory knock sounded on the chamber doors, somehow so essentially Inoa that I snorted out a laugh. Nakoa grinned in response, shaking his head in some exasperation, but he also gave me one last kiss and, tucking the sheet around me, got out of bed and donned his *kylte*. Glancing at me to be sure I was ready, he unlocked the door, stepping aside for an impatient Inoa and a stream of ladies bearing various burdens—including more buckets of water for another bath. Sticky again, I would not refuse that.

She kissed him on one cheek, patted the other, and told him to go to some other place I hadn't heard of before to bathe and ready for the day. The tones she used sounded like she anticipated it would be a long one, and not happily so. Nakoa endured her instructions with his usual affectionate patience, but didn't leave immediately. Instead he brought me a fresh garland, cupping the back of my head and kissing me deeply after placing it around my neck. With my body so freshly roused from the recent play, my heart accelerated and I had to restrain a moan of desire. Nakoa pulled away with a pleased—and mischievous—smile, so I thumped his chest.

"Oh, go on," I muttered, not dimming his smile one iota.

He stopped to kiss Inoa on the cheek, and left the room in great good humor, singing a cheerful tune even as his guard snapped to attention outside. The door closed and Inoa turned to me with an expression of gladness, clasping her hands together and bowing deeply.

"Thank you, my queen, for all you've given us. The future is gloriously bright."

I shifted, uncomfortable with her gratitude. I hadn't done a thing but indulge in an amazing sexual encounter with the most compelling man I'd ever met. One I intended to walk away from as soon as I could secure my freedom. Leaving the sheets behind, resolved not to give the bloodstains on them another thought, I climbed into the tub and sank in, thanking the maid who offered even more hot water.

It felt good to soak and even better when one of the ladies expertly washed my hair. It seemed to be longer, though that shouldn't be possible. They toweled me dry and rubbed oil into my skin. Apparently the tending hadn't been all due to my invalid status. Once again, Inoa and her ladies fell into a pattern of friendly chatter, assuming I could not understand. Much of it, in truth, I couldn't quite parse, as they did not attempt to go slowly or choose words I already knew, as Nakoa so thoughtfully did. They also spoke in a less formal, more casual shorthand, what I interpreted as familiar language.

Mostly they discussed the events of the day before, and the interminable challenge of entertaining so many guests. Chief Tane seemed to be spreading dissent, something that annoyed Inoa greatly. There was a continued problem of some islands being out of contact, again a mention of birds.

None of them had any doubt over what had happened between Nakoa and me. The dragon flew in the sky, which heralded the return of a golden era. That last using the same word and intonation I interpreted as "beautiful." Several of the women commented on my great good luck, and I tried not to contemplate which of those casting me envious glances from their liquid dark eyes had been ones to taste Nakoa as I had—or to tutor him into knowing how to pleasure a woman's body so well. A ridiculously possessive concern to have—and not at all like me. Particularly regarding a man I had no intention of keeping. I knew well that jealousy was a sign of insecurity, but then . . . I'd never been all that secure in the realm of sex. Or men. Might as well face that.

Still, I wished I knew what drew Nakoa to me. Magic? Fate? Something else entirely? Such a stretch to believe he'd recognized me on the ship because he'd somehow seen me before. And that he'd sent me rain so I could live, three decades before. Andi was able to scry long-distance, and into the future, but she'd never said how that worked. She had recognized Harlan from visions, however.

Possible, I supposed, that a wizard king who could make it rain could also have seen me from afar.

Though that still didn't address why me, some orphan girl of a minor noble family of a people and culture entirely different from his own. If we were connected, how could that be?

Perhaps Akamai could assist. Surely something in the library would give some clues. I made a mental list of where I'd look first, as soon as the ladies set me free.

But it was not to be, alas—which became rapidly clear as the ladies laid out what I was to wear. Apparently I'd advanced to a new level, a further step from my former self, and deeper into Nakoa's world. All the better to immerse myself, I kept in mind, stilling the uneasiness as the ladies dressed me in a light skirt of copper silk panels that hung low on my hips, caught there by a girdle of golden chains. They gave me breast plates of a similar shade, tooled with intricate scales, along with arm and ankle bands of twining dragons, much like Nakoa's.

While two of the ladies set to work decorating my hands and

feet with a red-black dye, drawing intricate designs on me, Inoa herself brushed my hair, attempting one of the elaborate braids I'd seen on some of the other women.

"Like silk," she said, both admiring and frustrated as the fine stuff slipped away from her efforts. "Pretty, but too short, yes? It will grow."

"Perhaps in the prosperous future," I agreed, to keep her happy. I knew well how impossible my hair was to style, which was why I never let it get past shoulder length. It always immediately fell out of any coil I tried to put it in. Eventually Inoa gave up, settling for weaving in flowers that matched my garland.

"King Nakoa KauPo says you can walk?" She spoke slowly and formally, frowning in earnest concentration. I nearly broke down and let her know that I could understand better than she thought, but circumspection won out. I learned a great deal from listening to their conversations. Look at me—perhaps I made a decent spy after all.

"Yes, thank you, Inoa." I started to bow to her, partly to expatiate my guilt and apologize for the injury she had no idea I gave her.

She stopped me, though. "No, no! Queen." She raised her eyebrows significantly and bowed deeply to me. "See?"

Inoa showed me the final result in a mirror the ladies brought carefully in, the frame distinctly Dasnarian in design. A precious import, then. The image in it looked equally exotic. Though I was still fair-skinned in comparison to the Nahanauns, and despite the days spent indoors recuperating, I'd tanned a fair amount, my skin a golden brown shades lighter than my hair, though my freckles remained darker points. The gold jewelry echoed similar sunstreaks in my hair, my brown eyes that had always been unremarkable picking up the shimmer of amber, eerily evoking a memory of the dragon, sailing silently down the volcanic air. I looked as wild and barbaric as Nakoa—and perhaps as queenly as I'd badgered Ursula into looking.

Advanced in rank due to one night of wild sex. The way of the world in some places, but still it rankled. I'd done nothing like my true queens had done to deserve their kingdoms. They could dress me up as a queen, but I would still be an imposter. *You are no queen.*

I'm having a big piece of jewelry stuck on my head, Ursula had said before the coronation. The one I'd meticulously crafted for dramatic effect on every level. Could she have felt this, too? She'd stared at herself in the mirror so long, so soberly, much like this. Looking for the truth of it in herself. Or seeing the lie in it.

I insisted on adding the knife belt Jepp had given me but allowed Inoa to adjust it so the drape fell along the same lines as the golden girdle. The only splash of red in the metallic scheme, the ruby seemed to be the one note that anchored me to home, to where I truly belonged.

Inoa accompanied me as we walked through the corridors, soon bound in a new direction that I suspected would be where Nakoa held court. Everyone we passed bowed deeply to me, making gestures of reverence and joy, murmuring blessings all shaded with tones conveying fruitfulness and prosperity.

How long before Ursula's ships would arrive? Days more, at best. It had taken us that long to get here and we'd moved far faster than most groups could, plus the weather would only have gotten worse. The *Hákyrling* had been gone three days—it could be that they still worked on navigating the barrier. Zynda might not have even made it to Annfwn yet. I could be playing this role for weeks more, Nakoa working his devastating magic on me every night. By the time rescue arrived, I might believe the lie.

If you don't want Ursula going to war over you—as she no doubt would—then you'll have to hold him off. However you manage it.

What was I going to do?

We entered an open-air hall, the grandest I'd yet seen, formed primarily of a thin gold-and-copper arching roof, held up by pillars of carved obsidian. All dragons, in various sinuous poses. People—all of higher rank, by their clothing and jewelry—stood assembled, grouped in various contingents according to the colors they wore. They bowed in a rippling wave as I entered, Inoa falling back to trail behind me.

At the front of the hall, Nakoa stood from a throne woven of living vines and branches, all in flower. The typically stern lines of his face radiated pride and affection as I walked toward him, uncomfortably aware of how like and not like Ordnung's throne room this was. If any of those courtiers saw me at this moment, they'd shout me down for being presumptuous, for rising above my station. *Little better than a servant.* More than one person, even Ami, had said as much. For it was the simple truth.

As I drew closer, I spotted Akamai, seated at a table near the companion throne to Nakoa's, my journal and other papers neatly stacked there. He gave me a deep obeisance, driving home the irony of the moment. I should be sitting at that table, taking notes and observing the goings on, not . . . whatever I'd be doing.

As they'd all clearly waited on my arrival.

Nakoa took my hand and guided me to the throne on his right. With my back to everyone else, I gave him a suspicious frown, which he ignored, settling me in my seat and keeping my hand in his. The chairs were truly works of art. Ursula's had been carved to look like this, but these seemed to grow out of the ground. The floor, of inlaid wood in intricate patterns that mimicked dragon scales, radiated out from the sturdy trunks, densely interwoven, but seemingly rooted in actual soil.

Irreverently, especially considering how solemn the occasion seemed to be, I wondered about the servant assigned the task of watering and grooming the thrones. Near the hand not held by Nakoa, a blossom like those in my garland fluttered in some wayward draft, the ruffled petals moving almost like the wings of a butterfly. If only I could snatch my journal from Akamai and take a moment to sketch it.

But no. Far less enjoyable, Chief Tane stepped up before the thrones. He dipped in a bow that barely met the demands of their usual customs, his demeanor polite on the surface but seething beneath. I'd had no opportunity to discuss strategy ahead. If Nakoa wanted me up here playing queen, then he'd have to spend some time filling me in on the politics.

"King Nakoa KauPo," Tane began in a ringing voice, one he apparently loved the sound of.

"And Queen Dafne Nakoa KauPo," Nakoa corrected, steel in his tone that he'd lacked the day before. I risked a quick glance at him. Though his grip on my hand remained relaxed, even gently protective, his expression had gone as thunderous as I'd ever seen. Enough that I must have flinched, because he turned his head slightly to take my measure, then lightly stroked the hand he held.

Tane had more spine than I, because he added the greeting to me without missing a step, and with no apologetic tones. "What assurance do you bring that . . ."

I began to lose the thread of his remarks, though I picked out that he spoke of me and the dragon. More about tests of the ancestors. Missing islands. Important information for me to understand—and I needed to devote my mind to parsing a strategic response, not verb tense. Having enough of this, I gestured Akamai to my side. Tane paused, puffing in affront, though I'd been subtle in my movement. In Ordnung, such a thing would have caused no offense. Had I misstepped?

I looked to Nakoa, who only watched me with interest. The tamped-volcanic fury there behind his opaque gaze still, but not focused at me.

"Akamai will translate for me," I told him quietly enough that no one but the three of us could overhear. Not sure how Nakoa would take his secret being revealed, but figuring I'd be better off for laying it on the table. "Via Dasnarian. Subject to your . . .

pleasure," I substituted, not certain of the phrasing for acknowledging his ultimate authority to deny me.

A glimmer of warmth showed in his eyes, the human variety rather than the harder, volcanic kind, and he bent his head close to mine. "You are my pleasure, *mlai*." He turned back to Tane and gestured to him to continue. Considering the permission implicit, I beckoned Akamai closer and he began whispering the translation.

Between Tane's oratorical embellishments—he was making quite the speech—and Akamai's less than perfectly fluent Dasnarian, this method fell short of ideal, but I got more than I would have otherwise. Tane acknowledged that Nakoa and I had attracted the dragon, but he questioned our ability to keep her from "going wild," which I took to mean rampaging through the population. Fortunate for me to have a delay on processing that accusation, as I had no idea how to tame or restrain a dragon. Or what one ate. Meat, certainly, but . . . human? Big as she was, wouldn't she need a lot of food, as in big animals?

Tane went on, citing a long list of trials in Nakoa's kingdom, reminding me very much of the Aerron ambassador Laurenne's propensity for waxing on in excruciating detail about her kingdom's woes. Not that she wasn't justified, but she seemed to think that repeating the information enough times would produce the result she wanted. Perhaps it had, as Ursula's first request of Andi had been to send rain to Aerron.

His pet topic seemed to be that some of the islands in the archipelago had not been in contact. Apparently this had happened in their history—with islands sinking into the sea, never heard from again. Messenger birds returned with their missives undelivered. The great satisfaction of finally understanding what they discussed dimmed considerably as I realized what had occurred. Almost certainly the magical barrier had cut off those islands. Something Ursula had specifically told me not to discuss with Nakoa, goddesses take it.

Nakoa, now my lover, if not husband and king. How could I be loyal to both? A headache glimmered to life behind my eyebrows.

It quickly became clear that Tane aimed to undermine Nakoa's rule by implying that he knew not of his people's suffering and had not bestirred himself to see their troubles for himself, or done anything to ascertain the fate of these islands, because he'd secluded himself in the palace.

Devoting himself to caring for, and then seducing, the tender-footed foreign witch.

Akamai downplayed that last in his translation, but I caught the intonation well enough. No surprise that my less-than-tough feet elicited bemused contempt. The euphemism Tane used evoked an infant who'd not yet walked on her own, neatly adding the sideways implication that I might not be much more intelligent than that.

There was also a repeated reference to the treasure that prophecy promised the dragon would deliver that had not materialized. If Nakoa were truly a king and if he truly controlled . . . Akamai floundered again. We would have to discuss accurate translating over worrying about offending me. Tane insulted me just fine on his own. It sounded, however, as if he somehow referred to both me and the dragon as one, both needing to be leashed to the service of the people.

Something he implied Nakoa might not be man enough to do.

Much like the volcano, Nakoa silently rumbled beside me. I nearly expected smoke and ash to puff from his ears. Because that gave me cause to laugh, which could be useful at the moment, I let it out, disrupting Tane's momentum and causing both men— along with the assembly, who'd been whispering in tones of consternation—to focus on me.

Tane wanted to paint me as empty-headed? I'd learned enough from Ami to take advantage of those tricks. *Oh, please. Underestimate me again—for entirely the wrong reasons this time.* I'd fooled

Tane into thinking I could wield a blade. He had no idea where my true weapons lay. But to use them, I needed more knowledge.

"This is so boring." I pouted at Nakoa, who regarded me with a flicker of incredulity, which also took the edge off his imminent explosion. "Can't we do something else?" Easy enough to deliberately mangle the words. Inoa, who'd taken a place in the front row of nobles, looked more obviously astonished. The rest of the assembly ate up my performance, murmurs turning to dismay.

Nakoa picked up my hand, kissed it, and stood, waving a hand to dismiss court. "As my queen wishes."

Tane gaped in utter shock—quite comical, though I concentrated on awarding Nakoa with a besotted smile—then burst into protests that court had only just convened, something Nakoa had severely neglected.

Brushing him off like an annoying insect, Nakoa regally ignored him, along with several other nobles who attempted to snag his attention. He even waved off Inoa, announcing to all that his new queen had been bedridden and deserved more entertainment on her first day out than the dullness of politics.

I almost believed him myself.

With my hand tucked in the crook of his arm, Nakoa led me out of the hall and onto the broad escarpment overlooking the sea, where the celebration had been held. He pointed out sights, comparing them to my beauty, for the benefit of the few onlookers who trailed along. And who finally gave up in baffled resignation when he took me down the steps to the beach, where the sand made for fine—and clearly very private—walking.

"Your feet are not sore?"

"No, the ocean feels good." The crystalline water lapped around my ankles, cooling the warming soles as we walked well out of anyone's eavesdropping range.

"What do you wish to know?" Nakoa asked. Not much got past him. Amazing, really, that he already read me so well to know what I'd been about. If I was truly his queen, we'd likely work very well together. Pushing the wistful thought aside, I fluttered my lashes in my best Ami imitation.

"Maybe I was truly bored."

He snorted out a laugh, turned, and picked me up to kiss me soundly before setting me on my feet again. "Tell me another tale."

24

"You don't always have to pick me up," I complained, to cover my unexpected emotional flutter at the kiss—and at his unshakeable faith in me, a woman he barely knew.

"I like to." He tucked my hand in his arm and resumed our apparent pleasure stroll. "Or you can stand on a chair."

"I'm not *that* short," I muttered in Common Tongue, and he slid me an amused glance. Truly, it made me happy to see the edge off his anger. Perhaps the break was good for both of us. "Can you explain about the dragon? What is Tane's . . . complaint?" I substituted the Dasnarian word, suspecting Nakoa would know it.

He nodded and pursed his lips, thinking. "I do not wish you to worry. You are new in this place. Still tenderfooted." He cast me a teasing look at that.

"An infant, yes. I understood. Better to worry me than I not understand court and the . . ."

"Complaint," he told me, in both Dasnarian and Nahanaun. "Apologies to you, *mlai*. This morning was not to be avoided. People needed to see you as queen, now that you truly are."

Which I wasn't, but that argument would divert him from the current conversation and wouldn't convince him anyway, as stubborn about it as he'd been thus far. "I understand."

"This is difficult to explain, in words you know."

"Can we ask Akamai to translate?"

He shook his head. "These are things only for you and me. Tane thinks he knows, but he is not wise in this."

"Or anything."

Nakoa smiled, stroking my hand. "You are as wise as you are beautiful."

That wasn't saying much, but I took the compliment in the spirit it was intended.

"This is . . . private. Never tell another, yes?"

Swear to keep the secret—but what if it affected the Thirteen? I'd be honor bound—by an oath of fealty, even if I disregarded everything else—to tell at least Ursula. Of course, I was also honor bound to tell Nakoa about the barrier affecting his kingdom. Nakoa picked up on my hesitation immediately, stopping to take my upper arms so I faced him. "Make your vow." He used the Dasnarian word for it, all softness and amusement gone. How unerringly he seemed to see through me.

"I owe loyalty to my queen first."

The words dropped like rocks into the still pond of his waiting silence.

His hands tightened on me slightly, dark gaze severe. "No. To me first. Always this was so. You to me and I to you."

"Oh, don't give me that mystical claptrap," I snapped in Common Tongue, but he'd read me well enough.

He cocked his head slightly, narrowing his eyes. "Make your vow, *mlai*."

Suddenly this had become about much more than just these secrets. I fumed at him, shrugging off his grip and stepping away, all sweet emotional flutters burned to ash in my frustration. I switched to Dasnarian. "Don't you try to corner me, Nakoa. I've had about enough of this. I need this information to make informed choices and you're the one who stuck me in this situation to begin with. You can't just command my loyalty."

He folded his arms, implacable. "Make your vow, *mlai*," he repeated, strengthening the command tonality.

Maybe we wouldn't work so well together. The man possessed zero ability to compromise. Not that remaining as his queen had ever been a viable possibility, but it had been interesting to contemplate. Now he'd just pissed me off—and reminded me of all the very excellent reasons I had to keep him fenced off and not let him affect me so.

I folded my arms in turn. "No."

"Yes," he insisted.

I threw up my hands. "Fine. Don't tell me about the dragon. I'll find out on my own." In sizzling frustration I stalked past him, intent on returning to the palace. If there had been information in Annfwn's library, there would be in this one.

"Dafne." Nakoa's voice held a warning, and I ignored him.

He stepped in front of me, not touching me, but making it clear that he'd block my retreat. "Do not run," he said in a soft voice that nevertheless carried the promise of menace.

"Or what?" I put my hand on my knife. I wouldn't use it on him—probably—but I felt braver for it, and less intimidated by his scowling bulk.

"Or I will show you." He growled the words, anger rising also.

"You wish!" I hissed, in a full flood of anger, not even entirely sure why anymore.

"Yes. I wish." He moved on me and, my courage faltering utterly, I broke and ran. I only made it a few steps before he overtook me, swinging me up in his arms, slinging me over his shoulder, then headed down the beach away from the palace in great, ground-eating strides.

I shrieked in pure fury, pounding at his back with my fists, kicking at him and wrestling against his iron grip. He laughed and patted my rump, infuriating me further, if that were possible, climbing with agile grace over some rocks. I'd never been so angry in my life. I'd read stories where people saw red, and now my vision pulsed with it. Something not helped by my upside-down position. In the distance, the volcano rumbled.

"Put me down!" I yelled, adding every insult I could think of in every language I knew.

"Yes, Dafne *mlai*." And he did, setting me on my feet, his face and voice as bland as if he hadn't just dragged me off literally kicking and screaming.

Beyond infuriated, I punched him in the rock-hard abs. It hurt my hand, but I wasn't about to show it. I should draw the thrice-damned dagger. Taking a deep breath and a few steps of distance, I tried to calm my unprecedented rage. He'd brought me to a little cove, walled off on three sides by rocks, open to the ocean on the other. I'd have to climb or swim to escape and he'd undoubtedly catch me first.

"You are angry," Nakoa said, sounding not at all bothered by it, but simmering with some of his own.

"You think?" I spat back.

"I understand."

"But you won't let me go."

"I cannot." His jaw had that determined set to it as he ground out the words. "You will make your vow, *mlai*. Speak the words your heart already has."

I wasn't sure I understood him correctly. My heart had nothing to do with this, despite my uncertain emotions, unstable as the rumbling volcano. "I don't understand."

"You will." The quiet words were all the warning I got before his hands were on me, lifting me, then bearing me to the sand.

"Nakoa, thri—"

His mouth closed hot and demanding over mine, cutting off my curse. "No words. Feel."

I couldn't fight the flare of desire, the fire he seemed to be able to call up in me faster each time we came together, especially with the morning's session still warm in my mind. I found myself kissing him back with wild intensity, all of my frustrated fury alchemically transformed into the crazed need to touch him. We rolled over the sand together, nearly frantic with it. I scratched and bit at him, venting all that emotion, and he snarled in return, fastening his mouth on the flesh he revealed with his tearing hands.

"You want me," he growled against my skin. "Real. No game."

I dug into him. No denying it. "Yes."

Sand. Sea. Sky. Nakoa. The images flickered, blending into one. The taste of salt and skin, his hands up my skirt, ripping away the pantalets, and fingers thrusting into me with none of the gentle skill he'd shown the night before. I screamed, an echo of my enraged curses, calling his name and—as if the frenzied urgency escalated my responses that much more—climaxing immediately.

"Yes," he grated in my ear. "Feel. I am yours. You are mine. First."

He rolled onto his back, spearing into me in the same movement, gripping me by the waist as he thrust up into me. Then held me there. I thrashed, needing to move, the sensation too exquisite, but he held me still.

"Mine," he insisted, rocking himself inside me.

I shook my head, biting back the words that sprang to my lips. The traitorous desire that urged me to say it, too. That I wanted him to be mine alone, this man spread beneath me, wild lightning-streaked hair like an aura around his head on the pale sand, his brooding face tight with an edgier emotion. Desire, yes. Also determination and need. Foolishly, I wanted him to truly want me and for this not to be some sham. Those sloe-eyed ladies couldn't have him because he belonged to me.

No. No, I couldn't give him the vow he wanted. His hands moved up to my breasts, the metallic cups long-since lost somewhere in the sand, and I moaned a plea, rocking my hips, the inescapable pleasure rocketing through me.

"Nakoa . . . ," I gasped, bracing myself on his chest, finding that sweet spot.

"Yes. Yours. Take me, Dafne *mlai.*"

I dug in my fingers, spearing the tattooed dragon's scales, and he made a sound, tightening his hands on my breasts, pinching my nipples. Driving me wild. Challenging me with his night-black gaze. I moved on him, finding the rhythm I wanted, raking him with my nails. They'd grown longer in the last week, satisfyingly strong. He arched under me, lifting me with it, piercing me with sweetest pleasure.

I growled. Fierce and predatory, hot-blooded like the dragon. Mine.

"Yes. Say it." Nakoa met me with his own ferocious demand.

I raised myself on his cock and slammed down, hard enough to make him gasp and arch again, pinching my nipples with a pain that radiated through my mind, obliterating everything else. "Mine," I said.

"Yours." In a flash, he rolled me onto my back, taking control of the coupling, slowing the tempo so I became the one to writhe beseechingly. "Mine. Each to each. Me to you, you to me."

My heart thundered. I was the dragon, the volcano, Nakoa. Each to each. I lost myself in the frenzy of it, now clinging beneath him, thighs clamped around his hips, ankles locked to keep him there, chanting crazed commands to take me under utterly. Then on top of him again, his face contorting as the pleasure rode him hard.

We devoured each other whole.

Immolated in a blazing sun of endless climax.

At last, utterly spent, I collapsed over him, his skin hot and slick under my cheek. Heartbeat thundering. With him inside me still, it seemed the boundaries between us blurred. His hand trailed up and down my spine, a comforting caress. So at odds with the nearly vicious way we'd taken each other—for I could not excuse my own behavior—and yet somehow another face of the same emotion.

Just as my fury had somehow been the reverse side of my desire.

I had no idea how to feel and, tired of thinking about it, I let it go for a few minutes, letting the kaleidoscope of our furious love-making spill back in sensory fragments. For it had been both—full of fury and love. *Speak the words your heart already has.*

I didn't believe it. All afterglow, as Jepp called it. And yet . . .

"Nakoa *mlai.*" I murmured the words against his skin and his hand came up to cup my head, threading through my hair.

"Understand," he said, not quite a question, because he knew it wasn't. I understood all too well. Completely without knowledge, I still understood. He was first for me, whether I wanted it that way or not.

"You have my vow not to speak the secrets," I said on a sigh of resignation. "I might ask you, if I think I need to tell, though."

"I am always here to ask."

His simple words struck me. He would not always be there, because I would have to leave him eventually. How I'd manage that, however, without causing war but still escaping his determined possession, I had no idea. Perhaps he'd be satisfied with the piece of my heart I'd leave behind, against all expectation.

Magic bound us together—I couldn't deny that. But that wasn't real love. It made for a nice fantasy, to lie against Nakoa and imagine a true marriage, but I couldn't trust my own heart, or his. I'd never known what real love felt like, but I knew that it grew between people of like minds. Not striking like lightning from the sky, ripping one open, the way I'd been with him just now.

Maybe I could fulfill this role, help him with the dragon and this treasure, and that would satisfy whatever *geas* connected us. The smoke and ash from our fiery union would dissipate, our minds clearing of this induced emotion. That had to be the case, because I'd never felt any of these things before. I sat up, groaning at the protests of my body, aware I wore only the jewelry and the knife belt, with the dagger I'd never drawn. Nakoa touched my cheek, a bit of a wince in his expression. "Sorry for sore."

I contemplated him. "We both . . . lost our heads." I tried the translated euphemism, not sure if he'd follow.

He did, with a smile both rueful and full of male satisfaction. "Yes. And now your head is found again."

I sighed, not at all certain of the truth of that. I seemed to have lost all rationality. But I could at least gain the knowledge I'd paid this price to have.

"Tell me about the dragon."

Nakoa watched me gather up my scattered garments, as he sat cross-legged, the *kylte* he'd never removed—and wore nothing under, I'd discovered—draping over his lap.

"She is very old and slept a long time under the volcano. Long ago there were many dragons; then they died." He looked full of sorrow. "Many, all at once."

"You saw this?"

"No. Not me. Not my parents or their parents. Long, long ago—understand?"

My skin prickled with unease, as I recalled the illustrations I'd seen. "There was magic. Then there wasn't."

His face lit with appreciation that I'd followed. "Yes. Not all at once, but as the rains do."

Dwindling away in the face of drought. I nodded, thinking of the scrolls I'd seen in Annfwn that might have indicated when and how the barrier was first erected. Had that ancient sorceress realized at all the impact of her actions? Whether of malicious intent or accidental, the result had been the same. And the knowledge lost.

"My ancestors"—he made a grasping motion—"took what magic remained." He swept sand together, piling it into a cone. "See?"

"Into the volcano?" I pointed at the quiescent mountain, copper brown against the blue sky.

"Yes. The dragons, the magic." He cupped his hands protectively over the cone of sand. "The secret, passed from king to king, queen to queen. The dragons slept, so as not to die."

So like the Tala secrets for controlling the magic, passed from mother to daughter. Fascinating parallels.

"And then the magic storm came."

"Yes. I understood." He tapped his temple, then gestured to me. "The dragon awoke, but"—he bumped his fist against a sheltering palm—"could not open."

Awake, but trapped inside the volcano. How awful. For all her fierce strength and ancient majesty, she'd been as caught in her prison of stone as I had been in mine. A chill crossed my skin despite the heat of the sun.

Nakoa nodded, as if he followed my thought. "I needed you. And you came here."

"To help release the dragon."

He nodded, a wary look in his eye. I knew exactly why. "I did not 'come here,' Nakoa. You sent General Kral to take me." I used his grasping gesture, expecting a return of my former anger. It seemed I'd spent it all, however.

Nakoa held his palms up and shrugged his shoulders. "You did not know. I waited. I saw you, but you did not know."

"How did you see me?"

He frowned slightly and waved his hands. "As I feel the rain, ready to fall."

"Why didn't I see you?" It seemed eminently logical, that if we'd been magically or mystically connected, I would have seen him.

"Not your magic."

"I don't have any magic."

A slow smile spread across his face. "You are *mlai*. You have woman-magic. Not man/rain magic." He infused the concept of rain with something more, similar to the tones for storms and also masculinity.

I wasn't going to argue that because we'd only go in circles. More than we were already. "What does Tane want you to do with the dragon?"

"You and I, though he does not believe. He thinks to see us fail and then be king."

"Fail to do what?"

His brow knit. "Open . . . her treasure."

Kral's treasure. Goddesses take him. He'd thought the Thirteen had worked the storm to take it, then backpedaled when he realized we knew nothing about it. Suddenly the Dasnarian Empire's keen interest in these islands made much more sense.

"Is the treasure how you got Kral to bring me here?"

"Not to take, to invite."

"You promised him treasure?"

"What he believes and what I promise are not the same."

"Just as you know more Dasnarian than you let on."

He grinned. "They are not wise. I told him if he could get past the dragon, he could have access to the treasure. But I needed you for the dragon first."

"How did you tell General Kral who I was?"

"I painted a picture. You, in your white palace."

I had to believe it, as impossible as it seemed. "Okay. So, Tane wants us to try to open the dragon's treasure, thinking we will fail, as he thought to make you fail the test of the ancestors." I pieced it together, Nakoa nodding slowly as he followed my mix of tongues. "Tane wants the treasure. The Dasnarians want the treasure. The treasure belongs to the dragon."

"The dragon keeps it for the people," Nakoa clarified.

"Nice of her. What *is* the treasure?"

He held up his hands and shrugged.

The problem with passed-down secrets—they still left out the salient bits. "How do we release it?"

Nakoa tilted his head meaningfully. "You know."

"No, I don't. That's why I'm asking."

He reached over and tapped over my heart. "Here."

25

More of the mystical claptrap. "Nakoa . . ." I sighed out the frustration. "I don't know any of this."

"You know. This is yours to know." Nakoa spoke with quiet urgency, taking my hands in his. "I bring rain and you bring this."

"What is 'this,' though?"

Nakoa rubbed his thumbs over my hands, frowning at them, then huffed out a sigh. "It was not told me. Not for men. It's said it comes from the mothers."

A terrific thing to tell an orphan. Though my mother, a minor nobleman's daughter in Columba, could not have known these things to tell me, even had she lived.

Nakoa shrugged with a rueful half smile and tapped my heart again. "This is yours to know. Not mine. Why I need you. I cannot do it alone. You are here and our hearts are one. You have it in you."

That heart he spoke of so glibly shuddered a little. It would be infinitely preferable if Nakoa didn't affect me so. It made no sense that I felt so strongly about him. Of course he was fascinating, a compelling enigma of a man, but I'd been around powerful men all my life. He possessed keen intelligence that he seemed to use for the benefit of his people, along with all the charisma of a ruler—a trait I could admit to myself that had always been attractive to me. Perhaps I looked for in others all the confidence and decisiveness I lacked. No doubt much of the source of my tangled emotions for him was tied up in him being my first and only lover. Even with my body sore and throbbing from our encounter, a hunger for more of him hummed deep inside, as if I craved to make up for the starvation of a lifetime.

I didn't need for him to love me—particularly as I could not stay—but I perversely wanted this man, the only one I'd ever been truly attracted to, to truly want me, too. Not for some prophecy or the other half of this magic he expected us to work. But because he liked *me*.

All foolishness. I'd thought I'd long since reconciled myself to the glaring truth that no one wanted me—only what I could do for them. As if having my family and home cleaved from me had rendered me somehow not a full person. Not someone worth having on her own. All along I'd understood that Nakoa, like everyone else, needed me for particular, if obscure reasons. My own fault some part of myself had wandered away from that rational understanding and began creating romantic fantasies.

I was plenty old enough to know that sex and love were decisively not the same thing. Even more so when politics were mixed in.

If I accepted what he was telling me—and what choice did I have there?—then the sexual connection between us served to also affect the dragon. Magic didn't always fit into logical lines, so I'd have to suspend disbelief and go with that reality. The solution, then, would be to do what Nakoa and his people needed. Open the treasure, solve this puzzle of a destiny, and then go on my way.

Perhaps at that point, he wouldn't even object to my departure, as I would have done what he needed me for. Leaving this place was what I wanted, so the idea shouldn't make my heart ache.

"Dafne?" Nakoa's brows drew together. "What is wrong?"

"I'm fine. I want to go to the library. May I?"

He gave me a funny look. "You are queen. You do as you like."

"I mean, you don't need me in court? To be seen."

"You were seen. Tane will sow his seeds of storm. But the books do not hold the answers you seek."

I wasn't at all sure I agreed. "Is there more you can tell me?"

He thought, then shook his head regretfully.

"Then books it is."

We rinsed off in the sea, the water blissfully refreshing even if the salt stung in my abraded tissues—which included a few bruises and bites from Nakoa that I hadn't noticed at the time. Nothing like what I'd left on him, and he, in the midst of washing a deep set of scratches on his chest, caught me watching and grinned. "My dragon queen."

The term caught me off guard, hitting home in a disorienting wave, like when I felt as if I'd already read a book that I well knew I'd never before laid hands on. Did he know we'd called him the dragon king? Not possible, and yet . . .

Further rocked, I quickly dressed again, my skimpy outfit doing nothing to hide the sex marks. Nor on Nakoa. "Everyone will see and know," I said ruefully.

"It is good." He lifted my chin, bending down to kiss me. Perhaps mindful that I'd complained about being picked up all the time. "Beautiful."

He meant the sex, not me. I felt sure of it.

We walked back to the palace, he holding my hand until we parted at the hall that forked to the throne room. "You'll go back to court?" I asked, feeling vaguely guilty to be skipping out on my responsibilities.

"Yes. I will see you in our rooms tonight." He gave me a distinctly smoldering look, as if he hadn't just thoroughly sated himself with me. My body, already well attuned—absurdly so, given a lifetime of abstinence—heated in answer. Only a short time ago I hadn't understood how Jepp and Kral could have gone at it all night. Now I couldn't seem to go even minutes without thinking about wanting more of Nakoa.

"To play *kiauo*, yes," I replied in a flippant tone to cover the need, making him laugh.

"That, too." His smile turned wicked. "We shall see who wins—and the *kama*."

He'd certainly won that exchange. Flushed, I took myself off before I could get into any more trouble.

Akamai joined me in the library, clearly sent by Nakoa and thoughtfully bringing my journal and papers and laying them out as I'd last had them. An excellent memory he had.

"Don't you have to be in court?" I asked in Dasnarian, relieved to abandon my stilted fumbling in Nahanaun. The height of irony, that Dasnarian felt so comfortable in comparison.

"No, Queen Dafne Nakoa KauPo. I am your servant in all things." Akamai beamed at me. "I belong to you now."

"Belong? You are no slave."

"True. But you took responsibility for me, so I belong to you."

"What about your family?"

He shook his head. "They all died when I was a baby, in a great storm. I was found washed ashore, so the people brought me to the palace. But I have nothing. King Nakoa KauPo allows me to serve in the library. Then you took responsibility for me." He bowed deeply. "I am grateful, as I am otherwise vulnerable."

"Vulnerable how?"

"I have no status. No wealth of my own. I would leave here if I could." He shrugged. "But I have no means to do so. I am happy to serve you, Queen Dafne Nakoa KauPo."

Far too close to home on many levels. Dwelling on it wouldn't make him any happier than it would have me. "All right, then. You can help me find everything this library holds on dragons, no matter how incidental."

My feet barely bothered me—almost miraculously so—and it was such a treat to be able to explore the library under my own power. Akamai explained the organization, how the books, scrolls, and other texts were grouped first by subject, then by culture of origin, then by age of the document. Astonishingly I found copies of texts not only from various kingdoms of the original Twelve Kingdoms, but from some of the bordering countries and even from Annfwn. Some I'd never seen before and might be the only copies left in existence. All were in nearly pristine condition, too.

I felt terrible touching them with bare hands, but when I asked Akamai for gloves, he said he didn't know that Dasnarian word. It made sense on one level—no shoes and socks, no gloves. But how did they keep everything in such good condition?

A huge proportion of the library was devoted to materials in another language altogether, a style I recognized as quintessentially Tala and yet not that at all. This written language, much as it evoked the simple forms the Tala used, seemed to be hugely more complex. A scan of the variety of characters used made me think it could be hundreds of times more dense. What the Tala language might look like in written form, if they'd ever cared enough to give up their devotion to oral histories and make a scholarly pursuit of recording their language. Over and over, I recalled those scrolls I'd barely had time to study in Annfwn.

A tingle of intuition thrilled through me. "Akamai—what is this language?"

He didn't even have to look, pursing his mouth ruefully. "N'andanan. An ancient language we no longer know how to read."

"Who collected all of these, then?"

"The people of N'andana sent them for safekeeping, before their land disappeared."

"Disappeared?"

"Yes. To preserve their knowledge, since their people were doomed."

"What happened to them?"

"Perhaps the books say."

"The books no one can read."

I growled to myself when he nodded at that. This was important. I knew it in my bones. Why would a people facing disaster go to so much trouble to preserve all of these texts without providing a key to translation? There had to be one. In this library, somewhere. Or had been.

"How long ago did this happen?"

He merely shrugged in that relaxed Nahanaun fashion, saying the books had always been there. As he seemed to be no older than twenty, at best, and as everything I'd seen predated that, I'd no doubt it would appear that way to him.

It took stern self-discipline not to lose myself in side research, each new find as tempting as an array of pastries, each begging to be devoured immediately. For the first time, instead of wanting to hurry the days until rescue arrived, I entertained a wistful desire for them to slow, so I'd have just a bit more time to try to decipher N'andanan. As if I didn't have enough riddles already. Ironic that I wouldn't allow myself to indulge in a similar wishfulness to shirk my duty and vows of fealty to stay with Nakoa. That lay in the realm of impossibility. But studying this ancient language . . .

The difference lay in that I understood and knew how to study a language. I could spend my entire life in this library and not get through all of the materials preserved in it. Conversely, I did not understand Nakoa or being with a man at all. He wasn't for me, something I needed to continually remind myself of. Much as that dreamy, recently discovered romantic corner of my heart might dwell on the fantasy of spending my days in study and my nights melting in the crucible of Nakoa's embrace, the long-practiced logical part of my mind knew it couldn't be. Life didn't work out that way. At least not for me. If I'd learned nothing else, I knew that much. My role in the world—a good role, one I'd become good at—was to open the doors for others to walk through. Believing otherwise caused only heartache.

I had plenty of empirical evidence for that. I only needed to keep it in the forefront of my mind.

Akamai went back and forth, carrying the texts I pulled and arranging them on my table. As Nakoa had indicated that first day, nothing directly referencing the *mo'o* in Nahanaun seemed to be present. In a moment of unexpected and extraordinary triumph, however, I found exact copies of the scrolls I'd seen in Annfwn, the ones I'd thought of the moment I'd seen Nakoa's island volcano and—even more exciting—several others stored in the same cubby.

Good research takes a level of intuition. I wouldn't call it magic, exactly, for I had to be the least magical person alive. But for me there was always a moment, a kind of intellectual frisson, when I drew close to the information I sought. I'd felt it back at Windroven when I discovered the original designs from the builder. Or the day Andi walked into the library at Ordnung, barely knowing who I was, and I knew before she asked what books to give her. Exactly the same as at Annfwn, when I first saw the scroll with the dragons, the volcano, and the N'andanan text.

I unrolled the ones I knew, refamiliarizing myself with the drawings.

There a quiescent volcano, with its perfect dome. No broken lip. The jungle foliage I'd come to know. Paying more attention to the details this time, I noted that the lines seemed to continue off the top of the scroll. A thrill as keen as the brush of Nakoa's mouth on my skin rippled over me. Carefully I unrolled one of the other scrolls. It matched—not at the top, but to one side. Anchoring the curling parchment with other books to keep them flat, I lined up the images. The new scroll continued the scene, showing not just people, but animals in the . . . could it be rain?

Or a way of showing the magic barrier.

Excitement rippled through me. Forcing myself to work slowly and with care, I unrolled another, which matched the other side. It showed a landscape without the rainfall and, drawn in distressing detail, the limp bodies of dead dragons, wings collapsed, and people weeping. Having seen the dragon in flight, I nearly wept also, the corrosion of their glittering beauty so dreadfully clear.

Then, holding my breath and sending a prayer to Danu, who is also the goddess of wisdom and thus safeguards knowledge, opened the final scroll.

It fit to the top. And—blessings to Danu—was the one showing the dragon flying above the volcano.

Rendered lovingly in a metallic paint, which also served to contrast with the mortal gray pallor of the dead dragons, she could be our dragon. A surge of fierce, hot-blooded joy flooded me, much as it did when I joined with Nakoa and sensed the dragon. The night before I'd felt as if I looked through her eyes. Now it felt as if she looked through mine.

Impossible, but no more so than any of the rest of it.

I studied the script that circled the flying dragon, as if focusing my eyes on it could resolve the meaning. To no avail, of course. Still, I had ahold of a thread and would keep tugging. The key lay here, I felt sure of it. So many puzzle pieces. The dragon. The treasure. Dasnaria. Deyrr. Annfwn. The magic, coming and going. Lost N'andana.

I went back to the section of the library where I'd found the scrolls, sending Akamai to comb what had to be thousands of documents from N'andana, looking for anything related to dragons. On my authority, he recruited several other librarians to search—a job that could easily take months, if not years, even if any of us could read the texts we located.

Hours later, we'd covered every available surface with documents of all varieties, some with only fragments of the script, others with full pages. And nothing to match them with. I frowned at the one I studied, which looked to be a poem in stanzas, a dragon improbably holding a quill pen sketched in the margin. My eyes ached and I moved one of the lamps Akamai had lit to examine it more closely.

A warm mouth kissed my bare shoulder and I jumped, banging Nakoa in the nose. He rubbed it, giving me a look of mild reproof. "Tonight you do not like my kisses?"

"Sorry. No—I was . . . far away."

He surveyed the piles of books and scrolls with a bit of incredulity. "Did a storm hit the library?"

"Ha. It's in better order than it looks. And you have to see this." Without thinking I grabbed his hand and tugged him over to the table with the original scrolls. Only when he gave me a bemused smile did I realize I'd never reached for him on my own before—and that one didn't drag a king somewhere, even if he was your lover. I tried to let go. "I mean, if you wish to."

He held on, lacing his fingers with mine, smile moving into a tender affection that made my heart, which had settled down considerably until this, flutter irrationally. "I wish."

In triumph, I showed him the scroll with the dragon. "See?"

He moved a lantern closer. Full night had fallen as I worked, and apparently all of my assistants had fled when the king arrived, as they seemed to have a habit of doing. Or he'd sent them off. I'd been deaf to the world in my concentration. Nakoa bent over the painting, tracing the design with a finger, and I had to restrain myself from saying he really should try not to touch it. He grunted and cocked his head at me. "You found it."

Yes. Yes, I had. I beamed under his admiring gaze, delighted to have surprised him. "I can't read this." I indicated the text. "Can you?"

He shook his head. "It is in N'andanan."

"You know this place?"

"Yes. Though it has been . . . gone many years."

"Gone?"

"Some say it was . . . never real, understand?"

A myth. My skin shivered with that intuitive sense that we drew close to the answer. I went over to the table with my journal and maps, opening the one I'd brought of the Thirteen Kingdoms. I showed it to Nakoa and laid my hand over the blank space at the border of the mountains, where Annfwn should be. "Here?"

He frowned at me in puzzlement, so I unearthed the big map that showed his island archipelago and Dasnaria, then lined up my map to approximate what I guessed the physical distance would be. The maps were drawn to different scales, but it should get the point across.

"Dasnaria. Nahanau. N'andana?"

His face cleared and, though his clearly interested gaze went to the rest of my map, he shook his head again. "Not there. Here?" He put his hand between Nahanau and where the Annfwn coast should be, narrowed his eyes, and moved the map of the Thirteen a bit farther away, and his hand another two lengths down. "Here," he said, with more confidence. "A long time ago."

"Long ago—before the dragons died?"

He gazed at me thoughtfully. "Perhaps. The tales say N'andana disappeared first. Much later the dragons began to die."

It "disappeared" because of something that happened that resulted in the long-ago Tala sorceress creating the barrier. But what? My heart thumped with the excitement of discovery. If only Ursula hadn't told me not to discuss the barrier with Nakoa. Could I bend that rule? I shifted from foot to foot, both uncomfortable with my thoughts and abruptly aware of my aching feet.

Nakoa's eyes narrowed in suspicion and he reached for me. Had he discerned that I was lying to him by omission? But no— he simply picked me up and seated me on an uncovered corner of a high table. "Enough standing," he told me, then used both hands to push my hair behind my neck, stroking it as he searched my face, thinking hard about something. Like this we were very nearly eye to eye. I held my breath, terribly afraid of what he would ask me and how I could possibly answer. "Dafne *mlai*. In all of this"—he waved a hand at all the stacks, which did indeed look as if a storm had blown through—"did you find your answer?"

Not at all what I'd feared. Except most of what I'd found pertained to answering questions for the Thirteen, not to solving the problem of finding and opening this treasure. Guilt assailed me and I glanced away so he wouldn't see it. "Some? Yes. I have more . . . pieces to the puzzle."

"But no answer to the question in your heart."

I frowned. I could make a long list of all the questions I had. "I am closer."

He tugged on my hair to make me tip up my chin and nudged between my knees, moving close enough that I felt the heat of his skin like the wood stove in my old library at Ordnung. "I have an answer for you," he murmured and brushed his lips against mine, soft and sweet.

My breath sighed out, and he kissed me again, breathing it in with a sound of pleasure. He deepened the kiss, bracing his hands on the table as I wound my arms around his neck, losing myself in the drowning sensual haze he drew me into with so little effort. My heart slowed, finding his rhythm and syncing with it. Even as I heated, longing for more and more and more, a kind of peacefulness settled over my mind. A nostalgic sense like the warmth of a summer day, a picnic in a meadow and Castle Columba in the distance. My brothers chasing my sister as she ran, deliberately slow, shrieking with giggles, my parents watching with indulgent smiles.

The last time I'd felt love.

26

I awoke in the bright moonlight, Moranu's nearly full moon shining in the balcony windows with silver-bright brilliance. Beside me, Nakoa lay still and soundless. Too still. With a pang of dread—didn't people die in their sleep sometimes?—I reached out to lay a hand on his chest. It rose and fell, very slowly, the rhythm of deep sleep. Silly of me. Something about the dark hours before dawn always made me less rational. I hadn't had the nightmares for years, but I still came awake like this, full of worry, the memory of grief so sharp and fresh that it felt like a premonition of future tragedy, rather than memory of the past.

In my old life, I'd light a candle and read to distract myself until I could sleep again, but I didn't wish to disturb Nakoa. He'd carried me out of the library and back to our rooms, where we'd had sex as hot and driven as on the beach that morning. Then he had servants bring food, making sure I ate while we played *kiauo*. When I lost atrociously—I might have had too much of my mind on the riddle of N'andana and the dragon's treasure—he claimed a *kama* from me that had me blushing at the memory.

Better than remembering old things best forgotten. Or fretting over a future I had no good reason to dread.

294 • Jeffe Kennedy

I slid out of bed as quietly as I could and slipped on the gown I'd worn while we played and that Nakoa had tossed to the floor after. Something about that poem I'd been looking at when Nakoa interrupted me still niggled the back of my mind. I wanted to take one more look. Then I could tuck it to brew in my thoughts when I could fall back asleep. Sometimes the mind worked that way.

Nakoa's guards, playing some sort of game with tokens, looked startled that I'd unbolted and opened the doors, then came to attention, bowing to me.

"I wish to go to the library," I stepped out and said, once I'd closed the doors behind me. They conferred, the leader sending two men with me, keeping two behind on the doors. It seemed overkill to me, as I hadn't needed to be escorted by guards on other trips to the library, and the palace always seemed to be such a peaceful place, but I didn't mind their silent company on the way through the empty halls, and it paid to be cautious. A few shielded torches remained lit here and there, probably for midnight wanderers such as me. For the most part, however, particularly in the outdoor courtyards, moonlight gilded everything in silver. Moranu's presence seemed quite near. A night for shapeshifters and magic.

The guards took up positions inside the library doors while I lit a few of the lanterns and found the poem that had been bothering me where I'd left it. Perhaps my fanciful mood would help unlock its secrets. If the people of N'andana were related to the Tala, as it seemed they would have to have been, given the proximity of the lands and the language similarities, then they would belong to Moranu. I didn't normally feel the presence of the goddesses as Ami claimed to, but I welcomed Her assistance in this. Moranu was also the goddess of intuition, which I'd need at full strength to penetrate this riddle.

I settled into studying the poem, looking for characters or whole words that matched those in the main drawing. The stillness of the palace lent itself to allowing me to focus on the documents without distraction. I very nearly had the key to understanding. It felt just outside the reach of my mind, as in when I wanted to remember some obscure fact and couldn't quite. Striving never seemed to work, only relaxing and biding my time until my memory offered it up. The quiet, shadowed night enhanced that mood, and I let the words drift through, waiting for them to reveal their secrets.

A whisper of sound caught my attention and I looked up, thinking that Nakoa had likely awakened and come to look for me. But no—the doors to the library remained closed.

And the guards were gone.

My tranquil mood shattered into full-blown panic. I'd heard their leader. The guards would not have let me out of their sight. The formerly peaceful deep shadows took on a malevolent feel, crowding in on my small pool of light where I sat for anyone to see and attack.

I started to put my hand to the dagger, only to remember I'd never put it—or any of the little ones—back on. Jepp would lecture me for years for this failure. Imagining her wrath gave me a small burst of courage and I pretended to return to my study of the poem, while I listened over the frantic pounding of my heart.

That sound again. The slither of a boot on the floor. Why hadn't they attacked already? I was easy pickings. Though maybe they didn't know that. This had to be planned by Chief Tane, and he thought I actually knew how to use a knife—not that I'd exhausted my one parlor trick. At least I could endeavor not to make this too easy.

I reached for a pen, then changed my trajectory at the last moment, snuffed out the lantern, and slid off my chair to the floor, crawling immediately under the table to another. Then sat and listened.

My skin went clammy. Crouching in a dark cave under the table, another memory came back to me. The roar of the catapults, the screams of the dying. Blood, hot oil, and pitch. I'd crawled deeper and deeper, rocks tumbling around me.

Don't think about that. Focus on now. Listen.

Nothing for a moment. My hunter listening for me. I breathed through my nose as Jepp had shown me, concentrating on keeping soundless and still. When they moved, I moved. They'd expect me to go either to the doors or away, so I went tangential.

A muffled curse. Two Nahanaun men conferring. *Don't light the lamp.*

A whisk and click of flint.

Damn it.

No longer trying to be stealthy, I darted from under the table and ran full speed to the doors as a torch flared. They didn't shout and it hit me that I should. I wasn't a child hiding from pillaging soldiers. I was among friends who would race to my rescue.

Nakoa would.

I took a breath to scream and a weight hit my back, slamming me to the floor, a sweaty palm that stunk of fish oil clamping over my mouth, holding my jaw tight so I couldn't bite. Not that I could have screamed, bit, or even fought much, with my lungs frozen from the fall—and from the building panic. They'd found me. I'd die like my sister, Bethany. An image flooded my brain, one I hadn't understood at the time and had forgotten. The way the soldiers tore off her clothes and her screams as they hurt her. I'd fled our room, crawling out when they weren't looking. Leaving her in my terror and selfish determination to save myself.

I moaned. I hadn't wanted to remember that. One man held me as the other bound my hands and feet. They stuffed a cloth in my mouth and bound it with another length of rope, then rolled me in a rug. I didn't resist, paralyzed by fear, as I'd been that night Castle Columba fell and I abandoned Bethany to be raped to death.

After a while, I became aware that I rode on a swaying platform. My head ached and my gut roiled, while I sweltered in the claustrophobic heat of the rug. A heat I recognized, along with the sulfurous stink, and an angle that climbed.

Back up the thrice-damned volcano.

My captors moved fast. Not as quickly as the bearers who'd jogged with me to save Nakoa. At least I'd done that much. A bit of expiation for the guilt I'd blocked out all those years and yet still carried in my heart, waiting to burst out in fits of panic. *Oh, Bethany.*

My captors stopped, rolling me off the litter and onto hard rock. I stayed limp, hoping to at least eavesdrop on their conversation if they thought me still in a faint. Or in whatever fugue state had taken me over.

By the sound of it, a knife cut more ropes, the heavy fabric fell away, and air flowed in, blessedly cool in comparison. I barely managed to resist drawing in a great lungful. They cut the ropes binding me and the gag, and I managed not to whimper with relief.

"She is no dragon queen," Tane sneered. "Look how weak. A boneless infant. Addled in the head."

Points to me for correctly identifying the culprit. Not that it gave me any advantage. A toe prodded me, then kicked harder. I had to bite down on the gag not to react.

"Now what?" one of his men asked.

"We wait for her to wake up."

"Do we have time? It is nearly dawn. She will be missed."

"True. Wake her, then, if you are so certain how."

Quiet for a moment. Then cold water dumped over my head. Shocking enough that I couldn't disguise my reaction. No one would stay passed out through that anyway, would they?

Acting more confused than I was—if Tane wanted to continue to underestimate me, then fine, though he'd seen what Nakoa had not, that I was a fraud—I sat up and pretended to be terrified. Well, it didn't take much playacting. The bitter taste of fear and guilt still lingered in my dry mouth with the residue of the cloth they'd stuffed in there.

We'd gone much higher than I had before, the crumbled lip of the volcano not far above. And a cave opening before us about my height, the shadowed interior impenetrable after a few feet. My vision grayed at the edges, panic that hadn't quite receded fluttering in my chest.

"No, no, no," I whispered, then realized I spoke aloud in Common Tongue.

Tane yanked me to my feet. "Go." He pointed, in case I didn't understand. "Call the dragon, get the treasure, and you can live."

Oh, right. I absolutely believed *that*. It would be very easy to pitch my body into one of the lava pits and return to the palace. There would be no sign of what had become of me. All Nakoa would know was that I'd risen from our marriage bed and disappeared. He'd likely think I left deliberately, that I'd escaped him at last.

At least the thought snapped me out of sinking into that place of formless fear again. Barely. "I cannot," I told him. "I am afraid." No playacting necessary.

His face contorted with contempt and he slapped me. Not terribly hard, but shocking tears to my eyes. "Infant. Put her in the cave. We'll block it up and only let her out when she says she has the treasure."

The man hesitated, giving his chief an uncertain look. "That will take time and—"

"Did I ask for your opinion? Do as I say. You will stay here and I will go back to the palace, offer my services to help search for the queen." His face split in a nasty smile. "So flighty, these foreign witches, running off like that."

I considered bolting, nearly shaking with the need to simply run, even knowing they'd immediately recapture me and likely hurt me worse. But I couldn't be blocked up in that cave. I'd go insane. Felt like I was already, at the mere prospect. I had nothing left to lose. Time to stop dissembling about how much I understood.

"Chief Tane. If you let me go, I'll leave this island forever. I am protected by a wealthy and powerful ruler who will pay—"

He slapped me again and I tasted blood. "I care not. The treasure is in there with the dragon. Get it. If you don't, it will be your tomb. Take her."

They seized me and I screamed, thrashing as I hadn't mustered the ability to do in the library. Not that any of it did the least thing to dissuade them. With grim efficiency, they ignored my struggles to escape. One man hauled me inside the cave mouth and held me there while twenty or so of his tribesmen gathered heavy stones, grunting with the effort of moving them. The one keeping me inside kept glancing nervously down the tunnel, as if expecting attack from behind.

The dragon?

"Please," I tried. "My queen will reward you. Nakoa would reward you! Take me back and you'll be a hero."

He ignored me as if I hadn't spoken. The wall of rock nearly filled the opening and one of the other men called him to come out. He pushed me aside with enough force that I fell, then climbed up and wedged out, the remaining hole barely big enough for him to squeeze through. I tried to follow, begging them not to leave me, no pride left. He kicked at me, knocking me back. Another banged my fingers with a rock when I tried to reach through, the pain brighter even than the terror.

In despair I watched as they sealed away the morning light, leaving me in utter blackness. Walled in. Outside, more rocks clunked, creating a barricade I could never hope to move.

My legs gave out and I collapsed to the floor.

I sat there a long, long time.

Long enough for the air to grow close and the sulfurous stink to burn my lungs. I'd die from lack of oxygen before anything else. Better than dying of thirst, which would take a few days but would be grueling to suffer. I wasn't there yet, but I would be—and I remembered that, too, with new clarity. Opening the door to those few memories allowed them all to come through. I'd been so thirsty it hurt. My tongue had cracked, filling my mouth with blood, as it was now, and my head had ached with the dry heaves of my stomach.

Then the rain had come, trickling down the rock, allowing me to lap it up, bit by bit.

I saw you. I sent you rain.

Nakoa.

Would he see me now? I didn't know what to believe or hope for. There was no reason he wouldn't believe the worst of me, that I'd fled my captivity. I couldn't even reason to myself that he'd know me better than that, as I would have done that very thing, given the opportunity.

But he had called rain from a cloudless sky. I'd seen other magic I couldn't explain, both terrible and wonderful. Andi said she could feel Ursula thinking at her—maybe *she* meant that literally.

Trying to reach him mentally at least let me think about something other than being trapped in this cave. I certainly wasn't going any deeper inside the mountain. I closed my eyes against it and sat cross-legged, in one of the meditative poses some of the Hawks and other followers of Danu used. Concentrating on the feel of Nakoa, the shape and scent of him in my mind, the distilled essence, I thought at him.

Nakoa. Help me.

Over and over.

I imagined pictures of where I was and what had happened. And repeated my mantra, fueling it with all the emotion he aroused in me.

Nakoa. Find me. Help me.

Something shifted in the composition of the air. Not fresher. Hotter.

Stubbornly, I kept my eyes closed. I didn't want to see.

Something snuffled. Then a soft gravelly noise, like a snake sliding over sand.

Or a dragon, moving over lava rock.

Perhaps I'd hit some point of terror where I couldn't become any more afraid. I'd reached the peak and simply remained on that knife-edge of it. I opened my eyes, expecting blackness—and had to blink against the glow.

The dragon filled the cave beyond. Or rather, her head did. The narrow passage I sat in opened up farther on and the dragon watched me from ruby-red eyes that shone like twin suns, shedding a pink-shaded light over the glitter of golden scales. She rested her chin on the floor, nostrils as high as me flaring as if she drew in my scent.

She made no aggressive moves. If anything, she seemed to be making an effort not to startle me. Could I ascribe intelligent actions to her like that? The Nahanauns worshipped the dragons and valued them. The lovingly rendered drawings of the death of the dragons showed that much.

And, logic aside, I'd looked through her eyes and she through mine.

We were connected. I knew it in my heart, even if it made no sense.

Moving slowly, my limbs stiff, muscles cramping—another symptom of early dehydration, I noted automatically—I managed to stand and face the dragon.

27

How did one talk to a dragon?

Respectfully, for sure.

I bowed to her, in the style of Nakoa's people, the unreality of the moment making me feel suspended in some space apart from the world I knew. Not a dream, but a different place. As if I'd stepped into one of Zynda's parallel realms, leaving my usual shape behind.

"Greetings, Your Majesty." Best to go with the highest honorific. Scaled lids as big as the Vervaldrs' shields blinked slowly over the ruby glow, casting me into darkness and then light again. Curious to know if it would make a difference, I tried the same thing again in Nahanaun.

A sense of amusement rustled through my mind, dry and leathery as the sound of scales on rock.

Greetings, Daughter.

Goddesses!

Had I heard that? Stunned beyond comprehension, I stared at the great beast, who returned my gaze with an almost human expression of amused fascination. The words in my mind weren't in any language, but still I understood.

"Why do you call me daughter?"

She huffed, searing breath heating the narrow space more. A laugh? *An imprecise term, but our families intertwined ages ago. You are my descendant.*

"Our families . . . in Annfwn?"

Close. My ancestors came from a land called N'andana. Some moved away to Annfwn.

Startling, but . . . it fit. The Tala, N'andana, my family sharing a Tala border for so long. I'd been able to cross the barrier due to some long-ago Tala relation. Nakoa had insisted we were linked— to each other and to the dragon. The connection clicked into place. It made sense that the people of N'andana would be shape-shifters, too.

"Do you . . . have a human form, then?"

Clever daughter. No longer. Once I walked the earth as a woman, much like you. I had many shapes, gathering them through my life. I grew aged. Rather than pass from this world, I committed to this form. As was the way of my people.

"Why a dragon?"

This body is very strong, nearly indestructible. I need no food, as fire sustains me. The animal mind is large and allows my human one to persist, for the most part. The form has drawbacks, but mostly it is perfect.

"What kind of drawbacks?"

We get very hot. Her mind-voice sounded wry. *And I was a scribe when human. I miss having hands to write with. But virtual immortality is worth it.*

"Not immortal once the magic was sealed away."

A sense of immeasurable sadness swept through me.

No. The youngest went first. We tried to reach the Heart, but it was locked away from us. Finally we used the last of the magic to seal ourselves in stasis, awaiting the change that would awaken us.

"Us?"

There were a dozen or so of us who bedded in various places.

Hopefully they will soon wake also. Liberated, as you and my son freed me.

"Why did it matter that Nakoa and I . . . were together, to liberate you and for you to stay?"

Amusement flickered through her thought-voice, kindling crackling into flame. *It is how we built the spell, fueling it with sexual energy—the most basic of human creative magic, the kind that never changes, no matter how language or culture shifts. When my people choose this final shape, we anchor to a family, to a bonded couple. The women talk to us, relay our wisdom. The men bring rain, to keep us from burning up. You, my daughter and my son, along with your daughters and sons, will be my human family. I will relearn what I've forgotten and give it back to you.*

"Why didn't you speak to me before?"

The mental equivalent of a shrug. *My mind has been slow and I've forgotten much. Being in your heart, feeling with you, has brought much back to me.*

"Fascinating," I murmured. "I hate to ask this, but—do you have a treasure?"

Treasure?

"Gold, jewels. The legends of dragons often speak of treasure hordes."

Laughter bubbled in her thoughts. *Perhaps true dragons did. I don't know. But no, what would I do with gold and jewels?*

So much for that. I swayed on my feet. Definitely light-headed. "I want to talk more with you, if you'll allow it, but for now I need water. Can you help me?"

Follow me.

I didn't want to go farther underground, but the greatest danger lay in staying where I was, where I'd either die or face Tane's men. And yet . . . the thrice-damned wail of old fear kept me rooted to the spot.

It takes more courage to examine the dark corners of your own soul than it does for a soldier to fight on a battlefield. I wasn't sure if that was the dragon's thought or mine, because she echoed it, agreeing.

She was already moving away, the shadows falling in her wake. I forced myself to take a step. Then another. The rock beneath my feet was warm and smooth, easing my path. Small mercies. The dragon turned her bulk, reversing on herself as a snake would, legs and wings folded against her body as she slithered along the tunnel.

I kept my gaze on the tip of her forked tail, noticing as my eyes adjusted to the dimmer light that all of her emitted a golden glow, as if lit from within like a lantern. As we descended, the air grew hotter, sweat that beaded on my brow drying immediately. Then I stopped sweating, a dangerous sign that I was entering more severe dehydration. The increasing heat made it worse. How long had I been in the caves? Perhaps a full day.

Perhaps longer.

Nakoa had not come for me.

"My Queen?" I called out, my voice cracking so I had to try twice.

I hear you, Daughter. And my name is Kiraka.

"The heat . . . it might be too much for me. I don't have your strength."

So frail, the human form. Come, climb up on my back.

I moved along her side as she glanced back, holding still and shedding ruby light. She partially unfolded a wing, making a ramp of it to her back. Batwing thin and translucent gold, the membrane felt like softest leather. Or like Nakoa's skin. So soft it seemed I could easily put a foot through it, even barefoot.

"I don't want to hurt you."

That rustle of mental laughter. *You will not. With the magic flowing, this form is indestructible.*

I climbed up her wing, still moving with care. The bones of her wing, like the fingers of a hand, formed a ladder for me and I made it to the flat space of her back between her wings. Dizziness swamped me and I wondered how I'd manage to hold on to her without fainting. I'd have to, if I wanted to survive.

Kiraka moved carefully, barely jostling me, and I rested my cheek against her surprisingly smooth hide. Her scales were as fine as a snake's, and lying against her back, the pattern of her golden scales shifting as she moved, I fancied I was back in bed with Nakoa, as I'd fallen asleep with him last—lying atop him, his heart slowing beneath my ear, the tattooed scales shimmering in the candlelight.

He felt near at that moment. Maybe it was my rising fever. Maybe we were truly connected through Kiraka, because I almost scented him, felt the loving trace of his hand down my back, heard him murmur in my ear. *Mlai.*

Mlai.

Wake up, Daughter.

"Nakoa?" My throat creaked soundlessly around his name, my tongue too thick to move.

Here is water, but you must climb down.

My eyes felt like rocks as I blinked them open. We'd emerged into fresh air, blessedly cool on my skin, which felt as if I'd baked in an oven. It was night, Moranu's moon high overhead. Two more nights and it would be full. It rose an hour later every night, so it had been a bit over twenty-four hours since I'd slipped out of Nakoa's bed.

Are you awake, Daughter? Focus your thoughts and speak to me so I can hear.

Yes. It looked impossibly far, even with Kiraka crouched as flat as she could get. And I was both stiff with muscle cramps and swimmingly dizzy. I moved slowly, but my bruised and bloodied fingers wouldn't grip right. In a tumble, I fell to the ground, buffered somewhat by the curve of her wing. Sand, fine and white, grated against my cheek. She'd brought me to the beach.

Salt water. I nearly wept at the crushing defeat. Might have, if I hadn't been so parched.

Drink, she urged.

"I—" My voice was gone. Burned away. *I can't drink seawater. Oh. I have forgotten much while I slept. Can you climb back on?*

She towered over me and I could barely lift my head. *I don't think so. No.*

A cloud scudded across Moranu's face, bright and beautiful. From a distance I considered that I might be dying. I should have been able to make it at least three days without water and I'd lasted barely more than one. I made such a lousy adventurer. Kiraka's ruby light blended with the silver from the moon, and I wanted to ask her to tell Nakoa what happened to me, so he wouldn't always wonder, but my throat had closed down. If she could even talk to him as she did with me. So many questions to ask her. Things he needed to know, too.

So much time used up. All those years I'd won, by cheating the death that took my siblings, my parents, all of them. Had I used them wisely? *Hlyti is playing a fine game with me.* Maybe I wouldn't change a thing, as at least I'd had this time with Nakoa. Any turn in the path might not have brought me to him. He might not have had a choice in our marriage either, but he'd been good to me. And I loved him with brutal intensity. Almost from the moment we met, he'd stirred such strong feeling in me. I hadn't known what to do with it. Ursula had tried to warn me . . . *the emotional wounds leave scar tissue that keeps us from being able to feel like normal people do.* Everything I'd felt with him—the lust, the anxiety, even the rage—had all been about falling in love, and I hadn't had the tools to recognize it. Or handle how I felt.

A little more time and I might have figured it out. That and all the puzzles I'd left unsolved. So much left undone. At least Ursula was High Queen. I'd done that much.

Maybe enough to have made my life worthwhile.

The night grew darker. No. More clouds gathered over the moon, hiding her light.

Then the rain began to fall.

Nakoa. My lips shaped his name in hope, in prayer. *Mlai.*

Rain ran into my open mouth, easing the cracked tissues, a gradual moistening. My skin drank it in, too, it seemed, the wetness easing the burning heat. The rainfall increased, drenching me, and I gulped it down. Too much, too fast. Water hit my aching stomach and it convulsed into heaves, bile rising into my throat in a burning cough with it. Afraid I'd choke to death, I wrenched myself onto my side, spitting it out. Then turned my face to Nakoa's rain again, rinsing my mouth and drinking, closing my eyes to concentrate on making myself go slow.

"Dafne *mlai.*" Urgent hands patted my cheeks, stinging my burning skin. "Wake up!"

I opened my eyes, the rain feeling like tears running from them. *Nakoa mlai.*

His breath, already uneven, as if he'd been running a long distance, whooshed out in relief and he sat, gathering me up into his lap, leaning his forehead against mine, hair falling around my face. He took several deep breaths, just as I'd gulped at the water.

"I was so afraid," he whispered. "I couldn't see you. For so long I could not see. Then suddenly here you were. Can you speak?"

"You sent me rain," I croaked.

"Always." He ran his hands over me, skidding across my rain-soaked skin. "Are you injured?"

"Thirsty," I managed.

"Of course." He cupped his palm to the rain, then fed it to me, holding me in the crook of his arm with gentle care. Easier to take it in gradually that way. I leaned against him, savoring the feeling of coming home. I would not treat the gift of him lightly again. How I'd satisfy all of my obligations, I didn't know, but that would be a riddle for another day.

For the moment, I wanted to enjoy being alive.

Finally it felt like enough. I stayed his wrist when he moved to gather more rain. He glanced down at me, concern creasing his face, smiled a little, then turned a wary eye to the dragon again. I'd forgotten Kiraka's presence. Or rather, that her being there would be strange to Nakoa. She lay like a cat on the sand, her forelegs stretched forward, tail curled around herself, and wings mantled against the rain. Ruby eyes glowed with what I would have to call affection.

"Kiraka," I told him. My voice was rusty, each word clawing at my throat.

Nakoa gave me a bemused smile and caressed my cheek. "How do you know?"

I shrugged a little. "She said." I tapped my temple. "Here."

"Ah," he breathed the exclamation, then kissed the spot. "So clever, so wise. You have found what is yours to know."

"Not yet. Soon." I had things to tell him. More important than this. A fit of coughing took me that racked my burned throat.

"No words, *mlai*. We have all the prosperous future for words. Drink."

Nakoa—of course—insisted on carrying me back to the palace. I would have protested but had no voice or strength for it. And he simply scooped me up and started walking as the sun rose, burning off the last of his rainstorm. Kiraka said she'd stay behind, to watch the sunrise and enjoy the cool.

As the light grew, it became clear that we were on the opposite side of the volcano from the palace. How had he found me? How had he come so far, so fast? No wonder he'd been out of breath. Then again, I'd been lying in the rain a long time. Exhaustion overtook me and, though I tried to keep alert, my head kept nodding, until it would hit Nakoa's shoulder, startling me awake again.

"Rest, *mlai*," Nakoa finally said with a frown. "Heal."

One day I would be back to full health, with no injuries, and I'd make sure to stay that way. But I took Nakoa's suggestion— or rather, couldn't fight the dragging sleep anymore—and gave in to it.

He woke me occasionally, each time the sun a bit higher, to drink more water. Once he tried to give me some fruit, but my stomach rebelled and even Nakoa's thunderous frown couldn't make me try it again. When I awakened on my own near midday, a contingent of his guard had met and surrounded us, and we approached the harbor from the far side, away from the palace. Not at all abandoned now, it bustled with ships, all with sails showing colors and symbols of the various islands, some I recognized and some I did not.

Nakoa noted my increased alertness. On some of those other awakenings, I'd barely kept my eyes open long enough to drink the water. "Better?" he asked.

"Much." I felt like I'd never be not thirsty again, but I was far better than I'd expected. My throat no longer burned and my tongue no longer felt like a brick in my mouth.

"Good. I have sent guards ahead to fetch healing help for you." He hesitated. Unusual for him. His face carefully blank, he asked. "Where were you—can you say?"

"Inside the volcano. Tane walled me into a cave, so I would get the treasure for him."

Nakoa gave me a dubious look. "You do not like him, but it was not him. He is at the palace searching for you."

I snorted a laugh, but he didn't join in. "He went back, to make you think so. His men may still wait—outside the cave. High up. I'm not sure where. Kiraka found me and brought me out. It was . . ." Terrifying. Unbearable. My worst nightmare come true. And yet, I'd survived.

"I shall send guards to see."

"And to contain Tane."

"No. He has done nothing wrong."

What? "He tried to kill me!"

"If he had wished to kill you, you would be dead. If he did as you say, he only attempted to use you. A challenge within his rights."

So much about this culture I still didn't understand. Then the import of what he'd said dawned on me. "Are you saying you don't believe me?"

Irritation flickered in his eyes, along with something more. "I don't know what to believe."

"How can you say that?"

He sighed. "Dafne *mlai*. It is no secret you wish to be free of me."

I didn't know what to say to that, except the truth. "I didn't leave you. Tane and his men grabbed me in the library and carried me up there!"

"You were in bed with me." His face set into brooding lines.

"I woke up and couldn't sleep, so I went to the library. Ask your guard at the door."

"They have been asked. They say only that you left. Which I firmly told you not to do. The two who went with you cannot be found."

That didn't bode well. Dead or defected to Tane's side? "When did you tell me not to leave the room?"

He ground his teeth. "I said you were safe with me, but perhaps not the guard."

"I misunderstood." I wanted to clench my own teeth. "I still don't understand everything you say perfectly."

He didn't reply to that. I felt terrible that I'd been foolish. "I'm sorry, Nakoa."

For once he didn't tell me not to be sorry. He simply gazed into the distance, scanning the harbor and ships.

"Do you think I did this to my own hands?"

He didn't respond immediately, squinting at something in the harbor. Or the bay beyond. A runner came up to him panting, speaking the tumbling words so fast all I caught was the pitch of alarm, of an unexpected storm.

"What's going on?" I asked.

Nakoa gave me a look that was, if anything, darker, possibly betrayed. "A ship is arriving and we do not recognize the sails. Friends of yours?"

"How—how would I know?"

"Perhaps this is who you set out to meet."

"I told you, I—"

"Now is not the time. We will talk more."

Yes. Yes, we would.

28

My friends, indeed. The ship flew Ursula's hawk, along with the one for the Thirteen Kingdoms, with thirteen interlinked rings forming a chain within the three overlapping circles of the goddesses. A swell of pride made me unexpectedly weepy for a moment. No doubt much of the jangling emotional aftereffects of the last terrible day and the fight with Nakoa, but also seeing the symbol of what we'd accomplished. On top of all the nostalgia for home.

I was a mess. With Nakoa fuming in betrayed anger and me torn between outrage that he didn't believe me and plaguing guilt that I'd put myself in harm's way and that I'd entertained doing the very thing he blamed me for . . . well, the timing couldn't have been worse. How in the Thirteen had the ship gotten to Nahanau so fast?

I managed to persuade Nakoa to remain at the harbor as the ship pulled in, instead of taking me back to the palace, mainly by dint of arguing that he needed me to translate. At first he replied that anyone understood the point of a knife at their throats, and I very solemnly told him that if he hurt someone I cared about be-

cause he wouldn't let me help negotiate, then I would never forgive him. Who knew who Ursula would have sent to argue for my
release, but I would do everything in my power to prevent blood-
shed.

It made Nakoa even angrier, but he gave in. With ill grace. He
also refused to put me down.

"No. You had your way in staying. I will have my way in this.
Compromise."

"That is not how compromise works," I muttered furiously.
"And don't you ever get tired?"

He gave me a burning look of warning. "Yes. I am tired, *mlai*.
I will be more tired before this is done. Don't fight me in this."

"Does that mean I get to fight you on other things?" I snapped
back.

A hint of amusement lightened his visage. "I expect nothing
other—unless you shed your skin and become someone else, my
dragon queen."

I refused to let that mollify me. "You're only insisting on this
to make a show to my people that you think I belong to you."

"Yes. You do belong to me." He nodded at my growl of frustration. "But not only that. You are still weak and not well. I can
do this for you."

"I could sit," I pointed out.

He shifted me in his arms, pulling me closer and nuzzling my
neck. "What is the pleasure in that?"

Incorrigible man. How I could be both furious with him and
full of love for him escaped me, but that seemed to be my new reality. At least he gave me glimmers of hope that we could find a
way through this. "Fine. Make your show, but when it comes time
to negotiate, I need to stand on my own."

"We will see." All teasing gone, he studied the ship with a
granite expression. If he perceived any threat to me—or to his
keeping me with him—this would go sour very quickly. I would
have to play the conversation with utmost skill. Much depended on

who Ursula had sent. Hopefully someone patient and not likely to bristle at Nakoa's overbearing ways. She would have thought of that, known that the situation demanded tact, someone who put rational diplomacy before action.

The ship docked and the gangplank extended. I caught the metallic gold flash of a crown next to bloodred hair, dashing my hopes for someone reasonable. I groaned mentally. Ursula strode down the plank, hand on the hilt of her sword, followed closely by a grim-faced Harlan.

"This is your queen?" Nakoa asked in a low tone.

"Yes. Let me handle the introductions, Nakoa. I mean it."

He studied her. "We will see."

At least by obstinately keeping me in his arms, he couldn't draw on her and she wouldn't attack him for fear of hurting me. I hoped.

She surveyed Nakoa's warriors lining the pier; then her steely gaze found me, face tightening with anger and concern. She appeared to dismiss Nakoa the same way she seemed uninterested in the guard—a calculated strategy on her part I knew well—and focused on me.

Her eyes shone with cold rage, the talon scars on her cheek going white and pulling slightly. "Dafne—what in Danu happened to you? Are you hurt?"

One day people would stop inquiring after my health before anything else.

"I had quite the night, but I'm fine." I tapped Nakoa's shoulder. "Put me down, please, Nakoa *mlai*."

He gave me a long look, but complied. My legs wobbled a bit and my head swam, so I appreciated his steadying hands on my waist. Now he and Ursula stared each other down over my head, the tension between them as palpable as if I were standing between two infernos.

"King Nakoa KauPo of Nahanau, Her Majesty High Queen

Ursula of the Thirteen Kingdoms. You are allies, not enemies." I said it twice in both languages.

Nakoa's hands flexed on me, but he did not speak. Ursula gave me an incredulous look and spoke in Common Tongue. "Danu take that, Dafne! This man abducted you. Zynda told us everything. He will release you or die."

"He is a dead man, regardless," Harlan promised, as boilingly angry as I'd ever seen him, despite his eerily quiet pronouncement, "for his transgressions against you."

"No. He is my husband. All that has transpired between us has occurred within the marriage customs of these people."

"Not within ours," Ursula ground out. "He abducted and raped you. That's all there is to it."

"That's not true, Your Majesty. I . . ." I couldn't tell them I loved Nakoa before I told him. And it didn't matter that I loved him, because I couldn't stay. It might be better for him if I let him continue to believe I didn't. "I have feelings for him."

They both regarded me with sympathy that edged on pity. "This happens," Ursula said, more softly. "It's common and part of what goes on in the mind in abductions of this kind. You only believe this because of what he's done to you. Once we have you safely away from him, you'll see."

I set my teeth against the frustration of it. The doubt that wormed into my heart, dividing it between them. "We will have that conversation. But look at where you are. You have but one ship. As fierce as you both are, you are surrounded by greater forces. This will be solved diplomatically and I will translate. I am unharmed."

"Are you saying that he hasn't . . ." That flash of old pain in her eyes as she searched for the words.

"I'm all right. I promise. We can talk more, privately, but only after he is reassured that you are here to parley, not to attack."

Not happy, but knowing the truth of it, finally she acknowl-

edged Nakoa. "King Nakoa KauPo. We have much to discuss."
She still said "discuss" like she meant "cut your throat."

I translated for him, resisting the urge to shade the words with
more promising pitches. He heard Ursula's tone well enough as
it was.

"I will hear her words," he replied.

I repeated it exactly and Ursula eyed him, then me. "Here?
I'm not letting you out of my sight."

This time I turned to Nakoa. "Where shall we have this conversation? She is a powerful ruler, a warrior to be wary of and
very angry on my behalf. Not the throne room. Someplace . . ."
Neutral. "With level ground."

"Tell her to follow. Only her and her protector. No one else."

I relayed the instructions and she nodded without surprise, eyes
narrowing a bit, however, when Nakoa caressed my cheek. "Will
you insist on walking, my dragon queen, or may I carry you?"

I felt much better, though my mouth was already parched
again and the headache had returned. A concession, too, for him
to ask, which made it far more bearable, as undignified as it made
me. I held up my hand, unfolding my fingers to show him my
open palm, a sign of appreciation that made him smile, ever so
slightly. "Please carry me, *mlai*. And if I could have more water?"

He swept me up, barking out commands. A young woman immediately ran up with a bowl of water, which I drank, offering her
my thanks. Without further words, Nakoa headed up the trail to
the palace. Ursula and Harlan followed behind, heads bent together as they conferred, Nakoa's guard falling in behind.

He didn't go far, taking a fork from the palace path to one that
led to a clearing on a ridge overlooking the harbor and palace
both. A flurry of servants had placed a table there with four
chairs—and a footstool for me, of course—and set it with pitch-
ers of water and wine, along with platters of food.

Nakoa set me in the chair and I relaxed into it, feeling as if I might never get up again. One of Inoa's ladies hastened up, giving Nakoa a fresh garland for me. I'd totally forgotten that mine had broken in the library. He made more of a display than usual, holding it so that I had to bend my head to accept it. Once I did, he picked up my hand, held my gaze with not quite a smile, then pressed a kiss to the inside of my wrist before letting me go so Inoa's lady could minister to me.

She immediately lathered the numbing cream on my feet. The rest of me hurt so much, I'd forgotten about them, so the relief came nearly as a shock. I drank down more water as she worked to clean them. Then let her do the same with my hands.

Nakoa sat beside me, observing her work, Ursula and Harlan across from us. Ursula made a visible effort to choke back her seething temper, while Harlan's anger seemed to have abated, leaving interest behind, as he observed Nakoa with a neutral expression.

"Maybe we should start with why you look like you've been dragged behind a horse through a forest fire," Ursula suggested in a dry tone that didn't fool me for a minute. She'd watched Nakoa's ritual with ill-concealed hostility and clearly itched to take her blade to him, and Danu take the consequences.

"It's a long—ow!" One of my fingers sang with bright pain and Inoa's lady looked aghast. Especially when Nakoa questioned her sharply.

"It's likely broken." Harlan eyed my hands from across the table. "Possibly several others. Will the king allow me to set them for you?"

He'd done that for Ursula, straightening the nose Uorsin had smashed. The memory still made me queasy and I wasn't sure I'd be brave enough. Still he'd done a good job of it.

"Nakoa *mlai*, this is Captain Harlan of the Vervaldr, the High Queen's . . . protector. He has healing skills and offers to help me."

Nakoa gave Harlan a distinctly unfriendly once-over. "Dasnarian?"

Harlan inclined his head and replied in that language. "By birth. Not by allegiance, King Nakoa KauPo."

Nakoa grunted a non-reply but nodded his agreement and made room for Harlan, dismissing Inoa's lady. "For you, *mlai*."

"I know. Thank you. Thank you for all of this." I gestured to the refreshments and Ursula. "Will you be patient more and allow me to tell her what's happened in our language?

He smiled, a minute twitch of his set mouth. "You are meek when you want something. I shall remember that, in the future. Tell her what she needs to know. But you will eat and drink as you talk." He sat back, arms folded, watching Harlan kneel beside me to take my hands carefully in his big ones.

"It might be better," Harlan said, raising an eyebrow at Ursula, "to get Dafne taken care of first, and save the negotiations for later."

"It would be *better*," she snapped, "to get Dafne on the ship and take care of her there."

"Nakoa would not stand for it," I snapped back, echoing her tone. "Work with me here. I'm doing the best I can to keep you all from killing each other. Your Majesty," I added.

Harlan swallowed a laugh and she considered me with some surprise. And more than a hint of betrayal. "Dispense with the formalities and give us the story already."

I told her the tale, picking up from what Zynda had relayed to her, having to pause now and again when Harlan's ministrations grew impossible to ignore. Though they were broken in three places, the two smallest fingers on my left hand were "only" fractured, he said, which meant they wouldn't need to be reset, to my great relief. Using supplies from the packs on his belt, he splinted my fingers and bandaged them, listening without comment as I spoke. My hands free, and at Nakoa's pointed glare, I tried eating some fruit. Thankfully my stomach didn't rebel, so I continued to nibble, taking it slowly.

When I finished—telling her everything except personal details, like talking to the dragon and the other pieces I'd promised not to share—Ursula tapped her fingers on the table, assessing Nakoa. He returned her regard with the even stare of a man poised to fight.

"Stupid of you not to have your blades on you," she finally said.

"Thank you. How very helpful of you to point that out. *This* is where you want to start?" I was more than a little tired of feeling bad about getting kidnapped. Twice.

She sighed, looking as if she longed to remove the crown. Which I was frankly impressed she'd worn. "I don't know where to start," she admitted. "It's all so . . . fantastic and difficult to take in. Dragons. It seems like there's more that you're not saying. Things you aren't telling me. Which is not like you."

Always so thrice-damned perceptive, noting my evasions. "I need to do more research on them. There's a great deal I don't understand still. It would be good to consult with Zynda, if she came along?" Maybe the Tala had legends of these ancient shapeshifters.

"She stayed behind to work with Andi," Ursula replied a bit absently, still in deep thought, considering me with her sharp gaze.

"And yet *you* came here, when you should not have left the High Throne. I expressly told her to remind you of that. You've put yourself in danger by coming here."

"Maybe one day you'll listen to me," Harlan murmured.

"What's the point of being High Queen if I can't do what I want to?" she retorted, annoyed but with a hint of amusement at quoting Ami. Relieved to hear her sounding more herself, I pursued the topic. Anything to keep her off my divided loyalties.

"And how did you get here so fast anyway?"

She raised her eyebrows. "We took a shortcut."

Through Annfwn. Of course. "The Tala have sailing ships?"

"Rayfe still plays a cagey game with me, but I have to admit, when we heard what happened to you, he held back nothing." Reminded of that, she leveled her glare on Nakoa.

I wanted to hear what else had gone on, how things fared with adjusting the barrier, but by the burn of Nakoa's gaze, he would lose the last of his patience soon. We needed to reach some kind of détente before we could move ahead. Ursula's uncertain temper wouldn't make it easy.

"Here are the other things you need to know. You and Nakoa must come to terms on how the kingdoms will intersect. The barrier has cut off some islands and they don't understand why."

"You haven't told him?" She seemed to be asking more than the surface question, but I wasn't sure what.

"I haven't told him any of this yet, but that should be the first order of priority."

"Seeing to your safety is my first priority."

"No. The obligations of the High Throne come before I do. You know full well you shouldn't have left, but since you're here in person, then let's get this treaty handled."

"You want me to negotiate with the man who treated you this way?" Her voice carried a keen edge.

"That's not a question for you. It's between Nakoa and me."

"I don't agree. Look at you. If nothing else, he's clearly failed to protect you from his enemies. And he's transgressed against you, my adopted sister and a woman under my protection."

"We're handling the question of these enemies. I'm handling where I stand with him. I'm asking you to give me the respect of letting me do that. If I need your help, I'll ask for it. In the meantime, what I'm asking of you is that you establish a level of good faith with him so he won't view you as another enemy. For the good of the Thirteen, Your Majesty."

She pressed her narrow lips together. "I promise nothing, but we can set it aside for the moment. Tell me—why haven't you told him about the barrier?"

"First, because I'm still learning the thrice-damned language and haven't had the nuance to explain all this. Second, because you told me not to without your direction. I wouldn't go against that."

"I wasn't sure where your loyalty lay," she answered softly, a glint of betrayal in her gray eyes, not at all unlike the way Nakoa had looked at me. I hated that I'd put it there, for either of them. Totally different people, the two of them, yet so alike in many ways.

"You will always have my loyalty, my Queen," I told her. Then I reached out to take Nakoa's hand. He eyed me curiously, but cupped my bandaged hand in both of his. "But I owe him certain promises also." *First.* "If you will align yourselves as allies, as I believe you can do, then I won't have to choose."

"You can't be loyal to us both. You will have to choose, no matter what is decided today." She pressed the point home with lethal precision, laying open my heart. "I'm not at all convinced he hasn't messed with your mind in some way. All this magic. We know it can be done. Remember Illyria—she affected your thoughts then."

I almost couldn't draw a breath, as if my lungs burned with sulfur still. "I promise to consider that. Let's get the politics out of the way first. It has to be dealt with, regardless. Please."

"And the question of your loyalty to the High Throne?"

Harlan shifted, as if he wanted to touch her, but thought better of it.

"I honestly don't know." I held her gaze. "Don't make me face that decision, Ursula. I'm asking you for that."

She wasn't at all happy with me. I'd seen her furious—and betrayed—with Harlan, her sisters, various others, but never like this with me. It took a great deal for me not to back down in the face of that. Standing behind her, Harlan gave me a sympathetic nod.

"Fine." She faced Nakoa directly, closing me out. "Translate, then."

Concentrating on the moment, I focused on doing my job.

It took several hours just to get past the explanations. I nearly regretted pushing for this conversation to happen so soon. Already prickly and suspicious of my actions, Nakoa did not receive Ursula's explanation of the barrier and its movements well at all. It did not help that she was beyond aggravated herself and wavering in her trust in me, which made her impatient with my slow translation. Or that I searched for words to convey a number of concepts that hadn't come up in conversation thus far. She didn't understand the scope of Nakoa's island kingdom and he expressed incredulity at the concept of the magical barrier and plainly regarded all of it as an aggressive move on Ursula's part. Understandable, as she told him that his kingdom was part of hers whether he liked it or not, so he'd better start liking it.

At one point, they were both snarling at each other across the table, nearly about to leap over and throttle each other. Harlan finally put a restraining hand on Ursula and spoke in her ear, earning such a malicious glare from her I expected he'd be in for trouble later also. She called a break, which Nakoa agreed to, and walked off a ways to stand at the edge of the precipice.

I took advantage of the reprieve to send for Akamai to help with translation—and to bring the big map. It might not help, but the negotiation was failing miserably and I didn't know how to resolve their differences.

Particularly when their main difference was me, and who held my allegiance.

"Holding up all right?" Harlan asked me.

Nakoa had stepped off to talk with some of his guard and messengers but hadn't taken his eyes off me. "I'm beginning to feel like a piece of meat being torn between two lions."

He laughed, oddly making me feel better that he could. "They both love you and have to come to terms with that. The politics will sort out. You're doing a fine job."

"You think Nakoa loves me?"

Harlan regarded me with some surprise. "How can you doubt it? He treats you as a treasured wife."

"Yes, but there are other things going on. He does that for any number of reasons—all very complicated."

"It's not complicated at all, librarian." Harlan glanced at Ursula's back. "A man doesn't look at a woman as the king does you, doesn't read her smallest gesture as he does, if he doesn't love her. Trust me, I know."

"What did you say to her, to back her off?"

He made a wry grimace. "I told her she sounded like Uorsin."

I goggled at him. "A low blow."

"I save it for extremes." He assessed her rigid spine. "Sometimes she needs to hear it, as I need to hear when I'm in the wrong. This is what lovers do for each other."

"Will she forgive you?"

"Oh yes." He grinned. "I know how to get through to my Essla. Just as I imagine you know how to deal with your king."

"I don't know. I don't have much experience with this." I hesitated. But when else would I have the opportunity to get a man's advice on this? "He's really angry with me and I don't know what to do. He thinks I meant to leave him on purpose."

Harlan's face softened in sympathy. "The more we love someone, the more they can hurt us. He will listen to you."

"The thing is . . ." I had to sip some water to wet my mouth. "I will leave him. I have to. My place is serving Ursula."

He studied me thoughtfully, then patted my shoulder. "That is something for you to sort out, then. But I will do what I can to ease your way. She will cool off. Eventually." He glanced at Ursula again.

Doing my own assessment, I looked in Nakoa's direction, trying to make it seem unconnected to my conversation. His white-streaked brows had lowered and he glared menacingly at Harlan. "Maybe you should start making up to her—and let the king see."

"Ah, yes. We can remove at least that concern." He stood, poured a glass of wine, and went to her. Running a hand down her back, he offered her the wine, then brushed her temple with a kiss, saying something that made her unbend. She turned her head, profile sharp against the sky, and replied with a rueful shake of her head, then leaned in when he put an arm around her.

I hadn't meant the display of their status to be quite that obvious, but at least Nakoa looked more thoughtful than brooding. He even gave me a hint of a smile and came to sit beside me.

"You are tired," he said.

"So are you," I replied. "And we will be more tired before this is done."

He didn't smile exactly, but his gaze softened from its stony intensity. "Your queen loves you."

"I tried to warn you."

"Yes." He took my hand and held it. "I do not always listen."

"Tell me another tale," I tried to tease him, but trouble lurked in his gaze as it went to Harlan and Ursula.

"The Dasnarian is more than her protector—he is her husband? Not king?"

"Her lover, yes. It is not so . . . straightforward with them. There are rules."

"It is straightforward." He got that obstinate look, then touched my garland. "They are *mlai* as we are. No rule is greater than that."

"Nakoa . . ." I didn't know what to tell him. Harlan was wrong. I had no idea how to talk to this man, to get him to understand.

Sure enough, his face darkened, a cloud passing over the sun. "We will discuss later. Tell me one thing. Which of us do you argue for?"

I sipped more water. Ursula's question again. "You are both

precious to me. There need be no winner or loser. You can work together and I don't have to choose."

"You will have to choose, *mlai*," he said softly, an echo of Ursula. "Do you promise me this is true, about the magic barrier?"

"Yes, I would not lie to you."

"Not about that." And he turned away, just as Ursula had done.

29

By the time Ursula and Harlan returned to the ship for the night—as all agreed that would be the best place for them—I was ready to bash both her and Nakoa's heads together.

I was also skull-poundingly exhausted. Though Nakoa carried me back to the palace, we did not speak. I suspected he was as tired of arguments as I.

The big break had come when I convinced Ursula of Nakoa's power to make it rain—though I did not mention that he'd sent rain as far as Ordnung's environs, which might only make her more wary of his abilities—and when Nakoa agreed to help beleaguered Aerron in exchange for a tentative agreement on an allied kingdom status, based on what we'd worked up for Annfwn. I'd thought Rayfe had been stubborn on points, but he had nothing on Nakoa. Though we'd had Andi to smooth the way with the King of the Tala and I had no such power over my dragon king.

After our brief talk during the break, Nakoa seemed less angry with me, but I couldn't shake the lingering sting that I'd disappointed him. As I'd disappointed Ursula. It seemed that, no matter what I did, I let one or the other of them down. Keeping a promise to one meant breaking my word to the other.

I had no idea how to come to a solution that would please everyone.

Fortunately Nakoa simply dropped me off in our rooms, where a bath and a number of ladies waited to help me, and left again with a comment that he'd be back later. I needed the time to think. Or not think, more precisely.

To my utter shock, the mirror that remained a fixture in my rooms showed that I did indeed look like I'd been roasted in a fireplace. My eyebrows had singed to nearly nothing and my hair had crisped on the ends. The golden tan had deepened further, making my eyes look lighter by comparison, almost amber. The flimsy gown I'd had on for far too long was rent in places and filthy.

No wonder Ursula thought I'd lost my mind.

Maybe I had.

I loved Nakoa—no escaping that realization—but Harlan's glib reassurances that Nakoa loved me also were not something I could accept as readily. Nakoa had other reasons for his possessiveness, ones I'd sworn not to reveal. Some tied to Kiraka and her gifts. Others part of his admirable dedication to the throne and his people. Maybe some, as Ursula pointed out, due to the mind-clouding effects of magic. Certainly our relationship had been intensely overwhelming from the beginning. Neither of us loved for rational reasons, built on friendship and mutual regard.

And, in the end, did it matter if he loved me or if I loved him? I didn't belong in Nahanau. He clearly counted on me to be his queen and have his babies. Two things I couldn't do. We would have to part and the time had come for it. Maybe it was better that he was angry with me and felt I'd let him down. It would make it easier to sever this ill-advised liaison of ours.

I would get over him eventually.

I felt tremendously better to be clean, though not at all looking forward to the coming arguments. I considered waiting for Nakoa on the balcony, with the evening going from golden to violet. The bed, however, looked so inviting that I decided to lie down and close my eyes, for just a few moments. A bit of rest to fortify myself for the fight with my dragon king.

I awoke to early morning sun, still in my light gown, but under the sheet, the net curtains drawn around the bed. I'd slept straight through the night because Nakoa had never come back. My heart lurched into panic. Had something happened to him? Or was he that angry with me?

I sat up, thrusting off the sheet, ready to go look for him. But he was there after all. Farther away in the bed than usual, deeply and silently asleep. I lay down again, relieved. Then edged closer, carefully, though he hadn't awakened at my abrupt movements so far.

He lay on his side, facing me, the white sheet draped over his hip, and even in sleep he still looked tired. Less forbidding, though. Younger, somehow, with none of his usual stern lines. A different face of him. The volcano as it had been when it was serene, no crags from the eruption. No broken lip. Perhaps he'd looked more carefree before he'd endured so much for his people. We knew so little about each other.

I lay there, studying him in this unguarded moment, as I so rarely had the opportunity to do, and as if I could somehow see into him if I looked long enough. It felt oddly peaceful, just to be near him, listening to the rising chorus of birdsong out the windows, so unlike any others I'd heard before. Along with that strange chirp that I felt sure wasn't a bird, but kept forgetting to ask about.

I was tempted to touch him. To reach out and establish some kind of physical contact to bridge the distance between us, if it could be bridged. I stopped my hand before I touched him, letting it fall to rest between us. What I truly needed to do was think about what I could say to him. But, as they had been doing lately, words evaded me, fading before they formed, leaving my mind as empty as a blank page.

Nakoa opened his eyes. Such a deep color in his still peaceful face. He didn't seem at all surprised to see me watching him sleep. He simply put his hand over mine where it lay on the sheet between us, lacing his fingers between mine.

We stayed like that, neither of us speaking the words that would break the peace of the moment. Though we'd have to. The sounds of the palace rose beyond the windows, a different kind of song, and a reminder of the world we were obligated to rejoin before much longer. Still, I clung to being silent. Maybe if neither of us said anything, if we simply stayed in that moment, we could work a magic to let us stay there forever.

Nakoa shifted, parting his lips. But not to say anything. To kiss me. He drew me to him, kissing me softly, speakingly. I answered as best I knew how, pouring all of the love I felt, but could not responsibly confess, into returning the kiss. He let go my hand to cup my head and I indulged in touching him then, smoothing my hands over the intricate scales of his tattoos.

Brushing the narrow straps of the sleeping gown from my shoulders, he slid the fabric down, slowly, almost lazily, then followed the path with his hands, stroking my skin as he revealed it. I reveled in it, drinking in his touch, as thirsty for this as I'd been for water. It quenched something in me in a way I feared nothing ever would again.

Feeling desperate for him, as if we'd already parted, I pressed myself closer, crushing my bared breasts against his chest, the fragrance of bruised petals from my garland entwining with the scent of him, filling my head. His heartbeat thudded through me and, as if he understood and felt the same way, he pulled off the rest of the gown and held me tight against him, his big hands splayed on my back and bottom.

"Nakoa *mlai*," I gasped, and he murmured something, a phrase I didn't recognize. He coaxed a hand over my bottom, lifting my thigh over his hip, fingers dipping into my cleft from behind. Finding me more than ready for him, he slowly entered me, eyes black as a moonless night boring into mine. He filled me deliciously,

and my heart ached with it all. Where I'd been thirsty, now I
swelled to the breaking point. He rocked his hips and I cried out
with it, the pleasure so exquisitely intense it was nearly painful.
More than that, though. He was so much bigger than I that we'd
never been so face-to-face as in this position. The intensity of the
connection seemed deeper, sharper than ever before. Maybe he
did see into me, because I felt laid bare, unable to look away, even
when I came apart.

We finally untangled ourselves and Nakoa got up to bring me
a cloth, watching as I cleaned his spilled seed from my thighs. He
took it from me when I finished, wordlessly wiping himself off.
Then tossed it aside and looked at me, both of us naked, most of
the bed between us.

"I suppose it's time for us to discuss now," I said, the waiting
more painful than the dread.

"Yes. Put your gown on. We will talk over breakfast."

"I'm not really hungry," I said to his retreating back as he went
to the door. He only threw me a look, some of the forbidding
frown returning to his brow. Fine, then.

I dressed and brushed my hair. Soon the servants streamed in,
bringing all manner of food and drink, setting it up on the balcony. Obediently I sat and filled my plate. Nakoa did likewise and
the silence stretched on. No longer peaceful, but full of all the
words we both hesitated to speak.

Deciding not to wait for him to voice whatever accusation
lurked behind his increasingly stony expression, I took the initia-
tive. "I did not leave you, Nakoa. You were sound asleep and I
was awake. I went to the library to study."

He sighed. Broke a roll in two and handed me half. "There is
no blocked-up cave. None of Tane's men missing. No sign you
were in the library."

"So they cleaned up!"

"No one saw you go."

"I was wrapped up in a rug. Ask the servants if one is missing."

His jaw took on a stubborn set. "How did I not awake? I am trained as a warrior. None can sneak up on me."

"You sleep very deeply, Nakoa."

He shook his head. "I do not. Never have."

"You do with me. Look at this morning."

He didn't reply to that, simply simmered.

"Fine, then. What is your explanation for what happened?"

"I don't have one. However, I do not disbelieve you. The details will sort out. You were hurt, but not killed. Tane may have challenged you, but the win is yours."

I hadn't thought of it that way. I suppose I had defeated Tane.

"This is not the most important problem between us," Nakoa added.

The water I'd guzzled turned chill in my stomach. "What is?"

He set down the roll and wrapped his fist in the other hand, leaning his chin on them, regarding me soberly. With sorrow, even. "Perhaps I was wrong to make you stay."

I didn't need anyone to tell me he didn't admit to being wrong easily. I wanted to tell him he hadn't been wrong, but he had. At the same time, I couldn't blame him for his actions. Not in the same way I once had. Tongue-tied, I gazed back at him helplessly.

He nodded, confirming something in his own head. "You never wished to be with me. I see it in your face. All along, even when you are closest to me, you think of how you'll leave. You promised I would be first with you, but I am not. Your queen is and you wish to return with her."

"Nakoa . . ."

He waited, but I couldn't think of what else to say.

"Do you deny it?" he asked gently. "Is there another truth I'm not seeing?"

"I—I can't be who you want me to be, Nakoa. I never was that person. I never would have . . . accepted your garland if I'd known what it meant. I'm not meant to be a queen or work magic or talk to dragons. I'm good with books, history, knowledge—not this." I waved a hand between us. My fumbling through this conversation was a perfect example of my lack of ability in this arena. "I'm too old to have babies. All my life, I've known my place. And . . . this isn't it."

"You feel nothing for me. I am not *mlai*." He said it neutrally, no question in it, his face an implacable mask.

I wanted to tell him I did love him. I wanted to weep. All along I knew it would come to this inevitable conclusion, but with the moment staring me in the face, I wanted to fight it. I could. It would be easy to tell him I wanted to stay. But then I'd have to break my promises to Ursula, destroy her faith in me, after all she'd done for me. Not something I could do, however much I wanted to. This was what I'd worked for since we arrived on Nahanau and I had to take it.

"I will help you seal the bond with Kiraka. I think I understand what she needs. When we've finalized the discussions with Her Majesty, I'll go to the library. I might know where to look for clues to the treasure. I won't leave you with your throne in question."

"And then you'll leave with your queen."

"I have to. Will you let me go?"

"I will let you go, *mlai*. If you ask, I will say yes." He gave me a somber, searching look. "I will not fight you in this any longer. But I will continue to hope that you will not ask."

A knife thrust to my heart. I couldn't keep doing this. "I'm asking now."

He looked away then, gazing out over the glittering ocean. "Go, then. If all that is in your heart is a wish to part from me, then you shall walk onto the ship and your feet never touch the soil of your home again."

"This is not my home, Nakoa. It never was."

"Perhaps this is so, Dafne *mlai*. I thought I was wise in this and it seems it's not so. Many things have been broken. Perhaps this is also."

My heart felt sliced open. "I would change this, if I could. But I can't abandon my responsibilities any more than you can."

He nodded, still not looking at me. "We all do only what we can."

We received Ursula and Harlan in court this time. I sat beside Nakoa in my full regalia, playing the part of his queen, intensely uncomfortable doing so, particularly in front of them. We needed only to formalize the treaty agreements, in the full eyes of Nakoa's nobles. Ursula's keen, assessing gaze rested on me far too much through the ceremonial greetings. No doubt disconcerted to see me playact in her usual role.

When Nakoa announced the nature of the treaty, Chief Tane objected.

No surprise there. In fact, I'd been watching him surreptitiously, waiting for his move. He'd been watching me, too, more openly, with oily hatred in his gaze. Twice now I'd defeated him. I resolved I'd see him set back a third and final time. I could do this much for Nakoa, if nothing else.

"I object to this alliance." Tane postured boldly.

"On what basis?" Nakoa asked, sounding quite bland. He'd presented the situation as such—an alliance with another powerful realm, to keep the Dasnarian Empire at bay—and had not revealed the reasons that made it not only necessary, but a forgone conclusion.

"You are not truly king, thus have no authority to do so."

I'd had enough of this. "King Nakoa KauPo *is* king. He has proved himself as no king in recent past has done. Not in generations have the people of Nahanau seen the return of the *mo'o*. She is here now, to enjoy the king's peaceful rain, to bring bounty to the people again, as ancient legend promised."

He blinked at me, taken aback for a long moment. So did many of the nobles. *Not a silly airhead, after all, you dolts.* I thought it with vicious satisfaction. In the back of my mind, Kiraka agreed in affectionate amusement.

"There is no proof—"

"You want proof?" The moment of truth. Ursula and Harlan stood back, both watching me for clues to what transpired. *Kiraka—are you ready?*

Yes, Daughter.

Come show yourself, gracious lady.

She laughed. *Gladly.*

I put my hand on Nakoa's. "Show them, my King. Call the dragon so the people may see to understand."

Despite the gulf between us, despite my broken promises to him, he didn't question me. Instead he stood, bringing me to my feet also. He raised his hands, as he'd done bringing the rain, keeping mine joined to his, and I echoed him. Thunder rumbled. The ground vibrated beneath our feet. Ursula raised her eyebrows. In the distance Kiraka trumpeted. Moments later, she arrived, landing with spectacular grace on the escarpment beyond the hall, neck curved coyly and tail arched. Clearly enjoying herself.

Is this enough?

Yes, Kiraka. Thank you. You look beautiful.

As do you, Daughter.

"Do you need further proof, Chief Tane?" Nakoa asked, more gently than the man deserved. Just as he'd been with me.

To my surprise, Tane bluffed no more. Truly, he seemed shaken. He turned his gaze on me, then Nakoa, and inclined his head.

"No, King Nakoa KauPo, Queen Dafne Nakoa KauPo. The people await the treasure your reign will bring."

After that the discussions went reasonably smoothly. Especially as the enchantment of a playful Kiraka distracted everyone. With her permission, people went out in groups to meet her and touch her smooth scales. Before long, children clambered over her, shrieking with laughter. Elders greeted her with shaking hands, crying that they'd never expected to live to see her return.

The nobles who did focus agreed that the terms of the treaty were considerably better than what the Dasnarians had attempted to inflict on the Nahanauns. I'd made sure to introduce wording that prevented the High Throne of the Thirteen—or whatever the number would be, once the islands were all counted up—from laying claim to any of Nahanau's wealth, now or in the future, however it might be defined. Trade, yes. Tithing, no.

I'd borrowed that piece entirely from Rayfe, who'd demanded it to protect the abundance of Annfwn. Ursula gave me a hard look at that clause, likely wondering what was to be had from the storm-ravaged islands, but signed off regardless.

Kiraka might not have gold and jewels, but I wanted to be sure that whatever wealth she did bring would belong to Nakoa and the Nahanauns. Disloyal of me, but there it was. And Ursula was no Uorsin, to pillage the kingdoms of their best, to elevate Ordnung. Else I could never have supported her.

The main difference between the agreement with Nakoa and the one with Rayfe was that this one was not predicated on marriage uniting the royal families. Ursula had made it abundantly clear the day before that she regarded my marriage to Nakoa as void to begin with, consummated or not. In a more cautious mood today, she stopped short of accusing Nakoa of rape, or of forcing me to marry him under duress, but she also refused to acknowledge the connection.

The day before, Nakoa had fought her on it. No more. He simply let it pass without comment. *I will not fight you on this any longer.*

With the treaties in place, Ursula magically transformed from invading enemy to—if not exactly a treasured ally—at least an honored guest. Exactly as I'd hoped it would work. Kiraka stayed for a while longer, frolicking in the sea, happy to be with the children. She flew off again as court adjourned, saying to call if I needed her.

Nakoa and Inoa took Ursula, Harlan, a group of Hawks, and Tala sailors from the ship on a tour of the island and palace. I begged off to work in the library, though the irony didn't escape me that they would have seen more of the island than I. It gave me a pang that Inoa stepped so easily back into the role of playing hostess for her brother, but that was how it should be.

Akamai went with them, performing the laborious three-step translation from Nahanaun to Dasnarian, which Harlan then relayed to Ursula in Common Tongue. I tried not to feel guilty about it and poured that energy into studying the N'andana texts. I was missing something about the root of this magic and what the promised treasure could be. Though Tane had backed down, I hated to leave Nakoa with anything for the chief to use as an opening. If only I could find the key to being able to read the language, it would possibly answer so many riddles. How magic propagated. Why the barrier went up in the first place. How to manage it in the future.

"It seems I'm meeting you on your territory this time."

Startled by Ursula's voice, I looked up to see her standing across the table from me.

"Your Majesty! I apolo—"

"Oh, shut up with that, Dafne. Or, I suppose I should say, Queen Dafne Nakoa KauPo."

I groaned and scrubbed my face with my hands. "Please don't."

"How are you feeling?"

"Surprisingly good, actually. I seem to heal quickly these days. All the island sunshine, perhaps."

She studied me a moment. "Can I sit?"

"Sorry! Of course. Or we could go somewhere—"

"This is good. Quiet. Private." She sat, adjusting her sword as she did. "The dagger goes well on that knife belt—is it Jepp's?"

"Yes. She gave it to me just before she left. It wasn't her fault, Your Majesty, that she left me here. She had no choice."

Ursula didn't answer immediately, pursing her lips in thought. "If you call me 'Your Majesty' one more time, I might run you through. Since when are we not friends?"

I gaped at her, scrambling for a reply. First Nakoa, now her. I couldn't seem to get anything right. "I'm sorry. I didn't mean to—"

"And stop acting all humble and contrite!" she snapped.

"Stop interrupting me!"

Unexpectedly, she grinned. "That's better."

I shook my head at her. "It's just been . . . such a mess. I let you down. I got myself embroiled in this mess. You had to come rescue me and I still know nothing more about what you sent me to find out. I expect you to be angry and disappointed with me."

"I did not *have* to come rescue you. As you pointed out, I should not have. I could have sent someone else to extricate you."

"Why didn't you?"

She looked thoughtful. "Gut instinct? First of all, as I told you before you left Ordnung, I consider you part of my family. You know how I feel about protecting the ones I love. For good or ill, it's how I'm built. I couldn't have made myself stay behind again. It nearly killed me to do it once."

"Who did you leave in charge, anyway?"

She smirked. "Groningen."

"Oh." I thought about it. "Good choice."

"Yes. He agreed on the contingency that, in my absence, he would be revoking every one of Uorsin's policies he hated the most. In order."

"Goddesses." I was surprised she'd agreed to that.

She followed my thought, too, and shrugged. "He's a savvy king. Any policy or law he hates likely should be abolished—and he'll save me doing it. It worked out well. I get some distance from being tied to the throne and he gets to destroy his enemy's legacy."

"I should have known you came yourself in part because you wanted adventure."

"True. It wasn't easy to sit tight with tedious details instead of being the one out seeing what was going on. But . . . I also had a feeling that I needed to handle the negotiations myself. Having seen what I have, I'm glad I did."

"Because Nakoa is difficult to deal with?"

She smiled slightly and tipped her head in acknowledgment. "That. Though I know you smoothed the way for me considerably there—thank you. I apologize that I didn't think to tell you so yesterday."

"I'm sorry I couldn't do more. That I let you down."

"That's the second time you've said that." An illustration on the table caught her eye and she turned it slightly to see it better, then glanced up at me. "You've never let me down. If anything, I let you down yesterday by jumping to conclusions and saying some unfair things. I'll apologize for that, too. I was in a temper and not at my best." She grimaced ruefully.

"Harlan give you a talking-to?"

"Considering he's the most loving, gentle man I've ever known, he's sure good at kicking my ass."

This is what lovers do for each other.

"At any rate," she continued, "I have . . . certain scars that blind me sometimes. I was so worried about you and what you might have been forced into that I failed to see how much you love Nakoa and how much he treasures you."

"But . . . But you insisted that the marriage doesn't exist."

"It doesn't," she replied in a crisp tone, rapping her knuckles on the table. "You are my subject, my ward, my adopted sister, and my councilor. A foreign king has no right to abduct you and make you his bride without my say-so. I discussed as much with Nakoa before coming here to find you."

Which meant translated through Akamai and Harlan. I wanted to bang my forehead on the desk, thinking of the four of them discussing my sex life. This was worse than anything even Jepp had put me through.

"It's a bad precedent," she said, a smile in her voice. "My councilor would have been the first to say so, once upon a time."

"You have a point." She was right. I'd been so muddled, I hadn't even considered that aspect.

"So I offered to negotiate your hand in marriage and suggested a number of concessions that would come along with aligning our families." She watched me, keen-edged silver in her eyes.

Uh-oh. I swallowed my trepidation. "What did Nakoa say?"

She folded her arms on the table and leaned in, every inch the predatory hawk Harlan liked to call her. "He thanked me for the generous offer, said that he wished he could accept, for his benefit and for his people's, but that you and he had discussed it and you planned to return to Ordnung with me."

"Well—"

"Is it true?" She cut me off. "Yes or no?"

"Yes."

She straightened, truly flabbergasted. "When Danu grows pink roses, Dafne!"

30

"What? But you said yesterday that—"
"I know what I said." She waved it off. "And I'm sorry I interrupted you again, but I can't listen to this foolishness."

"My promises to you are not foolishness!"

"No." She said it quietly, her face softening. "They're not. But I release you from them, regardless. I also release you from your vows of fealty, which you can renew—if you wish—as Queen of Nahanau, ally of the High Throne. I even wrote it down, as I know you're fond of records." She fished out a scroll and set it in front of me. I didn't touch it.

"Why?"

"Dafne." She reached over to touch my hand. "Do you remember what I asked you that day, before we got word of Kral's forces?"

"You asked me what I wanted out of life and I said to serve you and the High Throne."

"And that you never met anyone you liked enough to marry. Now you have." Her smile broadened at my consternation. "Not that being married to Nakoa will be a picnic. Fortunately you have experience managing irascible and obstinate monarchs. You're perfect for the job."

"But . . . Ursula." I found myself gripping her hand. "I can't be queen."

"Why not? You'll probably be a better one than I am. I was watching you. You're much more calm and level-headed. Bringing in the dragon was a stroke of brilliance. It intimidated even me."

I laughed at the thought of anything intimidating her. Here I'd thought she'd been seeing how woefully wrong for it I was.

"I'm not a princess, though."

"So?" She shrugged. "Uorsin was a sailor. If it would make you feel better, I'll adopt you officially as my sister and give you the title. I should have done so already, but I've been busy. I did declare Astar heir, however, which should make you happy to cross off your list."

"Now you're just teasing me."

"Well . . . yes." Her grin took on a mischievous glint. It struck me then, how much happier she'd become. No longer so exhausted or worn down by care. It helped to have Uorsin gone, yes, but also Harlan had done that for her. *This is what lovers do for each other.* "About your endless lists, not about you or Astar."

"I don't know what to say."

"You're welcome. Now, go make up with Nakoa."

"That might not be easy."

"Never is, when you wound someone who loves you. All you can do is be honest, try to make up for it. Groveling helps. Danu knows I have."

I sighed, surveying the texts strewn before me. "I suppose, if I'm not leaving with you, this puzzle can wait."

"What do you work on?"

I chewed my lip. "I can't really tell you."

She laughed. "You and Andi, with all your magic secrets."

Something niggled at me. Andi and the Tala. "Do you remember, when we arrived in Annfwn's cliff city and that elder in their council spoke to you? She said, 'Annfwn did not expect to feel your feet upon her stones.'"

Ursula nodded slowly. "I recall thinking at the time it was unusual wording. Of course, Common Tongue wasn't her native language."

"This thing I'm working on—how much did Zynda tell you about what happened when we arrived?"

"I made her tell me in detail, several times, before I let her leave for Annfwn," Ursula replied in a dry tone.

Poor Zynda. "My feet got injured because Nakoa insisted on taking off my stockings and I wasn't used to going barefoot. Something happened when I stepped off the dock and my feet touched the soil of the island. And Nakoa said something to me this morning like that, that if I wished to part from him, I would walk onto your ship and my feet would never touch the soil of my home again."

"Ouch," she commented.

"I told you he's unhappy with me."

She smiled ruefully, a mirror of mine, and we shared a strange camaraderie in that moment. "He'll forgive you," she said. "I've done much worse to Harlan and he manages to forgive me."

You promised I would be first with you, but I am not. He'd been right about that and I wasn't at all sure how that could be forgiven. "The point is, I think this magic is all interrelated. These documents are from another island or set of islands that the Nahanauns call N'andana. There are similarities to the written Tala language, so I think they're related, but this one is far more sophisticated, much more complex than the Tala have. Probably much older. In fact, the Tala language might be a relic or offshoot of N'andanan."

"And you think the cultures are connected?"

"Yes. If N'andana still exists. See, I think that Nahanau, N'andana, and Annfwn were all interconnected long ago. I think I share common ancestors with Nakoa—which has to do with the things I can't tell you—because of the relationships reaching from the islands, to N'andana, to Annfwn and my Mailloux ancestors. There's something in that magic that has to do with our feet touching the soil, connecting us to the land. I know it sounds crazy."

"No crazier than the other magics we've witnessed. So why haven't we heard of N'andana?"

"I don't know. When the magic barrier was erected around Annfwn, it cut off N'andana from Nahanau, so it seemed to them that it disappeared. The people here greatly suffered from the loss of magic."

"Wait, are you saying this N'andana might be inside the barrier?" She looked thunderstruck. "I may have yet more people to feed? Danu stacks the challenges deep indeed."

I gave her a weak smile. "We haven't had much time to talk. Did the Dasnarians get through the barrier?"

"We don't know. They got to it, after some minor troubles; then Zynda traveled to Ordnung to report on your . . . felicitous union." She smiled with a wry twist of her narrow lips. "She was anxious about Jepp, however, so she went ahead while we rode to Annfwn. Then she, Andi, and Rayfe, along with some others, set off to meet the *Hákyrling*, with Zynda guiding them to the spot. They left a ship waiting for us not far from the cliff city."

"And that wasn't the plan in the first place, because Rayfe didn't want us to know he had ships."

Ursula curled her lip. "Apparently a whole navy, the wily shape-shifter. We'll discuss that more, I can promise."

"You know, if I stay here with Nakoa—"

"Which you will. Don't pass up a chance for real happiness."

"But I won't be able to go to Dasnaria to unearth the information you need."

"Jepp will be there. I sent instructions with Zynda for her." She cocked her head meaningfully. "Along with explicit orders not to beat herself up for what happened here. I managed to figure out that much on my own, even before you said so."

"Apologies."

"Not necessary. You're good to protect her. She must think very well of you to have given you her mother's knife belt."

"You knew?"

"Yes. Quite the story that goes with it, though it's not mine to tell. You'll be interested, if you can extract it from her. Whiskey helps. How was she getting on with our favorite Dasnarian general?" She asked it casually, in case I didn't know the intimate details.

"Not well. She told us what happened. They were at each other's throats most of the time."

"It will be interesting to see how that sorts out over time. Harlan is of the opinion that Kral will still help her in Dasnaria, regardless of his personal feelings."

I nearly told her of Kral's role in bringing me to Nahanau, but thought better of it. It might just anger her again and she'd greatly dislike any implication that she'd been manipulated. "Jepp is an excellent scout and will be a great spy, but—she can't read Dasnarian. She speaks it quite a bit better now."

She shrugged philosophically and looked around the vast library. "We can't have everything. And I certainly don't mind having you here amid all of this accumulated knowledge. It's a tremendous treasure, unlike anything I've ever seen. You're hardly isolated here. Taking the shortcut through Annfwn, and with an embarrassment of ships to choose from, we can establish regular trade and communication." She had a speculative glint in her eye that made me feel ever so slightly sorry for Rayfe.

"I should warn you—there's probably a hibernating dragon like Kiraka under Windroven. She says there are others like her, and if it's been rumbling . . ."

Ursula eyed me warily. "Do you know how to release it?"

"Maybe?"

"Perhaps you'd better compose a message to Ami. I can send it back with Andi."

"You're not going back to Ordnung after checking the barrier?"

She grinned. "Not just yet—and don't look at me like that. One of Nakoa's shipmasters has offered to go with us to map the barrier and help determine which of the Nahanau islands are inside and outside of it. Then I think we have to go search for this N'andana. Though I have no idea how to look for it."

"I do." When she raised a brow at my immediate reply, I nodded at her belly. "A star to guide you. If all this magic is interconnected . . ."

"Interesting." She drew out the word. "Perhaps so. See? I *have* to go personally!"

"I concede the point, Your Majesty."

She chuckled, amused at us both. "I assume you'll continue to research? Any information you can dig out will no doubt be useful in the days ahead."

"Of course."

"Our first step will be to see if the *Hákyrling* is still there. We'll check in with them and perhaps come back through here. Any messages for Jepp and Zynda?"

"I would love to send some with you. Thank you." *If* I didn't go with her. Knowing she would go to catch up with the *Hákyrling* only made it worse. I could go with them and complete my assignment. Maybe, once I did, I could come back here and . . . *All along, even when you are closest to me, you think of how you'll leave. I am not first with you.*

No, I couldn't suggest that. It was entirely possible Nakoa would not want me to stay, not after this. But if he forgave me, I'd abandon the mission. If only I could send Jepp some ideas of where to look. If only—"Wait! Akamai."

Ursula raised one eyebrow. "The translator?"

"He's more than that—he's a librarian. One who knows documents, reads Dasnarian, and longs to see the world. Maybe he would go with Jepp. He's most unobtrusive. People underestimate him. He'd be a terrific spy."

She nodded, considering. "Many of the same reasons I picked you. But what if the *Hákyrling* has already passed through?"

"He could ride back with Nakoa's shipmaster."

"All right. I'm willing. He can report to you and you can pass along what I need to know. That way we still have your hands and experience in the game, as well. I'll leave it to you to put the idea to Nakoa. I suggest doing so *after* the makeup sex."

"Ursula!" I was blushing. I knew it.

She grinned easily. "I owed you that one, for all the times you smirked at me."

"I suppose that's fair." I sighed.

"Courage, soldier. I'm sure you know how to get through to him."

I narrowed my eyes at her. "That's exactly what Harlan said."

She stood and hooked her thumbs in her sword belt. "What can I say? The man knows whereof he speaks. Thank Danu for that. Speaking of which, I'll go see what he's doing. I owe him some beach time. I'll see you when we set sail in the morning?"

"One way or the other, yes."

Though it was tempting to stay in the library a bit longer, to avoid facing Nakoa, I finally had to admit that I was no closer to answering the riddle. I had no idea how to get through to him, how to apologize. But I had to try.

I left my things where they were and found Akamai reshelving some of the texts I'd finished. "Did you have an interesting afternoon?" I asked him in Dasnarian, and he smiled broadly, but rolled his eyes.

"Yes, but I felt tugged at times, like a piece of meat between two dragons."

"Believe me, I know the feeling."

"Even after practicing with you, my Dasnarian is . . . creaky. I shall have to get better."

"You might have the opportunity." I filled him in on the plan, watching his intelligent dark eyes shine brighter. "I have to discuss it with Nakoa, but—"

"Why? I'm your subject now. The king has no say over what I do. I belong to you, Queen Dafne Nakoa KauPo." He bowed as he said it.

I winced inwardly, understanding the whole taking responsibility for him better. "Akamai. I know you were there for the conversation this afternoon. You heard what the king said, that he would not have me as queen."

"A discreet translator does not remember what is said."

"You'll be a good spy all right. But I know he said that. I might not be queen."

"He said you would not have him. There's a difference. However, I belong to you, queen or not."

I would have to be very careful about this in the future. "I suppose the decision is made. If you can be ready to leave when they sail in the morning?"

"I am ready now."

"Thank you." I turned to go.

"Queen Dafne Nakoa KauPo? The king likes that you are fierce and as stubborn as he. He respects that." He grinned. "Not that I remember anything that was said."

Turning his words over in my mind, I considered my strategy. Despite my delays, I returned to our rooms earlier than usual. If Nakoa held true to pattern, he would not arrive for some time. If he came to see me at all. Inoa stopped in to see if I needed anything, and I couldn't discern from her polite demeanor how she felt, or if she even knew my relationship with Nakoa was precarious. She happily agreed to arrange what I asked for and wished me a pleasant evening.

If I stayed, I would have to devote time to getting to know my sister-in-law better.

The ladies happily prettied me up, including shading in my much-reduced eyebrows and trimming the crisped ends of my hair. I considered wearing the transparent negligee but decided that was trying to distract Nakoa instead of being honest. Besides, if I had to go looking for him, that wouldn't work at all.

Hopefully, however, he would walk into my ambush.

I sat on the balcony, watching the light decline, reading back through my journal instead of taking notes. So much had happened since I'd started it. In fact, it had become so unwieldy that I should start a new one. Apropos for starting a new life. Or perhaps not a completely new life, simply a new chapter. Why hadn't I seen it? Ursula was right—I could continue to do much of what I needed to from Nahanau. I could still write the history I'd been planning. Living in the palace with what might be the most complete library in the world, I'd be able to provide information on a vast array of knowledge. It wouldn't be unreasonable to recruit more operatives like Akamai, or even Jepp and Zynda.

The spymaster operating where she felt most at home—in the library. Not having adventures. Though the adventures had brought me to this place, and I couldn't regret them. It made for a bright future.

If I could convince Nakoa to trust me again.

The doors opened and Nakoa came in, his stride halting as he spotted me, a rare expression of surprise on his face. He hadn't expected me to be there. And Inoa had not told him. She'd known, then—and had acted to help me. Goddesses bless her.

Setting his face into remote lines, he came out to the balcony, taking in the game of *kiauo* I had set up. "What is this, Dafne?"

No *mlai*. My heart ached for it, but I lifted my chin and tried to make sure it didn't show. "I thought we'd play. When I win, I will exact a *kama* from you."

He lifted his white-streaked brows but didn't smile. "I already gave you what you wish—you may leave. I will not stop you. I expected you to be on your queen's ship already."

"Not until I've beaten you at this game."

"The game is not important."

"It is to me. Please, Nakoa *mlai*."

"What *kama*? You have already claimed more than I can bear to give."

I had to press my lips against the tumble of apologies. "You think I will win so easily, then?"

He hesitated at that, stern mouth softening ever so slightly. "You have not so far."

"Then you have nothing to lose." I gestured to the other chair and poured some liquor for him.

"I don't agree," he replied, but he sat, inviting me to make the opening gambit.

The game took hours. I threw every bit of strategy I possessed into it. I'd thought about it quite a bit since our last game. Especially during those long hours wrapped in the rug and trapped in the cave. The game was not only about the pieces and the rules, but knowing your opponent and how he or she thought. Like Ursula, Nakoa tended to be protective of what he considered his responsibility, and his strategy reflected that. I kept him off-balance with erratic moves, cornering him into protecting his most precious pieces out of reflex.

Then I sprang my trap and, in three swift moves, captured the dragon.

He frowned at the board in astonishment. Then at me.

"I win. I am wise in this."

Conceding the victory, he inclined his head. "The wisdom of dragons, indeed. What *kama* do you claim?" He sounded resigned and challenging at once. For a while during the game, the shadows of disappointment had fallen away. Now he regarded me with a guarded expression, bracing himself.

The moment of truth. The dark corners of my soul cried their cowardice. What if he said no? Any sane man would.

If so, I'd gather up the pieces of my heart and go on with my life. I'd had a good many moments with him, to treasure in my memory forever.

Nakoa eyed me warily as I got up, came around the table, and knelt before him. It took me three tries to find my voice. "I'm asking you to forgive me for breaking my promises. For not believing in what is between us. I want to stay, if you'll let me. You are first with me. You were right, that you weren't before, but you are now. I'm . . . wiser than I was. Even if you say no, you always will be. I didn't see. Or listen."

He didn't move for a moment, looking like one of his statues. Then he lifted a hand and caressed my hair, running his fingers through it. He smiled sorrowfully, and my heart clutched. Maybe there would be too many pieces to pick up.

"You are not wise in this, it is true," he said. "You do not see the truth before you, unless it's in one of your books."

Tears pricked my eyes. "I know," I whispered. "Perhaps I could stay and we could . . . begin again. Start afresh. Let me try to do better by you."

"The world does not work this way. What has gone before is always there."

Like the bones of Castle Columba, forever buried beneath Ordnung. I sighed for the truth of it. For my aching heart and how I'd bungled everything. "I withdraw the claim to my *kama*, then."

"Yes. That is for the best."

I stood, my legs like waterlogged sand, and started to step away. He stopped me, putting his hands on my hips.

"Dafne," he said in patient tones. "You are *mlai*. This means I am always yours. You do not have to ask for me. Here I am."

The tears welled up, blurring my vision. "But you said to take back my *kama*."

"Yes." He spread his knees and drew me between them, using his thumbs to wipe away the teardrops. "So you can use it for something else. What do you want to do to me, my dragon queen?"

31

Much later, we lay in the dark of night before moonrise, skin to skin. Though it had been my *kama* to claim, Nakoa had been the one to plunder me, taking me over and over with a thorough ferocity that left me in no doubt of how he felt.

"I love you, Nakoa *mlai.*" I whispered it, in case he slept.

"What does this mean?" he asked, stroking a hand down my back, and I realized I'd said it in Common Tongue.

"I answered the question in my heart."

"I know." He laughed softly when I thumped his chest, capturing my hand and lacing my fingers with his. "I heard it all along. You were the one who did not hear."

"Oh, hush." I kissed him, drinking him in as I had the life-giving rain. He returned it, holding me tenderly, as if I were precious to him. I supposed I was. He'd told me as much.

But, for the first time, I truly knew it. It felt good, to lie there with him in our bed, as if I'd come home at last. I would learn the place as I'd learned his body and his moods.

"What is that chirping sound—the high one, there. Birds?"

"No, *mlai.* Like *mo'o,* only small, bright as jewels. As a boy, I would capture them and keep them to sing in my rooms."

Frogs? How interesting. "Will you show me?"

He kissed my hair, smoothing it. "Of course, Dafne *mlai*. You have only to ask."

"Then I have one more thing to ask."

He waited silently.

"I must get up and write some letters to go with the ship in the morning, but I don't wish to disturb your sleep. Still . . ."

Growling low, he wrapped a hand in my hair and tugged my head back for a long and thorough kiss. "Write your words, over there, where I can see you if I wake. Otherwise I shall sleep, knowing you are here, with me."

"Always, Nakoa *mlai*."

The morning dawned bright, Glorianna's sun shining on the harbor as we bade Ursula and Harlan farewell. Nakoa had seemed amused when I asked about sending Akamai with them, saying that he was already my responsibility. I did not mention my plan to extend my network of information with others. With Nakoa it worked best to give him information in small doses.

I blinked my eyes against the grittiness of the long night. It had taken hours to complete my letters—the most difficult explaining to Ami about a possible dragon under Windroven and what might be done about it. When I returned to bed, Nakoa had pulled me sleepily into his arms and . . . well, there had been no sleeping for me after that.

"I have a gift for you, Akamai." I took out the bit of silk and handed it to him.

His eyes widened in astonishment. "For me? I am over-whelmed."

"You might need them. When you meet Jepp, ask her to teach you how to use them."

He unwrapped one of the silver daggers and held it with reverence, studying the script etched on.

"In my language, it says, 'This is why it's perilous to ignore a librarian,'" I told him. "Use them well."

"I will, Queen Dafne Nakoa KauPo." He bowed several times, then hastened onto the ship with a last wave, leaving the four of us there.

"I still have the others, and this one, of course," I told Ursula, putting my hand on the ruby-hilted dagger.

"Good." She nodded, then gave Nakoa a flinty look and said in Dasnarian, "Use it on my heart-brother, if he doesn't treat you well."

I choked on my laugh, shocked both that she knew the words and that she said them to Nakoa. He gave her a thunderous frown, then released it, his smile breaking through like the sun through clouds.

"If I do not treat my queen well," he replied in careful Dasnarian, "I deserve the knife, Heart-Sister."

"I'm glad we understand each other." She handed me a scroll with a wry smile. "All in writing, so you can put it in your library, as I know you like to."

By mutual accord, we did not linger at the harbor. Instead Nakoa and I walked back to the palace and ascended the tower where we'd watched the *Hákyrling* sail away an age ago. When Ursula's ship passed through the great dragons guarding the harbor, Nakoa lifted my chin to survey my face.

"No weeping this time?"

I wrapped my hand around his, holding it while I placed a kiss on the inside of his wrist, one of few places he did not have tattoos. "No. I am happy. I am where I want to be. You are precious to me, Nakoa *mlai*. My home."

He smiled, close-lipped, but radiantly enough to banish all the stern lines. Almost as carefree as in sleep. "You are my treasure, also, Dafne *mlai*."

The word he used and the way he colored it. *Treasure*. Not at all the same as the Dasnarians used it. The pieces shifted in my head. Moving into new patterns.

The wisdom of dragons.

The women talk to us, relay our wisdom.

It's a tremendous treasure, unlike anything I've ever seen.

That scroll I'd seen back in Annfwn, with its vivid illustrations—and the unlikely one of the dragon and human, heads bent together over a scroll.

"The library," I breathed. "That's the dragon's treasure. Knowledge."

"This sounds true—this is yours to know."

"Kiraka can teach me to read N'andanan. She was a scribe. She holds the key to translating all of those books!"

He mock scowled at me. "Now I shall never pry you out of the library."

"Yes, you will." I stood on the low wall, to be eye to eye with him, giving him a long, heartfelt kiss. "You'll just have to make it worth my while."

The babe you'll bear, Daughter. The beginnings of your family for me to help raise and train up properly. I'll begin with respect for ancient dragon ancestresses.

I brushed past that, full of hope. "I'm too old to conceive."

No, Daughter. She sounded more kind. *This is what I bring to you. Your body is healthier for proximity to me. Younger, even. You will heal quickly and live a very long time, if you stay out of volcanoes. You may have many babies.*

Stunned, I wrapped my mind around it. If a girl, I'd name her for Bethany. If a boy, Gailand Fayne, for my brothers. A bit of life for them again. I couldn't wait to tell Nakoa.

Though, by the way he'd kissed my stomach, just over my womb, before I left the palace that morning, he might already know. Incorrigible man. I would have to extract a *kama* from him, if he'd known and hadn't told me.

Enough mooning, Daughter. Time for your lesson.

In agreement, I sat down and focused on my work.

Epilogue

I hiked up the volcano, a bag of texts on my back. My feet had toughened from all the abuse and it felt strangely natural to go barefoot. As long as I was careful to avoid hot spots.

Kiraka waited for me at our usual spot, ruby eyes lighting with interest at what I brought. It wasn't the simplest solution, for me to go to her, but her presence elicited too much attention at the palace for us to get any work done. N'andanan was complex, indeed, but I was beginning to get a feel for it. The more I learned, the more I thought it might be a perfect language. The language of the ancients. Full of magic and power.

Greetings, Daughter.

"Hello, Kiraka. How are you today?"

I am well. The sun is bright and I am feeling fat, sleek, and satisfied.

"I'm glad to hear it."

You are looking sleek and satisfied, also. Though not fat. Yet. Her mental tone held smug amusement.

My heart fluttered, a new beat in it I'd hardly dared give credence to. "Don't tease me, Kiraka. What are you saying?"